Amanojaku

DAMIEN LUTZ

First Edition, 2016
Second Edition, 2016 (Amendments and added illustration)

ISBN-10: 0-9946275-0-5
ISBN-13: 978-0-9946275-0-6

ACKNOWLEDGEMENTS

Thanks to my friends, who are still my friends, after I disappeared for over a year to write this book. And to the members of The Fiction Workshop, thank you for your continued advice and inspiration.

Amanojaku (天邪鬼), n :

a demon-like creature in Japanese folklore,

able to provoke a person into perpetrating evil deeds.

CONTENTS

ILLUSTRATIONS

"You still don't know you're a bad machine. To know yourself is to know God, my friend. The factory knows, that's why they put you here. You'll see. You'll find out. In time, you'll know."

- Ahmet, Midnight Express

"A lot of life is dealing with your curse, dealing with the cards you were given that aren't so nice. Does it make you into a monster, or can you temper it in some way, or accept it and go in some other direction?"

- Wes Craven

"Temper is a weapon that we hold by the blade."

- James M. Barrie

"Don't forget to love yourself."

- Soren Kierkegaard

.

BRULLE

2032 (ORIGINAL BUILD)

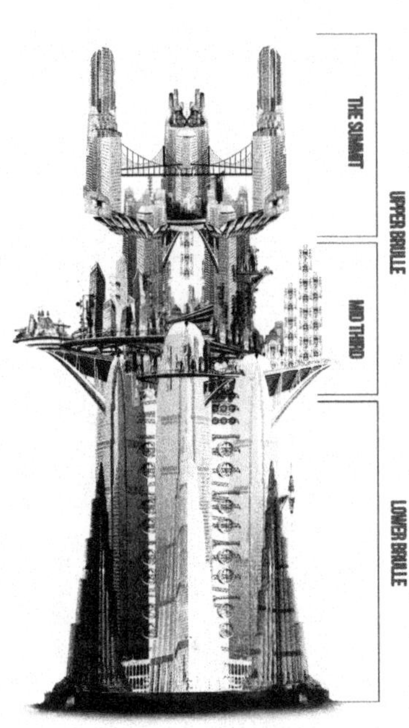

2040

PART ONE

SPIKY HAZE

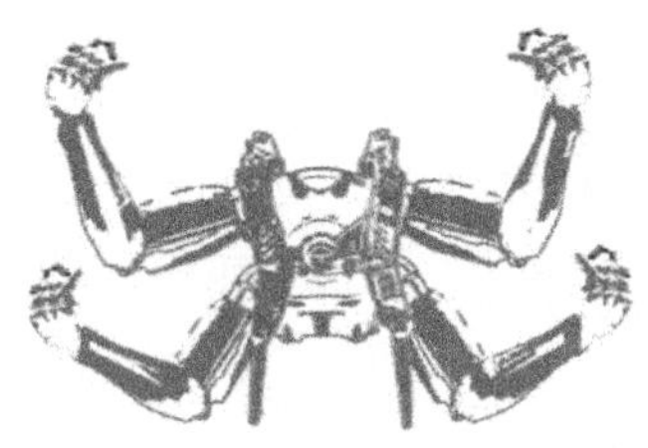

Birthday

All Andre Cross wanted was some peace and bloody quiet.

Strapped into his robotic four-armed harness, he dangled like a spider from the horizontal shaft's ceiling. The harness motor purred, but another noise—a frantic shrill in the left gripper's connector socket—squealed in his ear with mosquito persistence.

That's gonna drive me nuts.

Three times, he'd asked Dirk to service his harness. Three times, the farm manager had blown him off.

Cool air brushed against the back of his neck. At first, he mistook the sensation for a twitch of the implant embedded against his cervical vertebrae. He checked his recent thoughts for any aggression that might have activated the device but gave himself the all-clear.

Just my mind playing tricks.

Shaking off the chill, he focused on completing his last job for the day, when the synthesized voice of the farm's AI echoed through his visor.

"Operator 77. Two minutes remaining. Please report."

He gritted his teeth. If he took longer to fix the lift than the time allotted by Control's algorithms, those same damn algorithms would dock his Reliability Rating. The Baron did not like delays, and Control ensured the workers never forgot.

Yeah, yeah, Control, hold your horses.

The alignment mechanism in the lift's motor had slipped, of course. They all came loose at the intersections. Suspended inside the lift's motor cage, he reached down and slotted the mechanism back into place. Signaling with shoulder gestures, the grippers—the two upper robotic limbs on his harness—contracted and hauled him out of the cage, dangling him just above the lift. He flipped the cage panel shut, and the helpers—the two lower robotic limbs—screwed the panel back into place. Rolling his shoulders, the grippers hauled him clear of the cabin.

"Control, this is Operator 77. Lift Omega clear."

"Copy, Operator 77. Running lift diagnostic now. Standby."

But he didn't standby. Andre had been working on lifts since he was sixteen. He knew the cabin was good to go. His twelve-hour shift was done and dusted, and so was he, physically and mentally. Thinking of a hot shower, he headed toward the trunk exit.

Rolling his shoulders again, to activate the grippers, he swung along the shaft like a six-arm monkey. As the swing steadied, he withdrew his vape from the inner pocket of his overalls, clicked the lighting switch, and sucked the sweet vapor deep into his lungs.

Doctor Steele had advised him to quit smoking—along with an extensive list of other habits he should break—to avoid aggravating the implant. But ever since the Doctor implanted the roach-shaped device, Andre wanted to smoke more. Anyway, he had quit, hadn't he? For four long months. So he'd ticked that one off the Doctor's list of don't-dos and got back to doing what he wanted to do.

He blew a chain of vapor rings that distorted and floated away behind him and enjoyed the solitude. As one of the few remaining non-machine employees, he rarely saw another human during his shift.

Come to think of it, I haven't seen Jackson all day.

And that suited him just fine. Six years of solitary confinement had ingrained in him a preference for being alone.

The steady swinging rocked him, like a baby in a cradle. He yawned, never feeling so exhausted at the end of a day. Every shift in the tree-towers was a long and strenuous one. Some days he felt like he was just a device for survival, on autopilot, no different from the harvest drones in the greenhouse.

Still, a job was a job, and Implants couldn't be choosers. If he hadn't spent his prison labor time working on the Dock lifts, he would not have landed his lift-mechanic job on the farm. At least he got to work inside the tree-towers where there were always four walls to cling to. Out beyond the shafts, in the greenhouse itself, mountainous space sprawled above and below, with precarious branches spinning all around, the air pungent with the sickly sweet smell of the Blue Eye plants. As far as Andre was concerned, the greenhouse was Jackson's gig and he could keep it.

Twelve fantastic months, he thought with sarcasm, as he swung along the shaft. Twelve months since he'd accepted the implant to walk free from prison. Sure, he still had to manage the violent urges that had put him into prison in the first place, and the implant wasn't 100 percent accurate, sometimes mistaking panic or fear or excitement for the bad thoughts. The worst days were a spiky haze of temper flares and heavy sedation. But, so far, the device had recognized his violent urges and auto-medicated him before they'd eventuated into action. He was on track with his Plan, and well on his way to becoming a Good Citizen. That, at least, was worth a celebratory vape.

Happy nineteenth birthday to me.

Captain

The squealing noise in the left gripper socket lowered and contorted into a loud, harsh grinding. Heat from the friction burned his aching shoulder. He slowed his swinging to give the laboring limb a chance to cool down and to take the stress off his weakened muscles.

He didn't mind the pain in his shoulder, even if it did slow him down. At least it reminded him that he could still feel something, in some small way—a dull ache, just enough to keep him half-alive, just enough to not wake the implant.

No, he didn't mind the pain. As long as it didn't force him to take time off from work, trapping him at home in his small apartment like a bird in a cage with a broken wing. If he wanted to maintain his saving schedule, and afford the fee to Anchora, he needed to stay on the job. Being smuggled out of Brulle and into Anchora was his number one priority. His Plan to become a Good Citizen, and to put his past behind him, depended on it.

As far away as possible from the memories.

—Breathe, Boss. Keep your focus.—

The second voice, the reassuring, commanding inner voice, belonged to the Captain.

During the twelve months since Andre had been released—since he laid down on the crisp, clean sheets in the Titan facility and let them cut open his neck—he had remained conscious of his thoughts, watching his mental processes and correcting them when necessary.

"Keep your thinking-brain front and center, Boss," Doctor Steele had advised. "It controls the primitive and emotional brains. You can let those two out in moments of crisis, but day-to-day, you've got to think. You've got to remain rational."

And that was exactly what Andre did.

Rational as right and wrong.

After three months of counseling to strengthen his willpower, and clarifying his sense of right and wrong, Andre developed the Captain's voice.

The voice had been with him since he was ten years old, since the day… No, he wouldn't think about that. The voice had been with him a long time, but he hadn't always listened to it, and he hadn't heard from it during the six years he had been in jail. The Doctor's counseling brought back the voice. It was Andre's rational voice, his thinking voice, his right and wrong voice, telling him what to do and keeping the wayward ship of his mind on course. Most of the time.

Andre didn't tell Doctor Steele he'd given the inner voice a name. What was the point? Did the Doctor believe him when he'd said it wasn't himself controlling his temper that made him commit those violent acts? No. When Andre had talked about the day his brother gave him the dark thing, the fastidious Doctor Steele just warned Andre against the fragmentation of his mind. Andre had hazed out at the rest of the doctor's psychological mumbo jumbo. The only voice Andre had any worries about was Jeremy's, and he hadn't heard from his dead brother since the implant went in.

No, as far as Andre was concerned, the Doctor didn't need to know Andre had his very own manager—a separate entity, a higher voice— driving the mechanics of his mind. Because even if the Captain didn't keep him on track, the implant sat at the base of his brain, ready to synthesize a sedative from his own proteins and shoot them into his nervous system. He had everything he needed to keep the dark thing inside him in a permanent state of suspension. As long as he avoided the memories.

"Operator 77. Lift Omega diagnostic complete. Reactivating. You are… fifteen minutes behind schedule."

Damn it.

—You did your best, Boss. You're done. Time to head home.—

Andre puffed another vapor ring and shut his eyes, when Control's polite voice interrupted his attempt to relax.

"Operator 77. Final job downloading now."

What? "Wait a minute, Control. Omega was my final job."

"Negative, Operator 77. Malfunction on farm maintenance droid. Branch 15.5. Inside greenhouse."

The greenhouse? Where the hell is Jackson?

The thought of all that overwhelming space and light deconstructing his focus sent spiders of apprehension crawling across his back. This was not a good way to end the day.

"Ah, Control, I don't usually work in the farm. Try Jackson, Operator 4."

"Operator 4 unavailable. Urgent attention needed on Branch 15.5. Malfunctioning GPS and suspected crop damage. Please attend immediately."

For cryin' out loud. Is one damaged bush gonna dent the billions the Baron makes from these bloody flowers?

—How bad you wanna get out of Brulle, Boss?—

He bit hard into his lip.

Bad enough to give half my pay to a sly old dog like Dirk to smuggle me out of here.

—Then let's suck it up and get this done.—

He didn't have to accept the job. A faulty harness was a valid reason. But refusing one job would result in another drop in his Reliability Rating. He'd be sure to lose shifts. That meant less savings, and a longer time before he could leave Brulle. The Captain was right, as usual.

"Operator 77, please respond."

He huffed. *Son of a bitch, Jackson, you better have a damn good reason for not being available.*

"Accepted, Control."

The outline of the tree-tower refreshed on his visor screen. A pulsing blue circle marked his location inside the lower branch, and a red dot pulsed on an upper branch outside the tree. Next to the map, a timer estimated six minutes until he reached the droid.

"Operator 77, coordinates delivered. Proceed to Branch 15.5 and report on droid's status. You have … eighteen minutes."

Sucking back on his vape, he picked up the pace and swung toward an intersection to take a vertical shaft up. But as the grippers clutched and released in their graceful momentum, the grinding noise in the left gripper's socket spiked to a screech and his harness jerked to halt.

Not again, he seethed, his blood simmering.

The left gripper refused to release its hold from the scaffolding, and the right gripper pulled him forward, twisting his torso into a painful angle. Sharp spasms speared down his spine and zigzagged all the way out to his fingertips. In an attempt to reactivate the stalled robotic limb, he swung back and forth, but the stubborn gripper wouldn't budge. The motor squealed like a mad monkey in his ear.

Let go, you piece of shit.

After a few more swings, the stuck gripper released, the right grabbed hold simultaneously, and the swinging momentum re-engaged. But the monkey noise persisted.

If I have to tell Dirk one more time this junked-up harness needs fixing, I'll…

—*Breathe, Boss. Watch your thinking.*—

He swore and sucked hard on his vape. A little part of the old Andre stomped its feet.

Watch, think, listen—that's all I've been doing for the last twelve hours. Now I've got to do another job, in the damn greenhouse.

—*Breathe, Boss. It's just one more job.*—

He knew the Captain was steering him toward his fabled state of good citizenship. But after a long day of Control's voice telling him what to do, and the frustrating screech stabbing him in the ear, he was tired and irritated.

I'm not good up there. I don't LIKE the fucking greenhouse.

—*Boss.*—

And, since he was being honest with himself—*because that's what rational people do, right?*—he wished sometimes he could just let the rage take over. He still remembered the feeling. And he missed it.

—*Breathe. Forget the feeling.*—

The implant never quite removed that, did it? His thoughts quipped at the Captain, letting out his secret pet hate for the device crouching on his spine. He squeezed his vape and clenched his jaw.

And no little robot insect sucking on my proteins and living off my own goddamn body is going to stop the memories completely, is it? They'd have to kill me to do that.

—*Breathe, Boss. Stay in the front room.*—

And there it was, right on cue, the Captain stepping in with his warning phrase, letting Andre know he was close to activating the implant.

—*Forget about the past, Boss. Focus on the job. The sooner you get this done, the sooner you go home.*—

Andre stopped the harness swinging forward and held still. The screeching noise dropped into a grating, but less irritating, hum.

Yes. That's right. Stay in the front room.

He took another deep inhale from the vape, exercising his breathing technique with his vice (for right or wrong), and calmed his thoughts to examine his inner chatter. He was letting the bad thoughts in and goad him toward memories that would stir the dark thing. And if the dark thing started scratching in its sleep, like a clawed, sharp-toothed animal having a bad dream, he would likely lose contact with the Captain altogether. Then the really bad thoughts would roll in, and the implant would activate a Big Dose. Dropping into the medication's haze would mean kissing all his structured thought goodbye. Not a good state to be in when working on the spinning branches in the greenhouse.

—*One more job, Boss. Last one. Then you're home and hosed.*—

With his perspective reset, he took in one more long draw of his vape, flicked it off, and packed it away in his pocket. Redirecting his focus to the hot shower awaiting him, he put both the harness noise and his shoulder pain out of his mind and swung down the shaft to head to the high branches.

Right. Let's get this over with, before anything else goes wrong.

Mutiny

Reaching the shaft junction, he tapped into the panel on his chest. With a clunk, the robotic arms activated themselves, turned him around, and swiftly scaled the vertical shaft. Hanging off the back of the harness, as if he were the machine's backpack, he bounced as it carried him toward an access platform, where he could take a lift the rest of the way up.

Rocked into a brief moment of relaxation, his weary mind sat back in his skull and thumb-tacked an image to his brain, the way Jackson had stuck a dog-eared postcard of some generic tropical island on the inside of his locker. The image projected across Andre's mind, however, was not an island swallowed up long ago by rising seas. His mind's eye swept over a sprawling city hovering above a twinkling expanse of water. A colossal tower protruded from the city's center and disappeared into the clouds.

Anchora.

It wasn't Anchora's space elevator that attracted him—although that certainly guaranteed him work. It was Anchora's *flatness*, the absence of the ups and downs of Brulle's lifts, that appealed to his search for inner balance. More than anything, it was the distance that living there would put between him and all the bad memories lurking in Brulle' corners just waiting to ambush his Plan.

If he did his calculations correctly—and he sure as hell did, because he went over them every day, like a monk doing his morning mantra—he could afford Dirk's fee within a year.

—One year, Boss. One year and you're outta here. You got this.—

Although unconvinced all would go as planned, he didn't argue with the Captain. He'd had enough of the voice for one day.

Reaching an access-way connecting the lift shaft to the trunk's internal corridors, he tapped into his chest panel again. The harness swiveled around to face him toward the opening and swung him inside. Landing in a crouch, he stood and rubbed his aching left shoulder. The harness reconfigured and folded in its arms, settling like a dog-sized spider playing dead on his back.

A lift arrived at the platform, opened its doors, and Andre stepped inside. The cabin jolted, and so did his heart. He breathed through his discomfort and rubbed his hands together, when his wristlet vibrated. He checked the screen and a message appeared.

Deliver tonight? 2 would be good

It was Finn, his best customer. His *Best and Only Customer*.

Being paid partly in credits, and partly in Neura—the liquid drug produced on the farm—Andre initially struggled to save for his ticket out of Brulle. (His implant didn't allow him to use Neura. The drug would send his nervous system into overdrive, and no one, not even the know-it-all Doctor Steele, knew how the implant would react.) Not wanting to see the Neura half of his pay go to waste, Andre visited known meeting places for users and dealers to sell his stock to wealthy citizens from Upper Brulle.

Not that Neura was illegal. On the contrary. Everyone in Upper Brulle had Neura running through their veins. Neura was the main ingredient in a blood-enrichment supplement for the citizens on Upper Brulle's exclusive health plan. Titan also used it in the bio-blood fueling borg prosthetics.

Everybody knows the girl Neura.

The problem was, everybody wanted more. They wanted it pure, and they were all as hungry for it as Finn.

As the lift sped up the tree-tower's inner shaft, Andre recalled first arriving on the Neura scene with his pure, uncut product.

He'd met Finn on the first night he'd visited the smoky Alta Tavern. Finn wasn't hard to recognize as a Neura abuser. Dark circles hung underneath beaming eyes and an ecstatic grin was on his face: 'the mask of Neura.' Andre must have stood out like the other sore thumb on that pair of hands, staring wide-eyed at the busy environment with the telltale overwhelmed look of someone recently released from jail. By the time he had squeezed between sweaty patrons up to the wet bar, and ordered a beer, Finn had parked himself beside Andre and asked if he was selling. Finn's face had sparked a faint familiarity in Andre, but his conscious mind couldn't validate how he could possibly know anyone outside of his limited world. He had put the sensation down to it being an omen, that this guy would be a good customer. Within minutes, and without a haggle, Finn had bought everything Andre had.

From that day on, Finn was Andre's *Best and Only Customer*, and it suited Andre just fine. Maybe Finn was marking it up and selling it? Andre didn't care. All he cared about was saving the seven thousand credits as fast as he could to secure himself a seat on Dirk's secret ship to Anchora.

Twelve months down, twelve to go.

Every shift he took on at the farm deposited a few more credits into his account and cut that much time off the next twelve months. And the profits from feeding Finn's bad habit shortened that time a little more. Having dropped off a vial to Finn only two days prior, however, Andre had only one left until next payday.

I'm not going to keep up with the greedy bastard's orders at this rate. I can't risk losing my Best and Only to someone else. Maybe I can ask Dirk about sacrificing more of my credits for more Neura.

The lift eased to Level 15, and he stepped out into a glass-enclosed sealing chamber. As he approached another set of doors, a green light glowed above them and they slid open. The cool, dry air of the climate-controlled environment rushed in and brushed against his face. The rich smoke and cherry scent of thousands of ultramarine Blue Eyes punched his nostrils. His stomach churned.

Walking out onto the exposed platform, heat from the artificial lighting above beamed down and stung his arms. Dark blue pollen twinkled all around him, like anti-stars, spored from the Blue Eyes straining their green stems toward the spotlights. Looking up, he squinted into the merciless glare and tried to make out the insect-like harvest drones nesting behind the lighting. He imagined them rubbing their front cutter blades together–like hungry flies rubbing their legs–waiting for the Blue Eye petals to drop and reveal their naked capsules.

The other tree-towers loomed around him, and, behind them, the pink-lit wall of the greenhouse surrounded them all. Slowly rotating branches, covered in pods of the navy-flowered plants, made little sounds as they cut through the air.

Snit-svit-snit-svit...

That sound. He hated that sound. It reminded him of his brother's switchblade flicking in and out.

—Focus on the job, Boss. One more, and you're done.—

Breathing through his mouth to avoid the pungent odor, he pushed back his vertigo and stepped to the platform edge as the branches slid past. He told himself not to look over. Never having much self-control, however, he looked anyway. Nauseated by the dizzying view of the tree-tower trunks disappearing beneath their turning branches, he immediately regretted not taking his own advice.

The red light in his visor pulsed, reminding him of the droid he was there to retrieve. He tapped 'Branch 15.5' into a lectern-style terminal by the edge of the platform and stared straight ahead.

Each branch consisted of two parallel levels. Blue Eyes covered the lower garden level, and scaffolding ran parallel above the garden. The scaffolding provided swinging access to the length of the branch, while keeping the workers out of the garden and minimizing chance of damage to the Baron's precious plants. Access-ropes hung from the scaffolding, and its minimalist structure allowed artificial light and rain to reach the plants underneath.

While he waited for the branch to come around, a light appeared in a large, elliptical window embedded in the greenhouse wall directly opposite him. In the golden eye, behind the glass, a suited figure cut a silhouette so sharp it seemed to slice through the fabric of reality. He caught his breath.

The Baron.

Tower lights reflected in the window and twinkled like stars in the Baron's silhouette, giving him the appearance of some inter-dimensional being struggling to contain his disguise as a well-dressed human.

Ever since Jackson had told Andre the Baron's story, Vadim Grekov, Baron of the Neura Farm, had become Andre's idol citizen. After all, Andre reasoned, Grekov and he were similar. Like himself, Grekov had spent much of his childhood in prison.

—The Job, Boss, shouldn't you be concentrating on the Job?—

The row of branches stopped in front of him and locked Branch 15.5 at his feet. But Andre was lost in the moment, remembering how Grekov, unlike himself, had tamed his inner darkness.

He doesn't need implants or voices or goddamn breathing techniques to deal with his dark thing, Andre thought with admiration. *No. He controls it. He is an Extraordinary Citizen.*

Andre nodded toward Grekov, as if they were good old buddies from way back. But the lights in the Baron's room dimmed and went out, and Andre was sure he heard a loud locking noise echo throughout the farm. He put the noise down to his mind playing tricks on him. It did that.

—Are you quite done just standing there like a broken android, Boss, imagining how so alike you two are? Why don't you just ask him out for espresso martinis? This is the precise time you should be looking busy.—

Damn it, Andre swore at himself. *You're right.*

—I'm always right. That's why I got the top job. And you better start listening up more, Boss, or maybe you think you can do this all on your own.—

Andre blinked. That didn't sound right. The Captain didn't make threats.

Is the thin air getting to me? I knew this was a bad idea.

He really did not like being out in the farm. The yawning space above and below messed with his head, distorting the delicately structured mental architecture that maintained who was who and what was what.

—Move, Boss.—

He checked the time on his visor. Seven minutes had passed, leaving him eleven minutes to retrieve the droid. He raised his arms to splay his robotic limbs, checking their responsiveness in preparation for swinging out along the branch. He crouched and jumped upward, bringing in his arms, and the grippers latched onto the rope. As he hauled himself up to the scaffolding level, the branch resumed its slow turning.

Staring straight ahead to avoid the temptation to look down again, he checked the droid's location on his visor and swung out to the center of the branch. By the time he got there, however, the fugitive droid had moved. The red light on his visor map now rested near the branches' tip. Swearing, he climbed to the end of the scaffolding, only to find the last rope caught up in the beams.

Jesus Christ Almighty, is this day ever going to end?

—It's a manual pick up from here, Boss. Short and simple.—

After twelve long hours, he wasn't in the best head space to handle walking out along the slow-turning branch.

—You got this, Boss.—

Resigning himself to just getting the job finished, he unstrapped his harness, climbed out, and left it hanging from the scaffolding. He scaled down the nearest access rope, dropped to the plant branch, and tiptoed through the Blue Eyes. Although he didn't look down, he could see in his peripheral vision the flowers mesmerizing, white-dotted, poppy-like capsules staring up at him. Their zombie-bruise color and the branch's slow spinning made him dizzy, so he kept his focus forward on the branch tip to maintain his balance. Still light-headed, he breathed in through his nose, as his technique demanded, only to be nostril-punched again by the flower's sickeningly sweet smell. Furious at the unexpected overwhelming nausea, he cursed himself for being so—

{weak}

A familiar voice bobbed up out of his subconscious, like a dead body surfacing in a river. Shocked out of his rising discomfort, he froze. He didn't know how the nasty voice got through the Captain's presence, but he knew who it belonged to. Even after all these years, he recognized his brother's voice, and all his childhood anger rushed back and filled his body with stabbing tension.

—The droid, Boss. Finish the job.—

He shook his head and checked the visor map. The malfunctioning droid had reached the end of the limb. Taking a deep breath—this time through his mouth—he stepped with tightrope-walker care between the precious plants and tried to force his thoughts back to completing the task on time. But his brother's voice was not going anywhere without a fight.

As soon as I collect the droid, I'm gonna—

{rip its guts out}

—head home and take a long, hot shower.

{and smash it}

He stopped and squeezed his eyes shut to push back his brother's persistent intrusion.

Just shut up, Jeremy.

He reopened his eyes and pushed on, the droid only meters away.

—Stay in the front room, Boss.—

Oh, yeah. That's right, Captain. I'll stay in the front room. So how 'bout YOU keep Jeremy quiet? That's YOUR damn job, isn't it?

The Captain didn't reply. A tingle flared where the implant lay, the first light of anger reaching over the horizon of his reason. The spinning branches cut through the silence.

Snit-svit-snit-svit…

Great. Some Captain you are, pushing me out here and then disappearing when Jeremy turns up.

He envisioned the implant sitting like a gargoyle on his spine, just below his brain, waiting to pounce on his thoughts and gobble them whole. He clenched his fists and dug his nails into his skin, resisting what brewed in his mind. But the bad thoughts rolled in anyway.

Maybe, when I finally get home, I'll take a knife and cut out that little shitty piece of metal myself.

An animal, with sharp teeth and razor claws, shifted deep in his psyche. Its rusty jangle reverberated through his bones and up into his skin.

{yesss, do it, little bro}

Shut up, Jeremy.

{do it}

Shut up!

He pounded his temples with his fists to fight the mutiny in his mind. The helpers on his harness mimicked his motions, smacking against his head.

{do it}

"Just die!" he cried aloud, his words echoing throughout the greenhouse. The sound of his own voice startled him into a moment of clarity. He paused, the only noise in or out of his head now the *snit-svit-snit-svit* of the branches.

Just finish the job, he told himself. He pushed forward, not daring to look at the vast space dropping away around him. Dripping with sweat, he reached the branch tip and found the malfunctioning droid burrowing into the red soil. He picked up the wriggling machine—its six legs running in the air—and regarded it with disdain.

Gotcha, you little son of a bitch.

The droid's legs continued to paddle and an abstract thought popped into his mind: *I bet that's what my implant looks like.*

{do it}

In a moment of pure, delirious confusion, his tired, wrought grip on the rational finally slipped loose from reality. He saw his own implant in his hand. Before the real implant could register his intent, he punched into the droid's base with his helper arm and ripped out the droid's motor. Wires and cables dangled from its belly like intestines. A distant part of him rejoiced. It was a mean joy that filled him, like the one blooming in a child when it breaks another's toy because it can't have its own.

"Operator 77, please report."

The heat in his neck flared into a sting, and his implant blew its whistle. Teeny-tiny bells rang throughout his mind as sedative chemicals jumped into their cellular fire engines and sped throughout his nervous system. The medication relaxed his muscles and lightened his head, and he smiled like a baby.

"Problem neutralized," he reported to Control, barely hearing his own disembodied voice. Control said something in reply, but the medication's haze muffled its words. He dismissed it the way a drunk does a call for last drinks, his mind swirling around one goal: *finish the job.*

He took the disemboweled droid and headed back down the branch. In the haze of sedation, however, the space and the light became giant, rocking waves. His head spun and his legs wobbled. Swaying, like a stick insect in the wind, his balance left him and he toppled back toward the edge of the branch.

Damage

In spite of his sedated state, or because of it, he spun and swung his right arm forward. The momentum of his swing, with the weight of the droid clutched in his hand, pulled him away from the branch's edge and sent him crashing into the soil. Landing on his hands, helpers, and knees, he stared at the ultramarine petals littering the soil. He stayed there for a moment, trying to grasp how close he had come to falling to his death. Collecting himself, he lifted the helper still clutching the droid and faced the mangled, blue-spotted mess of a crushed Blue Eye plant.

"Oh, shit."

He straightened the plant as best he could, several branches damaged and limp. He knew what that meant for his Reliability Rating, but, in the relaxing haze of the sedative, he couldn't help but chuckle at his plight.

Well, I can at least finish the job on time.

A loud, clunky, locking noise broke through his haze and echoed throughout the greenhouse. A familiar voice called from deep in the well of his mind.

—Swim—

He shook his head, trying to compose himself, sure that the medication was playing tricks on him.

Tricks on tricks. That's all it is.

Standing and stretching out his arms and robotic limbs to keep his balance, he stumbled through the plants, obliviously stepping on every second one.

—Swim… swim—

The voice again. It sounded like the Captain, but far, far away.

What the hell is the Captain talking about?

He reached the spot below his harness and checked the time. Three and a half minutes to spare.

I can do this. I got this.

After a few clumsy swipes, he latched the busted droid onto his belt and hauled himself up the access rope. Strapping himself into his harness, he arched back to activate the grippers, when one solitary ultra-blue petal fluttered slowly and delicately past his face. Then another, and another. He focused on the petal, following it all the way down to the branch below, and faced hundreds of them littering the soil. Apprehension scattered a kaleidoscope of butterflies inside his stomach. In his daze, he hadn't noticed what had been staring at him the entire time—the plants had dropped all their petals. Their shiny, one-eyed capsules stood naked and ready for harvesting.

"Next harvest in three minutes." Control's voice made him jump in his harness. "Operator 77, this is your second warning. All Operators must evacuate the field immediately."

He froze with terror. He *had* heard a locking noise. But it wasn't locking, it was *unlocking*, and it had come from above, from the nest of harvest drones.

Flexing his mind to think clearly, he squinted up at the army of artificial lamps hiding the drones. One automated sap-harvester on its own was precise and delicate enough not to damage the produce, but the thought of being caught in a descending swarm of thousands horrified him half out of his haze.

Another clunk echoed throughout the greenhouse. The butterflies in his stomach morphed into bats, flew up into the rafters of his mind, and battered the inside of his skull. The Captain's voice, clear and loud, came booming into his mind's frenzy.

—*Swarm!*—

Swarm

No, no, no.

—*Breathe, Boss. You got to keep it together. You don't need another med-shot to slow you down right now.*—

Encouraged to have the Captain back on board, Andre breathed in deep through his mouth and exhaled slowly, three times, and the implant remained quiet.

He focused straight ahead on the tree-tower trunk and rolled his shoulders to activate the harness. The robotic arms jolted, then froze. His heart dropped and his stomach lurched. The high-pitched whirring noise screamed in his left ear. Another kaleidoscope of butterflies fluttered in his gut.

He corrected his movement and swung his body weight. The right gripper clutched onto the scaffolding and pulled him forward, but the left, again, refused to release, twisting his body and organs into a knot of sharp pain.

"No, no, no, not now!"

He couldn't move. His harness held fast. His focus, however, slipped, like numb fingers clutching at ice. The harvest drones buzzed above, preparing to drop. Another screeching colony of bats freaked up into his skull.

"Jesus fucking Christ almighty. Control," he yelled into his visor, "this is Operator 77, Branch 15.5. Harness malfunction. Abort harvest. I repeat, abort harvest."

"Negative, Operator. Harvest must proceed on schedule. Harvest in two minutes. Proceed to exit immediately."

"Control, operator in the field. Harness malfunction. I repeat, operator in the field!"

"Analyzing harness now."

The drone's buzzing suffused through the air, vibrating the tiny hairs on his ears. Looking up into the light, he forced his breathing into a slow and steady rhythm. As if mocking him, the stuck motor screamed in chorus with the buzzing.

"Operator, your harness has malfunctioned."

Andre elbowed his harness in frustration. "No shit!"

—Stay in the front room, Boss. Keep it together.—

"Abort harvest!" he yelled again. "Control, abort harvest!"

"Negative, Operator 77. Harvest activated. Abort unavailable. Initiate manual evacuation."

He shot a glance down the branch to the platform, gauging the distance and time it would take to swing out manually. His aching shoulder would slow him, but with his harness going nowhere, he had no choice.

Reaching back with his right arm, he stretched for the harness clasp and twisted as far as his burning muscles would allow. Contorted by the frozen gripper, his reach remained short, the silver buckle teasingly beyond his fingers. His fingers strained and wriggled, like spasming spider legs, until, with a final twitch, his index finger tapped the release mechanism. The strap slipped free and he dropped. As he fell, his left hand grabbed hold of the strap's end, jerking him to a halt, and flaring fresh, hot pain through his back.

Swaying, like a palm frond in a tropical breeze, he twisted around to assess his situation. With the plant branch below too far to drop to, and the ropes on either side too far to reach, he would have to climb back up and swing along the scaffolding.

"Harvest in twenty seconds," advised Control through his visor. "All Operators must exit immediately."

Jesus mental Christ!

—You gotta breathe, Boss.—

Breathe your fucking self!

Fear and anger exploded inside him, setting off another round of flash fires throughout his nervous system. The implant obliged, sending out its chemical troops. As he pulled himself up to the branch scaffolding, his mind and body relaxed, gagging his instinct as it tried to shout *Run*.

"Harvest in ten seconds. Environment sealing."

Fighting through the sedation, he focused on the chamber ahead and swung along the scaffolding. Lean muscles, developed from years of lift-work, operated in perfect synchronicity. But his lungs were out of shape from smoking, and the medication dulled the synapses in his nervous system, hampering his speed. Forearms burning, palms stinging, and his shoulder feeling as if it were about to blow out of its socket, his entire body formed a union and threatened to strike.

The buzz above thickened into one loud, whirring hum. The harvest drones, all eyes and sharp blades, dropped through the light, the first round engulfing the tree-tower opposite him. Their insect-shaped bodies hovered around the branches, scanning the plants and calculating maneuvers. Tiny spinning blades at the end of their arms sliced the air as they swooped, filling the greenhouse with a sinister twitter.

Snit-svit-snit-svit…

He passed the halfway mark, sweat stinging his eyes, pain biting both his forearms with the sting of twin Chinese burns. Out of nowhere, he thought of the Baron. Summoning a hidden reserve of determination, he drew on his mounting pain and anger, and swung harder.

"Abort!" he cried into his visor through gasps of air. "Abort… harvest… Opera… rator… in… field!" Straining with every swing, he almost laughed at his broken speech, but terror took over as the buzz of the second drone-tsunami cascaded down.

"Connect me… to Human… Monitor… now!"

"Connecting you now," Control obliged.

But 'now' didn't happen immediately.

Andre reached the trunk platform and swung out to grab on. His shoulder muscle spasmed, his left hand slipped, and he grabbed nothing but air. Falling down into empty space, his stomach floated in zero gravity. There was nothing he could do but flap his arms, like a mime artist trying to fly.

For one drawn-out moment, he was sure he was plummeting all the way to the bottom of the farm. But his body slammed into something solid, knocking all the air out of his lungs, and he realized the platform below had broken his fall.

He dragged himself to his feet and stumbled toward the sealing chamber. He banged the palm of his hand on the door control, but it didn't respond. He slammed again. Still nothing. Stepping back, his gut sank as he spotted the flashing red light above the door.

The air exploded into a hail of spinning blades.

Crack

"Control," he screamed, swatting the drones away and banging on the glass door panel. "Open the sealing door!" He pressed himself against the glass, but still couldn't avoid the spinning, razor-sharp cutters slicing and biting his back.

Snit-snit-snit-snit…

With his mind wrapped in a blanket of medication, he struggled to think of the number of the branch he'd fallen onto. "Fifteen! Open door fifteen!"

—You're on fourteen, Boss. Four-teen.—

"Fourteen! Open fourteen!"

The tiny monsters ebbed and circled around the branches in a starling wave, scanning the plants and coordinating their harvest. As soon as they turned back, their down-swarm would rip him to shreds.

"Open all the doors! Open all the doors on tower three!" He smashed his fist against the door, praying with every impact that the safety glass would give way before the drones dropped again.

"Safety procedures require you to confirm—"

"Screw your fucking safety procedures! Open the goddamn doors!"

The hissing reached a crescendo, and the swarm dropped, submerging him in a world of slicing, biting pain. Defeated, he fell to his knees, curled in a ball and pressed himself as close to the glass as he could. The droid attached to his belt dug into his side, and an idea flashed through his mind.

He stood up into the swarm, ripped the droid from his belt, and smashed its hard body against the door's thick glass, as fast and as hard as his sedated muscles would allow. Cracks splintered the door, but his motions confused the drones' delicate algorithms, drawing more toward him. His violent actions activated the implant, its mini-medicine factory working overtime, pumping more sedative into his body. Assailed from outside and within, he collapsed against the cracked glass.

Slipping into unconsciousness, a whistle of a rising wind filled his ears, muffling the sound of the drones. His brother's nasty voice spat into his mind.

{Do it, little bro. Finish the job.}

Everything around him blurred and pain faded from his immediate sensory field. Slapped awake by the closeness of the voice, he clenched his fist around the broken droid. He stepped back among the spinning blades, numb to the cuts and tears in his skin, and dove, droid held in front of him, through the cracked door.

Shattering the glass, he landed on the floor in a shower of falling shards. Confused by the motion, the drones swarmed in, bouncing off the chamber walls and ceiling in a deadly ricochet. He rolled back onto his feet and sprinted toward the waiting lift. With one final burst of anger-fueled energy, he dove again and crashed into the lift corner, tumbled over, and kicked the close button. The lift door slid shut behind him.

Just as sudden as it emerged, the rage left him, disappearing under the haze of the implant's massive dose. Confused drones smacked their little heads against the outer door, their tiny razor-sharp blades snipping at the safety glass.

Spiking out of his sedation, pain screamed through his shoulders and tore through his back. Warm blood trickled from his fingertips onto the lift floor. Exhausted, he slumped onto his hands and knees, and threw up.

"Dirk here," came a gruff, human voice through his visor. "What's the problem?"

Andre could not respond. Deep in his bones, his anger shifted and pushed against the implant's chemical cage. He wondered—not for the first time—if the implant was strong enough to keep the dark thing restrained forever.

As the lift slid down the trunk shaft, he floated inside his body, his mind submerging deeper under the heavy fog of medication, and his thoughts retreated to the deep recesses of his memory.

Egg

Andre's fragile ten-year-old mind had been slow cooked in the steam of residual hate left behind by his dead father; the hate crouched in his mother's eyes from behind her bourbon glass, and the hate nestled in his brother's bitter heart. That was family.

Jeremy, five-years older and soaked with dark energy, used his size and age to his advantage, taking things from Andre, threatening him, beating him, dangling him over the walkways. Andre had fought back, but being smaller and weaker, his futile efforts were frustrating and emotionally debilitating. Dismissed by his mother as brotherly behavior, Jeremy's tormenting became ever more brutal and sadistic. On the morning Jeremy held his switchblade to Andre's throat and slit the skin of his little brother's neck, he did it with a laugh, as if they were best of friends sharing a special moment.

"We've got no room for weakness in this house," his mother had slurred, when Andre went crying to her, blood soaking his shirt. "You got to stand up for yourself, Andre," she insisted, leaning so close to his tear-stained face that the sweet and sharp smell of alcohol on her breath stung his eyes, "or this world is gonna eat you up."

That was just how things were. That was family.

By the time he was twelve, Andre stopped feeling anything, certain that was how things would be forever. Until, on one perfectly still, baby-blue-skied day, everything changed.

That day began with Andre rising early to avoid Jeremy's morning volatility, and panned out like every other day—library, recreation hall, back to the library, then down to the cages in the e-waste district.

Lined in rows of towering wire-mesh rectangles, the cages were filled with Upper Brulle's discarded technology, to be sorted and recycled into new devices. Upper Brulle's insatiable consumer habits had flooded the recycling facility until it spread into an entire district spanning a platform connecting all four Stems. Stacked by automatic drones, and monitored by inadequate and badly maintained security, the district became Andre's perfect escape from his tormented home life. He spent every afternoon crawling through the cages, searching for anything still working that he could take home and use as a reason to hide in his room. Other scavengers collected outdated devices and parts to hack and modify into their own hybrid gadgets. Not Andre. He wanted things ready to use that would entertain and distract his increasingly chaotic mind.

On that day—with its misleading promise of a clear sky—he found an old wristlet, one of the first designs. He used his circuit tester to confirm it was in working condition, booted it up, and wrapped it around his wrist.

"I'll swap you."

The light voice from behind startled him. He spun around to face a thin, pale boy, hunched forward by the weight of a bulging pack on his back. The boy eyed the gadget on Andre's wrist. Andre shrugged.

"What you got?"

The boy slid off his backpack and pulled out a silver, flat, rectangular box. "I found a working DVD player." He pointed at Andre's wristlet. "I'll swap you this for that."

Andre hesitated, already comfortable with the gadget against his skin. "Nah."

"Finn!" a voice called from in the distance. The boy looked around, a worry in his eyes. He withdrew a small plastic container from his pack and held it forward. "I got a box of DVD's, as well. They're old Hollywood movies from last century. You can have these, too. All of 'em." The boy shook the container.

There's gotta be fifty discs in there, Andre thought. He had never been good at math but he knew that fifty DVDs meant many hours of escape from reality. He was sold. He made the exchange, and the boy raced off toward the voice calling him, without a thank you or goodbye.

Bloody scavengers.

Clutching his precious player, and the hours of entertainment imprisoned in its shiny discs, Andre forgot the boy in the cages and raced home. Eager to immerse himself in the cinematic world where heroes were winners and bad guys came last—and there wasn't ever a question about who the hell was who—he burst into his room and pounced onto the floor to set up the archaic machine.

Opening the box of DVDs, he discovered a 1980's movie that would become his favorite—Superman II. He slid the disc into the player, sat back, and immersed himself in the struggle between good and evil. The costumes were ridiculous, but the faces of the villains—General Zod, the beautiful and deadly Ursa, and the docile mute Non—pressed flat against the claustrophobic, two-dimensional Phantom Zone prison as it spun through space, pleasantly terrified him. He let out a loud sigh of guilty relief when, after Superman threw a terrorist's bomb out of the atmosphere to save the world, the detonation inadvertently shattered the Phantom Zone and freed the three Kryptonian criminals.

Yes!

He knew he shouldn't have been cheering a bad man like Zod, but many times after, he really wished there were another version of the movie where General Zod won.

Knees tucked under his chin, arms hugging his legs, he stared mesmerized as Zod forced the President of the United States to kneel before him. Engrossed, Andre didn't notice his brother stride into the bedroom until Jeremy stood by the small TV and kicked it off its bench. The screen shattered, just like the glass of the Phantom Zone had when it released Zod.

Rage filled Andre like helium in a balloon. His hands clenched into fists and his head shook. Before he could react, however, Jeremy said, "Shit, bro, sorry 'bout your TV. Hey, you wanna come for a walk?"

Stunned at the offer from his brother, Andre could only stare at him, as if flowers had sprouted from his ears and spirals spun in his eyes. Instead of those words coming out of Jeremy's mouth, they may as well have been a lizard-long tongue unrolling itself with lollies pouring out like the winnings of some crazy jackpot machine.

"A walk?" *Together?*

"Sure," Jeremy replied, shrugging and glancing at the broken TV. "If you're not doin' anything else. I wanna show you somethin'."

Andre's anger faltered, deflated, and seeped out of him in a slow release. He had never done anything with his brother besides fight. And here was Jeremy, asking him to hang out, like they'd been doing it for years. The invisible tendril of hostility that had bound the brothers and slowly dried out Andre's heart to charcoal, seemed to just let go. Untethered, released, he felt ashamed of his aggression toward his own brother, as if maybe the tension between them had all been his own fault. The last of his bottled-up hatred rushed out of him and vanished in a puff of magician's smoke.

Awash with emotion he had never allowed himself to feel—was it love?—Andre dared a smile, and followed his brother out of the apartment into the nightmare that would change him forever.

As Jeremy led Andre through the alleyway between Olive and Net Towers, Andre couldn't take his eyes off the switch blade in Jeremy's hand, hypnotized by the metal blade sliding in and out of its sheath.

Snit-svit-snit-svit...

"Where are we going, Jez?" he asked, his voice bouncing with every step, and his feet almost floating off the ground.

Jeremy didn't reply. He just kept walking down the twisting and turning stairways, flicking his blade in and out. He led them deeper and deeper into Lower Brulle, the sky vanishing above them behind the city spires. The walkways narrowed and steepened into claustrophobic crevices. Andre had never been down so far, and the tight spaces made his chest heavy, his breathing becoming labored. Finally, light filtered up from below.

Coming to the bottom of the steps, he followed his brother out into the soft light of an underground park. Giant mirrors suspended overhead reflected the distant sun above, allowing trees and plant life to grow under the towers. The leaves and branches drooped heavy, however, like the ears and tail of a pet kept in a basement.

Smells bad, Andre thought. *Smells real bad down here.*

The contained earth squelched beneath their feet, and the smell of stale water seeped up through the ground as if the irrigation had failed.

—Turn back.—

The voice came from nowhere, like a scuba diver popping up out of the ocean when there was no boat around. Somehow, he knew he should listen to the voice—wherever it came from—but the magnetic pull of his brother's promise drew him forward.

"Is this where we're going, Jez?"

"Not long now, little bro. I'm gonna show you something," Jeremy teased, not looking back. "Something just for you to see."

"Just for me? Really? What is it?"

Again, Jeremy didn't answer. He just trudged across the sodden grass toward a grove of trees, all the while flicking his blade.

Snit-svit-snit-svit…

As the brothers followed the path into the dense area, the trees thickened and branches leaned in. The stale earth smell filled Andre's nose, bringing with it some other sulfuric odor. He stopped and watched his brother become a shadow in the dimming light.

"Jez." His voice came out broken, teetering on the back of his throat, barely making it into sound before almost falling back down into the thing twitching in his stomach. "Should we go back, Jez?"

Jeremy stepped off the path and pointed down into the ravine running around the edge of the park. "We're here." He squatted and chuckled. "Come on, dopey. Come here. Light's going."

Andre's hands shook and his heart pounded its bloody drum. His legs quivered and he hated it. He didn't want Jeremy to see him afraid. This was his moment to show his brother how strong he could be, but he was terrified by the way Jeremy hunched like a giant toad by the ravine. Willing his legs to move, Andre hobbled to the edge and peered over. An indiscernible shape fidgeted in the shadowy bottom of the ravine.

"What is it?" His mind strained to recognize the shapes. Then, he heard a childlike voice.

"Hello, will you help me?"

Andre stepped back in shock, but Jeremy's hand was faster, latching onto his little brother's arm.

"It's just a child-bot, dummy. It's an old one. Probably someone from Upper Brulle got bored of their Christmas present and dumped it over the walkways." Jeremy chuckled again. "Look at it."

Andre's vision adjusted to the darkness. The battered child-bot lay in a twisted pile of limbs and torso, its head facing backward. Components hung out of its side like guts. A red strip—appearing like dried blood in the low light—ran across eyes sparkling in the dark. A wave of prickles itched over his skin.

"How's it still alive?" he asked his brother, attempting to stall whatever Jeremy had planned.

"It's not alive, stupid. It's just a machine. Still got some power left in it. But they really should'a finished it off."

Jeremy let go of Andre's arm and offered him the knife. Andre looked at the dark silver of the blade, then at Jeremy, unsure of what he was doing. He had never been that close, in such a still moment, to see so deeply into his brother's eyes. There was nothing in Jeremy's eyes, nothing but a bottomless darkness.

"And I'm letting you do it, Andre, cause you're my little bro."

Those words, they hugged Andre's heart. He wanted to believe them. But Jeremy's eyes weren't dead anymore. They vibrated with a greedy, vacuumous quiver, as if they were sucking the last light out of the city and keeping it all for themselves. In the black-hole emptiness of Jeremy's pupils, Andre glimpsed the dark thing that made his brother so angry. Its tentacles reached out and wrapped around Andre, as if it had lured him down into a trap.

Icicles of adrenaline shot through his nervous system. His empty hand clawed in anticipation. A short, ridiculously high-pitched cackle escaped out of his terrifying joy, out of the car crash mix of all the emotion he was too young to understand. He let his desperate desire to believe in his brother's camaraderie override the fear that he had been tricked into doing something terrible, and he took his brother's knife. *Jeremy's own switchblade!*

"Go on, bro," Jeremy whispered, smiling. "Finish it."

Andre's body shook as he forced his legs to carry him down the ravine. Reaching the small, helpless android, he glanced up at Jeremy to make sure his brother was watching. "I'm gonna do it, Jez."

Jeremy was but a black blob on the edge of the pathway, a gargoyle in the twilight. "Do it, little bro. Finish the job." His words fell to the ground, heavy and final.

Andre turned back to the child-bot staring up at him.

"Hello," it said, trying to turn its head around the right way. "Will you help me? I'm—"

Andre raised the knife into the air and plunged it into the android's eye. Sparks sprayed the fading light. The child-bot convulsed and arched up in a spasm, a synthesized wail squealing out of its open, childlike mouth. Andre pulled back in terror.

It looks so human.

Jeremy's sadistic chuckle floated down the ravine and sat on Andre's shoulder. "Remember what Dad use to say, little bro? 'If you're going to tell 'em once, you might as well tell 'em twice.'"

Andre raised the knife again, but the child-bot's head shook from side-to-side, its wail grating against his raw nerves.

"Yes." Jeremy's voice slid into Andre's mind, as if his brother had turned into a lizard and curled up in his ear. "Do it."

"Will you help me?" the android gurgled.

I really need you to shut the hell up.

All the anger, all the frustration, all the raging fury he thought had vanished from his heart welled up like an underwater explosion and released itself. He stabbed the twitching android in the chest.

"Kill them, Andre." Jeremy's voice echoed through the darkness of the ravine. "Kill them."

{Yessss}

Wrapped up in his frenzy, Andre never questioned who Jeremy meant by 'them.' He didn't notice Jeremy's hissing voice had moved inside his head. He plunged the blade into the child-bot's soft, artificial skin again and again. Sparks flew out of its eyes and oils seeped out of its insides. He stabbed and he stabbed, no longer caring if it screeched or squealed. In that moment, as he raged against all the times Jeremy had hit him, all he knew was the satisfaction of the stabbing, and the strength it imbued him with. He no longer saw the android's face. It was Jeremy lying there in that ditch, smiling up at him through sparks and oil. Andre stabbed and stabbed, and the violence creeping around the caverns of his brother's black-hive heart quietly laid its dark egg in his.

PART TWO

OMENS OF A FEATHER

Mo Da

As the lift settled to a stop and slid its door to the side, Andre's mind slipped back to the present. The empty space in the open doorway stared back at him.

End of the line, buddy. You getting out, or what?

Slumped in the corner, his hands shook and his heart banged against the inner walls of his chest. But his pain sat behind a black shape in his thoughts that shifted its form every time he tried to identify it.

What in the hell just happened? Did the dark thing just sneak out of the implant? Did I let it out?

So much static crackled in his head. He couldn't be sure what really happened, or what might have been tricks of the medication's haze.

Jeremy. Jeremy did it.

Thinking sapped his energy. He blinked away the remnant memories littering his mind, pushed his hands against the sides of the lift cabin, and pulled himself to his feet. The ominous shape behind his thoughts disappeared, and the stinging pain in his back came alive.

He stepped out into a neon-lit hallway and headed to the infirmary, focusing on steadying his wobbly legs that made the floor seem soft and squidgy. He arched his back and pushed out his chest—as if that would ease the pain—and oxygen made its way into the medicated corners of his body. His heartbeat settled and the shaking stopped. By the time he reached the infirmary door, the thumping in his head had abated, his thinking had cleared, and the world around him had settled back into its solid form.

He swiped his wristlet over a control panel, and the door slid open, revealing a long room with four metal-framed beds huddled in the center. A glass wall at the opposite end of the room looked out to the tree-towers, their lower branches swinging close past the window. Harvest droids swarmed between the trunks, as they reconfigured maneuvers, before smothering the branches again like aphids.

Relaxed by the sense of safety from being behind the glass wall, he slumped onto the stained mattress of the first bed and searched around for the medi-bot. Machines lined the left side, a high-pitched beep repeating every few seconds from one of them. Tables and benches lined the right, with tools and smaller machines stacked on top of and crammed under them, and cables dangled in loops from the ceiling. Repairing both androids and people, the infirmary seemed more like a robotic workshop than a place to treat human wounds.

Finding a control board attached to the bed's rail, he punched commands into its keypad. A cable hanging beside him jolted and hummed to life. With a clunk, a spherical medi-bot lowered from the ceiling, expanding and retracting its seven arms, as if it were an obese Swiss-army knife stretching before a workout. It floated down next to the bed, and a red laser shot out from the eye on its top-right side.

"Hello," a voice crackled from its speaker. "Please state the location and nature of your concern."

Andre ignored the medi-bot's request and let it make its own assessment. He winced at the ghost pain of the laser running over his back. Completing its scan, the medi-bot settled in front of him.

"You have severe lacerations on your back and shoulders. Would you like treatment?"

"Proceed," he confirmed. A screen lit up on the medi-bot's panel, and he pressed his thumb against it to register his identity.

"Thank you. Please prepare for some discomfort." The surgical robot extended an arm and swabbed his cuts one at a time.

Just hurry up so I can get out of here.

The infirmary door slid open, and a female android walked in, carrying a limp technician in her arms. Andre recognized Jackson immediately.

Where the hell have you been?

At first, Andre thought his co-worker had also been caught in the swarm. But Jackson's body bore no visible wounds. As the android placed him on the third bed, Jackson shook and twitched in his unconscious state.

The medi-bot swabbed a deep cut in Andre's shoulder. "Ouch," he exclaimed, pulling away.

"My apologies," the medi-bot responded. "Would you—"

Andre waved away the robots attempted offer to stop. "Continue."

Leaning back, and gritting his teeth, so the medi-bot could proceed, he looked over the naked form of the PrePAC inserting a drip into Jackson's arm. He didn't care much for the Baron's archaic, misogynist pension for female PrePAC staff. They all appeared the same after a while—only their names printed on their necks and the occasional different facial markings, gave them any individual identity.

Truth be told, Andre hated PrePACs. He hated their human-like appearance and abilities, enabling them to steal human jobs. He hated them because they were too human, perfect humans. Except that, even though they were aware, the Mesh that controlled them kept them somewhat vacant, like extremely polite zombies—and that was not natural. But most of all, Andre hated the way Upper Brulle treated androids better than they did the migrants, forming relationships with them, falling in love with them.

The PrePAC paused her procedure and looked up, tilting her head to the side. One red stripe ran across her eyes like a perfect, bloody brush stroke.

Andre froze with embarrassment, as if she'd caught him stealing something. A strange mix of panic, regret, desire and despair beat separate drums of anxiety in his chest. Sound disappeared from the room for an instant, as if sucked into an invisible vacuum, and the white noise of rushing air filled his ears. His heart flickered erratically in time with the overhead lights, and one thought flashed into his mind:

It's the child-bot all grown up…

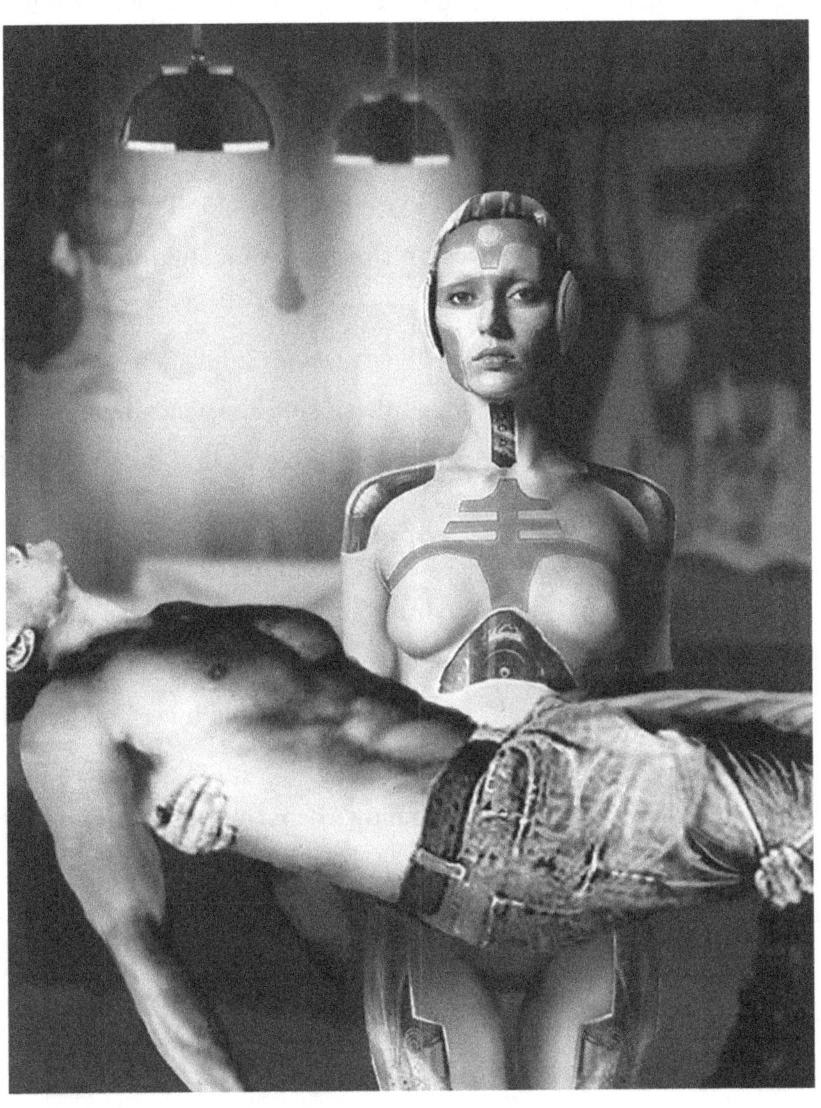

Connection

But of course, it wasn't. The red eye strip was a common adornment on PrePACs.

And PrePACs don't grow up. They don't even die. Unless they're murdered.

He tried to turn away from her eyes, but he couldn't. She *did* look like an older version of the child-bot, his memory of it still lurking in the shallows of his mind.

Why do they all have to look so bloody similar?

Raw guilt bloomed from a dark garden inside him, catching him off-guard and overwhelming him. An unrecognizable feeling dominated all his other internal sensations.

—It's just an android, Boss. Pull yourself together.—

He was being stupid, but the disturbing familiarity of the android leaned on a big, red 'don't-touch' button in the core of his being.

"Excuse me, sir," she said, jolting him out of his inner conflict. "I detect a spike in your heart rate. Are you in shock?"

"What? No. No, I'm fine. Mind your own damn business." His cheeks flushed with heat. Being rattled by the android frustrated him even more, and his inner swelter intensified.

—Stay in the front room, Boss.—

Stay in the front room, he repeated to himself.

—Jackson doesn't seem well, does he, Boss?—

Andre diverted his attention back to his co-worker.

"What happened to him?" Andre asked the android, unable to resist another glance at her face. The name on her neck read 'Mo Da'.

"Operator 4 has suffered an allergic reaction to ingested chemicals," Mo Da explained, her pale and delicate hands rolling back his sleeve to reveal a gangrenous wound surrounded by scaly flesh. The crocodile skin around the wound's edge formed deep fissures threading through his arm.

Geez, Jackson. "What the hell is that?"

"If you are referring to the scaling on his left arm, he has been injecting zilla."

Andre recognized in Jackson's face the same gaunt look of drug users in the Stems, his dark skin having had hid it well until now. Jackson had always been scattered and unreliable—did he even have any Reliability Rating left?—but drug addiction had never entered Andre's mind.

"PrePAC, what is zilla?"

Mo Da hovered her hands over Jackson's arm, light emanating from her palms, as she scanned his wound.

"Zilla is a combination of Neura and Troplamid, an over-the-counter pain-killer, and is injected into the vein. Dangers are paranoia, hyper-arousal, and rage-induced psychosis." Her innocent delivery of something so horrific fascinated him. "Regular use damages the tissue of the injected area, causing the skin to scale. It is for these reasons users term this concoction 'zilla', after the fictitious Japanese monster, Godzilla—"

"Yeah, yeah, okay, I get it."

He could have listened to her talk more, but his own stomach cramped in retaliation to his morbid delight.

He'd heard about dealers making their own home-brew, cutting Neura with dangerous ingredients and selling it to the migrants who couldn't afford the pure drug. He'd considered mixing his own, but when he met his *Best and Only Customer*, he didn't need to worry about stretching his stock or making it more affordable. Besides, mixing was risky, and a dead customer was not a good customer.

That's just not good business sense.

Mo Da completed her scan and swabbed Jackson's wound.

"Will he be alright?" Andre inquired, more as a reason to look at Mo Da again than out of any real interest in Jackson's well-being.

"It seems Operator 4 did not follow the correct Neura-Troplamid ratio. Such an error is ninety-two percent fatal."

"Quiet," a gravelly voice demanded from the doorway. A burly man with a beard, in a sleeveless black shirt and black cargo pants, strode in to the infirmary. A strip of stark white ran through the middle of his dark hair, and a rifle hung over a shoulder that glistened with the synthetic skin of a prosthetic.

A borg.

Andre loathed PrePACs, but borgs prickled his skin. Tortured by the presence of the implant in his head, he could not fathom why anyone would willingly replace healthy limbs with prosthetics.

Standing over Jackson's unconscious body, the borg guard grabbed the technician's other arm and rolled up the sleeve. More scaling.

Jesus Jackson, what the hell have you been doing to yourself?

"Prepare for injection in your left shoulder," the medi-bot warned, startling Andre with its automatic and toneless voice. He'd forgotten it was even there. A needle protruded from one of its appendages. Hovering by his shoulder, it tilted forward and jabbed the needle into his skin with a sting.

"Sir," Mo Da said to the guard. "I found this with Operator 4." She held out a small, glass vial. "This is Troplamid, an over the counter painkiller. Users mix this with Neura to extend its supply and potency—"

"I know a zilla user when I see one." The borg's words lacked emotion, sounding as robotic as the medi-bot. He paced around Jackson's bed, stroking his jet-black, shovel-shaped beard. As he turned, the neon light fell on his hand, revealing the unmistakable stylized black eagle design of the farm's security insignia. Only one man in the farm wore that tattoo—Strato, the Baron's Chief of Security. A heady mix of fear and contempt filled Andre. To him, Strato was nothing more than another robot, Grekov's tool. But the borg's violent management of the farm's security was well known. Titan might have owned the farms, but Grekov and his iron fist, Strato, controlled them.

Andre panicked, wondering if Strato was there to deal with him for damaging the Blue Eyes. *Did Dirk finally crack it and rat on me?* He hunched over and lowered his head in an attempt to not draw attention to himself, when the medi-bot blasted his back with a dry spray. He shot upright and cried out in pain. Strato blinked and turned his dark eyes on Andre.

Shit.

"What are you doing here, Operator?"

The repetitive beep from the machine ticked over the seconds as Andre searched for words to respond. He finally opened his mouth, but Jackson spasmed, arching up on the bed like a person possessed. Strato's hand clutched his rifle as he spun back to Jackson's convulsing body.

Thanks Jackson. Now we're even. Time to get out of here.

Jackson threw back his head, arms springing out to the side, and his hands clawed at the bed. A guttural sound rattled from deep in his throat. With the scaling on his arms, he looked like some half-human, half-reptile mutation.

"Medi-bot," called Mo Da, "sedative required."

The medi-bot pulled away from Andre, leaving his treatment unfinished, and slid along its railing to hang above Jackson's bed. Mo Da restrained him, and the suspended robot injected Jackson with a clear-liquid, but his body continued to convulse.

"Enough," stated Strato. He slipped the rifle from his shoulder, flipped it to face the handle forward, drew back, and swung at Jackson's throttling head. But before the handle hit its mark, Mo Da's hand shot out, like a bullet, and grabbed the rifle. Halted mid-swing, Strato fell forward with the momentum and into the barrel end of his weapon, and bounced back.

Andre's heart thumped, his palms sweated. Mo Da's focus, her indifference, her exotic deadliness thrilled him.

In one precise and fluid movement, Strato ripped his weapon free from Mo Da's grip and kicked the android's legs out from under her. By the time Mo Da hit the floor, he had flipped the rifle again and pointed the barrel end at her beautifully impervious face.

The overhead neons flickered, as if the infirmary took a snapshot of the special moment—cyborg and android in a standoff, mutated human convulsing at their side.

Andre's exhilaration morphed into fear and panic, and his heart pounded like a jungle drum. Before he could even think, he jumped from the bed and called out, "Wait!"

"Sit down, Operator," Strato snapped. He did not flinch, did not take his eyes off Mo Da. The finality of his words slapped Andre out of blind reaction, and the Captain's voice popped up out of its hiatus.

—Sit down, Boss. Sit-the-fuck-down.—

Shaking, Andre lowered himself back, like a blind man feeling behind himself for a seat. The medi-bot swung back to his bed and settled beside him. A faint wave of the medication's haze washed over him, as if the excitement had activated the implant.

What the hell am I doing?

"Sir," Mo Da explained, holding up her human-like hands from her position on the floor. "Please forgive my interference. I am programmed to protect human life."

For a moment, Andre thought he heard the click of Strato's finger pulling the trigger. He flinched, as if Mo Da had been shot. In his mind's eye, her head exploded, like the Phantom Zone, releasing three angry, otherworldly criminals to fly around the room and rip Strato to pieces. But when she spoke, it was Andre's hallucination that shattered, dissolving back into the stark reality of the infirmary.

"I would be forced to report this to the Mesh," Mo Da continued, tilting her head and widening her hands in an explanatory gesture. Andre watched Strato with stunned anticipation.

Did she just threaten him?

"Like all PrePACs," she continued, "I share my experiences with the hive mind of the Mesh, to better predict human needs. Any witnessed crime is automatically reported."

She was simply stating what she had been programmed to do. But her timing, her gesture, her tone—*android's don't have tone*—they all hinted at feigned ignorance and calculated delivery.

—You're imagining things, Boss. She's just an android.—

Strato stood poised to blast her head open. His self-control unnerved

Andre more than if the borg had pulled the trigger. Only Strato's eyelid quivered to betray his doubt. Andre envied the borg's self-control as much as he feared it.

Making up his mind, Strato stepped back, slid his rifle back over his shoulder, and walked toward the door. "Take the Operator to the holding cells," he ordered calmly. "Immediately." As the door slid shut behind his hulking frame, the room itself seemed to breathe a sigh of relief.

Jackson, still unconscious but settled, lay panting on his back, his face and body drenched with sweat. Mo Da rose and placed a hand on his wrist. As Jackson's sweat released the zilla from his skin, a stink like burnt plastic and urine filled the room. Mo Da looked up at Andre.

"Thank you for your assistance."

Conflicting emotions besieged him. Embarrassed by his own excitement at connecting with the android, he couldn't deny the thrill of being a part of what had just happened.

—Connecting? You're 'connecting' with a machine? Are you keeping it real, Boss? She almost got you killed.—

You're right. Damn PrePACs are too real. They're too bloody real.

The medi-bot swung around in front of him. "Please avoid operating heavy machinery or performing hefty lifting for two hours. Should you experience fever or vomiting, please report to your GP. Thank you for your patience." The medi-bot folded its arms back into its orb body and drew itself up into the dock in the ceiling. The dangling cables swayed and clanged, and the anonymous machine along the wall repeated its beep.

Eager to escape the pungent odor emanating from Jackson's body—and to get away from Mo Da's disturbing effect on him—Andre eased off the bed and pulled his overalls carefully over his shoulders. As he tightened the straps, his wristlet vibrated and he checked the screen:

Can you do it or not?

He cursed at forgetting to respond to his *Best and Only Customer*.

—*You want to get your mind back on the Job now, Boss?*—

Mo Da picked up Jackson's unconscious body and carried him across the room. His limp foot knocked the empty Troplamid vial from the bed, the glass cylinder hitting the floor with a defiant ting and rolling over to Andre in a perfect arc. It stopped with a dull clink at his boot, label side up.

Hi, I'm Troplamid. Call me Troppy. That PrePACs's sure got sumthin' extraordinary about 'er, don't she?

Andre snatched the empty vial from the ground and squeezed it quiet.

"Android," he called to Mo Da, refusing to look at her, refusing to say her name aloud, as if that might affirm the affect she had on him. "What is the safe ratio, of Neura to Troplamid?"

Keeping his back to Mo Da, he heard the door slide open. In his mind, he saw her turn in the doorway and tilt her head.

"The safe ratio of Neura to Troplamid is 5.7 to 4.3. Although not illegal, sir, I do not recommend it. Dangers of paranoia, hyper-arousal—"

"Enough," he said, waving her away.

"Good day, sir," she replied, and the door slid shut.

A muffled clunk echoed from outside the window. The drone swarm gathered upward and disappeared behind the lights high in the ceiling, back into its nest. A branch whooshed past close to the window, and blue petals floated through the air. The farm stood quiet with the finish of the harvest.

Until the next harvest. And the next. How many until I get out of this hellhole. That's if I don't get myself fired, or worse. What was I thinking, standing up for her?

—*It's just a machine, Boss.*—

Something new stirred in his heart, something fluttering and delicate; something that activated his implant, but was not his temper. Terror gripped him. The giddying sensation lay right next to the dark thing, like twins in a womb.

If I don't get the hell out of this place, I'm going to go mad.

—*Don't even think about it, Boss.*—

He slipped the glass cylinder into the inner pocket of his overalls and tapped a reply to Finn on his wristlet:

I'll see what I can do

Price

He headed down the corridor with a new sense of purpose spearing out of the medication's haze. Perhaps mixing zilla was too much of a risk, but he kept the idea in the back pocket of his thoughts, and let his Plan run a subconscious risk assessment. Just the availability of an alternate option relieved some of the mounting pressure.

In fact, the day's events only made him more determined to do whatever he had to do to escape Brulle. As fast as he could. The solid structure he thought he'd built in his mind had revealed itself to be riddled with gaps. If a strong wind came, those gaps were bound to make a lot of noise.

His wristlet vibrated, snapping him out of his planning. He cursed Finn for his impatience, but the message was from Dirk:

See me before you go

He cringed. Facing Dirk for the crushed Blue Eyes, before the old coot had a good night's sleep to calm down, did not bode well for Andre's Reliability Rating. As much as Dirk wanted Andre's credits for the smuggling fee—a customer is only as good as the credits in his account—he had put his own job on the line several times covering for Andre's regular stuff ups. And although Dirk seemed to hold a soft spot for him, Andre knew the sly old dog would stick his neck out only so far. Andre sensed that line drew near. Then it would be *adiós job* and *astalavista Anchora*.

As he rode the lift up three levels to the control room, the lift's wall screen showed a sprawling city hovering over a twinkling expanse of water. Seductive aqua-marines reflected in his eyes.

"Anchora," the voice-over said through the lift's speakers. "Your platform to the stars." The image zoomed in on the base of a cylindrical tower protruding from the city's center. A lift cabin shot up inside the tower rising through the clouds, sped through the opalesque thermosphere, and came to rest at the Orbitor platform twenty kilometers above sea level. Space planes launched from the runway, transporting people and goods toward the ISS and Moon Village. "Third release visa applications now open. Only seven thousand credits, on approval."

Andre rubbed his shoulder and rummaged through his thoughts, searching for an argument to sweet-talk Dirk out of deducting his shifts. His shoulder muscles burned, distracting him, until he cursed his harness, and—*bingo!*—he found his angle: Dirk's failure to service his harness. If he played the confrontation right, he could turn the situation to his favor. As long as he didn't have to explain why he acted like a drunk out in the farm that morning, he would be fine. He hadn't told anyone about his implant, for fear of the questions it would generate. His past was a titanium box he didn't intend to open.

Inhaling lungs full of confidence, he marched into the dark control room.

A fly eye's configuration of monitors surrounded the window looking out over the farm. Data and information displayed across the window's glass. But Dirk slouched in his chair facing a TV in the sidewall. The reflection of flashing advertisements fluttered across his haggard, sleepy-eyed face. Catching Dirk in a moment of inattention was a good starting point for Andre's argument.

Perfect.

"You," Andre snapped, pointing at his lounging manager. "You nearly got me killed out there."

Dirk's heavy eyes flicked open and he sat up straight. A cloud of thin, red hair clutched for life around the sides of his shiny head. He unfolded his thin arms and turned to the data display on the window.

"Don't you start blaming me, boy," he snapped back. "I followed protocol. I responded as soon as I was alerted."

"If you'd been doing your job and watching the data on the screens instead of the TV you wouldn't need to be alerted."

"Hrumph." Dirk made the familiar noise he made whenever he couldn't admit he was wrong. "Well, you're alive, ain't ya?" A tight, raspy cough wracked his lungs.

Andre stopped at Dirk's side, and saw deep, black crescents weighing down the old man's blood-shot eyes.

"Anyways," Dirk continued, "I got your harness retrieved. It's in for service. You can pick it up in the morning. Now, about the damage—"

Andre laughed, cutting off Dirk's attempt to avoid the harness issue.

"I've been telling you that for the last week. That's four times that hunk of junk's stuffed up on me. This time could have been my last."

Dirk wiped sweat from his forehead and tapped into the table's interface. "Can't be sending it off every time you hear a little squeak."

"I got ripped to shreds out there today!" Andre turned to show his bandaged back and shoulders.

Dirk only glanced at Andre's wounds, and scoffed. "That's the way the world works, boy. Puts on a big birthday party for you when you first arrive, then follows it with ticks and tocks and hard knocks as it counts down your time." He burst into another coughing fit and fumbled for his water bottle. Whatever disease had been eating away at the old man's chest for the last twelve months had settled in and started feeding on the rest of him.

"Here," Andre offered, sliding the bottle across the desk so Dirk could reach it. He had no idea how old Dirk was, but he couldn't have much longer. His skin had paled to a sallow grey, and weight had been abandoning him by the week.

A far cry from the jovial character I met a year ago.

Even then, when Andre started working on the farm, Dirk had a face like a crumpled-up old map. But he was solid and vibrant. Always frowning and huffing, with a long, red beard that coiled over his barrel body, he looked like a feisty dwarf lost out of some fantasy world. Now he was more a wraith from a B-grade horror comic. Once, Andre had inquired about Dirk's health, curious why an old man so close to death focused so much on wealth. In return for his concern, Andre had received a verbal tirade about privacy and gossip.

Andre lowered himself gently onto the seat next to his ailing manager, careful not to bump his own bandaged back. "Just another twelve-hour day, old man. No problem," he obliged, feeling pity for him.

"Now," Dirk said, plonking down the water bottle, as if it were a nuisance. "Let's talk about what happened out there today."

Old devil softened me up.

Dirk poked a swollen finger right in Andre's face. "You ever damage a bush again, and Grekov will hear about it. You got me?"

Andre nodded. Another rattling cough shook Dirk. Andre pushed the water to him again, and Dirk snatched it away.

"Why, Dirk?"

"Why what?" Dirk barked before gulping the water.

"I know I'm a risk for you. And I know you're doing me a good price on the ship to Anchora. Jackson told me what you were charging him."

"'Were' being the operative word there. Shame about that. He was outta here in five days." Dirk took another sip of the water and turned his blood shot eyes on Andre. "You're not a very trusting person, are you, Cross?"

"Come on, you know what I mean. If Grekov finds out the number of times you've covered for me, you'll be gone, too."

"S'pose that's your way of saying thanks. Lot easier just saying thanks." Dirk wiped water droplets from his wiry mustache. "I been here a long time, Cross. I know the look a man gets when he's got an implant spittin' its poison into his brain."

Andre's heart jumped. His titanium box of secrets had materialized and opened in the middle of the room. Dirk waved away his surprise.

"Don't be gettin' your knickers in a knot. I won't be telling nobody." He leaned forward, peering into Andre's eyes, his breath pungent with the sweet, dirty smell of coffee and bourbon, and Andre saw it, for the first time. Dirk's eyes had dulled to the same listless glass that Andre met in his own each morning in the mirror. "You're an Implant, too?" he asked.

Dirk sat back, almost proud. "One of the first."

"I…I had no idea."

Dirk's brow bunched down, his expression dropping into seriousness. "With that thing in your head, your future isn't looking pretty, boy. But, believe me, it's a lot prettier than if you don't have it.

Embarrassed by the revelation of his secret, but touched by the man's sensitivity—and surprisingly relieved to share his secret with someone— Andre realized the crazy old bastard might be his only friend.

Dirk squinted. "It's not easy, I know. For you. It's gonna be harder. Whatever crazy thing you did to get yourself that implant, it's still haunting you. I can see it in your eyes. If you don't get out of this city soon, you're gonna flip. Right, boy? You know it, don't ya? And by the looks of your hacked-up rig, that might be a lot sooner than I first gave you credit for. Now, I don't know if runnin' away is gonna *get* you away from it, but it sure as hell is gonna give you a better chance than stayin' in this shithole." The old man's cough again hijacked his lungs.

Andre patted him on the back, but Dirk brushed him away.

"Why didn't you say something before?" Andre asked.

Dirk gulped down the cough. "It's a man's choice whether he wants to talk about it or not. Not everyone's gonna be okay with you havin' a robot roach on your spine. I get it, but other folk will think you're a borg. And unless you're a guard, like Strato, if you get borg status you won't last long in Lower Brulle. We both know that."

Andre dared a question he thought he would never ask another. "Do you ever … has the implant ever …?"

Dirk smiled. The dark circles curving under his eyes blackened. "You might think the implant can't handle what's going on in your head, boy, but I can tell you, it gets stronger over time. And if you don't tame your crazy, you'll start needin' the meds, like a junky does zilla. If you don't get in control, that thing will feed off you, like a parasite, and eat you from the inside out. Best thing to do is to not aggravate it. Get as far away from the source of that aggravation as possible. That's the implant's purpose, isn't it, to stop you gettin' angry?"

Andre nodded. Dirk understood things better than he realized. Anchora's sprawling cityscape flashed again in his mind. Twelve more months in Brulle seemed like a lifetime. No, a life sentence.

"It's just … here, this farm, this city. The memories …"

"Yup. I know about that, too. If I was in better shape, I'd get outta here myself. No point now. My wife being too sick to travel. But for an Implant like you, well, I'm sure it's worth a lot more."

Dirk's words snapped Andre to attention. "A lot more than what?"

"Well, you're right about one thing, young fella. I ain't doing nuthin' for nuthin'. A ticket to Anchora is worth a lot more to someone with an

Implant than someone without one, right? And anyway, with Jackson's fee out of the equation, I need to compensate."

The penny dropped, and it was a Godzilla-sized penny.

"You slimy, old—"

"Ah, ah." Dirk waved his fat finger. "Favors aren't free, boy, no matter how much I pity ya. Like you said, I'm risking a lot more than you're payin'. Business is business."

Anger lit a match under Andre's implant and blew on the flame.

—Breathe, Boss. Breathe. This old man is your ticket out of here. Don't fuck it up.—

"How much?" Andre asked.

Dirk gulped back the raspy rattle rising in his throat. "Fourteen."

"What? Fourteen thousand credits? That's double what a visa costs!"

Dirk's lips spread apart and tore his face like a rip. "But you ain't never gonna get a visa, are you, boy?"

Andre's chest heaved with the breathing techniques he was getting sick and tired of practicing.

"That's settled then," Dirk said, sitting upright and tapping onto the keypad on the desk. "Anyways, I need you in early tomorrow. Since I can't trust you out near the plants, I got Smythe covering Jackson's shift in the greenhouse. You can take Smythe's shift in the lower levels. You might not appreciate it, boy, but I *do* look after you."

Andre pressed his fingers against the table's surface until their tips glowed white. The pressure helped him fight back the thoughts of what he wanted to do Dirk's weathered head. Dirk glanced sideways at his hand clawing the table.

"You might want to see about that anger problem of yours, boy."

—Get up and go, Boss. Now. He's not worth it. You got this.—

Andre flexed his mind to keep the violent thoughts and his implant at bay. He stood without speaking and trudged out the door.

"Oh, and boy?" Dirk called. "Don't fuck it up tomorrow. 'Cause my kindness only goes so far."

Laughing, Dirk burst into another spasmodic cough, his death-rattling bark following Andre all the way down the hall, chomping away on Andre's resistance to taking a risk.

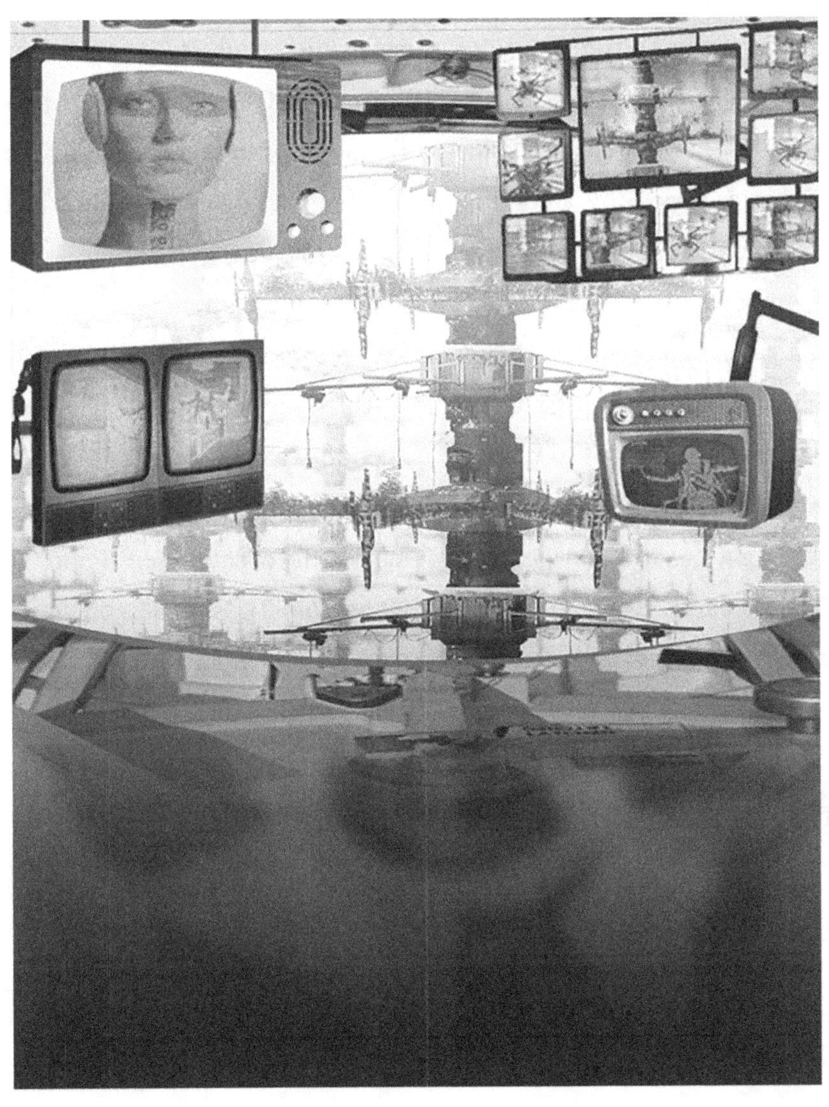

Host

Before the great loss of biodiversity turned the world's weather into a swarm of shape-shifting banshees, a menagerie of species, of all shapes and sizes, inhabited the oasis surface of the planet. One of the most hyper-diverse and beautiful creatures, the scorpion wasp, survived since before the Jurassic period by utilizing a terrifying survival technique that transformed its prey into zombie incubators for its young.

Equipped with a stinger-like appendage, a scorpion wasp would target a juvenile orb-weaver spider and lay an egg on the arachnid's back. Staying attached, the egg hatched a larva, which secreted chemical signals into its host, directing it to reshape its web into a cocoon-like structure. Protected from predators by the manipulated spider, the larva grew big enough to eat its surrogate mother and finished the cocoon itself. From the murdered spider's hijacked web, an adult scorpion wasp emerged, to fly off and hunt down the next juvenile prey, perpetuating the vicious, primordial instinct that knew only killing and eating.

Annihilation of global ecosystems reduced the hardy yet delicate wasp to but a memory in the world's digital libraries. However, the cunning and violent survival instinct that had kept the wasp and other species alive for millions of years endured as DNA junk in the primitive part of humanity's brain.

Andre didn't know anything about wasps, and he'd never seen a spider beyond the pixels of his TV, but he had been stung by his own parasitic demon of violence—the invisible stinger of his hate-filled family, slowly needling into his psyche over the years of his childhood. Penetrating his vulnerable, weakened, young spirit the day his older brother coached him into stabbing the child-bot, the dark thing's egg grew inside him and hatched the morning he committed murder. But before the dark thing drove him to continue the cycle of violence by provoking and embedding it in another, the authorities imprisoned Andre in solitary confinement and took away the dark thing's next prey.

Due to the nature of his crime, Andre's trial had been dealt with swiftly, after which he was immediately delivered to CRX—Brulle's 'correctional maximum' prison.

Built into the Docks at the base of the Stems, CRX imposed the highest levels of fully automated isolation upon an epidemic of convicted criminals, in an effort to detain them with minimum ongoing management costs. Rarely seeing another human being during their incarceration, many prisoners did not survive the brutal psychological trauma of extended solitary confinement.

On Andre's arrival, a soundless floor drone led him through the prison's vacant halls, past endless blank walls. For some reason he had expected arms swiping through gaps between cell bars. He had prepared for heckling, and threats, and all sorts of rancid smells. But when only a silent, sterile nothingness greeted him, he feared he'd walked into something worse than any place of violence. Violence he could survive— he still had the dark thing awake in him at that stage—but a total lack of stimulation or conflict threatened madness by spiritual vacuum.

Led to a nondescript panel in a wall, he stepped into a small separation room, then entered his cell—a cell within a cell. Two by two and a half meters in dimension, barely larger than his mother's king size bed.

After the first few weeks of utter peace and quiet, he found himself becoming obsessed with small things—the flicker of the light, dust in a corner, a faint mark on a wall. His moods swung, and without any visible change in his environment—except the food arriving in the delivery hole, and the water flushing in the toilet—he had no tangible thing to attach his mood swings to.

With no prey, the dark thing receded, slipped into a coma, and left Andre alone in a six-year hell.

He struggled to maintain his sanity on a day-to-day basis, and isolation panic set in. Imaginary sounds emerged out of the endless silence, frustrating him day and night. He lost his focus and reliable memory recall. His irritation became anger, blooming into a simmering rage. His actions, he realized, were calling to the dark thing, the power that had led him there. But in his complete isolation, the sense of strength and fearlessness that the dark thing had awoken in him did not return. To his great distress, the only thing that had ever needed him, abandoned him.

Fortunately, the compulsory 'rehabilitation' work on the Dock lifts provided a welcome relief from the confines of his cell. He climbed through the Dock's maze of empty shafts for hours, repairing stalled cabins and degenerated tracks. After years of his intrinsic human desire to be social completely denied, he made the shaft walls and the cabins his companions and familiars, with whom he discussed the day's meaningless events in detail.

With only irregular hours of lift work to break up the confinement, however, the isolation further pushed him into a terrifyingly empty place, completely destabilizing him. He began to question his very existence. He did outrageous things, harming himself, just to prove to himself that he was still there, that he could still have an effect on the world by provoking physical punishment from the robotic correctional systems.

Long after time had lost meaning, and teetering on the verge of madness, Andre awoke to an angel walking into his cell. Arriving from the other side of the nothingness, it stunned him further by engaging him in normal, everyday conversation.

"How are you, Boss? Have you been keeping busy?"

Andre wasn't sure how long he'd been talking before he realized the angel was not an angel but a man, a doctor, and he was offering Andre a way out. Doctor Steele had come on behalf of Titan, explaining their mood-control implant solution. As soon as Andre grasped the reality of the situation, he seized the chance at freedom.

The implant wasn't an instant solution, however, Doctor Steele advised. To ensure Andre would be a good candidate for the implant procedure, Titan would first monitor his activities. And the implant had its imperfections. But neither of these factors meant anything to Andre.

What's a few loose bolts on the only bridge out of hell?

Over the following seven months, he focused his purpose-starved attention on imposing upon himself a strict personal order. He adhered to a disciplined schedule of breathing and exercising to prove, to Titan and himself, that he was fully rehabilitated and ready to become a Good Citizen. His desperation empowered his ability to fool himself for a very long time.

Following a further three months of Doctor Steele's one-on-one counseling—in which time Andre developed the Captain in secret—the unseen mind of Titan determined Andre Cross was, indeed, at eighteen years of age, fit to return to society as an Implant.

After he signed some digital documents he didn't understand, Titan guards swept him through a kaleidoscope of foreign doors, corridors, rooms, and vehicles that seemed to move around his stationary self. He fell out of the transfer blur onto the crisp clean sheets of an operation bed in Titan. The implant procedure was quick and performed while he was still conscious. Following just a few days of tests, Doctor Steele released him back into the Stems.

The system set him up in a small apartment in the West Stem, where he stayed inside for days, afraid to leave. The chaos of the outside world overwhelmed him. To his surprise, free at last, he found himself longing for seclusion, for the safety of walls close around him. But Titan had plans to ensure he became a productive, successful Implant and organized him a job on the Neura farm. His lift experience on the Docks made him an ideal mechanic for the farm's tree-tower multi-lifts.

After initial trepidation, he submersed himself in routine and welcomed the return to a maze of shafts. His first paycheck—one hundred credits on his wristlet and a vial of Neura—was a foreign concept that beared no significance to him. All that mattered was that he had walls to cling to. He felt home.

Days turned to weeks, weeks to months, and the dark thing remained in its coma like a hibernating alien in the belly of an astronaut. Andre convinced himself he was glad it was gone. Moments of anger came, but they were mere sparks that quickly vanished under the firm rule of the Captain. He had purpose. He was on a direct course to becoming a Good Citizen.

Almost a year passed before the change in his internal rhythms, activated by the presence of others around him, agitated the dark thing. Trivial things began to annoy him, drawing him down mental tangents to where memories were kept like demented children in a basement.

While the darkness inside him waited patiently to provoke and embed its violence in another—someone alone, fragile, and desperate, just like he was when Jeremy put the blade in his hand—Andre's resolve began to waver. The Captain's reliability slipped. His temper got the better of him more regularly, and the implant burned often as it converted his proteins into its sedative medication. His moods shot up and down and slid sideways, like the lifts he spent his days fixing. His ship of hope veered far off course. He feared he was headed for the edge of madness again, when his co-worker, Jackson, told him about Anchora, and how Dirk could smuggle him there.

A light flickered on under the darkness of the past creeping back over his mind, and it shone a little clarity on his situation. His memories were his prison. Brulle was his jail keeper. The implant was an effective medicine, but what he needed even more was a prevention—one that only distance from his memories would provide.

With the promise of an achievable goal, a business-orientated aspect emerged in the Captain's voice. With that as his guidance, Andre spotted a new destination and swiftly mapped a course to reach it—get out of Brulle and get away to the vast flatness of Anchora.

Fresh winds of determination blew his sails and put him back on track to becoming a Good Citizen. He buried the corpse of his past under the floorboards of his internal vessel. He took on extra shifts, saved every credit, and sold all his Neura to his *Best and Only Customer*. He had the Plan, and he was determined to reach it as fast as possible.

But the dark thing had its own plan. The perilous reef of madness was the destination it had in mind for Andre, and destabilization was its trick.

When his biorhythms spiked on meeting Mo Da, Andre didn't notice the prickling release of the dark thing's predatory chemicals. Distracted by a sense of something he had forgotten—but which had not forgotten him—his steeled mindset again edged off its carefully plotted course. The dark thing leveraged his confusion, hijacked his rising emotions, and manipulated his actions to weave its cocoon, fooling Andre into believing he did things out of choice and good intention.

Omen

Exiting the lift, Andre crossed the farm's atrium and left via the main entrance. Every muscle in his body ached, the cuts on his back stung, and his head floated in the medication's residue.

Two more years of this. Two more years to save Dirk's greedy fee.

Craving a vape, and avoiding the crowds on the transport platform, he took the stairways clinging to the side of the tower cluster. On his way down the first set of stairs, he sparked up his vape and pulled the empty Troplamid vial from his pocket. He rolled it over in his hand and again raised the idea of mixing zilla.

He'd always sided with the Captain against risks. But that was a stance he'd taken twelve months ago, when he'd just gotten the implant. Stepping out of prison was like stepping onto a little sailing boat, a jar of optimism on deck, and his devotion to being a Good Citizen firmly grasping the wheel. His cramped apartment seemed like a luxury, and the prospect of a job blew like wind in his sails.

But that was twelve months ago. Twelve months of navigating the spiky haze of impulse versus implant. His optimism had been knocked over and broken so many times it was more cracks than solid. The constant repairing of that crumbling vessel distracted him. He spent more time veering off course and steering back to it than actually sailing on it. And since he was having this straight-up conversation with himself, he took a long hard look at the waterline around his Plan and admitted he was sinking. Because even though—*and let's just get right to the point shall we, Captain?*—he had covered it over with a false bottom, the zombie of his past lay under the floor of the lower decks, and, somehow, the undead thing itself was taking on water.

As he descended the stairs, passing a hive of hole-in-the-wall stores and bars billowing vapor, he slid the Troplamid back into his pocket.

He came back from reflecting on the twelve-month stretch behind him, and tried projecting the same time frame ahead. Then, he doubled it. He didn't need to be mathematical genius to work out where his Plan would be by then. On the bottom of the ocean. Even if the spiky haze didn't drive him mad, or the unreliable mechanics of the farm didn't rip off one of his limbs—*or, worse still, Boss, get yourself killed trying to be a knight in shining armor for a PrePAC; let's not forget that little twist on things*—he feared he'd end up a walking, talking, coughing husk, like Dirk.

He stopped at a viewing platform overlooking a patch of tower clusters clinging to the North Stem. Twinkling lights blinked across soot-blackened walls, and cleaner-bots scaled their sides in their never-ending eating of the anti-tech graffiti.

Brulle was the problem. His little jar of hope was no match for Brulle's monolith of memories. He needed to haul up some new sails while the fresh winds of opportunity blew and get back on course.

If 5.7 to 4.3 is a safe mix, then, hell, why not? Maybe this is the break I need. I should buy that Mo Da a drink.

He didn't doubt Finn would buy more from him. The reclusive hacker loved nothing more than staying in his seedy apartment, getting high, and tinkering away on his machines. *Just a little mix, maybe, from time to time.* Finn might notice the zilla's weaker affect, but Andre was sure Finn's addiction would get the better of his common sense and allow him to believe the zilla was Neura. *Maybe just a low ratio mix each time. See how that goes.*

—*You sure you wanna take that course, Boss? You get the ratio wrong, you could lose more than a customer.*—

True. But I can be careful.

—*And what about when he starts seeing those scales on his arm, Boss?*—

He's a user. What does he expect? He can use the other arm.

—*And if the Baron finds out you're bastardizing his product, you can bet your implant that your harness will be the least of your worries.*—

Maybe Grekov would be proud, Andre rebuffed, tired and frustrated by the Captain's anchor of sensibility, and slipping into an irrational defense. *Maybe Grekov will pat me on the pack and say, 'Hey. Very entrepreneurial, Andre. Want to set up shop for me in Anchora? I'll fly you there and hook you up.' Maybe taking a risk is what it takes to be an Extraordinary Citizen?*

Andre stood at the edge of his decision, like a virgin skydiver balks at an open plane door. He wasn't making sense and he knew it. He drew back on his vape to find it empty.

Stepping away from the viewing platform, he continued down the stairway and headed for Alta District where he usually bought his vape supplies. He reached another stairway and pushed through the jostling throng of people to reach the Best Top Pharmacy. Ducking under its neon sign hanging askew—the 's' and 'Top' flashing and sparking spasmodically as if zapping mosquitos—he turned sideways to squeeze through the doorway and into a crowded aisle, leaving the noise of the world behind him.

In the musty Zen garden quiet, floor to ceiling shelves—packed top-heavy with everything and anything—teetered over like ancient rock formations threatening to avalanche. Whatever Andre wanted, Bao—the store's bonsai-sized owner—was sure to have it. Her searching often took some shuffling and ladder climbing, but she always delivered. Best Top Pharmacy was more than just a pharmacy, more than just a two-dollar shop with pills; it was a retired genie bottle passing its twilight years, granting the humble wishes of the everyday citizen.

"Hello, Mr. Cross," Bao chimed, the happiest Chinese lady in history, smiling and bowing from behind the counter. "Welcome back to you!"

A circle of bamboo hung just above her head, covered in a web of string and adorned with beads and feathers. Every time she bowed, her puffy red hat bumped the hideous thing, making the feathers jiggle like drunk showgirls called to stage. Repulsed, Andre couldn't take his eyes off it. It was the most disgusting thing he had ever seen, like a bird had shredded itself flying through a spider web of steel.

"You want one or two, today, Mr. Cross?" Bao called, as she brushed the mobile aside and backed in among the shelves to collect what he always asked for.

Reaching the counter, Andre held up two fingers. He figured that if he bought just two cartridges at a time, he would smoke less. Although this self-delusion had proven unsuccessful, he persisted with it anyway. Bao shuffled back to the counter, vape cartridges in hand.

Automatically, as if he'd made up his mind in another dimension, he withdrew the empty Troplamid vial from his pocket and placed it on the counter.

"Oh, and I'll grab some of these, if you've got any," he said, scratching his nose and sounding as casual as he could. He needn't have worried about a performance, however. Bao was either oblivious to Troplamid's part-time job as a Neura enhancer, or she was business-savvy enough to not concern herself with her customer's co-curricular activities. When she conveniently whipped out two Troplamid vials from under the counter and placed them on the bench, Andre figured it was the latter.

She tapped the vials and winked. "This one good one. You like."

Leaning forward to put the vials in a bag, Bao's head bumped the mobile again, sending the feathers into another dance routine. Andre's skin crawled at the thought of them coming loose and flocking at him. He hated birds. He hated anything that didn't have hands. *Animals with no hands do everything with their mouths. You can't climb or swing if you don't have hands.* And as far as Andre was concerned, that was downright disgusting.

"Oh, you like this one, too?" Bao reached up and shook the mobile, setting off electric shocks of repulsion in his atoms. "Dream catcher. Good for bad dream. You have bad dream, Mr. Cross?"

He screwed up his face and shook his head. Bao shrugged.

"Just one-twenty credit for you today, Mr. Cross, thank you."

He swiped his wristlet on the terminal, picked up his purchase, and thanked Bao as she chimed goodbye.

Mix

Doing the math, he would need several vials to cut his Neura into the two vials of zilla. And a measuring jug. And spare vials.

To avoid drawing attention to his activity, he visited several pharmacies down the side of the tower. Once he had everything he needed, he made his way across to his own tower cluster and caught the lift to his floor.

His one-room apartment sat right next to the lift-shaft, which was convenient for when he came home exhausted, but not great for sleeping undisturbed. He had hoped another apartment would become available, but, with the number of people he'd seen coming out of the one-bedrooms, he didn't expect a vacancy to appear anytime soon. The Stems were more packed than the shelves in Bao's pharmacy.

Stepping inside, the apartment's low ceiling brushed his head. He glared, as he always did, at the foldaway bed leaning out on its buckled hinge half an inch from the wall. *I'll fix you when I get some spare time.* Between working, dealing, and sleeping, however, he didn't get much time for spare time.

Late afternoon light squeezed through a small window in the opposite wall. Far from giving him a sense of space, the window's view of the red, over-mined plains made him claustrophobic, magnifying the device's presence in his neck and shrinking his sense of self to a tiny spot caught between the glass and the implant. Sometimes, he wondered if that was how general Zod felt, trapped in the Phantom Zone.

The sun dropped behind the horizon, fading rays captured in the underbellies of low clouds. Stars speckled through the sparse gaps in the overcast sky, reflecting themselves in the segmented fields of solar panels spreading out, like iridescent petals, from Brulle's base. Beyond, the world became a barren, desolate landscape, ravaged by drought and storm, littered with the skeletons of abandoned cities. No living thing, not even the super-human PrePACs, would survive for long outside a shuttle.

Floating through the dust of the storm rolling toward Brulle, a pair of red and white lights flashed; the landing lights of a migrant shuttle flying into the Docks below.

They just keep coming. Guess I can kiss a quieter apartment goodbye. Well, I've done twelve months in this hole, I can do twelve more.

Built as a high-capacity vertical metropolis, Brulle became a beacon to thousands seeking refuge from the extreme weather conditions degenerating older cities. The four staggering towers of the Stems propped up four shorter towers forming Mid Brulle, which themselves supported the single Summit tower. Wearing the Summit, like a young ruthless queen does her crown, Brulle stood for the resilience of human ingenuity and the merciless march of progress. Enticing migrants with utopian marketing images of the Summit, Brulle drew the migrants in under her glass and steel gown, only to trap them in an unrelenting social system that ensured they never lived any higher than the overcrowded Stems. Arriving with nothing more than their own petite jars of hope, Brulle worked them into her mechanics until their hope was ground to dust and their bodies could give no more.

The shuttle blinked its lights one more time and disappeared beneath Andre's view. He tapped on the TV built into the wall, lowered the volume, and dropped a tabletop down from the inside of the folded-up bed frame. An overhead lamp brightened, as it warmed up, giving him a perfect workspace to mix the zilla. He placed the Troplamid vials and measuring equipment on the table, lined them in a straight line, and pulled out his last vial of Neura.

Although sore and tired, his mood still trudging through the quagmire of Dirk's manipulation, he allowed himself a moment of excitement at the possibilities that his unexpected window of opportunity might bring.

He began the measuring and mixing process and turned his thoughts to the fourteen thousand-credit question: just how would Dirk smuggle him into Anchora? Would he hide Andre in the cargo hold of a migrant shuttle? Not likely, with the heavily monitored shuttles and immigration docks tighter than Dirk's wallet. Would Andre have to stand among the cramped, legal migrants, clutching a costly counterfeit ID, like the one he had found in his mother's room when he was eight?

Strangely, try as he might, he couldn't see his mother's face in the memory of the passport photo.

—Focus on the job, Boss. If you're going to do this, do it right.—

He poured the Troplamid into the second measuring jug, but his thoughts, already off course, continued on to their inevitable destination overlooking the gaping hole in his past—his father.

All Andre knew about the man was that he had been violent and died miserable working on Titan's mining machines in the Docks. All that remained of his father for Andre to get to know was the anger and hate left behind in his mother's drunk eyes and in his brother's bitter heart. They never spoke of the man. His mother had told him to forget about it. The few times Andre pressed to hear more, Jeremy had flown into a rage of fists, while his mother would sit back, sipping her cup of moonshine and shaking her head as if to say 'I told you so.'

And where is my mother now? he wondered, in a rare moment of permitted reflection. It pained him that she had never contacted or visited him during his time in prison, and he had done everything over the last seven years to avoid the heavy, unbearable, jealous-laden guilt of that question.

Upon his release, he had considered searching for her, but any social interaction had become anxiety arousing; his experience with it had eroded from his solitary confinement. He could not fathom how he would handle such a confrontation.

The apartment walls shook as a lift passed by. Last light disappeared behind the horizon, pressed down by the heavy hands of night. The apartment's light auto-activated and shot the room with equal light and shadow. A woman on the TV talked about the sighting of a bird, a rare occurrence since the crisscrossing streams of drones and hover traffic drove them from their migratory paths.

"Are they really extinct," pondered the young TV presenter, "or have they flocked off to some secret world they kept hidden in the higher realms of the sky, riding the tops of the storms, and never again touching ground?"

Andre cringed at the memory of the feathers adorning the dream catcher in Bao's shop. The handless creatures were gone, and Andre, for one, was fine with that. *You can't mix zilla without hands.*

He directed his focus back to the Job—doubling his stock to fill Finn's order. As he leaned forward to see the measuring line on the jug more clearly, he smiled.

I should have done this ages ago. Bigger risks equal bigger rewards. That's good business thinking.

—Boss, a living customer is a good customer, as Bao might say, and

she's the one with a successful business. Finn's a guarantee. You won't find another customer like that. This could end up costing you more than twenty-four months. How do you think your Plan will go then? —

With the Captain's last attempt at stark reasoning paralyzing him, Andre's hand holding the Troplamid vial hovered over the jug of Neura.

—*There's no turning back, Boss.*—

He looked out his small window, as if confirmation lay in the dust storms ripping up the barren horizon. Perhaps, if he strained hard enough, he could catch a glimpse of Anchora. If he did, that would be an omen, wouldn't it? *Omens are good for decision making and good for business.* He strained his sight, stars twinkling at the edge of his vision. For no reason, he wondered if there would be PrePACs in Anchora. Mo Da's face—he knew it was she by the tilt of her head—popped up in his mind.

At that precise moment, something small and hard smacked into the window. A bone-crunching thud echoed throughout the apartment and scuttled down his spine. His heart tripped a beat—the sound reminding him of the clunk of the harvest-droid's nest opening—and his hand jolted, tipping Troplamid into the mixing glass of measured zilla. Still in shock, and oblivious to upsetting the ratio, he put the Troplamid vial down and leaned close to inspect the splattering of blood on the glass. A red and grey goo—either guts or brains, or both—slid slowly down the window. A small black feather clung to the smear.

Andre sat back and grinned. *Now, THAT'S an omen.*

To be present, when he'd barely spend five hours a day in his apartment, to witness one of the rarely-seen, dirty creatures he hated so much smashing its delicate little skull into his window—well, that just had to be a sign, didn't it?

Yes, a sign, for sure. I gotta make a wish on something like that.

He shut his eyes and made his wish that the days of living in this shitty little sleeping hole would come to an end. But, he foolishly failed to define just how soon, or in what form, that end should come.

Reassured that the course he had set was the right one, he poured more Troplamid into his mix, stirred, and filled up two empty vials. He screwed on the caps and held one vial up to the light. As he turned it, he noticed the zilla slid more slowly down the glass than pure Neura did. *Nothing that Finn would notice*, he decided. Finn rarely looked at the Neura before he twisted the injector cap and squirted it into his hungry vein.

Feeling somewhat triumphant over Dirk's trickery, he tapped a reply to Finn into his wristlet:

All good. See you at 9

With an hour to kill before his *Best and Only Customer* would be home, he sat back against the polymer wall to catch the rest of the news: a lift in upper Brulle had blown a motor and shot its cabin straight up the arse of another. Thirteen people injured and two people killed.

Oh, well. A few less Borgs in the city isn't gonna do any harm.

A politician talked about the benefits of Upper Brulle expanding its boundary to encompass Mid Brulle, offering a complete overhaul of the lift systems.

Bastards. That'll push more migrants down into the Stems. We'll be sleeping in the damn hallways.

The interview cut to footage of protests outside a council tower where the expansion was being discussed. As Andre lost interest and nodded off, the news presenter turned to weather and promised storms.

Tricks

Thunder banged outside the window and rattled the glass.

He jumped awake, his heart pounding, anxiety prickling his body. Whatever dream he had just escaped from, he was glad he could not remember it.

Don't need your dream catcher, thanks Bao. I got a bad memory that does the job just fine.

Rain pelted the small window, the bird's blood and guts washed away. He wiped sleep from his eyes and checked the time on his wristlet.

9:45

Finn would have been home for a while and waiting for his fix.

Better that he's a little hungry and impatient so there's no chance of him noticing the zilla. He'll practically drink it out of the vial. And then, I'll let it drop I can get more. Just casually. It's all about creating demand.

His back ached from the cuts and fall, and his eyes burned with weariness, but determination pushed him off the bed. He slid the two zilla vials into his inner pocket and strapped on his boots. Stepping out of the apartment, and into the corridor, he let the door slam behind him, his sleepy mind not consciously registering the crack appearing in the window.

Exiting the tower, he waited on the transport platform. Hundreds of conveyors slid along cables strewn between the towers, shuffling along like giant fairy lights, while hover traffic wove between them. He'd had enough going up and down walkways for one day, so he caught a conveyor to Finn's tower cluster. The silver cabin rode its cable up between the four Stems and slid out into the vast, chaotic space under Mid Brulle.

Between tower clusters, a giant 3D holographic advert played out, showing a child running across an immaculate room, in front of a large TV. She jumped into the arms of a female PrePAC android, who lifted her up and embraced her, as if she were her mother. The advertisement's audio played through the conveyor's speaker system.

"Titan trans-humanist technologies—empowering individuals with technological innovation to architect every aspect of their lives." The child's mother, on the TV screen in the background, acted out the hug. The PrePAC mimicked the mother's movements perfectly, allowing the mother to hug her daughter from a distance. "Freedom from nature's limitations. Empowerment to be the best You you can be." The room scene faded away, leaving only a white outline of the PrePAC as it faced forward.

"The Titan PrePAC Android System. With the hive-learning intelligence of the Mesh, PrePACs are the safest, most intelligent pre-emptive androids on the market."

The PrePAC graphic faded back into the vision of the android placing the child gently on the floor. The child ran across the room and morphed into a woman, as the background changed into a city walkway. The hologram focus zoomed in on the woman's leg, x-raying to reveal robotic mechanics in her thigh.

"Titan Ultras. Advanced prosthetics, utilizing Neura-infused bio-blood, puts the Evolution of You in your hands."

The hologram zoomed out from the woman's leg, panned up to her head, and focused in on the back of her neck. A seed-like shape outlined itself under her skin.

"And Titan Customized Implants. Giving you complete control over your moods and desires."

As the fluid scene zoomed back out for its finale, the running woman darted off across a city scene, and the tall, curved glass structure of the Titan facility reared up to fill the hologram.

"Strength. Improvement. Control. This is what matters. Titan trans-humanist technologies give you all this and more. Put The Evolution of You in your own hands."

The conveyor shook as it slid back between the Stems, and the hologram disappeared from view.

If Titan is advertising down here, then Upper Brulle's expansion into Mid Brulle has already been decided. It's going to get bloody crowded and noisy down here.

Sensing the walls of his world closing in, he touched the back of his neck. Doctor Steele's voice came back to him, echoing up from the past.

"This is your chance to be a Good Citizen," the Doctor said, as he slid a touchpad in front of Andre on the day of his release. "Sign the authorization, and you'll walk out a free man, free of your limitation. That's Titan's promise to you."

Take the implant, or spend another fifteen years in prison. How could he have said no? He couldn't, of course, and that was Titan's plan, to empty the jails and make people responsible for themselves. Technological rehabilitation, they called it. Only, a year into his 'freedom,' he realized he hadn't escaped his limitation. He had to carry it, like a dead Siamese twin the good Doctor had forgotten to cut off.

*—Are you paying attention to your thoughts, Boss—*The Captain's voice yanked Andre back to the present.*—You're working yourself up. Breathe.—*

He closed his eyes, inhaled slowly, exhaled, and focused on a small point in his mind, to clear his thoughts. As it brightened, the point grew and defiantly split in two. He willed the lights to merge back together, when they enlarged into a pair of glassy blue eyes. A strip of red slashed across them. Mo Da's face floated up behind the eyes and held them in its sockets, like jewels. Her face faded away, taking the eyes with it.

His heart quickened. The implant warmed. He had to stop thinking about her, but he couldn't. His mind clutched at any thought of her, like an addict scrambling for its last vial of zilla. All the PrePACs were fundamentally beautiful, but what stood out about Mo Da was the way she seemed to possess a defiant courage, beyond the clinical self-preservation programming. She was so ... *human.*

—Boss. IT almost got you killed. No, YOU almost got you killed. Maybe you need to get your implant adjusted to catch sudden moments of stupidity. Twelve months. That's all. You got to keep your focus.—

He knew the Captain was looking out for him, but he told himself his fascination with Mo Da was normal. Even natural. She was made to be attractive, with her ivory skin, pink lips, and perfect proportions. Of course, he was attracted to her. Good Citizens are only human, after all.

—So you want to screw an android now? You want to get your business chewed off when the damn thing short circuits? PrePACs are

made to look perfect, but they're not. They're dead inside.—

{like you}

Shivers rattled Andre's spine, as Jeremy's voice returned from its banishment, intruding upon the Captain. Andre squeezed his eyes to block out his brother's voice, but Jeremy's snarling face bobbed up into the middle of his thoughts, out of the same darkness that had swallowed his vision of Mo Da. He pushed the image of Jeremy away and willed Mo Da's face to re-emerge. But her image rippled and slipped from his mind's grasp, like a desperate fish darting through his thoughts, and left only emptiness in its wake.

Tricks on tricks.

The conveyor jerked to a stop, and the doors slid open, but Andre remained. Eyes squinted shut, he stood at the edge of his mind and stared back into the darkness. An exquisite black, as vacant and silent as death itself, stretched before him in dimension-defying vastness.

What is she doing to me?

The answer alighted upon the unleveled ledge of his mind with the grace and ease of an ancient winged predator. Mo Da had aroused something in him, and whatever it was, it was something he was missing, something he had forgotten. And he knew, there and then, if he wanted an answer to her riddle, he would have to venture into the very past he was running from and wrestle it from the dark.

—Boss. Your alignment mechanism is out. You're stalled. Fix yourself up and get moving.—

He opened his eyes, pressed his hands against the inside of the lift, and pushed himself out onto the platform. Small puddles of rain dotted the ramp, like odd-shaped mirrors. His feet splashed through them as he lumbered across the connector bridge. Warm, sweet air rose up in its invisible release from the wet concrete.

He didn't look back at the conveyor, for fear he may see it full of the terrible darkness, Jeremy sitting in the middle, flicking his switchblade. He disowned the vision, abandoning any attachment to it so it could be transported away, deliberately ignoring the fact that all conveyors eventually came around again.

Finn

He reached the tower, and the crisp air flooded into his lungs, refreshing his body and cooling his head.

Deciding more of the fresh air would do him good, he avoided getting inside the claustrophobic lift, and took the stairways winding up the side of the tower. Holding the railing, he walked through the light and shadow maze of the zigzagging ramps until he reached Finn's level. At the end of the corridor he poked the intercom button and its tired buzz echoed throughout the apartment's rooms, like a gunshot ringing out through an abandoned world. The auto-door slid open, and a tall, stoic male PrePAC blocked the doorway.

"Good afternoon, Mr. Cross. I am Ki Po. Please come in." The android stepped its powerful frame aside and bowed. "Finn is in the downstairs workshop. Can I offer you a drink?"

There was no android in Finn's apartment the last time Andre had visited, so the only way it could know his name was if the apartment's AI had told it. Andre hated the way the city's walls and robots spoke to each other. Ignoring the android, he pushed past, took off his jacket, and stomped down the stairs in the middle of the apartment.

At the far end of the lower level stood a tall, transparent garden pillar in front of a floor-to-ceiling window. Tower lights outside silhouetted the glass pillar. The plant's leaf and root system wrapped around inside and pressed against the glass like an alien specimen in a transparent egg.

At the other end of the long room, in the chaos he called a workshop, Finn hunched over an L-shaped workbench. Wires, components, soldering irons, and electrodes littered the bench, peeking out from the shadows. Cocooned in a stark ray of spotlight, he faced four large monitors. Animated hieroglyphics of code ran across all four screens. Andre kicked the back of Finn's stool.

"You got yourself one of those metal bastards, I see."

"Hey, Andre." Finn spun around and laughed nervously. "Yeah. He's not the latest model, but he'll do." Finn's gaunt face glowed white in the spotlight as if he were a ghost emerging out from the monitors behind him.

Andre dumped his jacket on the bench and rummaged through the inner pocket. He withdrew the vials of zilla and lobbed them onto the keyboard next to Finn. "Seven fifty," he said, pushing a pile of components out of the way and leaning against the bench.

Finn's eye-brows raised. "Seven hundred and fifty credits? Gone up again? I can get this stuff—"

"You can't get stuff this good from anyone else and you know it."

Finn stayed silent in submission, wiping sweat from his dirty brow. He was typical of the wealthy addicts from Upper Brulle. Even though he could easily afford to live in the higher levels, he opted to live on the fringe, closer to Mid Brulle, for easy access to his habit. And although

Finn had built up the gumption to complain whenever Andre hiked up his price, Andre knew his *Best and Only Customer's* complaints were hollow. If Andre cut off his supply, Finn would have to frequent the dangerous bars again to find another dealer. That was never a fun, safe, or sure endeavor. And Andre delivered; that, of all things, kept the reclusive Finn loyal.

Finn snatched up the first vial and twisted the cap to extend the built-in syringe. He turned it until it clicked twice, treating himself to a double dose, and slid the needle into his vein. His eyes rolled back, his mouth drooped, and he slumped forward. Andre stood and unfolded his arms, worried he might have mixed too much Troplamid. But Finn gasped and sat bolt upright, his eyes popping open. He coughed, blinked, and shook his head.

"Oh my God," he exclaimed. "That shit's good."

Andre shrugged and sat back against the bench, trying to sound calm. "They've doubled my quota at work. I've got others asking for it, but you get first dibs."

The largest monitor on Finn's bench beeped, and a three-dimensional schematic of a PrePAC rendered. A prism spun in the PrePAC's head. Distracted, Andre leaned toward the monitor.

"And what do we have here?"

Finn sat up straighter, snapping out of his rush. "Ah, I'm kind of busy, actually," he stammered, reaching for the keyboard in an attempt to shut down the display. Andre grabbed Finn's forearm, his grip too tight to be friendly. "You hacking a PrePAC, Boss?"

Finn sighed, submitting to Andre's intimidation, like he always did, like Andre knew he would. Andre released his arm, and Finn gestured to the screen.

"I may have found a way to access the PrePAC's AI cage through an update."

"And what you gonna do when you hack that bucket of bolts? Don't PrePACs need the Mesh to tell them what to do?"

Finn licked his lips and raised a finger. "No, they don't need the Mesh. They share their learnings with it, and it refines their algorithms." His words came out faster as he pointed at a line of code. "But—and I'm pretty sure about this from my research—a PrePAC untethered from the Mesh should retain its learning ability. It might even learn faster, without the constant reconfiguration."

Is that what's happening to Mo Da? Is she trying to feel something more than the Mesh allows?

—You need to forget about the androids, Boss, and get Finn committed to buying more zilla. Stay focused on the Job.—

But Andre's curiosity was piqued, provoked by intoxicating thoughts of Mo Da. *Can Finn really hack them, and allow them to think? Would that make them human?* "Won't you have Titan banging on your door and dragging your hacker ass off to some integration room?"

Finn smiled, a little smug, as he tapped with zilla-speed onto his keyboard. The PrePAC model faded off and the flat, rectangular prism enlarged on the screen. He lost himself in presenting his work to an audience, pried from his solitude by someone showing interest.

"That's where the Mirror comes in. It's a little piece of software I'm designing to implant in the PrePACs code. It sends dummy info back to the Mesh. That way, the Mesh doesn't register the PrePAC's been hacked, and I'll have complete privacy."

The prism spun slowly on the screen. Andre's face reflected in the dark glass. For a second, he thought he glimpsed Mo Da trapped inside the prism, pressed against the surface, as if kissing it. His head began to spin like the Mirror. He blinked, stood away from the screen, and walked over to the garden pillar to distance himself from his hallucination.

"And why the hell does a geek like you need privacy?" he asked, trying to get his mind on track. "Going to get it on with your boy-droid?"

—Get back to the Job, Boss.—

Andre pressed his forehead against the pillar's cold glass to bring his thoughts back to central.

"Actually," Finn said, standing up, rubbing his mouth nervously. "I got some plans ... that include you. If you're up for it?"

Andrew shot Finn a glance. "What do you mean?"

"I mean, you help me, I help you. I could move a lot of Neura, fast."

Andre's eyes narrowed. "I just told you I'm getting double now—"

"No, I mean more. If you can get more, a lot, in one go, I'd buy it all outright."

Andre's neck itched just under his skin. He turned back to the orchids in the garden pillar, their roots pressed against the glass of their transparent prison. *Is he suggesting what I think he is?*

"I have a lot of mates in Upper Brulle," Finn continued. "They would pay a lot for your product. So, if I could get a ... a shipment ..."

—Careful, Boss. Remember what the Doc taught you; beware those trying to manipulate you. Don't get side-tracked. Stick to your Plan.—

Oh, I know when people are trying to manipulate me. I'm on to that trick. Jeremy taught me well.

"How much are you talking about?" he dared Finn.

"Ten."

"Vials?"

"Liters. It'll make you a big profit, Andre. And fast."

He damn well is. He's asking me to steal from the Baron.

Old rage, familiar and malign, rose its dark sunrise inside him. His hand wrapped around one of the delicate orchids.

Does he think I'm some weak-minded, spineless PrePAC he can program to do his dirty work? I got my implant and I got my Plan and I'm not gonna screw that up for this little shit.

—Breathe, Boss, Breathe it out. Keep your cool. You got this.—

But Andre's cool had well and truly left the building. His heart galloped. Goosebumps rose in fields across his skin, awakening the pain of his cuts, and his shoulder muscles tightened. He squashed the orchid between his fingers, then released it, its crimson petals springing back like crepe paper before falling limp on their stem.

—Stay in the front room, Boss.—

But the Captain's warning failed. Andre turned and strode up to Finn, forcing him to step back.

"I can get four vials," Andre stated coldly. "Per fortnight. That's it."

Finn blinked, the zilla giving him the confidence to hold Andre's glare.

"But you work on the farms, right? I just thought maybe you could, I dunno, find a way—"

Let's hear you say it then.

—Boss ...—

"Find a way to do what?" Andre demanded.

The smug look vanished from Finn's face as he backed up against the bench. "You need this Andre," he dared. "You need this as much as I do."

A flash burst forth from Andre's amygdala—the seed shaped storehouse of emotional memories snuggling deep in the primitive part of his brain. Sparks shot out through his nervous system. Too fast for the implant to react, his hand whipped out and grabbed Finn by the throat, shoving him down on the bench. The monitor toppled to its side, the 3D image of the prism on the screen breaking into static. Tools and computer parts scattered to the floor in a symphony of clangs. Andre leaned in close to Finn's panicked face.

"You stuck-up little shit. You think I'm just a poor farm-worker who's gonna jump when you wave your rich-boy credits around?" The first foot-soldiers of medication marched through his bloodstream, but his flash of anger had momentum. He squeezed Finn's throat, and he *enjoyed* it. "You think I'm gonna risk my ass just to feed your little habit?"

Finn gasped for air, clawing at Andre's vice-like grip. "Andre," he sputtered.

The foot soldiers moved into position and the heavy artillery came out. A chemical onslaught snuffed out the flash fires of Andre's anger, rounded up his rebellious emotions, and knocked them down. His grip relaxed, and he staggered backward.

"Shit, dude," Finn gasped, dropping to the floor and gulping in air. "It was just…just a suggestion. You really need some anger management, you know that?" Shock gave Finn even more courage.

Sweat trickled into Andre's eyes. He felt two-dimensional, trapped, and claustrophobic. His vision blurred and the world shifted, like the static on the monitor's cracked screen.

"I'm not your Neura mule," he muttered. He swayed away from Finn and shuffled to the bench. By the heavy waves rolling through his body, he had activated a Big Dose. A Doozie, in fact.

Finn hauled himself onto his feet. His eyes narrowed. "Andre, are you alright?"

Andre had to keep his implant secret from Finn. He had to leave. "I'm not doin' your dirty work," he snapped, his words slurring. He snatched his jacket off the bench and stomped up the stairs to the main level.

"Is everything alright, sir," asked Ki Po coming out of a room. "I heard—"

"Get out of my way, bucket," Andre growled, shouldering past Ki Po and hurrying out the apartment door.

Pushing through the sedative's dizziness, he ambled down the hall and out onto the walkways. A breeze raced up and slapped him in the face. He clutched the railing and breathed the cool air in deeply, feeling its chill hit his lungs.

Thousands of lights twinkled across the underbelly of Mid Brulle, shining through the maze of walkways crisscrossing overhead. The falling light forged giant geometric shapes out of shadow and blasted them across the towers in a frozen, matt explosion.

He stumbled down the walkways, but his body moved on autopilot. His thoughts bobbed up and down between reality and the deep, warm cloud of medication. Each time he dipped under the surface, empty spaces opened up in his mind and snippets of his childhood flashed on and off. His thoughts split, the past overlapped the present, and bad—*very bad*— memories slipped through the cracks and caught up with him.

Hatch

Violence comes in many forms. The explosive and reactionary are dangerous. But nothing is more sinister than revenge, carefully planned and calculated over a period of time, maintained and nurtured, like rows of Blue Eyes, tendered to bloom maximum damage.

Sounds of glass smashing and metal hitting the floor echoed from the back room of Andre's childhood home.

"Where is it?" Jeremy screamed. Another crash, and their mother's slurring voice begged Jeremy to calm down.

Andre crouched on his bed, his hands shaking. He slid Jeremy's switchblade out from under the pillow. He'd been playing with it, thinking about the child-bot, about how the blade had so neatly punctured its artificial skin. He wasn't sure how he got the switchblade. He couldn't remember taking it. All he knew was that his brother's knife was in his own hand again.

—You gotta put the knife back.—

The rational, calm voice bobbed up in his thoughts.

—It's not yours. You don't want it.—

But a part of him *did* want it, very much. Gripping the bone handle gave him strength. Tracing a finger along the cold, steel edge cleared his mind. He felt invincible. His brother was nothing without the blade; a nasty, spitting little toad that could easily be stomped on and slit open.

Andre's twelve-year-old mind was too young to realize just how deep his brother's darkness had worked its way under his skin. In the right environment, the dark egg in Andre might never have hatched, remaining dormant so long that it solidified, petrified, and fossilized. But his father's death, his mother's alcohol-soaked depression, and his brother's reckless violence created the perfect incubator for the larva of blind hate to grow inside him.

When Jeremy first stormed into the back room and accused him of stealing the knife, Andre froze in terror. But with the purity of the switchblade in his hand, he quickly recognized the reaction as a habit. It was like something inside Jeremy was daring Andre to fight back, goading him to rise up and fight. And when Andre didn't, when he kept the blade hidden under the pillow, that thing, that darkness in Jeremy, threw itself into a fit and spun him into a tornado of fists slamming down the hall.

Andre knew Jeremy would come back. He flicked the blade in and out, hypnotized by the sound, and waited with an ancient predator instinct hunching in his spine.

Snit-svit-snit-svit…

As Andre predicted, Jeremy's pounding footsteps returned down the corridor. Andre's grip on the switchblade threatened to squash the sheath's molecules. This time, he didn't hide it.

"I knew it," came Jeremy's cold, dead voice, as he stopped and seethed in the doorway. Spying the knife in Andre's hand, his eyes brimmed with equal hate and malevolent joy.

"Enough," their mother slurred, coming up from behind Jeremy. She cautiously patted Jeremy on the arm. Andre had never seen his mother touch Jeremy, never heard her stand up to him. But even this intervention was timid and weak.

She may as well pat him on the back and tell him 'good job', Andre thought, squeezing the knife until he couldn't feel it in his hand.

At her touch, Jeremy thrashed his mother away, his elbow smacking her in the face and knocking her hard into the wall.

For all the jealousy he held of his mother's love for Jeremy, his brother's strike against her shattered the prison of fear that had imprisoned him his whole childhood. The egg that lay in his psyche since he murdered the child-bot in the sticky wet leaves of the underground park cracked its delicate membrane and released a quiet, controlled rage that Jeremy would have been proud of, had he survived.

{Kill}

The voice rushed through his mind on a burst of wind. He recognized it as the voice he'd heard in the ravine—a guttural, animal voice rattling through his bones. He wondered fleetingly if it was really his own and then the thought passed. He stood and marched toward his brother, his left hand flicking the blade in and out of the sheath.

Snit-svit-snit-svit...

"Here's your blade, Jeremy," he said, his voice sweet and kind, as if he were calling his brother to dinner.

Jeremy smiled and lunged.

Focused and tight—the fear packed away in some taut, controlled place he didn't even know existed—Andre swung out and slit Jeremy's side.

But Jeremy didn't flinch. No pain registered in his eyes. Just like he hadn't noticed his elbow collide with their mother's face. He dove at Andre, tackling him to the floor, and pinned Andre's flailing arms down with his knees. Pummeling his little brother from every direction, he didn't seem to care about the blade anymore, or the bloody gash in his side. He just hit and hit and hit.

Unable to raise his arms to swing the blade again, Andre drove the blade up into Jeremy's inner thigh. In and up.

Riiiiiiip.

Jeremy howled and buckled over, collapsing to the floor. Blood spurt out from between his legs and sprayed them both. He looked like he was pissing blood, and Andre almost laughed. Clutching his inner thigh and squealing like a slit pig, Jeremy's face faded to a sickly yellow. Andre didn't need to be a doctor to know his brother would be drained dead in minutes. But the beast unleashed in Andre was not done.

He lunged onto Jeremy's writhing body and drove his knee into the gaping wound. Jeremy screamed a pathetic scream, a parody of his terror, and Andre reveled in hearing his brother's weakness.

But still the monster inside Andre wanted more. He threw the knife aside and dug his bare thumbs into his brother's eyes. He dug and dug and dug, until they popped with a squelch right out of their sockets.

Standing, blood dripping from his hands, Andre backed away from the body in front of him. Intense white noise enveloped his mind, calming and numbing him. His mother screamed and ran to Jeremy's punctured, bloody body, cradling him in her arms. She glared up at Andre, her eyes wide with terror and tears streaking down her face.

"You monster! What have you done? What have you done to my baby?"

Feeling nothing, Andre turned and trudged bloody footprints down the hall. Reaching the front room, he sat in the armchair and looked out the small window at the unusually perfect blue sky. His hands shook and he licked at the metallic taste of blood on his lips.

Must have got some in my mouth when his eyeballs exploded.

"What have you done? What have you done?" his mother screamed, her voice echoing down the hall.

His head ached from the thrill of the kill. If she didn't shut up, he was sure he was going to go in there and shut her up himself.

—Stay in the front room. Stay right there.—

The calm voice again—the one that told him to turn around when Jeremy led him to stab the child-bot. It spoke clear and definite in his mind. He could no longer hear his mother screaming, and a beautiful silence surrounded him. He stared out the window, wondering where the thumping in his head had come from. He put it down to having a hell of a day.

I'm just gonna stay right here. In the peace and quiet,

Blood dripped from his hands onto the wooden floor. Sweat poured from his skin and into his eyes where tears should have flowed. He sat there until the roar of hover engines came and took the peace and quiet away.

PART THREE

WAYWARD VICE

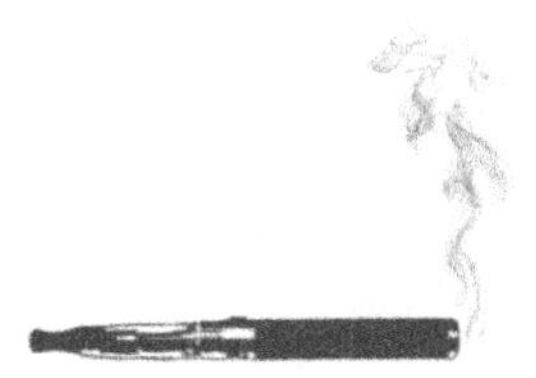

Purpose

The vertical city of Brulle protruded from sprawling flatlands, like the stinger of some giant robotic wasp. Magnificent and grotesque, its sixteen hundred meters of steel and glass glinted in the morning sun, defiant against the chaotic weather pummeling the earth.

One rogue sunray broke through the clouds over Brulle and pierced the crack in Andre's tiny window. Bursting fractured into the room, photons of the solar spear bounced off his forehead and scattered, failing in their cross-space quest to wake him from his slumber. The chiming alarm on his wristlet, however, did the job, shattering the dream that left little trace in his waking mind. Only a vague yet annoying sensation remained, attaching to itself a lingering significance. As he groped at the elusive memory in the shifting shadows of his psyche, the dream slipped further away, like skywriting letters blown into distorted shapes before their words were ever finished.

He gave up the futile pursuit, tapped off the alarm, and rolled over.

Staring across his cramped, musty apartment, waiting for his mind and body to wake up, he realized his lack of memory stretched back further than the dream. Try as he might, he couldn't recall walking home the previous night, or getting into his tower. He remembered stumbling down the walkways from Finn's apartment, high on a medication haze. The next thing he could recall was waking up, as if the meds had sliced time in two, removed twelve hours, and stuck the broken ends back together.

Panic fluttered through his being. Amnesia didn't happen often, and only sometimes after a Big Dose. He found some comfort in knowing the meds stabilized his behavior, but the gap worried him. He held up his hands. No marks, no blood. He rolled out of bed and checked his reflection in the kitchenette's backsplash. Apart from the bags under his eyes—rivaling Dirks dark crescents—he was clear of any signs of altercation.

Okay. No point in worrying, then.

He grabbed a glass from the shelf above the backsplash to pour himself some water and knocked an empty Troplamid vial. It rolled across the bench and clinked into the sink.

Damn. Did I even get my credits from him?

He tapped into his wristlet to check his balance and sighed with relief. Finn had put a payment through. A small increase in his savings this time, but by the next fortnight, with his zilla mix, he would double that.

So the Plan is back to twelve months. But that is still going to be a long twelve months. How many more blackouts can I survive without getting into trouble? Maybe… maybe I could mix it a little more. Save the credits in nine months. Maybe even eight, if I push it.

No, that would be self-sabotage, and he knew it. Unless he planned on doing something drastic to boost his income—*which I'm not*—he would have to stick it out. Mixing zilla was one thing. Stealing from Grekov, that was a whole other level of crazy.

—Twelve months will go by like a sand storm, Boss.—

He wiped the thoughts aside, refusing to let his memory gap fill in with doubts.

Actually, he felt well rested. His shoulder didn't ache. His mind had cleared overnight, as if sleep had dumped a whole lot of mental garbage into an alternate universe, zipped up the connecting hole, and wiped away all trace. His sense of self stretched out into a plateau of calm. He didn't really know what Zen meant, but the word floated through the stone garden of his mind. What a Big Dose took from his lucidity, it made up for in a deep and restful sleep.

"Window," he commanded. The apartment's AI lowered the window's tint where more light waited to come in. But it was not bright light, it was dull and heavy and billowed into the apartment like smoke. The overcast sky outside was the color of concrete. Dust rendered the land below invisible. The previous night's rain had washed the blood and guts from the glass, and in the middle of the window, like a tear in reality itself, floated a spider-shaped crack.

Andre leaned close, his own reflection emerging in the glass and split in two by the fissure. He ran a finger over the crack, but trapped and frozen, like a prehistoric mosquito in resin, it was deep inside the glass.

Nothing to worry about then.

Eager to get to the farms and clock up as many hours as he could, he dragged on his overalls and grabbed a protein bar. Life didn't seem so futile.

—You got a plan, Boss. You got purpose.—

Damn right, Captain.

Sliding open the apartment door, he put one foot out into the corridor, when he thought he heard a splitting noise behind him. He stopped and glanced back at the window, half expecting to see a hand-sized web of cracks, but the fissure remained invisible from the doorway.

He laughed at himself. *Tricks on tricks.*

He shut the door with his renewed sense of purpose and never saw his shitty little apartment again.

Omega

—One stepping-stone at a time to cross the river, Boss. Keep your focus, and keep your job.—

Aligning his thoughts with the Captain's mantra, he reached the top of the walkways and strode across Devlin Square toward the farm entrance.

Keep my focus. No over-mixing. Twelve months, and I'm outta here.

In the fresh light of his reset perspective, Anchora seemed only a hop-skip-and-a-jump away. He pictured himself in a low-ground neighborhood on the fringes of the flat city, jogging through a sprawling park. Flatness. Lots of flatness.

A horn blared and his heart jumped, ripping him from his postcard fantasy. He stumbled back from a black hover van zipping in from above as it merged with the ground traffic. He'd wandered into the buffer zone without looking, where cheeky drivers would dip under slow vans to overtake them.

"You're gonna kill someone," he yelled at the oriental girl driving the van as it zoomed past.

Stepping quickly back into the main pedestrian flow, he kept his head up and eyes forward until he reached the farm. He swiped his wristlet at the security gates and headed to the lift wells. Riding up to the prep level, the lift doors opened and he walked straight into her.

Mo Da.

His heart floated. Tribes of goose bumps rose from their hiding spots, dropped their weapons, and worshipped with their blind heads that which had called them.

"Please, excuse me," she apologized, bowing and stepping to the side before moving into the lift.

He opened his mouth to speak and caught himself. He didn't know what he was going to say, but his desire to say *something*, to strike up conversation, surprised and perplexed him. No words came to him, however. What could he possibly say? Ask her how she was? What did she think of the accident in Upper Brulle?

She's just a god-damned machine.

He put this head down and walked on, but the flustering rush both thrilled and infuriated him. How could a PrePAC quicken his heartbeat, activate his sweat glands, and make him *feel*?

—Don't look back, Boss. Keep moving.—

But he couldn't control himself. She was the edge he had to look over. He turned his head sheepishly and glimpsed her vanishing in the shrinking slit of the closing doors. Her clear eyes, sparkling with jewel-allure in her red face-stripe, disappeared like his elusive dream.

—Jewels? Are you kidding me, Boss? Are we working today or writing poetry? What's today's mantra? Keep your focus, and keep your job.—

I know, I know, I just—

"Cross!" Dirk's gruff voice snapped Andre out of his mental flurry. The old man drove down the wide hallway on a low transporter. He pointed two fingers at his eyes, then pointed them at Andre, while mouthing the words, "Don't fuck it up."

Sweating, clenching his fists, Andre nodded and strode forward.

Damn that android getting into my mind. Damn her! I'm keeping my focus and keeping my job.

—Welcome back, Boss. Now let's do this.—

Continuing along the neon-lit hall, he passed through a marching group of PrePACs, all spitting images of Mo Da.

Reaching the entry bay to the farm, he climbed into his harness and slipped on his visor. The visor's interior display lit up, the day's jobs downloading and listing on the glass. He swiped his wristlet, and the door opened, the access corridor to the shaft maze yawning before him. He stretched his arms and the four robotic limbs followed his motion.

So far, so good, harness. Better stay that way.

He jumped and waved his arms upward, the two grippers latching onto the lift guide running the length of the shaft wall.

"Okay, Control. Hit me with the first job."

"Good morning, Operator 77. Priority on Sub Level 2. Highlighting coordinates now."

Remembering Dirk had put him on the lower-levels to cover Smythe—who was in the greenhouse to cover the dearly departed Jackson—Andre ground his teeth at the change to his routine, and climbed down instead of up.

The pain in his shoulder remained dormant. He felt fine. He had purpose. He took the first intersection and swung along a horizontal shaft, traveling at a steady speed, and continued down, following the map outlined on his visor. He withdrew his vape from his inner pocket, sparked it up and clenched it between his lips. Not recognizing the area, he checked the map again. Deep in the lower regions under the farm towers, he estimated he was somewhere near the refinement plant. Climbing around a corner, he spotted his first job—a stalled lift in the next intersection. As he swung toward it, the lift's ID displayed across his visor: Lift Omega.

Omega, again, huh? This bugger keeps me busy.

As he approached, he discerned a high-pitched whirring coming from inside the lift's motor. He used his grippers to lower himself in between the lift and the shaft and opened the motor cage. Surprisingly, the alignment mechanism sat in place. His left helper arm moved in and scanned the brake pack. Data typed itself across his visor and revealed the problem: the lift's controller couldn't turn to allow it to transfer between the vertical and horizontal shafts.

"Control, we got a jammed brake system. Estimated delay, six minutes. Stand by for update."

Dangling from the ceiling, he puffed on his vape and tapped his palm with his fingers to extend out an assist tool from the helper. His forearms bulged as his callused, scarred hands reconnected wires in the motor's innards. With the wiring in place, his right helper reached in and extruded a welder from its palm.

Reconnect these babies, and that's job-one done.

He ignited the welder and sparks shot out in all directions, bouncing off his visor.

Snit, svit, snit, svit…

Out of nowhere, the dream that had eluded him upon waking that morning swam up to the porthole of his memory and flicked its tail.

Mo Da. He had dreamed of Mo Da.

As he stared into the bright blaze of the welding, he journeyed through its glare and back into the memory of his dream.

Walking through the twilight shades of a forest, silhouettes of trunks thinned around him until he stopped in a clearing. He stood naked, Mo Da appearing opposite him. They stared into each other's eyes, a sense of connection warming in his chest. She did not speak, but her mouth moved, making a terrifyingly familiar sound:

Snit, svit, snit, svit…

Distracted by his reverie, the helper limb moved too close to his own hand and sizzled his skin. Recoiling and swearing, his lips dropped his vape. The metal gadget clanked down into the motor cage and disappeared below the brakes.

Shit.

—Doc told you to quit, Boss—

Oh, shut it.

He peered into the cage and spotted the blue light of the vape wedged in the brake system.

I gotta get that outta there. That's got my name all over it.

While the helper completed the welding, he reached deeper into the cage. The pain in his shoulder awoke with claws, as if it had been waiting to pounce at the worst time. The farther he stretched, the farther the claw raked down his arm muscles.

—Keep your focus, Boss, and keep your job.—

"Operator 77. Job passing five-minute mark. Please report."

The blue light of the vape stared back at him. *Can't you reach me?* it seemed to taunt. He bit into his lip and stretched again, his shoulder on fire and the harness cutting into his ribs. Sweat dribbled down his arm and into his hand. He needed to stay on schedule with Control, but he had to get his vape out of the cage. There was only one thing to do.

"Lift Omega repaired," he informed Control. "Exiting motor cage now." Using the time it would take Control to run its diagnostic, he tapped into the harness' chest panel to set it on standby and climbed out to retrieve his vape by hand. Still upside down, he spidered to the cage floor and snatched the wayward vape.

Gotcha.

He slipped the vape into his pocket, zipped it shut, and began scaling backward, and upside down, up to his harness.

—Move it, Boss, move it.—

"Operator 77, diagnostic complete. Reactivating in ... eight seconds."

Andre's heart took off like a sprinter at a start gun.

Holy shit, that was quick.

He scrambled backward up the cage. The lift's motor revved into action.

"Seven."

A loud thud echoed from outside the lift, and he immediately thought of the swarm.

—That's stupid, Boss, and you know it. There's no insect drones down here. Get back into your harness and get out.—

"Six."

Through the wire of the motor cage, he glimpsed the large double-doors at the end of the shaft sliding open. Harsh, white light burst through the gap, momentarily blinding him. A rush of cool air blew against his body.

"Five."

The lift wasn't going anywhere, he reckoned, until the doors were fully open. He had time to get out. He blinked away the light stains on his retina, pushed his inverted body up, and strapped himself back into the harness.

"Four."

Another thud as the doors stopped in their open position.

—Get moving before the lift does, Boss.—

"Three."

As he tapped into his chest panel to restart the harness's power, the lift motor whirred into motion.

"Two."

—Now, Boss. Now.—

"One."

He slammed on the extract button, and the grippers yanked him up. But before he was clear, the lift jolted forward, knocking the back of his harness. The grippers lost their hold, and he dropped back into the cage. The armpits of the helpers collided with the rim of the opening, jerking his body to a halt, stopping him from falling all the way in. But he was stuck, held hostage by his awkward fall.

To his surprise, the lift didn't speed off; it cruised along the shaft toward the open doors. Instinctively, he switched off his wristlet and visor so Control couldn't track his unauthorized activity. He'd have to come up with an excuse later for being off-line.

The air cooled and blew against his face as the lift moved inside the chamber. In the calm of the lift's slow slide forward, he managed to push himself out of the cage with the aid of his helpers. Crouching on the cabin roof, he stared around in wonder at the cavernous insides of the chamber.

Monstrous automated packer-cranes silently crisscrossed the polished concrete floor, four booms extending from their tall, black, and yellow bodies. Wrapped in glistening plastic, crates dangled, like cocooned prey, from the end of the booms, each one loaded with large vials of blue liquid.

Andre's heart raced. He couldn't catch his breath.

Rows and rows of four-story-high shelves, stacked with pure Neura, disappeared in all directions—more than enough of the drug to supply the entire city, including all the migrants of Lower Brulle.

Hole-ly-shit.

He couldn't have stumbled into a more out-of-bounds area if he tried. He needed to back up and get out of there faster than fast. But before he could pry his eyes away from the gleaming hive, the large double doors behind him shut with a final, echoing thud.

Hive

He finally caught his breath and took a few desperate gasps.

If I get caught in here, no excuse is going to fly.

He flattened himself on the roof of the lift cabin, eyes darting from side-to-side as he scoped the chamber for workers or cameras. Or a way out. But the endless rows of shelves covered every wall, dotted here and there with gaps for large vents.

The cabin slid along a white strip on the chamber floor, heading toward a row of empty cabins, where the auto-straddles stacked them with Neura crates.

—Keep your cool, and keep your job. This isn't a problem.—

Oh, yes, this is a problem. This is a big fucking problem. I should NOT be in here.

The cabin reached the stacked row and jolted to a stop. To his great relief, there was not a human in sight. The whole system was automated, running off programming and floor sensors. That explained why he didn't see any cameras.

—See, Boss? It's simple. Stay off the floor, and stay out of trouble. Just follow the machines. They must go somewhere. You got this.—

An auto-crane approached, and the cabin doors creaked open. The hair on the back of his neck spiked. Glancing around the side, he spotted a camera high up on the chamber ceiling, aimed on another set of double doors to the right. He dropped to the cabin's side, out of view, just in case the camera turned toward him. As the crane moved away, he sneaked a peek forward. The sheer volume of Neura vials blew his mind.

There's enough Neura to supply the city for years.

The cabin spun on the spot, exposing Andre to the camera. Although it remained fixed in the other direction, he scrambled around the side of the cabin and swung into its opening. Giant, banana-sized vials of blue liquid glowed through the tight plastic wrapping. Finn's voice came back to him from the previous night:

"I just thought maybe you could, I dunno, find a way—"

No, no, no. This is nuts.

—Boss, if this ain't a wish granted by some cosmic genie, then I'm a monkey's uncle. Get yours, and get some now.—

His indecision, and its paralysis, persisted. It wasn't like the Captain to goad him into reckless choices. It wasn't the Captain's job. The Captain's job was to say things like:

You've gone bat-shit crazy, Boss. That's what you get putting little metal things in your head.

No, no, no. That isn't right, either.

The Captain never complained about the implant. It convinced him to let Doctor Steele put the roach on his spine in the first place.

Voices overlapped in the radio station of his head. He confused own thoughts with the Captain's. He squeezed his eyes shut and focused his attention on a tiny dot in the center of his mind. The channels fell silent, leaving behind a soft, humming static. In the quiet stretch of that moment, he felt two things at once: the exact same flutter in his heart that battered his chest with its butterfly wings when he first saw Mo Da, and a movement in his bones, the shifting in his marrow when the dark thing stirred, filling him with equal excitement and dread.

All he knew, in that moment, was that his whole life was a slow road to hell. If he didn't make some drastic change, he was never getting out of

—Brulle—

the chamber undetected, and his

—dark thing—

temper would get the better of him and his implant.

As fast as they emerged, the twin sensations vanished.

He opened his eyes and the vials stared back. The quiet swish of the cranes swept through the chamber, reminding him to hurry up and

—get some—

make a decision.

Heart pounding, hands shaking, like furniture in an earthquake, he reached out to the nearest crate and dug his fingers into the plastic. He tore the wrapping open with a rip that sounded like teeth tearing flesh. Blue vials sparkled in the light of their exposure, their silver capped ends shining. He snatched up a glistening vial and slipped it into his inner pocket. Cold, and surprisingly light, it pressed against his chest. Adrenalin pumped through his body. He grabbed another vial, and another. He took four in total—*that's got to be worth ten thousand credits or more*—and stuffed them into his overalls next to the first. His hands itched to snatch more, but there was no more room to stow them.

He zipped up his inner pocket, his ticket to Anchora heavy against his chest, when his vape tumbled out onto the cabin floor.

Oh, no you don't. Not again.

He reached forward and snatched up the elusive gadget, when the cold hard metal of an auto-crane knocked him from behind and sent him tumbling deep into the cabin. The doors slid shut and engulfed him in total darkness.

Promise

Rooted to the spot, his mind remaining as empty as the dark, he peered wide-eyed into the pitch-black. His breathing stopped. His heart stopped. He felt like *he* had stopped, his existence sucked into a black hole.

The cabin jolted into motion, throttling him out of his paralysis and forcing him to brace himself against the invisible crates. As the cabin moved, he jammed his vape deep into his smaller inside pocket.

When I get out of here, I'm throwing you over the walkways.

He crawled toward the door and felt for an internal latch, but found nothing. Knowing the search was futile, he sat and saved his energy.

The cabin swung to the right, and plonked down onto something hard. He hid behind the crate nearest to the door and waited for a chance to escape. The doors slid open, and a dusty, dry wind rushed in. He shielded his eyes as a crane boom reached in and scooped up the crate in front of him. Without hesitation, he opened his arms to bring them back together, and the grippers latched on. As the crane swept high into wind and light, he climbed onto the top of the crate and peered over the edge.

The concrete floor of another vast hall dropped away below. The breeze blew stronger against his back. Rows of lift cabins lined the walls, and auto-straddles unloaded them. He spotted more vents of to the side. He'd worked in the vents before. If he could reach one, he could climb through it and get out.

As the crate swung slowly around, he squinted at the buffeting wind, and blinked in disbelief. A row of transport shuttles perched like fat birds on a docking platform that opened out onto the barren landscape of the outside world. The cranes loaded crates into the rear of the ships, then reversed away, revealing panels across the back of the ships displaying the names of a city. Seven letters of tantalizing hope shimmered across the panel on the farthest ship:

A - N - C - H - O - R - A

Every part of him tingled. His mind struggled to make sense of it all.

A distribution center. This is how Dirk does it.

The cabin jerked and the crane slid in line with the others, all moving toward the ships.

Heaving with excitement, Andre made a split decision.

I'm getting on that ship.

Ducking, as the crane passed a low beam, he crouched in preparation to jump onto the platform. Two PrePACs walked around the side of the vehicle, however, forcing him to flatten back down on top of the cabin. The PrePACs—older, less agile models than Mo Da—appeared to be inspecting the cargo as the cranes loaded the ships. If he were still on the load when the crane lowered it to the cargo handlers, he would be caught with his pockets full of stolen Neura.

More PrePACs appeared on the platform. Panicking, he searched the bay for an escape route and spotted another low beam overhead. With a cautious glance down at the androids, he pulled himself back into a crouch.

1—2—

The crane passed under the beam, and he sprang toward it, arms splayed. His left gripper missed, his stomach rolling with terror, but his right gripper caught hold. Swinging, like a monkey in a zoo, he gestured for the gripper to haul him up, and climbed onto the top side of the beam to flatten down, out of site. The Neura vials clinked and snuggled against his chest.

For a few terrifying seconds, he expected to hear the calls of the cargo handlers below. But no alarm came.

He peered over the edge. The rear of the Anchora ship closed and the cargo handlers stood back. Red lights flashed across the bay. Engines roared into life. The shuttle hovered and launched into the air, vanquishing his brief moment of hope in the steam left behind.

He gripped the beam, pressed his forehead against its cold metal, and closed his eyes.

It's an omen. It's an omen. It's just not meant to be right now.

Reluctantly, he relinquished his hold on the missed moment and eased his grip to slink along the beam to the far wall. His disappointment morphed into determination. He scoped the area for a way out and spotted a vent just below. Careful to keep out of sight of the PrePACs toiling on the empty platform, he climbed down from the beam and dangled in front of the vent.

Extending a tool from a helper arm, he unscrewed the vent's seal, and it came away easily. He steadied himself in the entrance with his feet and used one hand to grab the side. With the other, he hit the fold switch to collapse his grippers into the harness and swung himself into the vent. With his desperation-fuelled focus still driving him, he held the vent's seal in place, slid a helper through the slats, and secured the seal from the outside.

With the vent in place, he looked back out at the empty bay. The red tail lights of the Anchora ship shimmered in the heat emitting from its engines. His fingers squeezed the vent's slats until he couldn't feel them anymore. As the ship disappeared into rolling clouds, a gravity yanked his heart against the inside of his chest.

Now what do I do? Do I stay here and wait for another ship? How long will that be?

He curled up on his back, like a spider playing dead, paralyzed by a mix of excitement, fear, and indecision.

Exit

—Okay, Boss. So what we got here?—

The Captain emerged out of his stalled thoughts. Andre was too desperate for direction to demand where the hell the Captain had been.

—Well, let me give it to you straight, Boss. You just stole a few thousand credits worth of Neura from the city's resident psychopath, to pay for a ticket on a ship that's owned by that same psychopath. You couldn't have screwed yourself any harder if there were two of you.—

I know, I know.

—So, let's break this down, Boss. One. You can't get anywhere near the ships with those cargo handlers around. There is no way, and you know it. Don't even think about it. Two. If you get caught wandering around in there, with or without Neura, you can kiss your job, and Anchora, goodbye. Three. Dirk said the next ship is in five days. You stay here that long, you can kiss everything goodbye.—

Okay, just let me think.

—You don't need to think, Boss. You just need to move. Now.—

Convinced by the sensibility of action over procrastination, he rolled over onto all fours and crept forward. His harness scraped the top of the vent, forcing him to lower himself like a lizard. The position awoke the strained muscles in his injured shoulder, but he pushed through the pain, focusing on using his bearings to find his way back to a lift shaft. Control would be looking for him, but it was still too soon to reactivate his visor-comm.

—Just breathe. It's not a complete mess. A few missing vials aren't going to be noticed for a while. Maybe not until the ship is unloaded at its destination. You need to get back to the shafts, act like you slipped and knocked yourself out, then walk outta here like your head hurts more than your shoulder does right now. Mix that Neura into zilla. Double it. Triple it if you have to. Make enough to make enough, if you get my drift. Contact Finn. Tell him the deal is on, and tell him he needs to act fast. Faster than

fast. Instant-fucking-noodles fast. Or he misses out on the deal of the century. Tell the same to Dirk. Just keep your cool, make the deal, pay Dirk, and get on the next ship outta here. You can do this, Boss. You GOTTA do this.—

So that's where the Captain had been—cooking up his crazy plan. But it wasn't that crazy, Andre had to admit. It was the same Plan he'd been following all along, only the Captain had turned it up to warp speed.

Encouraged, he crawled on. But after many turns, he arrived at yet another intersection and lost what little sense of direction he was building. He waited for some flash of sensibility, but the Captain had no more advice, silent again, perhaps lost somewhere back in the vent with Andre's bearings.

Frozen, he imagined himself wandering the vents until he starved to death, or drank the Neura out of desperation. *Okay, I really am goin' crazy now.*

As he struggled against indecision, a voice echoed through the vent and kissed his ears with hope. He half-crawled, half-shuffled in the direction of the voice, coming to a grill in the vent's floor. He held back from the light, lowered himself to his belly, and slid forward to peer through. Four metal framed beds sat side-by-side in the middle of a long room. Boxes were stacked up against the side of the walls.

The infirmary!

Another voice spoke, its tone rising and then the sound of the auto-door opening and closing. Silence.

—It's now or never, Boss.—

He pushed the vent seal down and lowered himself out onto the bed below. After replacing the seal, he jumped to the floor.

Okay, so now what?

—The main plan hasn't changed, Boss. A little detail altered, that's all. Dump your harness here. Hide it in the clutter. Then walk straight out the front door. But first, you gotta cover your tracks. Reactivate your coms, and tell him you've been sent home with an injury.—

Holy shit, that's brilliant. I HAVE got this.

He reactivated his visor and faced a barrage of messages from Control.

"Operator 77, we have lost contact, please report to maintenance."

"Ah, sorry Control, I, er, had a slip. Knocked myself out. I'm at the infirmary. Being sent home now."

"Event highly irregular. Reporting to the Monitor."

—Let them tell Dirk. Then you can organize the deal.—

Yes, perfect.

"Yes, yes, of course. Please notify the Monitor. Please have him contact me when he's available. Thank you."

He unbuckled his harness, slid it in under a bench, and stacked boxes in front of it. After taking a deep, settling breath, he stepped out into the hallway. With his head down, and a hand pressed against his forehead, he caught a lift down to the main exit. The four vials of Neura in his overalls pressed against his skin, their cold sapped out by the heat of his body.

Arriving on the ground floor, the lift doors slid open. Another deep breath. He walked across the atrium and headed toward the main gate. He swiped his wristlet on the security portal and breathed a sigh of relief as the light in the glass panels lit up green. With the transport platform in view, he stepped forward, but the doors stopped opening and closed back up. His stomach jumped up into his throat. The light in the door glass flashed red.

"Operator 77."

He could tell by its maddeningly polite tone that the voice behind him belonged to a PrePAC. He turned to face one of Baron's personal female androids. An older model, she lacked the realism Mo Da possessed, and her voice broke up among her words.

"Please accompany me to Level Zzix. The Baronzz would like to zzpeak with you."

Grekov

Andre's heart galloped in his chest, the beat drumming on his fear and rolling it into a greasy ball of nausea. He glanced around, his panicking mind considering making a run for it—toward the stairs or back to the vent—when two other PrePACs came through the gate and stood behind him. Although their embedded laws ensured PrePACs could not commit an act of violence, their firm grip could detain someone should their algorithms sense danger to their owners.

His pulse pounded so hard he thought he heard the Neura vials rattling in his pocket. He clutched his chest where they hid and tried to calm himself. With no other choice, he followed the PrePAC to the lift, the second two walking uncomfortably close behind him.

Arriving at Grekov's level, the lift doors slid open, and the PrePACs forward movement ushered him down a hall and into a grand room.

A large, elliptical window framed the spectacular view of the farm. With his back to Andre, Grekov stood before the window, his sharp, lean silhouette like a splinter in the glass.

Without acknowledging Andre, Grekov turned and moved behind a long, sleek table and tapped onto its smooth surface. The only item on the table–a large statue of an eagle, made from some smoky, transparent stone—sat frozen in a mid-flight attack at the end of the table, with a scorpion in one claw and a lizard in the other.

Having never been so close to Grekov, the Baron's appearance initially disappointed Andre. With a shiny, veined head pinched forward into a pointed nose, his physique tall and wiry rather than strong and solid, he was more immaculate than intimidating. His skin shone with a polished finish, and his glossy fingernails twinkled light delicately across them. His suit was the sharpest Andre had ever seen. It could cut diamond. The more Andre watched him, however, the more the Baron's attention to detail unnerved Andre.

Grekov did not possess the appearance of an ex-criminal. He looked far more calculating and cunning than that. He looked like a man who controlled things with his mind, from a distance, be it buying, selling, or murder. The intensity in Grekov's eyes, as he tapped onto the table, seemed to bore right through the table's surface, as if reading the table's DNA and calculating how he might reengineer it for his own means.

Giddy with fear and admiration, Andre's eyes lit up at witnessing first-hand the focus that must have enabled Grekov to tame his own darkness, to leash it so that it amassed him wealth and power over others. Containing his own violent urges and manipulating others with an iron mantle, Grekov was everything Andre wished he could be. Grekov was Superman and Zod in one deadly, slender, agile form.

Grekov walked from behind his table and approached, fixing Andre with his slate-gray eyes. His deep, velvety voice drummed out and echoed through the room. "Mr. Cross. I believe you had a problem yesterday with your harness?"

Andre dared a sigh of relief. Maybe his thievery had not been exposed after all. "Ah, yes," he stammered. "The left gripper's been freezing. It's no problem now, it's been fixed."

Grekov stood in front of him, his intense stare holding Andre in a trance.

Is he reading my mind?

He imagined Grekov's vision a tangible thing, twin spears piercing through his pupils, harpooning Andre's thoughts to drag them out into the light. He could feel Grekov shuffling through the boxes in his mind, searching for secret hiding places.

Is there a harness behind this one, hmmm? A stolen vial of Neura or two in this pocket, perhaps?

Andre imagined moving his thoughts outside his brain and shifting them around the room, where Grekov, deep in the dark attic of Andre's head, would never think to look.

Grekov nodded. "You know that's not why you're here. I've become aware of complaints about my product being degenerated and on-sold to citizens." He held up a half-full vial of Neura and tilted the vial. The thick blue liquid clung to the glass as it slithered down. "Does the degradation look familiar, Mr. Cross?"

Andre's stomach lurched. Bile rose in his throat. Grekov held one of the vials of zilla Andre had sold to Finn.

Son of a goddamn bitch.

Grekov twisted the vial's cap to extend the injector. He spoke with the calm tone of someone used to having things go his way for many years and expected that standard to continue for many more. He held the injector in front of Andre's face. "This is not good business, Mr. Cross. How can I assure the quality of your product? What if you make a batch that scares off, or kills, one, or several of my customers? This sort of disruptive activity just will not do." He gestured to a monitor on the wall, and Finn's face filled the screen. "This man, from Mid Brulle, was admitted to hospital this morning, from an overdose of badly mixed zilla. Know anything about this?"

Andre's tongue froze like a fish in a freezer. Grekov gestured to the wall screen again. Black and white CCTV footage replaced Finn's face, showing a looping snippet of Andre leaving Finn's tower.

So that's it? He's pissed at me for mixing? He doesn't know I stole the vials?

Andre dared to believe he had a chance of walking out alive, maybe even keeping his job. "I'm sorry, Mr Grekov. It won't happen again, I promise. I just needed some extra credit—"

"I produce Neura here to the best quality, a quality Upper Brulle has come to expect. This 'zilla' is very bad, Mr. Cross, for the users, and for my business. It might be fine for migrants like yourself, but not up here, do you understand?" He strolled back to Andre, until his lean body and gaunt face were only an inch from Andre's. "Do you know what zilla does, Mr. Cross? It not only eats my customers from the inside out, it eats at the organs of my business. Anything that threatens my customers, threatens my business. And I won't have my livelihood put at risk, do you hear me?"

Andre's face flamed, anger and terror knotting inside him. He bit into his lip. His hands twitched at the thought of grabbing Finn's pointed little skull and screwing it down into his body. Barely able to contain his fury, he was grateful when the implant tingled, recognizing his violent thoughts. Medication swooped out of its funnel-web hole and snatched his anger back into its cocoon. His temper spiked in resistance, and the implant responded again with a web of bittersweet sedation. His chemical levels shot up and down, like out-of-control lifts in a building gone berserk. As his anger melted under the meds, he thought he heard a primordial, reptilian hiss in the back of his head.

Grekov held up the injector to Andre's eye and twisted it until it clicked three times. "We all make errors in judgment, Mr Cross. But I am, first and foremost, a business man, and I cannot condone bastardizing of my product."

Grekov's top lip quivered. Andre's head floated in a haze as the meaning of Grekov's words tried to register themselves at the gates of his mind. A tiny droplet of zilla squeezed through the injector and perched on the tip.

The shuffling of movement to the side broke the moment, as Strato strode up to Grekov. The borg held his hand to the side of his head, as if listening to a communication device, and whispered into Grekov's ear.

"Sir, there's a problem…with PrePAC Mo Da."

At the mention of the android's name, Andre's attention focused and excitement replaced his fear. The Baron blinked, betraying his contained surprise. Even in his haze, Andre's head flushed with jealousy.

Was that surprise on Grekov's face? Or concern? Or … something else?

Grekov eyes closed for a second, then reopened.

"I want all the details," he commanded.

Strato nodded once and strode out of the room. With the flick of his hand, Grekov motioned to the PrePAC to clear his office and turned away, as if Andre had never been present. As the Android passed him, Grekov handed it the injector and commanded it to dispose of the vial. The PrePAC took the injector and moved to Andre's side, gesturing him toward the door.

His head reeling from how close he had been to a much worse outcome, Andre took his chance to escape Grekov's wrath and staggered out of the room. As sedated as he was, his mind fixated on what might be happening with Mo Da.

Breach

What did she do?

Concentrating on his concern for Mo Da, he stumbled as the PrePAC ushered him into the lift. The droid caught him by the arm with its free hand and helped him stabilize.

He still could not believe his fortune. Thanks to Mo Da.

What are they doing to her?

As the lift descended, an overwhelming anxiety assailed him. Lost in his medicated delusion, he withdrew his vape and clicked the light button.

"I'm sorry, szzir," stated the PrePAC. "Smoking is not allowed in the liftszz."

Andre drew back deep and blew a ring into the air. "Vapor isn't smoke—"

The PrePACs hand shot out and latched onto Andre's wrist, its grip digging its fingers into his skin. He cried out in pain as the android bent his arm down and backward, forcing his body into a twist.

"I'm sorry sir. Szzmoking is not allowed in the liftszz."

"Alright, alright," he shouted, attempting to thrash the android away. The PrePAC released him, and he stumbled back into the wall, rubbing his wrist. A single, dull clink sounded by his foot and echoed throughout the small cabin. The PrePAC looked down and Andre followed its gaze. His stomach dropped. A twinkling Neura vial lay by his foot. A second vial fell out of his overalls and plunked next to the first.

Andre and the android lifted their heads and faced each other with the timely grace of two performers about to embrace and dance.

"Breach," the droid announced, latching again onto Andre's forearm. "Breach. You are required to remain in place. Breach. Remain—"

Panic flashed through Andre's mind and body. Before he could even think—before his implant could register his primal, reactionary thoughts—he swung his arm up and forward, stabbing his vape into the droid's eye.

Sparks exploded from the android's face as it fell backward, arms flailing like a blind man swatting flies. Regaining its bearings, the android yanked the vape from its eye. The optic burst out of its socket with a blue flare, and the PrePAC collapsed forward onto Andre. He screamed at the vicious sting of something piercing his side. Yanking himself away from the droid's grip, he clutched at his wound, his hand closing around something cold and cylindrical protruding from his stomach.

That bastard stabbed me with my own vape.

The smoking PrePAC fell onto the floor, face-first, and lay still. A pleasant ding chimed through the lift, as it settled to a stop, and opened onto the main atrium.

Crossing his arms to hide his wound, he peered out to see an empty foyer. Three workers walked toward the opposite lift areas, but otherwise the way to the main gate was clear. Compelled by panic and desperation, he pressed the lift's basement button, to send the PrePAC away, and stepped out into the foyer as the doors closed behind him.

Pain burned where the vape still protruded from his side. A warm, wetness bloomed on his skin. Deciding he couldn't pull out the cylindrical device in the atrium without risking attention from the cameras, he crossed his arms over his stomach, wincing at the pressure, and strode forward. The main gate stood only fifty meters in front of him, its steel frame gleaming a promise of escape.

Halfway across the floor, his heart beat accelerating, the sharp spike of adrenaline shot through his body and flushed his skin with prickling heat. His head swam in a whirlpool of medication that refused to abate. Reaching the gate, he swiped his wristlet, and, to his great relief, the glass doors flashed green.

Stepping out into the morning sunlight, he shambled down the ramp toward the transport platform. He didn't know where he was going, he just knew he had to *go*. The more he tried to focus, however, the more his head floated and tossed, like a blimp in a gale. His vision shifted from blurred to vivid and back again. His skin crackled like ice. Something was not right.

Am I getting another dose?

The wound in his side burned with such ferocity he thought the vape might have somehow lit itself. With his arms still folded over his stomach, he pushed forward, but his feet began to drag. He stumbled toward the platform edge, and people waiting for the lifts turned. They stood back, their faces contorting with fear and disgust. Sweating and paranoid, he leaned against the railing, not daring to look them in the eye.

A lift arrived, its doors opening with a hiss. He pushed past the crowd and into the cabin. Disembarking passengers gasped and stepped away. He tripped and fell into the corner, and a woman screamed. The lift closed its doors and whisked him down the side of the tower.

Alone in the cabin, his body on fire and his throat swelling up, he feared his implant was malfunctioning. He struggled to decide if he should go to a hospital or just run for his life. As he fought to focus, he looked down to remove the vape from his side, and froze in horror.

The metal object sticking out of his side was not his vape. It was a Neura injector vial. Terrifying realization gripped him. The PrePAC had accidentally stabbed him with the vial, injecting him with his own zilla mix. And by the tornado of icy pain swarming through his body and exploding in his brain, he had taken in a Big Dose.

Door

His entire nervous system screamed, shooting fireworks of both pain and euphoria to the ends of his every nerve. As the lift jolted to a stop and opened its doors, his stomach convulsed and ejected his breakfast.

Wiping his mouth and hauling himself to his feet, he staggered out into Devlin Square. Thinking he walked forward, his disorientation steered him sideways in between parked hover vans. He fought his eyes trying to roll themselves back into his head. Spikes needled his skin, as if glass shattered underneath. His entire structure of thought crumbled at its edges, collapsing in on itself and threatening to bury him in an avalanche of darkness.

This is it. This is how I go. Exploding from the inside out.

Booming from his core, another tsunami of euphoria washed over him, wiping away his terror. Swamped by the intense pleasure, all sense of dimension abandoned him. He reached out to steady himself against a van, but his hand clutched at air. Sensations coalesced and distorted. Slipping in and out of lucidity, his vision splintered and reconfigured. His gut spasmed, clenching so tight he could barely breathe, and he generously sprayed the van with whatever was left in his stomach.

His hands found the wet side of the van and he held on. An urgent voice yelled something somewhere to the left. The nauseating euphoria ebbed back, his eyes refocused, and a clarity stretched out in his mind.

"This way," the voice called out, closer.

In the sudden moment of calm, he spied a parked hover van, only meters away, with its side door ajar.

He clenched his hands into fists, as he mustered all his strength, and staggered, like a child trying to run after stepping off a spinning ride. Colliding and bouncing off the hovers, he pinballed between the parked vehicles until he stumbled headfirst into the darkness of the open van.

"Hey! Get outta here!" came a high voice through his haze.

The euphoria came back in a wave. A hand grabbed his arm, and he looked up to see a lean oriental girl. Her face sparked a sense of familiarity. His euphoria morphed into something he had not experienced in a long time, something sharp and red and violent. Instinctively, he whacked her aside, knocking her off her feet and slamming her into the rear of the van. Her body slumped to the floor, leaving behind a dent in the door.

Confused and amazed by his clarity and strength, he stared at his hands as if superpowers had zapped out of them. Another voice yelled from somewhere in the van, but a wind rushed into his ears and blew the words away, dissolving them into bits of noise floating in a sea of distorted sound effects. The van disappeared, its floor becoming rock, hewn from chaotic winds and sharp rain. All his senses reached out and traced the spaces around him. The world he knew had been replaced by a dark, primeval landscape. His vision filled with the outlines of things creeping toward him, and a myriad of previously unnoticed odors filled his nostrils. His brain overloaded, his vision flickered, and his heart verged on bursting out of his chest. This world, this old, old world, he knew it, had lived in it a long, long time, and it stank of death.

Gunshots rattled the air, imploding the hallucination and snapping him back into the reality of the van. He sensed—no, he *smelled*—someone beside him. He *smelled* fear and danger. But before he could turn to face the peril, a blast of pain exploded in his head, shattering the vivid colors and smells and rage into tiny shards of light, until their disappearance sucked him into total darkness.

PART FOUR

GOD'S ZILLA

Grace

Floating up out of a dispersing fog, Andre pressed his face into the softness of an unfamiliar pillow. As he drew in a deep, savoring breath, his ears drank in the peaceful quiet around him. The sharp smell of bleach seeped through his bliss, however, and awoke a spearing ache threatening to crack open the top of his head. He tried to move, but his muscles resisted, as if lead had been poured into his veins. Flecks of dried vomit caked the back of his throat, and he licked his parched lips with a lizard-rough tongue.

Water.

Prying his eyelids apart, soft light flooded in. He shifted on a lumpy mattress and the bed squeaked, as if frightened mice lived in its joints. Something long and cold shifted beside him. He looked down to see it was his own arm, his right hand scratching bloody bandages that wrapped around his abdomen. He had been stripped down to his underwear. Pulling his scratching hand away, his fingers clawed up like the legs of an arthritic huntsman. As the connections between his mind and body reignited, an intensifying burn flared in his side under the bandage.

Touching his forehead to find a lump, he tried fathoming how long he had been out, but the throbbing pain in his skull destroyed his sense of time. He recalled being confronted by Grekov, then leaving with the PrePAC. The events that followed rushed back into his memory, right up to the moment his entire being vibrated with intense strength and energy. A vague hint of the prehistoric world he'd been transported to teased his sanity. He pushed the disturbing experience to the side of his recall and fast-forwarded to the last two things he remembered—something hard colliding with his head before everything went black.

"Welcome back."

A blurry, bespectacled face hovered over his. Blinking, Andre focused on an Oriental man he did not recognize.

"Be at peace," the man said. "You have been to a bad place, but you are safe here."

Andre tried to speak, but his vocal chords refused to vibrate, and all he could do was mouth a 'Thank you.' The man put a cup to his cracked lips, and Andre lapped feebly. As cool water trickled over his dry throat, he clutched the cup with both hands and gulped.

"Woah," said the man, pulling the cup away. "Take it slow."

As soon as the water hit his stomach, his insides spasmed and threw the water back up. He caught the regurgitation in his mouth and gulped it down, his throat so dry even his own sick refreshed him. Sweat trickled through Andre's hair and over his forehead, and the man wiped it away with a cold, wet towel.

"Where am I?" Andre managed at last, rubbing his forearm where his wristlet use to be.

"You are in The Heart of Grace. We are a community sanctuary, in the Stems. I am Tan."

As his focus adjusted, he looked around the room. Afternoon light fell through a row of tall windows along the opposite wall. He lay on a bunk in the middle of a row of similar bunks. A double doorway stood closed at the end of the dorm. On the bunk two up from his, a gaunt man lay on his back, his chest barely lifting. So wasted was the man's body, he was more skeleton than human. Weeping, infected-looking ulcerations colonized his arm and his skin scaled like a reptile. A sharp razor of anxiety sliced through the fog that had until then kept Andre's mind calm. Tan pinched Andre's chin and turned his head away from the sick man.

"Do not concern yourself with others. That's not going to happen to you. I can tell you are new to zilla. It's not usual to take such a dose, and through your stomach, of all places—although I've seen stranger things. If you're new to it, then you are an excellent candidate for rehabilitation."

Rehabilitation? "Am I in a hospital?" Andre asked, too groggy to explain he was not a user, too uncertain to know if that was even a good idea.

"No, dear, I told you already, this is a church."

"You're a Doctor?"

Tan smiled, flattered. He placed the wet towel on a table next to the bed and folded his hands in his lap. "Of sorts. I do what I can. But don't you worry, I know my work. God's will delivered you to the Heart of Grace. God's will has honored us with the fortuity to save another of Brulle's lost ones. For certain, had God not directed you into our arms, your soul would be forever wandering this awful machine we call a city, sucked into its mechanics like so many others." Tan pulled the blanket back over Andre's torso. "You certainly had a big dose. You've been out for twenty hours."

The double doors at the end of the room swung open with a bang, and Tan jumped to his feet. A tall, lean young man strode through the light and shadow cast by the windows.

"Brother Kade," Tan greeted, clenching his fists and rubbing his thumbs over his forefingers. "I was just going to let you know our new guest has awoken."

Brother? Kade didn't look like a priest. Stoic seriousness hardened the newcomer's handsome face, and his black cargo pants and fitted jumper made him appear more military than religious. As Kade stood over him, Andre pressed back into the pillow under the young man's piercing green eyes.

"Where have you come from?" Kade demanded.

Weak and dizzy, Andre could only blink against the confrontation. Kade leaned forward and ripped back the blanket, his eyes scanning Andre's body.

"You're not an addict, you haven't got the track marks. What were you doing near the farm?"

"I… I don't remember," Andre stammered. "My head—"

"Get him up," Kade commanded Tan.

"But he is still weak," Tan protested.

"He's been asleep for a day. We're not a hostel. The Keeper wishes to have dialogue with him. Now." Tan bowed and helped Andre out of bed.

Touching the cold floor, Andre's feet tingled and his knees struggled to hold his weight. Tan helped steady him while he climbed back into his overalls.

With a look of disgust, Kade grabbed Andre by the arm and ushered—no, he *pulled*—him toward the double doors, leaving Tan behind.

"They're no good to us if we don't let them recover," Tan called from beside the bunk.

"They're no good to us if they're hiding something," Kade retorted, shoving Andre out of the dorm and into a long, chilly corridor.

The cold of the stone floor bullied its way through Andre's bare feet and hitchhiked a ride on his blood stream to collide with the warmth of his brain. He could almost hear the hiss of steam rising from his head as the brisk walk refreshed him, and his headache abated. Passing closed doors of other dorms, he took note of everything he saw, and gathered his thoughts.

So, I'm somewhere in the Stems. I've been out twenty hours. That makes it about six pm. And, by the sounds of things, no one here is too happy about Neura or the farm. Especially this prick. I better come up with a story about what the hell I was doing at the farm, and fast.

"You remembering anything now, Liar Man?" Kade goaded, his taut voice creeping up behind Andre like a stalker. "Do you remember barging into our van in your doped-up state and breaking Aoto's arm?"

He did. At Kade's words, the scene replayed itself in Andre's mind, chopped up and rejoined, like a bad edit of a cheap movie. A warmth fluttered through his torso as he remembered the rush of the drug overriding his implant, sending him into a violent frenzy.

So it was Kade who knocked me out.

Kade ushered him onward, and Andre walked out of the dorm area along a balcony overlooking a lower entrance. From below, a distinct, toxic smell darted up into his nose, triggering a sense of familiarity. He sniffed, but the identity of the odor's sharp essence eluded him. Kade shoved him in the back, propelling him forward out of his dawdle.

"I asked you a question."

What did he ask? The van. I broke the girl's arm in the van. "Look, I'm sorry about that. I... I wasn't myself."

"Well I don't know about that, 'cause I don't know who you are. But it's Aoto you gotta apologize to. And the Keeper. You done more damage than you realize. If we weren't running for our lives back at the farm, I would have dumped your sorry ass there and then. Now you're here, the Keeper insists we help you. If it were up to me, you'd be out on your own."

"Glad it's not up to you then," Andre shot back, already tired of Kade's aggression.

Kade latched onto Andre's abdomen, and dug his fingers into the wound. Andre cried out in pain as he collapsed to his knees on the hard floor. Kade held him in the debilitating grip and spat his words into Andre's face.

"You listen to me, Liar Man, and you listen good. I don't like you. Not one bit. Something's not right about you. I know a liar when I see one, and I know you're got a whole lotta lying in ya."

Kade's fingers dug in deeper, biting into Andre's side like the clenching jaw of a crocodile. Andre felt a familiar twinge in his spine.

"And I'm gonna catch you out, Liar Man. You got that? I'm gonna catch you out, 'cause that's what I do. I catch out liars like you."

Kade released his hold, grabbed Andre by the arm, and hauled him back onto his feet. As Andre gasped at the dizzying pain in his side, Kade shoved him forward again.

"Now move it. Next door on your right."

Clutching his wound with one hand, Andre breathed in and out, deep and slow. No matter how crazy Kade seemed, Andre couldn't afford a dose from his implant. He needed his head clear if he was going to lie his way out of his predicament.

"Better start thinking up your story, Liar Man, and it better be a good one."

Kade's words voiced Andre's thoughts so well they burrowed into his resolve. He breathed through the biting pain, uncomfortable in the silence.

Hairs spiked across his neck as he noticed what else was missing. Not just his wristlet. The voices were gone. No Captain. No Jeremy. Just a beautiful and unnerving quiet.

Brother

Turning right through an archway, Andre walked into a bright but musty chamber and squinted at the dazzling view.

Beyond a large window in the end wall, hover traffic crisscrossed the vast space between three monolithic towers. The underside of Mid Brulle arched over, connecting the top of the Stems with a thick labyrinth of suspended structures and interconnecting walkways. A multitude of bottomless pools embedded in the architecture above twinkled, like scattered jewels fracturing light from the sky above and rippling it throughout the scene. Giant holographic advertisements moved between tower clusters, and lights of all shapes and colors dotted every facade like the aftermath of an exploded neon creature.

I'm near the top of the Stems.

"Welcome," boomed a brash voice from Andre's left, "to The Heart of Grace." A muscled, middle-aged man, with a short, sharply manicured beard, stood up from behind a circular table. A silver cross dangled around his neck. Next to him sat an Asian girl, nursing her right arm in a sling. She scowled at Andre, and he recognized her from the van outside the farm. He heard the crunch of her bone as he recalled slamming her into the back of the van. She might have looked like a little bird with a broken wing if she wasn't clutching a menacing, blunt-ended mace in her good hand. She pulled her bound arm against her body.

So, that's Aoto. No wonder she's not so friendly.

Bookshelves ran the length of the wall behind the table. Andre had never seen a book in his time in Brulle, all information stored in digital libraries. The room stewed in the rich smell of leather chairs and the dusty books, like a time capsule turned inside out.

As the bearded man walked around the table, muscles bunched under his black sweater. A generous smile pushed fine-wrinkles from the corners of his eyes up into jet-black hair speckled with gray. His stark gaze scanned Andre up and down as he reached out his hand. Two large gold rings twinkled on his fingers.

"I am Brother Elron, Keeper of The Grace." Up close, his face revealed a blotchy complexion and yellow teeth. "And I believe you have met our young Sister Aoto."

Andre nodded, offering her a feeble, apologetic smile. She scowled again, gripping the mace resting on the table.

"Amanojaku." She threw the strange word into the air.

"And you are?" Elron asked, hand still outstretched.

Andre eyed the Keeper's hand with suspicion before shaking it. "Andre Cross."

Elron smiled. "Be at ease, Andre. You are in safe place." Andre glanced at Kade standing beside the door.

"Are you sure?"

Elron's smile broadened, as he held Andre by the arm, and steered him toward the window wall. "Oh, don't let Brother Kade bother you. He's here for my protection. Some victims of Neura can become quite a handful." He leaned close to Andre's ear, his hot breath sweet with the scent of some herbal smoke that made Andre crave his vape. "You've broken something he thinks belongs to him. And she—Aoto—she's just a little superstitious. Your actions have delayed a project we have been working on. But, to be honest, a little extra time to ensure our intel is accurate won't hurt."

Elron's grip didn't release Andre's arm as he stopped him and faced him to the window. A large gold cross adorned the bulkhead. Elron sighed theatrically.

"Beautiful, isn't it? A grand achievement of humanity's ingenuity. A haven from the mess our bad habits created. Unfortunately, these same habits have followed us into Brulle. Although everything looks wonderful, the truth is, Lower Brulle is in decay. It is being eaten from the inside, much like the poor users of zilla." Elron reached his other arm around Andre and cupped the back of his head. "So much crime, it's become a way of life. With Upper Brulle offering only token support, this void is filled by community and volunteer centers, such as ours."

"Neura has a lot to answer for," Andre offered, stalling for time as he worked out what he would say when Elron started asking him questions. Elron laughed and slid his hand down onto Andre's shoulder, pulling him in close and squeezing.

"You know that's not the truth, don't you, Andre?"

Andre stiffened, afraid Elron knew he worked on the farms. The Keeper leaned in closer.

"Neura is just one facet of the dark jewel drawing us all in like a black hole does the stars. It's not just the drugs, my Brother. It's what lies in the DNA of Neura: technology. All these machines, these nano-bots and pharmaceuticals, they're eating us like spider babies eat their mothers."

Andre couldn't help a confused look at Elron. The Keeper laughed his hearty laugh again, sliding his hand down Andre's side and lightly squeezing his waist, as if reading the strength of his body. Andre flinched at the stranger's closeness, but held still for fear of offending his host.

"Oh, there's nothing wrong with technology, per se," Elron continued. "No, we'd be hypocrites to make such a claim. Technology is important. It's what will do our biding while we focus on our enlightenment. No, it's this incessant, narcissistic obsession with altering our God-given forms. 'Enhancing' and 'modifying,' as if we're nothing more than machines. And now, these trans-humanist borgs are replacing whole body parts with prosthetics. It's out of control. Brulle has an addiction to technology, whether it's drugs, or prosthetics, or sexual relations with androids. This sacrilege of allowing artificial life inside us, physically and spiritually, simply must stop."

Piecing together his own story, Andre smiled, only half-listening to Elron. The Keeper continued, his voice rising and dropping with the fluidity of a well-rehearsed performance.

"Oh, the citizens of Upper Brulle know not what they do. They think they are thriving on Neura. But they are not thriving, they are becoming addicted, reliant. The nanotechnology in the Blue Eye plant remains in the processed Neura, and embeds itself into their cells. The more they use it, the more technology colonizes their bodies and the less human they become. The less human they become, the weaker their connection with God." Elron clutched Andre's waist again. This time, Andre pulled away a fraction. *What does he want?*

"That is what the Church is here for, Andre. We are an extension of humanity's spiritual immune system, evolved to protect our connection with the divine." Elron stepped in between Andre and the window, silhouetted by the view, and grabbed him by the shoulders. "Brulle has a demon growing in it, Andre. We must draw it out into the light and face it. Brulle's rehabilitation begins here in the Stems, but this is only the beginning. It is the Heart of Grace's mission to free all in Brulle from its unnatural dependencies." He brushed Andre's cheek with his ringed hand. "Victim by victim."

Andre's chronic resistance to affection had had enough and yanked on the levers of his reactions. "Where are my things?" he demanded, pulling away again.

Elron did not flinch at the abrupt change of topic. He clasped his hands together, forming a dome of fingers, his rings becoming two golden satellite dishes. "All your belongings are safe and will be returned to you when you are well."

"I want my wristlet—"

"Apart from essential medications and equipment, any intimacy with technology by a church member—or guest—is prohibited, to minimize electromagnetic radiation. Radio waves are blocked from coming in or going out, to allow our spirits to cleanse themselves. So your wristlet would be useless. We are delightfully isolated here in the middle of the city. Isn't it wonderful? A sanctuary for you to focus on your healing. And you will be healed here, Andre. You will become strong."

"I'm not sick, I just—"

"Oh? You are not a user? Would you care to share with us your story, then? Are you ready to tell us about your implant?"

Andre's stomach dropped like a plummeting elevator. His brain froze with stage fright, and the story he'd formed in his mind refused to come out and perform. Elron smiled his perfect smile, and moved back to Andre's side to speak softly into his ear. He cupped the back of Andre's neck again and gave it a light squeeze.

"Yes, we know about your implant. Tan scanned you when came in. You have no need to keep secrets. You are not alone. There are others here, like yourself, innocents caught up in the perversion of humanity. I can help you, Andre. I can make you strong again. So, tell me, how did you get here?"

Andre swallowed back his unease, sensing Kade by the door listening intently for his lie. He "I'm a lift-mechanic. I work all over the city. And yes, I'm a user. I have a supplier at the farms. That's why I was there. I couldn't wait to get home for my next fix, so I had it there in the carpark."

"No." Elron lowered his voice and gently, almost lovingly, stroked the back of Andre's neck. "I meant, how did you get *here*, to this state of being that accepted an implant? What happened to you, Brother? What did the past make you do?"

Andre was utterly unprepared to explain his implant. He'd divulged his past to no one but Dirk. He'd spent the last seven years trying to hide it. "You don't ask someone that."

"I cannot help you if you do not open up to me, Andre. Without honesty and openness, you can't be rehabilitated. You've admitted you're a user. That's good. That is the first step. Now, what else do you need to confess?"

Andre slipped out of Elron's grip to face him, and hesitated. The silence in the chamber stretched out in all directions. The wound in his side throbbed, and his pulse pounded in his ears. He glanced at Kade, standing by the door, throwing back a glare that begged Andre to try to escape. Aoto leaned forward on the table, gripping her mace, her eyes pinning him to the spot with guilt. His resolve weakened his ability to lie, and he dropped his head in resignation.

"I hurt someone."

Elron did not reply, letting the silence draw Andre's darkness out into the light. Exhausted, weakened, he looked up and into Elron's understanding eyes, and the urge to confess his crime overwhelmed him. The walls of silence he'd built around himself tumbled down, and the truth spilled out. "I killed my brother," he blurted, a ghost weight lifting out of his body.

Elron nodded, encouraging Andre to continue.

"I was twelve. He was … violent. He threatened to kill me, and our mother, many times, over the stupidest things. And he would have. I had to do something. One day, I … I just went crazy." He couldn't admit to planning his brother's murder. He barely admitted that even to himself.

"And you couldn't control this rage?"

The discussion drained Andre's body of strength. His legs shook. "No. No, I couldn't. It was like a … a dark energy consumed me, took over me. I was me, but I wasn't me. It doesn't make sense, I know, it never made sense, but it's what happened."

Elron again brushed his gold rings against Andre's cheek. "It does make sense, Brother."

Brother. That word, and Elron's tenderness, pulled the remaining pins out of Andre's structured caution. "I killed him," he confessed. "I stabbed him with his own knife. That stupid, fucking switchblade of his, with that bloody sound it always made. I wanted it to stop, I *needed* it to stop, the sounds, the beatings, so I just…I stabbed him to death with his own stupid knife." Guilt and relief overwhelmed him. Tears welled in his eyes and sobs caught in his throat. Elron moved forward and put a comforting hand on his shoulder.

"But it wasn't what you wanted, was it, Andre? It wasn't what you really wanted. You wanted him to love you, didn't you?"

"I just… I wanted him to just… be my brother."

Elron gripped Andre's other shoulder. "To love you."

Andre couldn't say it. His whole body shook, and his legs threatened to give way. It took all his strength to not burst out crying. In Andre's moment of vulnerability, Elron swooped in and wrapped his strong arms around Andre's quivering body, hugging him into his muscled torso. He cupped the back of Andre's shaking head and spoke in his slow, soothing voice. His moving lips brushed Andre's ear, like the annoying wings of a moth.

"It's okay, Brother. It's okay. He did love you."

With those words, the last vestiges of Andre's resolve broke. All his guilt, all his hate, all his anger—all the years in prison and months of slaving on the farms, the constant medication, the voices, and the roller coaster ride of the previous twenty-four hours—flooded out in a tsunami of emotional release. He buried his face in Elron's solid shoulder and burst into sobs. Elron hugged him closer, and Andre hugged him back. For a moment, Andre was twelve years old again—not stabbing his brother, but hugging him, two brothers holding each other tight.

"He loved you, Andre." Elron continued stroking the back of Andre's neck. "He just didn't know how to show it, like you struggle to say it. He was possessed, affected by the demon in this suppressive city. Like you have been. You are not a bad person, Brother. And you are in a place that will help you believe that."

Andre's sobs subsided, just enough to return his emotions to the present. He tensed, suddenly awkward in the stranger's embrace.

"It's not a weakness to cry, Andre. It's brave, and it heals."

Andre fought his conflicting emotions, his thoughts arguing with themselves.

It is weak to cry. Jeremy taught me that. But Jeremy didn't cry, and he's dead.

Goosebumps spread out across his skin in an emerging armor. He stepped back and wiped the last tears from his cheeks. His inner defense systems reactivated, hauling up the drawbridges and lining the curtain walls with archers. The broken thing inside him pulled itself together and snarled. He hadn't felt that weak in a long, long time. He was in danger.

I don't know anything about these people.

Out of the re-established fortress of his resolve, defending his doubts and championing his suspicions, a question catapulted to the forefront of his thoughts. "What were Kade and Aoto doing there? At the farm?"

Elron avoided Andre's eyes, the red pigmentation on his cheeks flaring. Aoto looked at Kade, but Kade shuffled his feet and lowered his head.

"What were they doing there, at the farm?" Andre persisted. "I saw you," he said, pointing at Aoto. "In the van, earlier in the day. You nearly ran me over. If you're so against Neura, what the hell were you two doing there?"

Elron rolled his eyes and sighed. "Andre, as I have told you, the farm is part of the evil possessing Brulle. We … study its activities. If we are to beat this disease, knowledge is better than ignorance." Elron waved away the discussion. "Enough of this chit chat. You must be exhausted—"

"I want to leave."

Elron's faithful smile did not falter.

"Andre." He opened his arms, palms outward. "Once you enter the Heart of Grace, you stay until you are strong enough to leave. That is our promise to you."

"Are you saying I can't leave?"

"I'm saying you are welcome here, and we can help you. You may leave when you are well. But, you should know that I am required, by law, to advise the authorities of anyone leaving who I deem not fit to rejoin the community. You have been placed in my care by the hands of God. It is my duty to help you, and to protect the entire community. Do you understand?"

Their eyes locked with the impassiveness of the horns of fighting gazelles.

"Do we have an understanding, Brother? You do want to be better, don't you? That is why we have rules, to guide you back to health."

The rules were clear; there was only one real rule in the Heart of Grace—Elron made them all. Andre dropped his gaze to the floor. "Of course."

"Good." Elron moved back to Andre's side, put his arm around his shoulders, and ushered him toward the door. "You will find your strength here, Andre, I promise. That is what we offer. A second chance to those who might otherwise never get one—"

Cutting Elron's words short, the chamber door swung open with a bang. A young man, wearing the same military style clothes as Kade and Aoto, ran in.

"Keeper," he puffed. "The bill has been passed. Upper Brulle is claiming Mid Brulle."

Kade shot a worried glance at Aoto and then at Elron. The Keeper's eyebrow arched up, like the back of a cat, and his smile vanished. He clasped his hands and pursed his lips.

"Thank you, Max."

"Your Grace—" Max began, but Elron waved him away. Still catching his breath, Max nodded, bowed, and left.

"Now what do we do, Keeper?" Kade barked. "It'll be weeks before Aoto can climb again."

Elron regained his composure, spread his smile back over his face, and turned back to Andre. "While you are here, you will follow our doctrines. Rest well, Brother. We rise at dawn." He gestured to Andre to leave the chamber, and Andre stepped outside the room. Kade followed, slamming the door behind them.

In the cold hallway, Andre could think of only one thing.

That's plenty of time to get the hell out of here.

Boots

As he walked in front of Kade back to the dorm, the same faint, chemical odor that had teased his senses earlier assailed him. He couldn't nail down the olfactory mystery—something familiar, yet nasty and out of place—but it made every muscle in his neck tighten in alert.

A clunk echoed from the level below. The double doors swung open, and rain swooped two figures into the tiled area. One of the figures fell to the floor, while the other helped them back up.

"What's going on?" Andre asked Kade.

"Another 'lost soul' delivered into our care," Kade replied. "We might need your bunk soon. Move it." He shoved Andre down the corridor.

If that's the way in, then that's also a way out.

Reaching the dorm, Kade stopped him at the double doors. "Get your rest, Liar Man. You'll need it tomorrow."

"Thanks for your hospitality," Andre retorted, tired and fed up.

A nasty grin split Kade's handsome face. He leaned in so close Andre had to press himself back against the door. As Kade spoke, the heat of his breath stung Andre's eyes.

"Aoto's right about you. You got a whole lotta angry in 'ya, creepin' under your skin, sittin' in your mind. Makes you do shit you don't even know you're doin'. Like breakin' her arm. That's Amanojaku. Stirrin' people up so they do crazy shit in return. 'Cause as soon as they do, they let Amanojaku inside them." Kade poked Andre in the sternum. "You got a monster inside you, Liar Man. And we don't want it here."

Andre swallowed back a lump in his throat. "I do what I gotta do to survive, like anyone."

"Oh yeah? Is that why you killed your brother? Was that for survival? Or just 'cause you like stabbin' people?"

Kade's words punched Andre in the stomach, winding him with accusation, muting any reply. Kade leaned back, smiling and gloating in the silence. The dorm doors opened and Tan's bespectacled head poked through.

"Ah, welcome back. Thank you, Kade, I'll take it from here."

Kade shot Andre one last look of daggers before turning to stride away down the hall.

"You've met the Keeper then?" Tan asked, ushering Andre inside and closing the doors. "Isn't he an inspiring man?"

The smell of disinfectant greeted Andre, barely masking the lingering stench of human waste. He feigned a smile as Tan lead him to his bunk, unable to answer, still recovering from the punch of Kade's words.

"He survived the 2026 Great European Fire, you know?" Tan explained. "Fled to Russia to help rehabilitate the migrants driven from the emerging trans-humanist states. That's where Elron established the Heart of Grace, where he began his preaching. He will save this city's soul, rest assured. Yours also." Andre sat down on his bunk and Tan stepped back. "Anyway, I'm rambling. You must rest. We rise early for prayer. Sleep well, Brother." Elron's biggest fan bowed and walked toward the doors.

Andre glanced at the bunk where the zilla addict had been laying earlier, but it was now empty. The man's boots remained under the bunk, pushed under where only Andre could see them.

"Hey," Andre called to Tan. "What happened to that man?"

Tan scratched his nose. "He's in the arms of the Lord, now. Get some rest." Tan shut the door behind him, and the lights went out.

Andre got out of bed and tried on the man's boots. They were a little large for him, but they'd do. He would need them once he got outside.

He didn't know how he was going to get out of the church, but he sure as hell wasn't staying. Their surveillance of the farm, and their reaction to the bill being passed, bore characteristics of a growing insurgence, a sleeper cell just waiting to wake and wreak havoc. And their compulsory rehabilitation reeked of recruitment. But for what end exactly, Andre couldn't be certain. All he knew was, as dangerous as it was outside with Grekov after him, if Kade, or anyone of Elron's followers, discovered he worked on the farms—and dealt Neura *and* mixed zilla—his life wouldn't be worth the piss-stained sheets on his dirty bunk.

He lay back staring at the outside lights shifting across the ceiling and planned his escape. Glancing outside, he guessed by the daylight fading above the horizon that the time was around seven o'clock. If the church rose at dawn to pray, they would surely sleep early. That meant if he waited a few hours, when everyone would be asleep, he could go for the entry where he saw the addict being brought in. It was a loose plan, but it was a plan.

Okay, it's a very loose plan. There's probably guards by the front door, or some lock or something. I need a tighter plan than that. Captain, where are you?

He scrutinized what little he'd learned about the church and remembered the black van Kade and Aoto had been in.

There has to be a docking bay somewhere. And where there's a bay, there's another way out. Maybe I can take the van.

Weary as he was, he resisted closing his eyes, determined to stay awake and aware of the time. He focused his mind on what he would do when he was outside. But that vague, uncertain set of options stared back at him like a broken robot.

I don't even know where to start. I can't go home. The Baron's after me, for sure.

He rubbed his hands over his short-cropped hair, digging for ideas.

If I could get into the farm, maybe I could get on that ship. But ... there's no way. That place is tighter than an android's asshole. Goddamn it, I need a plan! He banged the edges of the bed with both fists, the jolt sparking the throbbing pain in his side.

Okay, breathe. Just breathe. I gotta put my thinking cap on it. Think like a Boss. What would Grekov do? From the nowhere of his desperation sprang a hazardous idea. *Maybe I can blackmail Dirk. Threaten to blow the lid off his smuggling gig if he doesn't smuggle me out. Jackson was going in five days. I could take his spot on that ship. If I can get to Dirk before then ...*

He struggled to imagine exactly how he would handle that confrontation. He tried thinking in Captain speak, to encourage the voice to come back—he could use all the help he could muster—but in so doing he turned on himself.

That's about the craziest idea you've ever had, Boss, and you've thought some crazy shit.

Yeah, well, I'm out of options. So, Captain, unless you wanna wake the fuck up and give me a better idea, that's the fucking Plan.

The Captain still did not respond, so Andre spent the next few hours sifting through every aspect of his minimal options, reconfiguring them, then pulling them apart again. He kept coming back to the same crazy scheme.

Out there, Grekov is after me. In here, Kade's out for my blood. Either way, I'm dead as long as I stay in Brulle. I've got to get to Dirk and get on that ship. I don't know how he'll sneak me into the farm without being caught, but he'll find a way. He'll have to.

The windows tinted and blanketed the dorm in darkness. Before Andre could catch himself, his exhausted mind and body relaxed their grip on his desperate strategizing and dropped him into a slumber.

Odor

The warm wave of sleep ebbed, exposing his awareness to the cold atmosphere of consciousness. His thoughts picked up where they left off, before exhaustion had dragged them under, and startled him awake.

Damn it.

He sat up and looked around, trying to gauge how long he'd been asleep. All sunlight had gone. The hover traffic had slowed past the peak period. Estimating the time was anywhere between eleven pm and five am, he decided he had to move.

He rolled quickly off the bed to minimize the squeaking and slid the dead man's boots out from under his bunk. Sitting on the floor, he laced them on.

Can't go running through the city in bare feet, can I, Boss?

Laces tied, he stepped quietly to the double doors and leaned an ear against one. He focused his hearing through the wood and out into the hallway. Nothing but silence. He tapped on the door, and readied himself to tackle whoever would open it, but no one responded. Examining the door handle, he found no lock. He tried it, and it turned. He pushed the door ajar and peered out into the empty, dimly lit corridor. Surprised to see only an empty chair down the hallway, he took his chance, slid out through the gap and closed the door gently behind him.

With a quick glance in both directions, he headed past the other dorms and down the hall. Reaching the balcony, he descended the steps to the lower floor and scoped the space. Two pillars stood in the center, between the steps and the main entrance.

He crossed the floor of the entrance chamber, when Kade walked out of a side hall, his arm around Aoto. Andre darted to the side and ducked behind the first pillar. As the lovers' footsteps and voices moved across the entrance, he circumnavigated the pillar, keeping himself out of view. The footsteps stopped, leaving Andre trapped in the middle of the chamber.

"I've got to get back to my shift." Kade spoke in a hush, the hard edge of his tone gone.

"When can we be together again?" asked Aoto, the light echo of her voice butterflying around the room. "You spend so much time with Elron. I think you like him more than me."

"No, babe, no. It's just, he's the Keeper. And I owe him. You know that."

"You don't owe him anything. He owes you, for all you've done for him. For what you *will* do for him tomorrow." Aoto paused. "And I should be with you."

"You should. But we have to act now. Elron says he has someone in mind to take your place."

"It should be *me*. It is my honor. Maybe, then, Elron would look at me as much as he looks at you."

The unmistakable wet sound of lips kissing echoed softly around the pillar. Andre shut his eyes and willed Kade and Aoto to move on.

"We are nearly there, Aoto. I will do Elron, and you, proud."

"I want him to be proud of me, too." Aoto's voice rose in pitch. "Who is this Andre? He fucked up our surveillance, broke my arm. Now Elron treats him like a pet. He brings Amanojaku here."

"I don't like it, either, babe. But don't worry, Elron gets tired of his fancies fast. I've seen it before. Then I'll make that liar pay for what he did to you."

Andre gave up trying to move them on with his mind and pressed himself against the pillar, anxious that someone else might come in or descend the stairs, and spot him.

"I've got to get back before Dimitri takes over watching the dorms," Kade continued. "I've been gone too long as it is." But they didn't move, Aoto's voice becoming breathy and seductive.

"Stay with me, just a little longer." Their kisses sounded like small animals eating.

Andre's anxiety got the better of him. He feared the echoes of their kissing might be footsteps coming. Searching the atrium for options, he spotted an arched entryway in the far corner of the wall where stairs lead down. He didn't want to be diverted further away from the main entrance, but his uneasiness refused to allow him to stay in his precarious hiding spot any longer.

Maybe that's the way to the dock.

Clenching his fists, he tiptoed to the doorway, keeping the pillar between himself and the lovers. He descended the stairs and walked down a hallway, sneaking past a closed door, when the chemical odor that had reeked the halls since he arrived hit him again and unmasked itself in his olfactory memory.

No. No, it can't be.

Compelled by disbelief, he returned to the doorway and peeked in. Although only the soft glow of monitor displays and strange machines lining the walls lit the room, he made out a large metal bench in the center, covered with some sort of distillation apparatus. Two empty metal-framed beds sat to the side. Tubes dangled above them, looped up to connect to the apparatus on the bench, and wound through scaffolding rigged across the ceiling. The tubes dropped down at the rear of the room and stretched into a shadowed corner.

It is. That's the same smell that came out of Jackson's skin.

Reflecting in the monitor light, blue liquid sparkled in glass vials stacked on the bench. Drawn in to confirm what his eyes could not believe, he moved to the bench and picked up a vial of Neura.

There's got to be three liters here. Or more.

As he twirled the vial in the luminescent light, an idea flashed in his mind.

Selling these to Finn to pay Dirk might be whole lot easier than trying to blackmail the old bastard.

On the bench, next to the apparatus, lay mechanical components and wires. Underneath them spread an open book, its pages showing anatomical sketches. Andre turned the book over and read the title: Robotics, The Future and You.

What the hell are they doing with Neura and this robotic shit?

Footfalls from the stairway resounded down the hall. Andre froze, unable to decide whether to run out the door and risk being seen, or hide in the lab. The footfalls neared and his indecision decided for him. He darted to the back, ducking under the tubes hanging down from the scaffolding, and crouched in the shadows. Two men walked past the doorway. Their voices echoed down the hall, and their footsteps fell away.

Standing to leave, he bumped his head on the low-hanging tubes, and a guttural moan emanated from the shadowed left corner. Frozen with terror and unable to look away, he squinted into the dark. Another moan. Emerging out of the invisibility of darkness, the left wall revealed itself to be, in fact, a large cage. Inside the cage, a shape of lumps and rounded angles dragged itself along the floor toward the bars. The tubes reaching into the cage quivered, as if attached to whatever was moving. Terrified, Andre wanted to run, but footfalls returned down the hall, forcing him to crouch back in to the dark corner.

Doesn't anybody fucking sleep around here?

Tan entered the room and tapped on a wall lamp. Dim light flooded the bench and ran right up to Andre's feet. The thing in the cage groaned again.

"Be quiet," Tan ordered, moving to the bench and tinkering with the apparatus.

Andre flattened himself against the wall, pulling into what was left of the shadows. He couldn't take his eyes off the thing crawling toward him, as it growled and edged into light. A bandaged arm fell through the bars, its clawed hand scratching at the floor. Every cell in Andre's body screamed at him to flee, but he refused to risk ruining his one chance of escape. He shrunk farther back into the corner and waited—and prayed— for Tan to leave. The prisoner moaned again.

"I said be quiet," Tan muttered.

Andre could just make out the caged man's battered and bloody face, and caught his breath. It was the man from his dorm.

What the hell are they doing to him?

In the edge of the low light, the gaunt face sunk into the shadows of its own concaving contours. Collared, the man was barely lucid. Wires protruded from a hole in the scaled flesh of his shoulder.

He's a borg?

A tube ran from the man's bandaged arm, up through the scaffolding, and draped down into a flask sitting on the bench.

They're drugging him. With Neura.

Growling again, the borg lashed out with a deadly swipe, his swollen face smashing in between the bars. Andre leaped up reactively and banged his head on the tubes, their movement rattling the apparatus on the bench. Tan spun around, a scalpel gripped in his hand and glinting in the light.

"Who's there?" he demanded, squinting, his voice quivering. "I can see you. Come out. Now."

Holding his hands up in a peaceful gesture, Andre stepped out of the shadow. "I … I'm sorry, I got lost," he stuttered, edging his way along the wall toward the doorway.

If I'm fast enough, I could probably out-think the implant and snap Tan's scrawny neck. But at the thought, the implant prickled against his spine. He knew he had to move fast.

"What are you doing out of your dorm?" Tan's voice shook as much as his hand holding the scalpel.

Andre was certain the little ferret would prefer not to have to use it. He decided to try a different tactic.

"It's okay, Tan, I just got lost. I don't care what you're doing down here. I don't like borgs, either." He kept talking as he backed along the wall.

"You shouldn't be in here. You should be back in the dorm."

Andre reached the doorway. "I know, I know, I just got lost. I'm going back now."

Tan lowered the knife and smiled. Andre thought he'd talked his way out the situation, but a heavy hand gripped his neck from behind and threw him to the floor.

He crashed down onto his wounded side, sharp pain shooting up his back. Rolling over, he faced Kade bearing down on him. Andre held up his hands in defense. "Kade, just wait—"

"I knew you weren't to be trusted." Kade bared his teeth in a hyena smile and lunged. Bending at the waist, he drove his boney shoulder into Andre as he staggered to his feet. The impact slammed Andre into the wall and knocked all wind out of him. Kade grabbed him by the throat and squeezed. "I don't know who you are, but I am not going to let you undo all our work."

Unable to speak, his windpipe crushing under the pressure, Andre flailed his legs and landed a hard kick into Kade's groin. Kade yelped like a puppy, fell against the bench, and collapsed into a ball. Glass flasks smashed into pieces on the floor, and the borg roared and rattled its cage.

"My equipment!" Tan screamed.

Kade rolled around as he huffed through the pain, clutching his groin, veins popping out of his forehead. Andre rubbed his own throat protectively as he gobbled in air and staggered away. Although immobilized, Kade lay in between him and the doorway. Instinctively, Andre jumped up, grabbed hold of the overhead scaffolding, and swung toward the door, right over Kade curled up on the floor. As he neared the doorway, he dropped to run out of the lab, but froze. Elron blocked the doorway, his muscular arms folded, his gold rings sparkling.

Enemy

Elron unfolded his arms and clapped slowly. "Bravo. Bravo, Brother. You're quite the acrobat. Impressive." Two young men stood on either side of him.

Andre recognized the one on his left as the man who burst into Elron's chamber earlier to report the bill being passed. He held a gun and pointed it at Andre.

Tan picked up pieces of the broken apparatus, whimpering and whining. Elron stepped forward into the lab, looking around at the mess on the floor, and waved at the room.

"I see you found our little project. Understandably, you're confused."

"I told you we couldn't trust him," Kade snapped from the floor.

"Dimitri." Elron gestured to Max's overweight companion to assist Kade. As Dimitri reached out to him, Kade shoved his hand away. Dimitri grabbed Kade by the other arm, hauled him up, and twisted his arm behind his back. Held in place, Kade growled. His eyes never left Andre as they flared, like those of a caged wild beast, measuring up all the ways he might try to escape just so he could rip out Andre's throat.

"What the hell are you hypocrites doing?" Andre demanded. "I thought you were *helping* people?"

"Oh, we help people," Elron explained. "That is our ultimate goal. But some ..." He glanced over to the cage where the borg's outstretched hand scratched at the floor. "Some, however, are beyond God's Grace. They're permanently infected. We can't help them, but they can help us. They are our gift from God, so that we may perfect our weapon of salvation."

"Don't tell him anymore!" Kade barked, spittle flying from his lips. Elron's contained demeanor cracked.

"Shut up, you fucking imbecile! If you hadn't left your post at the dorm to cavort the halls with your lover, we wouldn't be standing here now having this fucking conversation!"

Kade bit his lower lip and lowered his head in humiliation. But his passivity lasted only a moment. His eyes flicked up and held Elron with their gaze.

"I don't have to listen to this." He thrashed his arms free and Dimitri pushed him toward the door. Max trained the gun on him, but Elron waved his ringed hand.

"Let him go calm down somewhere else."

Kade flashed Elron a scowl. Edged with mad jealousy, his eyes betrayed the fear behind his anger. In that moment, Andre witnessed a connection between Kade and Elron, a favoritism Kade was used to, a benefit he feared he was losing. Kade disappeared out the door.

Elron took a deep breath and stroked his beard. With his composure fully regained, he turned back to Andre. "Upper Brulle is waging a war, Mr. Cross, against nature, against God. The migrants of Lower Brulle are the victims. Titan owns the Neura farm, controlling the wealthy citizens of Upper Brulle with its hedonistic drug. But Brulle is over populated, and Titan wants the city for trans-humanists only. So they facilitate the proliferation of zilla to degenerate the migrants into a sub-class, with the sole aim to wipe us out. And they're winning. The migrants feel wretched, that no one needs them, driving them to seek more relief in zilla, until it rots them from the inside out. Do you know the average age of a zilla addict, Mr. Cross? Between fourteen and twenty years old. Children. Titan are killing our children." Elron puffed his chest, pushed up his head, and paced across the room as if he were on stage.

"Neura, zilla, it makes no difference. As the Devil's merchant, Titan is the enemy. And I take enemies very seriously, Mr. Cross. Prayer is not enough. Peace does not come by intention alone. Peace will never be handed to us. As a progressive church, we don't just pray and preach. We attack." Elron raised a clenched fist, the sparkle on his rings reflecting in his eyes. "Peace must be *taken*."

Andre's heart raced. He was right about one thing; the Heart of Grace was a cult with military plans.

Elron picked up a vial of blue liquid from the bench and strolled toward the borg in the cage. "Tan has accumulated enough ingredients to develop a zilla to poison Titan's blood supply—both the borg's bio-blood, and Titan's enriched blood supplement that all its other citizens use. When the infected Neura enters their bodies, they will all feel the extreme effects of zilla. They will attack each other, and themselves." Elron looked down at the delirious borg. "We've been conducting tests on this one, using zilla we gathered from our clients when they first arrived. Tan has designed the most destructive mix. As you can see, it is very effective."

Andre couldn't believe what he was hearing. He suspected Elron's mind had been twisted by an extreme interpretation of his religion. But this? "You have Neura, and you've turned it into zilla? Into a bio-weapon?"

Elron walked back toward Andre, placing the vial back on the bench. "When the city sees what damage Titan's precious Neura can cause, Titan will be abandoned, discredited, and shut down. Upper Brulle will be in chaos. We will move up and offer our way as the only way forward, putting an end to all of Titan's interference with the human spirit. We will reclaim the city's true human spirit and reconnect it with God. And you, Andre, I think you can help us." Elron reached out and stroked Andre's muscled arm. "Don't you want revenge for what Titan has done to you—forcing you to rely on an implant, caging you in the crumbling Stems like a criminal in a shrinking prison?"

Andre lowered his eyes and glanced at the guard holding the gun. "Do I have a choice?"

Elron smiled. "Of course. We are all free in the eyes of God. If we forced you to join us against your will, we would be no better than Titan trying to force us out. No, you are free to make your own choice." Elron leaned forward, his skin pockmarked, like pumice stone, and his breath smelling of alcohol and smoke. "But surely you understand that this operation you have stumbled upon must remain secret until our plan has been enacted?"

Scenarios raced through Andre's mind. What would helping Elron commit him to? The longer he stayed with the church, the more at risk he was of them discovering he worked on the farms and sold zilla.

And Kade … Kade's determined to bring me undone.

Trying to think, his mind drew blank. He had run out of options. He'd fucked up his chance to escape.

"Why?" he asked, stalling while he worked out what to do. "Why are you asking me to help?"

Elron looked Andre up and down. "We can use your skills, Mr. Cross. You're strong. More importantly, you might find that the community work I offer proves to hasten your rehabilitation process. Committing your involvement would prove to me your awareness of the zilla problem. It would prove to me your commitment to fighting it, not just for yourself, but for the community. It will help convince me you are in the right mind and not prone to doing anything to jeopardize Brulle's, or your own, rehabilitation. Consider it a chance to prove to me I can trust you."

*—No, Boss, it's because he needs you.—*The return of the Captain's voice startled Andre.—*They can't do whatever it is they're planning to do without Aoto, and they can't wait six weeks for her arm to get better. They need you. You just got handed an ace, I'd say. One last chance to not fuck it up.*

Thankful for the Captain's rational thought providing some sense of direction, Andre let his survival instincts take over. He feigned a sigh and dropped his head.

"You're right, Your Grace. Zilla has ruined my life. I do, I do want to stop using it." He lifted his eyes. "I'm scared, alright? That's why I ran."

Elron stepped behind Andre and stroked the back of his neck. "No need to be scared, Brother. You are in good hands now. I believe in you. You must believe in me. And I promise you this. Once you have helped us bring down Titan, you will have redeemed yourself in the eyes of God. Then I will have Tan remove your implant, and you, too, shall be free."

The back of Andre's neck twitched. *Take my implant out?*

—Just play the game, Boss.—

But I don't know what I'm agreeing to.

—You don't need to know all the details right now. You just got to go with it and be ready to do what I say, when I say it.—

Andre nodded. "When do we start?"

Elron gave his neck one last squeeze before letting him go and stepping back. "Due to the bill being passed, we need to act fast. With your help, we can leave in the morning. Kade will lead. You will do anything, and everything, he says. Now, get some sleep. Tomorrow, Brulle's rehabilitation—and your own—begins."

"But what do I have to do?"

Elron waved his ringed hand in the air. "We'll discuss the details tomorrow. For now, it is late. We rise at dawn for prayer. We pray for our health and for the downfall of all who barter in the evil of zilla."

Hiding his unease, Andre nodded again, and Elron motioned to Dimitri to take him out of the lab.

"Oh, Mr. Cross," called Elron, his velvet voice laced with peril. "Make sure you tie the laces on those boots of yours. I don't want you tripping up tomorrow and disappointing me."

Heat rose in Andre's cheeks. He followed Dimitri out of the lab, back up to his dorm, and Dimitri shut the door.

Laying on his bunk, he stared through the tall windows out to the city's kaleidoscope of light.

What have I gotten myself into? I can't let them take my implant out. Can I?

—Put your business hat on, Boss. Bide your time. Do the Job, and do it well. When you've got the Keeper's trust, he'll relax his hold on you. And when he does, you take that Neura stash from the lab, and you run. I guarantee Finn will buy it. Getting high is all he cares about. And I guarantee Dirk will take the money and get you on that ship. Money is all HE cares about. That is the Plan. Things might look crazy right now, but you just gotta keep your head down and step on one stone at a time. As remote it may seem, that is your only way forward.—

At the same time as he listened to the Captain's advice, Andre explored Elron's offer to remove his implant. He rarely allowed himself to indulge his buried loathing for the device, but the threads of Elron's arguments dangled in front of him—threads he absentmindedly wove into a legitimate argument.

Maybe Elron's right about Titan's technology. Maybe I'm addicted to my implant. Instead of reducing my temper, maybe it's doing the opposite, rewarding me with meds every time I imagine doing something violent. Maybe I'm the implant's Best and Only.

He flipped the sides of his predicament over in his mind, like a monkey flicking a light switch off and on. He couldn't deny that if Elron found out about his connection with the farm, he would be thrown over the walkways. Or worse. Elron didn't care about Andre's murderous past. He blamed that, and everything else he feared, on his disgust at humans merging with technology. To Elron, that's what it all came down to— keeping technology as a subordinate, like migrants in the Stems.

—The implant is not your enemy, Boss. The memories are. These people are.—

But Andre hadn't heard a peep from his violent urges, or from Jeremy, since waking up in the church. As much as Elron invaded his comfort zone, a small part of him leaned toward the Keeper's brotherly solace. What did he have to escape to, anyway? Was it really any better than what he was trying to escape from? Elron said he believed in Andre, that he would help him.

In the light of his musing, his chances of getting back into the farm and being smuggled to Anchora seemed slimmer than Aoto's broken arm. Maybe this was a real chance to be a Good Citizen. And didn't he deserve that? Didn't he? Hadn't he had enough bad luck?

—You make your own luck, Boss. You make your choices. Don't lose your grip here. You're squashed between a rock and a hard place, and they're both closing in. But you've got to get out of here. I guarantee if you don't, you'll be getting intimate with more than just your biggest fan, Elron. I'm talking about Kade. He's got your number and he's counting it every minute.—

Kade was the splinter; Andre couldn't forget that. As much as Elron seemed to be partial to Andre's presence, Kade possessed a hatred for Andre that Jeremy would have been proud of.

Why? Why do I attract this?

—You got bit, that's why. You got bit by something when you were young. Same thing that bit your brother and your daddy. It put something in you, Boss. It attracts like for like. And you gotta know, there isn't a cure. The implant is all you got. You let them take that out, you may as well pull the pin out of a grenade and pop it in your mouth. But you got an ace up your sleeve, now. You got the Keeper of the church liking you. You got his protection. And he needs you for something. You know their whole deal, so you are in. And you know what else you got? You got a whole stash of Neura just waiting for the right time for you to collect it. You still got a chance to get out of Brulle, Boss. You can still be a Good Citizen.—

Andre rolled onto his side, the bed squeaking, as if the joinery crushed the imaginary mice. He buried his face into the pillow, banishing the light from his vision. As the monkey in his mind continued to flip the light switch off and on, he plummeted face-first into a deep, deep sleep.

Nightmare: Part 1

His feet plodded through thick mulch, the soaked, rancid ground squelching and sucking at his ankles. Although his feet moved in a forward stepping motion, his body slid sideways, dragged by some unseen force toward a dark forest of gigantic shadows.

"Can you help me?" asked a synthesized voice from somewhere in the dark.

The air thickened, solidified, and closed in. His pulse thumped like drums in is ears. His heart banged on the inside of his chest with the desperation of a kidnapped victim waking in a boot. As the curtains of mulch pressed in on him, he thrashed, but the mulch hardened into wood.

Doctor Steele's familiar face appeared and he held up a needle. His mouth moved, but the Captain's voice came out.

"You got this, Boss."

He was no longer upright, but lying flat on his back, scratching feverishly at the wooden panel above. Exquisite terror gripped him as he realized he had been buried alive. Hyperventilating, his vision blurred.

"... help me?" came the voice again, muffled.

The thumping pulse in his head threatened to pound him into madness, when something rough and scaled slithered next to him. He didn't want to turn, but he couldn't help following the dream's script. When he looked over, it was not the dark thing he saw, however, but two olive eyes floating in a red strip.

"Releeeeeeasssse meeee ..."

Prayer

A bell ripped Andre from the nightmare. He shot up in his bunk, gasping, and his body soaked with sweat. Kade's voice startled him to his core.

"Bad dream?"

Emerging out of the foggy remnants of the nightmare, Andre was so fundamentally shocked upon seeing Kade's face he almost pissed the bed. He swallowed, his throat dry as a bird's nest. Kade held a pile of folded clothes, like a big brother come to get him up for school.

"Yeah, a nightmare," Andre admitted, wiping sweat from his face. "But better than waking up to you." Pretending the nightmare wasn't as terrifying as it had been helped him quell the residual fear. "What the hell is that noise, anyway?"

Kade threw the clothes at him. "It's the prayer bell. We gather in the prayer hall in ten minutes."

Andre rubbed the sleep from his eyes, then opened them again to see Kade already leaving the dorm. His dream-riddled sleep left him more tired than when he had laid down, and his vape cravings had returned.

Maybe I shoulda took that damn Dream Catcher thing from Bao.

He swung his legs over the bunk and winced at the painful ache in his side. Lifting the bandage, he peered under and grimaced at what he saw. Green puss wept from angry red edges, the wound looking worse. *No thanks to Kade digging his fingers into it.* He initiated his breathing exercises, snuffing any thoughts of what he wanted to do to Kade before they bloomed into sharp roses of anger.

Unfolding the clothes—jeans, a t-shirt, and a jacket—he dressed and headed down the corridor. Young men and women, their faces tired and unenthusiastic, filed out of the other dorms. Scabs and sores covered the arms of some while others looked less damaged. They shuffled along in short, sharp steps, wide eyed and fidgeting.

It's like walking amongst the dead.

Entering a large, sparse hall, the followers knelt before a giant, down-lit cross hanging on the rear wall. Andre took a spot near the edge of the group, and a hand patted him on the back. He looked up to see Elron passing him to stand under the cross at the front of the hall.

Andre noted half of the group stared blankly forward, as if their brains were back on their pillows. They scratched their arms and faces and looked at anything but Elron or the cross. But a few straightened to attention, a fever in their eyes.

"Good morning, Brothers and Sisters," Elron greeted, spreading his arms. "Let us show our gratitude for another blessed day. Please, now, join me for a short prayer, for the lost and the weak." He bowed his head, clasped his hands, and cleared his throat. "Enter the homes, Lord, of those suffering from sickness and addiction. Heal them. Enter the homes, Lord, of those suffering in this world of depression, and suppression, and give them strength. Amen."

"Amen," the gathering echoed in unison, raising their heads.

Elron clutched the cross around his neck and paced the room, his voice booming through the hall.

"This morning, I would like to speak with you about that which controls us. I want to talk with you about the nature of addiction. We are all addicts in some way. Drugs, anger, the flesh. It doesn't matter the substance. When addiction bites you, it consumes you, hijacks your mind and takes over your actions. There is nothing new about this evil. This reptilian presence has tried to destroy humanity ever since God placed temptation with us in his Garden. It is the Devil, and the Devil has its seed in all of us, tempting us, testing us. Zilla is the latest incarnation of the Devil's temptation, weakening humanity to make it easier to seduce them."

Elron looked down, stroked his beard, then lifted his head back up.

"But you are not weak, Brothers and Sisters. For you have found solace in the Heart of Grace. You have found an ally in the Heart of Grace. Your demon has found its end, here, in the Heart of Grace. And let me tell you something else, my family. You have found *strength* in the Heart of Grace. And with that strength, you can take back the lives that have been taken from you. You can be something *extraordinary*. Do you believe in your own 'extraordinary,' Brothers and Sisters?"

Elron's words sailed up next to Andre and threw over a rope over to his lonely, desperately-lost boat.

I do.

"We start our lives crawling around on our bellies, like lizards scavenging off the forest floor, completely unaware of our power. As life digs into its wicked bag of lessons and throws its challenges at us, it forces us to defend ourselves, to dig deep into our own bag of tricks and pull out resources we never knew we had."

Oh, I know all about tricks. Tricks on tricks.

"After many losses, we earn a few wins. With the taste of our nascent power, we think the entire would is ours, and nothing can stop us. Infected with the hunger of over-confidence and greed, we harden our shells and defend with scorpion aggression any who come near us, or our possessions. Inevitably, chasing an insatiable goal, we overstep our mark, bite off more than we can chew, and stumble into a confrontation we cannot win. We're beaten, pulverized by the consequences of our greed. The true depth of our own perversion is revealed to us by the intensity of that defeat."

Jeremy's face flashed in Andre's mind.

But I had to. I had to kill him.

"Only then, if that doesn't kill us, do we have a chance to become something extraordinary. But there is still one more lesson. We must accept the evil we have seen in ourselves. We must see it and own it and carry it until we die." Elron's words led Andre along as easily as Jeremy had led him to the ravine. "Weighed down by this knowledge, we must find a way to rise again. Then—and only then—do we become the eagle, to soar above our weaknesses and become the extraordinary creature we are all destined to be."

Lifted to a teetering height by Elron's sermon, Andre slipped and cringed at the mention of the eagle. The bone-crunching sound of the bird slamming into his apartment window echoed in his mind.

Some damn omen.

Elron paused and resumed his place under the cross.

"You may feel as low as the lizard now, my family. You may carry the burden of the scorpion's regrets. But here, in the Heart of Grace, you will find your strength, you will beat your addiction, and you will soar. Grace be with you."

"Grace be with you," mumbled the followers in messy unison.

Elron bowed and threw Andre a smile before he left the hall. Andre's eyes followed him, the initial sense of safety he felt with Elron re-awoken by the insightful sermon. The followers remained on their knees for a silent moment longer before standing and bowing to the cross.

The savory smell of cooked eggs wafted in from a door on the left and made Andre's stomach growl. The followers moved into the adjacent room. Starving, he followed, when a something tapped him on the shoulder. He turned to face the heavy-set, young man who had subdued Kade in the lab. *Dimitri*. Sweat beaded across his brow and wet-patches bloomed from the armpits of his tight, grey shirt.

"The Keeper wishes dialogue with you."

Andre sniffed at the delicious breakfast smell pulling him toward the mess hall. Reluctantly, he followed Dimitri to Elron's chamber.

Guess it's time to find out what the hell I signed up for.

Plan

Inside the chamber, tinted window-walls blocked out the early morning. A quivering hologram of the city floated above the table's dark, reflective surface. Elron stepped into its blue light, the cross around his necklace winking as he moved.

"Brothers, please take a seat." He gestured to a bench against the wall where Max sat next to Kade. Aoto stood behind them, staring intently at the hologram. Max nodded indifferently to Andre as he sat down, but Kade glared at his arrival with disgust.

"You're all aware of the mission," Elron continued, "and why we need to bring it forward. I'll go over it in detail now for clarity." He put his hands into the hologram and made a pulling-out motion, causing the city image to zoom in to a large building in Mid Brulle. Andre recognized the Neura farm.

"From the intel gathered by Aoto and Kade, we know that every Wednesday Neura is delivered, by cargo shuttle, from the farm in Mid Brulle to Titan in Upper Brulle."

Elron tapped into a panel on the table, and a smaller hologram shimmered out of the dust in the air to form a large Titan shuttle. "This shuttle is our Trojan horse. When traveling along hover corridors, cargo shuttles use a three-sixty-degree proximity laser system, enclosing the entire vehicle in a secure bubble. The shield alerts the driving system, and the driver, to any vehicle or object getting too close. We will use a detour to re-route the Titan shuttle to a street-level inspection point, where the security system will be deactivated. There, we can access the shuttle from its roof."

Apprehension, laced with a rising excitement, crept over Andre.

Elron made another pulling-out gesture. The hologram zoomed in to a turn-off, where simulated hover traffic merged down into a tower-level street.

"Max and Dimitri will set up the detour corridor to intercept the shuttle here, at Point A, where the hover traffic merges with the street traffic. Max will direct the driver to pull into the underpass route here, at Point B, where Kade will keep the driver distracted with the vehicle inspection. At this time, the shuttle's power will be off, allowing us entry via the roof's access panels. Once inside, we will infect the Neura vats with Tan's zilla."

Elron paused and stepped toward the group, hands cradled in front of him.

"Now, as you know, Aoto, our most nimble member, who has been training for this exercise, has been injured."

Andre glanced at Aoto, and noticed a shame behind the fierceness in her eyes. He had taken away from her the honor of scaling the underside of the bridge and delivering the zilla.

"As you also know," Elron continued, "this injury was caused, by accident, by our newest guest, Mr. Cross, during his … deliverance to us. As God's plan would have it, Mr. Cross is himself a strong and experienced lift-mechanic, with exceptional strength and agility. Some of us have witnessed this first hand."

Max and Dimitri laughed. Kade did not react; staring wide eyed at Elron, his mouth open in disbelief at what he was hearing.

"Mr. Cross has offered his services to repay his debt to our Church. He will take Aoto's place today."

"What?" Kade and Andre exclaimed at the same time, their voices echoing together throughout the chamber.

"I didn't agree to that!" Andre argued.

"No way in hell," Kade yelled, jumping to his feet. "This is Aoto's mission!"

Elron bounced his hands, palms down, in placation. "I understand your doubts, both of you. Kade, you know we cannot delay the mission. The Council has awarded development approval to Mid Brulle. We all know what that means. We could lose our window of attack in a matter of days. Migrants will be pushed down into the Stems, effectively dissolving our operations here. We will lose access to the hover traffic. We must move now, with what we have."

Kade looked at the oversized Dimitri, dismissing him, then pointed to Max. "Max can do the climb."

"Max is the only one with a valid council ID. No one else can use it. We need Max to detour the shuttle."

"What about the residents Aoto is training?" Kade turned to Aoto, but she shook her head to let him know the residents were far from ready. He glared at Andre. "He's an Implant. Implants are serious offenders. We can't trust him."

Elron licked his lips and held up his hands. "We have all made mistakes, Kade. We all deserve a second chance, like the one I gave you when you arrived, remember? Forgiveness is key. That is what has given you the strength you have today, has it not?"

Kade scowled and dropped back to his seat on the bench. "This is a bad idea."

The same jealousy Andre witnessed in Kade's eyes the previous day laced the young man's words. Kade had a fear on him like a sickness.

"I am not breaking into a Titan shuttle," Andre interjected. But Elron ignored him.

"I see you are losing faith, Kade. Doubt will only deteriorate our chances. You must strike it from your heart. I need you to assemble yourself within. I need you, Kade."

Kade raised his head and faced Elron, frustration and adoration conflicting in his eyes. Elron stepped forward and knelt to his level, cupping the young man's face in his hands.

"We all need you. Every migrant in Lower Brulle needs you. This is the turning point. This is where we turn the Devil in on itself, and clear the way for God's chosen to ascend. This is what you have been sent for." Elron gripped Kade's biceps. "This is your test, to rise above these petty emotions and show God what you are really made of."

Elron released his hold on Kade, stood, and turned his back. As Elron returned to the hologram, he threw his last words over his shoulder like he was tossing out the garbage.

"Or you may as well walk out right now and go back to your hovel in the Docks, where I found you." Shame flooded Kade's face, but Elron was not done. "Only this time, you can overdose yourself properly, because if that is your choice, then you have no purpose left, and you are only part of the problem."

Silence fell over the chamber. The hologram sparked at its edges, as if sizzled by the tension. Kade sat upright and drew in a deep breath.

"I am assembled, Your Grace. I am assembled and present. I am devoted to the mission. Forgive me."

Elron smiled, his pocked face bathed in the cold, blue glow of the hologram. "You are forgiven, Brother Kade. And you are commended for your strength and bravery. The Devil continues to test you, yet you constantly rise above. I am thankful to have you with me. We are all thankful. Now, let us move on."

The Keeper pinched the hologram, zooming in on the underpass at the base of Mid Brulle.

"Mr. Cross, you will be positioned here, in the beams. You will scale down to the shuttle's roof by auto-rope. Using a de-locker device, you will access the shuttle's cargo hold—"

"Wait a minute! I'm not—"

"Mr. Cross. Do you want your implant out, or not?"

The question paralyzed Andre, giving voice to his deep-seated dislike for the implant. His uncertainty exposed, it split him in half like a glacier cleaving itself.

Do I?

Unable to speak, he lost the moment to argue. The two sides of him drifted apart. The last thing he needed was to get involved in another crime. But the unexpected opportunity to get on the next shuttle to Anchora, by doing just one job, proved too tempting to ignore.

—Stick to the Plan, Boss. It'll just be like dropping into a lift's motor cage and fixing the alignment mechanism. You got this.—

Elron nodded, accepting Andre's silence as acceptance. He reached into his robe to withdraw a large, glass vial. As he held it up into the light, by one of its silver-capped ends, crystals sparkled and twirled in dark blue fluid.

"Once inside, Mr. Cross, you will pierce the vat's seal with this injector and infect the Neura with zilla. Empty the vial, then exit the shuttle. Re-lock the access panel and retreat into the beams." Elron spoke as if the mission was nothing more dangerous than changing a rotator rod in a hover engine. He closed his hand around the vial and stepped toward the group. "Now, remember, shuttle drivers expect random vehicle checks, so this works to our favor. But, this also means they know how long an inspection should take. They are very particular about this. We have no more than thirteen minutes to get into the shuttle, infect the Neura vats, and get out—undetected."

Andre kneaded his palms and fingers, contemplating the task ahead. The thick calluses that had formed from years of lift work would give him the pain resistance to do the climb.

How hard could it be?

As crazy as the situation seemed, his desperation to get out of Brulle, and his unresolved resentment toward Titan, allowed his mind to get on board.

Thirteen minutes. That's easier than fixing a lift.

Standing before Andre, Elron held the vial teasingly in front of him. It was as big as the vials in Grekov's sorting facility. "I repeat, Kade will be able to distract the driver for thirteen minutes only. It is imperative the driver has no suspicion of the Neura being tampered with."

As Andre reached out for the vial, Elron moved it from his reach and handed it to Kade. As his hand wrapped around it, Kade smirked victoriously.

Returning to the table, Elron lifted his head, proud and determined, the hologram's blue light outlining him in a chilling glow. "You've seen what Tan's zilla did to the borg. It will enact the same effect on countless other borgs and Upper Brulleans. The infected sinners will be driven mad, becoming monsters, clawing at their own skin, attacking anyone and anything in their violent frenzy. They will literally tear each other apart." He glanced up at the summit of the holographic Brulle, his voice lowering to a reverent whisper. "Their deaths will be their wake-up moment, and our salvation. It will be quite beautiful to watch."

The savage plan thrilled and excited him. A holographic memory of the thrill of killing flickered through Andre's marrow. His implant tingled. He was sure he could do the job. He *wanted* to do it. Elron's brutish confidence and fanatical determination swept him along and out of the last of his uncertainty.

"Now," Elron said, clapping his hands. "The Titan van will pass through the rendezvous point in thirty-five minutes." He tapped off the hologram and deactivated the window tint. Morning light suffused through the room. He lowered his head, closed his eyes, and the team did the same.

"Grace be with us today. Give us the strength, oh Lord, to enforce your divine connection, so that your chosen may be healed, and your enemies destroyed. Guide us today, Lord, and lead us to victory. Amen."

The men echoed Elron's word with gusto, transforming the holy moment into a pre-war cheer.

"Wait," Andre interrupted. "Don't we do a run-through or something? What happens if I'm detected? What happens if they see me? What's Plan B?"

Elron returned to the obsidian table and tapped into a panel without looking up. "I've explained this, Mr. Cross. There is no Plan B. Were you not listening? Time is of the essence. There can be no failure. Suffice to say, your own successful rehabilitation depends on you remaining undetected. You have thirty-four minutes."

Andre didn't like the sound of that, not at all. He looked around to Max and Dimitri for support, but they were already leaving the chamber. Only Aoto remained, standing at the window, her head down, bitter disappointment visible in her drooping shoulders. He had not only robbed her of her chance to be hero, he realized, but to also be a martyr.

So they don't just need me to climb. They need a fall guy if something goes wrong.

—Nothing's going to go wrong, Boss, if you stay focused. You can do this. You need to do this. Remember the Plan.—

He took a deep breath and left the room to catch up with Max and Dimitri. Heading down the stairs and along another corridor, he followed them out into a docking bay. A black hover van—the same one that Aoto nearly ran him down with outside the farm—sat in the middle of the bay. Max and Dimitri loaded tripod-shaped devices into the rear. Kade walked over to the wall and tapped on a control pad, opening the two large bay doors, flooding the space with morning light. He walked back over to Max and Dimitri and handed them both something small. They each put the object into their ear and climbed into the back of the van. As Andre approached, he could see patched-up bullet holes in the van's side.

Kade turned to him and held up a small transparent sphere. "Put this in your ear. This is how we'll communicate. When you want to speak to the team, press your finger against it. The boys will give you the rest of your equipment."

As Andre took the device, Kade grabbed his arm, and his nasty smirk contorted his handsome face. "Don't fuck this up today, Liar Man. I only need one excuse to take you out of the team."

Kade released his grip and pushed past, leaving Andre rubbing his wrist.

—Don't let him knock you off balance, Boss. That's what he's trying to do. Stay focused. Finish the Job.—

Oh, I'm gonna finish it, alright. He gritted his teeth, pushed the communication device into his ear, and climbed into the van, shutting the door behind him.

Inside, Max and Dimitri had strapped the tripod devices next to tools on the left side. A cumbersome, archaic surveillance panel took up the rest of the wall. Max sat by the machine on one end of a bench running along the right side. With Dimitri's bulk leaving Andre little room in the middle, he squeezed in and sat shoulder-to-shoulder. Dimitri looked him up and down.

"You should feel honored to be part of this today. Not everyone gets a chance to do something extraordinary like this."

Inspired by Dimitri's enthusiasm, an undeniable exhilaration fluttered in Andre's stomach. He never thought he would be using his monkey skills for anything as exciting as taking down Titan. The word 'destiny' flitted through his mind. He chuckled inwardly at himself. Maybe he was *destined* to be more than just another Good Citizen.

Maybe I'm meant to be extraordinary.

Voices crackled out of speakers on the surveillance panel. As Max tweaked the controls, a woman's voice came through, chopped up by static.

"Titan Control … is Transport Four-Nine, departing farm … aboard. ETA, thirty-seven minutes."

Max checked the time on the panel and called to Kade climbing into the front of the van. "Target's arrival time at Point A in twenty-three minutes."

A sonic whoosh shot through the bottom of the van, as the engines lifted it off the floor and floated it out between the bay doors. The sides vibrated and the tools rattled in their racks. Andre gripped the seat, remembering how much he hated hover travel.

As the van rose up into a traffic corridor between the towers, Max and Dimitri lowered their heads and closed their eyes. Their hands formed a lotus pose, index finger to thumb. Impressed by their calm, determined focus, Andre wondered if perhaps Anchora was not his only option.

Detour

Peeking through the rear window, he noted the church's location before it disappeared from view. Just as he'd thought; the church sat near the top of the North Stem.

Kade swerved sharply, merging the van with the traffic moving up toward the base of Mid Brulle. Andre's stomach heaved, and sweat beaded across his top lip. As far as he was concerned, flying was for birds. People had hands for climbing, not wings for flying. He gripped the edge of the seat until his fingers glowed white.

The loud rumble of the engine and his rolling nausea reminded him of the last time he had been in a hover van—when he was taken from his home for murdering his brother. Even then, in his numb state, he vomited from the unsettling, gravity-defying sensation. In that moment he had sworn that he would happily go anywhere the authorities put him, as long as he didn't have to ever step inside another suicidal flying machine again.

Kade cursed at a driver for overtaking him, his bark snapping Andre back to the present.

Sweat trickling down his back, Andre told himself not to look out the window again, but he couldn't control himself. Below, walkways zigzagged between towers in a multi-layered, three dimensional web. Conveyors slid back and forth along taut cables in their endless puzzle. Above them, the underside of Mid Brulle stretched across the Stems in a rib cage of concrete and steel. From within the streaming lights of the moving traffic, the space between Lower and Mid Brulle took on the enchanting confusion of an old snow dome turned upside down.

This isn't so bad after all.

Next to him, Dimitri opened his eyes and exhaled. Sweating profusely and beginning to stink, he reached under his seat, pulled out a silver device shaped like a fist-sized suction cup, and handed it to Andre

"This is a universal de-locker," he shouted over the roar of the engine vibrating below their feet. "The shuttle's access hatch on the roof will be locked. Push this onto the opening mechanism and press the center button. Wait 'till the light goes green, then you're in. Remember to re-lock the hatch and take the de-locker with you when you're done."

Andre took the device, weighed it in his hand, and stuffed it inside his jacket. Excitement fluttered in his stomach. He was really doing this.

Dimitri then slid a coiled rope from under the seat and flipped it into Andre's lap. "And this—"

"An auto-rope," Andre finished, shouting back. "I've used one before, down on the Dock lifts."

Dimitri's eyes widened with admiration. "You worked on the Dock lifts? I heard they're massive. Dangerous. People die working on them.

Was that when…"

Andre nodded, enjoying the recognition. Being respected was new delight to him. "I climbed them for six years, since I was twelve."

Dimitri gave him a shy smile, looking over Andre's muscular arms as if they'd suddenly enlarged. Unfamiliar confidence and self-importance sprang up inside Andre, exhilarating him. The van bounced, throwing his stomach up into his throat and shattering his brief moment of glory. Not wanting to lose Dimitri's admiration, he sat back to hide his weakness and willed the giddy ride to be over.

Finally, through the front window, an overpass loomed ahead—one of the four monstrous arches connecting the Stems to Mid Brulle's base. The dark span stretched out and up, like a giant bat wing, absorbing light with its lifeless, matte polymer skin. Remembering a scene from an old B-grade Japanese movie, Andre imagined a rubber Godzilla-like doll poking up between the towers, dipping back and forth. He chuckled at the ridiculous image, momentarily forgetting his nausea. But Kade swooped, knocking the image out of Andre's mind, and steered the van down to merge with the tower traffic.

Veering into a turn-off, the van split from the main flow and drove under a pedestrian bridge. With a jolt, the van stopped and lowered to the ground. Andre released his grip on the seat and thanked Godzilla that he hadn't passed out in front of Dimitri.

"Let's do this," Kade called from the front.

Max and Dimitri jumped out of their seats and donned bright orange council vests. Taking several of the tripod devices, they exited the rear and headed up the street to set up the detour.

Andre climbed out and, for a brief moment, thought about running.

But immediately following that thought, he stopped and wondered where he would run to. He had to escape Brulle. He needed to get on Dirk's ship. He needed the church's Neura. He threw the auto-rope over his shoulder and looked up to assess the underpass beams.

—Just stick to the Plan, Boss. Stay focused.—

A hand slapped on his shoulder. Kade stepped in front of him and withdrew the zilla vial from a pocket on the arm of his jacket. "This is the zilla injector. Twist the bottom here. A syringe will extend from the top. Jab it into the seal of the Neura vat, and you're done. Don't leave anything behind."

Andre took the vial and twisted the bottom to test it was functioning. A needle popped out, just as Kade had explained. It was just a bigger version of a Neura vial. He twisted the bottom back into place and slid the vial into his jacket.

"Once I have the driver distracted," Kade continued, "and they shut off the engine, you'll be able to get inside. Remember, thirteen minutes. You'll hear a countdown from one minute in your earpiece. If we fail today, and Titan discovers our intentions, they'll come at us with everything they have. We won't get time for a second chance. Is that clear?"

Andre clenched his fist and dug his nails into his palm. "Crystal."

"Good." Kade turned back and pointed to the end of the road where Max and Dimitri set up their tripods. "The hover van will come down the same way we did, and stop here." Kade checked his watch. "We have ten minutes." He clasped his hands and offered Andre a lift up to the beams.

Andre hesitated, seeds of doubt attempting to sprout.

"We have ten minutes," Kade repeated.

Taking in a deep breath, Andre stepped into Kade's hands and jumped up with the momentum of the lift. Just as he thought he would fall back, Kade pushed him up higher, and he latched onto the beam. He hauled himself up, his wound smarting, and crawled along the top of the beam to the middle. He flicked on the auto-rope and watched it coil itself around the beam like a snake on speed. Pulling it tight to be sure it was secure, he attached the other end to his jeans.

This'll be just like lowering down from a maintenance branch.

Below, Kade took three tripod-like contraptions out of the van and set them up around the underpass. He flicked a switch on the first tripod, and a laser beam shot out, connecting the heads of all three to form a laser blockade in the road.

"Two minutes," Kade announced through Andre's ear piece.

He peered out from his hiding spot, reminded of hiding on the beam in the farm's distribution chamber, as the back of the Anchora ship faded into the distance.

I got this. In and out.

"Shuttle's arriving." Max's voice drew Andre's attention to the detour. Dimitri waved a white shuttle to the side of the travel corridor and Max approached it. The driver waved an arm out of the window in irritation. Max shook his head, pointing, urging the driver down under the bridge.

"What's the hold up, Max?" came Kade's impatient voice through Andre's earpiece. "Get them down here."

Andre licked his lips and gripped the auto-rope. Any second the shuttle would turn and drive toward him, and it would all be up to him. His anxiety hitched a ride on his rising excitement. His heart pounded, like the ominous beat of an old Hollywood action movie, and his mind took a crazy tangent.

Maybe I'm in one. Maybe I'm inside one of those old shiny DVD's, trapped like General Zod in the Phantom Zone, and the only way I'm getting out is by scaling down to the Titan shuttle, sneaking inside and poisoning the Neura vat. Just like a goddamn hero.

Adrenaline pumped through his body and his pulse throbbed in his ears. He no longer felt the pain in his side. The oppressive, impending doom that had been pushing in on his life for the last year vanished. He felt alive. More alive than he had ever felt.

The Titan shuttle hovered forward and veered down into the underpass, a string of red lights dotting its roof.

"We're on." Kade's voice crackled in his ear. "Don't fuck it up, Cross."

Kade stepped away from the laser blockade and approached the shuttle, guiding it to park under the beams, until it stopped with its access hatch directly below Andre's hiding spot. Andre tugged at the auto-rope one last time. As Kade reached the driver's window and leaned in, the engine cut out and the van lowered to the ground in a billowing cloud of steam. The red lights along the roof flashed twice and stayed off.

This is it.

He swung over the beam's edge, and the auto-rope silently extended itself and lowered him down.

I'm really doing this, he repeated to himself, breathing short, shallow breaths. *I'm really doing this.*

He slowed his descent as he neared the shuttle, subduing the swing in the rope, and eased himself to a soft stance on the roof. Detaching himself, he slipped the de-locker from his jacket, pushed it onto the access hatch and pressed the button. The de-locker flashed red, changed to a static green, and a click sounded from inside the cargo area. He pulled the hatch open quietly and swung down inside.

As his eyes adjusted to the low light, his stomach sank. The inside appeared to be empty. Squinting, he willed the outline of Neura vats to appear, when something moved in the shadows. He froze, recognizing a human form. He hastily retreated and squatted to jump up to the hatch. The person took a step closer, and light streaming through the hatch fell on a pair of olive green eyes embedded in a perfect strip of red. Andre's heart tripped on its own beat and fell down the stairs of his resolve. Mo Da tilted her head, her eyes twinkling like twin falling stars.

"I remember you."

PART FIVE

THE GLITCH

Ticket

Lush, exotic apprehension filled the air and rippled shivers through his skin. He remembered her name, but he had forgotten how flawlessly beautiful she was. Her translucent artificial skin, her glistening olive eyes floating in the bright red slash. He held up his hands defensively and glanced around.

"Don't move!" he blurted out in a whisper, wary that any loud noise might alert the driver. Mo Da took another step forward.

"Operator 77. What are you doing here? Are we back at the farm?" She cocked her head toward the hatch.

With his vision fully adjusted to the low light, he could see that, aside from Mo Da, the shuttle was indeed empty.

Oh, shit.

"Cross?" Max's voice echoed through Andre's earpiece. "ETA?"

He put a finger to his ear but hesitated. If he reported there was no Neura, Kade would leave him behind. Or worse. His hero fantasy evaporated and panic set in.

"Where's the Neura?" he demanded in another whisper. Mo Da stared back at him, her eyes glistening as if they were real. "This is not a Neura shuttle." She paused, lowering her head. "I am being returned to Titan for reprogramming."

Andre fumed. Kade and Aoto's useless intel was about to get him killed. He needed something, anything, to keep him useful to the church. Mo Da lifted her head again and held him with her gaze.

"Why are you here?"

He opened his mouth to reply, but stopped.

Just get the hell out of here.

He plucked himself out of his hesitation and crouched to jump up to the hatch. Mo Da's cold hand gripped his forearm.

"Please," she begged, her plea awkward in her polite tone. "Don't leave me here."

Andre yanked his arm away, but her grip would not release. A stupid thought popped into his mind—*I could use those arms on my harness*. Her grip tightened, snapping him back to attention.

"Please. Take me with you. Will you help me?"

Rearing up from the depths of his subconscious, the child-bot's face overlaid Mo Da's, the memory flooding him with guilt.

Will you help me?

"Get the hell off me!" He yelled as he kicked at her, but she deflected his leg with one hand. For some reason, even though he knew androids could not attack, he anticipated an offensive from her. But she released her hold on his forearm, dropped to her knee.

"Please. Forgive my interaction. I do not want to die. Will you help me?"

Will you help me?

Her human plea for her own survival transfixed him. His chest heaved with the pumping of his heart. His pulse throbbed in his ears, and his thoughts ricocheted like pinballs inside his skull.

—Androids don't die, Boss. They're not alive.—

"What the hell are you talking about?" he demanded. "What do you mean 'die?'"

"I am being returned to Titan for reprogramming. I … think too much. Does that not mean I am alive?"

Static from the implant scratched down the back of his spine. He felt the familiar tingle activating as Jeremy's voice slid along its belly out of banishment and into his prefrontal cortex.

{take her}

The air inside the van seemed to frost. Another ripple of shivers ran through his skin and vibrated down into his bones. Medication swam through his blood, nipping at his focus and loosening his joints.

—Maybe you should …—

A waver in the Captain's voice added to Andre's confusion.

Maybe I should 'what,' Captain? What are you telling me?

But the Captain did not immediately respond, leaving Andre paralyzed with indecision. Mo Da stared up at him and tilted her head. A flare lit in his heart.

"Please. Accept my service?"

*—hack her—*the Captain concluded.

What?

{yesss} Jeremy agreed. *{hack her}*

In the haze of the medication, Andre struggled to pinpoint where the idea had come from—was it Jeremy, or the Captain, or himself? It just arrived, like a swat team abseiling down his ears, ordering all his sensibilities onto the floor, and handcuffing them with military precision. Purpose of mission: Classified.

{Do it} The insistence in Jeremy's words echoed through his bones. *{Take her}*

His neck struggled to hold up his head. A wave of confusion gushed through his remaining thoughts and wobbled his delicate sense of reality. He grabbed the side of the shuttle as he groped for clarity. But the flat wall felt rough, cold and jagged under his hand, as if an invisible world of rock lay just behind his touch.

—*Hack her.*— the voice repeated, no longer recognizable as Jeremy or the Captain. The dark thing's designs seeped their chemicals into the holograms of his thoughts. Like a jack-in-the box, an image of Finn popped up in his mind, but the suggestion from inside his head refused to make sense. Mo Da did not move, waiting for a response.

—*How bad you wanna get out of Brulle, Boss?*—

Bad. I want it bad.

—*You need a ticket, Boss. And this it. Time to take a risk and get back in control. Get Finn to hack her, and Elron can send her into Titan with his zilla. You'll have a solution for Kade's balls up, and Elron will trust you. We'll be right back on schedule.*—The Captain relayed his radical idea with the perfect delivery of a newsreader. But Andre remained unconvinced, struggling to think through the haze.

A loud bang exploded outside the shuttle, ripping through the silence inside and echoing in terrifying stereo through Andre's earpiece. Mo Da cocked her head. Andre's heart pounded as the truth of the situation dawned on hm.

Kade's shot the driver.

Two more shots rang out.

"Abort!" Kade cried in Andre's ear. "Abort!"

But Kade wasn't talking to him. It was all over for Andre. They would shoot him and leave him there to take the blame. In the panic of the moment, and persuaded by the thought of keeping Mo Da by his side a little while longer, he convinced himself that the Captain's idea had a chance.

He's right. It's time to take control.

"Mo Da, service accepted."

Mo Da's eyes sparkled so bright they looked almost teary. She stood and bowed her head again. "By your word."

"Follow me." He jumped up to the hatch, but his legs gave way, and he stumbled to the side. Mo Da caught him and lifted him up to the opening. He clawed at the rim and hauled himself onto the roof, where second-guessing awaited him.

What the hell am I doing? Don't I have enough troubles?

—You got a bag full of 'em, Boss. But the android's your ticket out of them all.—

As Mo Da stood, he mustered all his strength and focus, and he scanned the underpass. Max ran toward them from the detour point, tripods in hand. Dimitri trailed behind, struggling to keep up. Their van sat only meters away, its rear doors open, but Kade was nowhere to be seen.

"Stay by me and do as I say," he commanded Mo Da. Draping himself over the side of the shuttle, he dropped to the ground, landing on rubbery legs. Mo Da dropped beside him, and they ran to the van.

As they neared the open rear doors, Kade walked out from behind, a gun in his hand. He wiped blood from his lip, and more blood dripped from a gash above his eye. On seeing Mo Da, he scowled and swept up his gun to point at her.

"What is this?" Kade yelled. "What is *that* doing here?" He jerked his aim to Andre. Mo Da stepped to Andre's side, closer to the van's open door. Kade switched his aim back onto Mo Da, then back to Andre.

"You screwed up, Kade. There wasn't any Neura in the shuttle," Andre yelled, pointing at Mo Da. "*She* was in there. But we can use her."

Kade spat blood on the ground. "We don't need a damn PrePAC, and we don't need *you* telling us what to do. It's Plan B, Cross."

Kade's finger pulled back the trigger.

Plan B

Mo Da slammed the rear door into Kade's arm, knocking the gun off aim as it went off. Andre covered his head and held his breath, but no bullet struck him, a ricochet sounding in the beams above.

Mo Da stepped forward, grabbed Kade's arm, and twisted. He growled in pain and his eyes filled with terror and disgust. She twisted his arm back farther, forcing him to his knees. (Andre imagined General Zod doing that to the President) Swearing and frothing at the mouth, Kade bent over until he dropped the gun. Mo Da kicked it away—directly to Andre's feet—and let Kade go. After a moment's hesitation, Andre snatched the gun from the ground and pointed it at Kade's chest. His finger quivered over the trigger.

I could end it now. Shoot Kade. Take the van. And Mo Da. I could—

Jeremy's voice slithered through his thoughts and scattered them.

{not yet}

—Get the Neura, Boss.—

He froze, unable to comprehend why, or how, Jeremy and the Captain would encourage him down the same path.

Is the medication making them sound the same? Nothing makes sense.

Shouldn't I just run?

{not yet} Jeremy's voice repeated.

—*Finish the Job.*—echoed the Captain.

Kade's eyes, brimming with furious hate, locked on Mo Da as he rose. "You shouldn't have touched me, you fucking bitch."

His threat to Mo Da snapped Andre out of confusion and into action. "Just shut up and listen! We can use her. She can get the zilla into Titan."

Kade pulled his eyes away from Mo Da and glared at Andre. His nasty grin returned, splitting his sweaty face. "You're sabotaging the mission, Cross. We can't leave a trace—"

"You sabotaged the mission when you shot the driver!"

Kade's gaze darted to the side, betraying his failure.

"You let her escape?" Andre demanded. "You let the driver get away?" Andre's heart lifted at the leverage Kade's bungle gave him. "Then it doesn't matter anymore. Titan will know the shuttles are targets. You fucked everything, Kade. Elron is not going to be happy with you."

The smile dropped from Kade's face as he looked down and rubbed his hands on his thighs.

—*You got him, Boss. Time to drive it home.*—

"We can still do this. We don't need the Neura shuttles. We can hack her, and use her to walk the zilla into Titan. They'll never see it coming." Andre took a deep breath. The details of the Plan unfolded by themselves, the words sliding from his mind and off his tongue. He lowered the gun and handed it to Kade. "You can tell Elron it was your idea."

Kade's eyes jumped from the weapon, to Andre, to Mo Da, and back again. He snatched the gun and pointed it at Mo Da. His head and hands shaking, Kade struggled to make a decision.

"Kade," Andre warned, "we need her."

Kade swore and dropped his arm. He pushed the weapon into his overalls, and held out his hand. Andre leaned forward to shake it, surprised by Kade's change of attitude, when Kade's words brought him back to reality.

"Give me the zilla."

Andre scowled. *Should've known.* He withdrew the vial and slapped it into Kade's hand.

"Get in," Kade ordered, spitting another globule of blood and storming off to the front of the van. Breathing a sigh of relief, Andre nodded to Mo Da. She stepped up onto the van's rear platform and paused.

"What did you mean by 'hacking' me?" she asked. "You cannot hack me. I am a PrePAC7—"

"Shut up," he commanded, shoving her forward and following her in. He pointed to the space on the floor between the bench and the radio console. "Sit. And don't speak. We're about to have some unhappy company." She sat on the floor and crossed her legs. "More?" she said, with the same suggestively sarcastic tone she had used when confronting Strato.

Andre needed her to be quiet so he could think through the haze and concentrate on pushing the Plan forward. "Mo Da, hibernate."

After a momentary hesitation, her eyes closed and her head dipped forward. He took a seat on the bench near her and braced himself, as Max jumped in, tripod in hand.

"Whoa!" Max cried, standing back, staring at Mo Da.

Dimitri waddled in behind, arms wrapped around the rest of the tripods. Sweat pouring off his wide forehead and too out of breath to speak, his eyes filled with fear and excitement at the sight of Mo Da.

"Shut the door," Kade called from the front cabin, as he fired up the hover engines. Max and Dimitri looked at each other, then back at Mo Da.

"There's a damn PrePAC in here," Max yelled.

"We're taking her," Kade called back over the roar of the engines. But the Brothers didn't move, mesmerized by Mo Da's presence.

"Damn it," Andre exclaimed, getting up and pushing Max out of the way. He hefted Dimitri in and slammed the doors shut. The van shook, as it levitated and leaned sideways to turn around, before shooting off through underpass to merge with the hover traffic.

Andre leaned against the door—his head fitting neatly into the dent Aoto had left—and wondered what the fuck he was doing.

Trace

The engine hummed, like a group of chanting monks. Dangling tools clinked against the metal interior with the delicacy of Tibetan chimes. Swayed by the rocking vehicle, Max and Dimitri eyed their unexpected bounty.

Squatting by the rear doors on his own, Andre gripped the handle as if clinging to a cliff ledge. With the excitement behind him, the ache in his wound returned with a nasty sting. Medication wrapped around his brain, like the tentacles of a blue-bottle jellyfish latched onto a child's leg. It wasn't a Big Dose, not by a long shot, but it had punch. And that left one big question draped over his thoughts.

What set off the implant?

He thought back to finding Mo Da in the shuttle, when the medication hit him. He was sure he hadn't had aggressive thoughts, too stupefied by the sight of her. In fact, since waking up in the church, he'd remained mostly calm and centered. For a second, he heard Elron's voice telling him that the peace and quiet in his head was some miracle of God. But Andre knew it was more realistic that the dose of zilla had drained the energy from his temper. His anger spurts would be back, he could be certain of that. But they had yet to return. So it wasn't his anger that had activated the implant.

That left only Mo Da, and how she made his heart race.

As the van swayed gently, the meditative quiet inside shone an interior light on the chaos she left inside him. Stones of guilt weighed him down from the child-bot memory she had conjured. Her ability to do that, just by looking at him — when she knew nothing about who he was — vexed him. But there was more.

He glanced at her, and his upper body flushed with heat. His pulse throbbed in his ears. He thought he heard a deep clunk echo through his bones, as if a dormant but fundamental cog had suddenly woken up and slipped a notch. An undeniable sense of vulnerability besieged him.

—*Stay focused, Boss.*—

He forced the feeling down to where he tried to keep his temper. Lifting up that trapdoor on the floor of his subconscious, he rolled the disturbing new emotion in like a dead body, slammed the mental trapdoor shut, and fled back to the present.

"What is she doing here?"

Dimitri's voice reminded him about the Plan — *get out of Brulle* — and Andre's erratic mind swung to the next idea. He couldn't clearly see the details of the web he was spinning, but the unusual excitement compelled him to weave blind.

One stepping stone at a time to cross the river.

"You might want to ask Kade about that," Andre replied in a low voice, careful so Kade could not hear him laying doubt. "Looks like his intel was wrong. That wasn't a Neura shuttle. That was a transport shuttle for this." Andre nodded to Mo Da. "Since this stuff-up guarantees Titan will increase security on their deliveries, we need a Plan B. I figure we can hack her and use her to take the zilla into Titan." Eyes wide and scanning Mo Da's body, Dimitri nodded.

"Can you do that? Can you hack her?"

The last part of the Plan formed itself on the run and popped into place as Andre said it. "No. But I know someone who can. Someone who will do anything for Neura."

—But you'll convince Finn to hack it out of guilt for snitching on you to Grekov. Then you'll SELL him the Neura, and hey, presto, you'll have the credit to buy that ticket.—

Andre's heart raced. *That's bloody brilliant. A hell of a lot smarter than trying to blackmail Dirk. But how is Dirk going to get me into the farm under Grekov's nose?*

—Boss, smuggling people in and out of places is what he does, remember?—

"We got plenty of Neura," Dimitri offered helpfully. "Plenty, from all the junkies comin' in." He frowned apologetically at Andre. "Sorry. I just meant, we got plenty. We don't need it all."

Andre nodded. "Sounds like a plan, buddy."

Dimitri nodded back and smiled. A quiet alarm beeped out from the surveillance panel. Max spun in his seat and tapped on the radar screen.

"What's going on?" Kade called from the front.

"Someone's locked onto us," Max reported. "We got a tail!"

Kade swore. As Dimitri scrambled for his seatbelt and stretched it around his bulbous belly, Andre peered out the rear window.

"I can't see any police," he called out to Kade.

"She's got a tracker!" Kade barked back.

Shit. Of course. Andre wondered how he could have been so stupid. But something didn't seem right.

"How did they get here so fast? It's like they knew we were coming …" His words trailed off. He rubbed the back of his aching neck, a terrible thought pursuing him.

"You really didn't think this through, Cross," Kade snapped. "Max. Get rid of it!"

Max grabbed Mo Da by the shoulder and dragged her over. Dimitri frowned at Andre, disappointed in his new idol.

"Open the door," Max cried out to Andre over the roar of the engine.

"What?"

"Open the damn doors and hold on."

"No!" Andre pleaded, the image of Mo Da plummeting to her end filling him with a sudden, unexpected mourning.

"Wait," Andre yelled, but Kade swerved the van a sharp left, sending Andre sprawling. Heat flared up his spine. For a split second, his world became two overlaid realities — one of the present time; the other, the same dark, prehistoric landscape that surrounded him when he was high on zilla. Then the van righted itself, and the worlds merged back into the one reality of the van.

Max slid a knife from his boot and jammed it into the back of Mo Da's neck, and a panel popped open. He stuck his fingers into the hole and ripped out a small, black, almond-shaped device. He held it up and scowled at Andre.

"You idiot. Open the door."

Kade swerved the van up into a sharp ascent, throwing Andre back into the rear doors. "No, please!"

Max tossed the tracker to Dimitri and pulled a gun from his jacket. "Open the door or I'll shoot the latch off right through you."

Andre braced himself between the floor and the ceiling. He took one, longing look at Mo Da's limp body in Max's arms and flicked the door latch. The right door fell open, and he gripped the walls as the wind rushed in.

Holding Mo Da with one arm, Max kept the gun pointed at Andre. Dimitri tossed the tracker through the open door into the traffic below. Relief and jealousy swarmed Andre as Max kept Mo Da held tight.

"Shut the door, idiot!" Max barked, snapping Andre out of his daze. He reached down and pulled the door shut. As the van levelled and veered into a solid stream of traffic, Max checked the radar on the surveillance panel and cursed.

"They're still on us!"

Kade accelerated and swerved through the traffic. "Can you cloak us?" he called from the front, steering the van toward a clearing between the Stems.

Max tapped furiously into the surveillance panel. "I'm trying!"

"Oh, shit," Dimitri muttered, yanking his seat belt tight. "You better strap in," he warned Andre.

Ignoring him, Andre peered out the rear window again. A silver van darted between the traffic behind them. He turned back to Dimitri. "What's going on?"

"Okay, got it!" Max cried out, strapping himself to the bench, close enough to reach the panel. "Three-two—"

Before Andre could register what was happening, Max wrapped his arm around Mo Da and slammed the control panel a final time.

"One."

The engines cut out, the lights went off, and the van dropped.

Gravity yanked Andre upward and slammed him into the ceiling. The sides shook and the tools rattled. The force held him pressed him against the roof.

Still holding Mo Da, Max reached over and tapped the panel. "Kade, you ready?" he yelled over the whoosh of the van falling.

"Ready!"

Max hit the panel again. The engines roared back to life, the interior lights flickered on, and the van bounced out of its fall. Andre slammed back into the floor, crashing on top of his wound, pain exploding through his side. The van shot forward as Kade regained control and steered it between tower clusters hugging the lower Stems.

"Max, report?" Kade called out.

Max let Mo Da go, unbuckled himself, and checked the surveillance panel. "We lost 'em."

Dimitri let out a loud, audible sigh and wiped sweat from his pale face. "I hate it when you do that, Max."

"Well done, Max," Kade said, tilting the van upward and heading back toward the top of the Stems. "Let's get home before they relocate us."

Andre leaned back against the rear, his insides wobbling like jelly and his whole body aching. "What the hell was that?"

Max slid his knife back into his boot and pulled Mo Da back over to him. "That's how we cloak. We scramble, shut off everything, and disappear. The tracer loses connection. Fun, huh?"

Andre breathed down his heart rate and held his bandaged side.

That thing's never gonna heal.

As Max stuffed two loose wires protruding from Mo Da's neck back into the compartment, he winked at Andre. But Andre was not feeling friendly. Max had just thrown him around like a bug in a jar. And now he held Mo Da in his arms, like they were young lovers in an old, romantic movie.

Max flipped the panel shut and leaned her back into his body. "They sure do make 'em real," he said, biting his lip, his struggle with the guilt Elron had surely embedded in him taut on his face. Andre gripped the door handle tight. Sparks ignited throughout his brain. He fought back at his desire to protect Mo Da, the rising emotion infuriating him.

Oh, yes, he was sure to get angry thoughts again.

"You better be careful with her," he warned Max, his tone deathly flat. "She's our ticket. You damage her, Elron is not going to be happy with you."

Uncertainty bloomed on Max's face. He glanced at Dimitri for reassurance, but Dimitri's gaze darted between him and Andre, and back again. Max seemed to decide the space was too small to risk setting off a certain crazy in the van.

And if you ever touch my ticket again, Andre thought to himself, not taking his eyes of Max, *I'll rip open the back of YOUR fucking neck.*

He sat back and waited for the short and sharp dose of medication that was bound to arrive. Kade eyed him from the rear vision mirror. Andre didn't care. He reveled in the light, groggy wave after his short moment of violent fantasy, as if drawing back on a vape after sex.

The Captain was right. Mo Da was an ace up his sleeve. And with Elron in his back pocket, he held a brilliant hand.

I just need to make the most of it before Kade pulls out a wild card.

Fortuity

Elron slammed his fist down on the obsidian table, jolting the full zilla vial laying on its side. His voice boomed with fury through the chamber. "You let the driver get away?"

Kade stood firm in the middle of the room, arms behind his back, and held Elron's blazing gaze. "It wasn't a Neura shuttle, Your Grace," he explained, warning Andre with a glance to keep quiet. "Titan must have changed schedules since we got our intel. This android was the only thing in the shuttle. It was being delivered to Titan."

Mo Da lay motionless on the floor by Andre's feet where Max had lain her down. Elron kicked back his chair to rise and strode across the chamber floor, stopping just short of Kade's face.

When he loses it, he really loses it, Andre thought to himself. *I can relate to that.*

"Tell me you burned the shuttle." A vein snaked from Elron's temple to his right eye and pulsed with his words. The pores on his face swelled like miniature sinkholes, oil oozing out of them and glistening on his skin. "Tell me, you didn't leave any trace that could lead back to us."

"No, Your Grace," Kade lied. "Of course not."

—You got even more over him now, Boss.—

Elron's eyes squinted, as if searching through Kade's words for evidence of deception. "And what good did you think bringing this *thing* back here would do us?"

"Since there's no way we can hit the vans anymore," Kade continued, as if he had the situation completely under control, "I decided we should hack the PrePAC ... use her to take the zilla into Titan."

Elron blinked with disbelief. "*You* decided? And how the hell do you propose we hack the most secure operating system ever made?"

Kade stuttered something and stopped. Andre took a deep breath and stepped forward. "I know someone, a hacker."

Elron shot him an incredulous gaze, his eyes running up and down Andre as if slicing him with laser beams. Andre quickly continued before Elron exploded.

"He's been working on hacking PrePACs."

At Andre's words, Elron's eyes grew huge and avid with a childish awe. His manicured eyebrows arched, pushing his forehead into greasy folds.

"Your Grace," Kade whined. "I told him this is dangerous—"

Elron held up his hand, silencing Kade without looking at him, and walked toward Andre. "Is this true. Can this be done?"

"If anyone can circumnavigate the AI cage, Finn can. He may have done it already."

Riveted to Andre's every word, Elron clutched at the folds of his vest, his fingers clenching the fabric as he bit into his lip. Every little movement was like some over-rehearsed piece of theatrical choreography. Delirious from the pain in his side, Andre almost burst into laughter.

"And how will you persuade this hacker to do this for us?"

"You could offer him Neura," Dimitri blurted, unable to hide his eagerness to be involved in the exciting plan. "All those Upper Brulleans want more Neura." It was like Andre had handed the big oaf a script.

Thank you, Dimitri.

"Is this possible?" Elron asked, not taking his eyes off Andre.

Andre nodded slowly, as if thinking it over. "That's not a bad idea. Dimitri's right. Finn would do anything for that pure Neura you've got."

Elron's eyebrows relaxed and his eyes narrowed. He paced across the room, his head down. He stopped in front of the window directly under the gold cross and rubbed his gold rings. After a long pause, he turned back to Andre.

"How much?"

Andre opened his mouth, and froze. He hadn't got those details of the Plan from the Captain.

Hello, Captain?

"You never said anything about Neura," Kade snapped at Andre. "Your Grace, he's up to something. He put this idea into our heads. He's manipulating us!"

Elron held his hand up to Kade, again without looking at him. "How much?" he repeated, as if everything—the success of the church's mission, his judgment of Kade's failure, and his affirmation of his feelings for Andre—hinged on Andre's next words.

—You need fourteen thousand credits, Boss. Finn would pay that for

four liters. You need four liters. —

Andre shrugged, and the words came out before he lost the courage to say them. "Four liters."

Elron pursed his lips and stroked his beard. "You're playing a very dangerous game, Mr. Cross. But we must make the most of this fortuity. Considering the failure of our recent efforts."

Elron turned his back and strolled to Kade's side. "Do it," he whispered, but loud enough so Andre could hear. "And do not let him out of your sight. The hacker receives the Neura only when we receive the hacked PrePAC. If the hacker does not do what we ask—if there is any deviation from this criteria—kill them both."

Kade smiled his vulgar grin as he eyed Andre. "Pleasure, Your Grace."

But Elron's hand swooped out from his robe and gripped Kade's arm, vanquishing his grin. "Your focus is clouded, Brother, and now you are infected with fear. It is rotting your resolve and weakening your mind. You will cut this from your soul and leave it outside, or you will not come back. Do I make myself clear?"

Kade stared at the ground in shock, his lips quivering and his nostrils flaring. He searched for words to respond, but failed. He could only nod, and Elron released his grip.

"Remove that thing from my chamber," he ordered Kade, pointing to Mo Da. Without a word, Kade picked her up, threw her over his shoulder, and left the room.

The door shut, leaving Elron alone with Andre. He strode to the bookshelf behind the table, lifted a decanter of amber liquid, and poured it into a crystal glass.

"The walls of this church are closing in, Andre. There is scarce time for doubt or rivalry. And there is no room for weakness in this house. Sometimes, however, a little tension weeds out the weaknesses. The stronger will prevail and restore equilibrium." He took a sip, licked his lips, and fingered a glistening drop clinging to the glass edge. "You've brought me direction from Kade's disarray. I'll do what I can to support you. But, ultimately, the success of your rehabilitation is up to you. I just hope this hacker friend of yours does not disappoint."

He paused, letting the silence hang as he took another sip, and turned to look out the window. Finally, he waved his ringed hand in the air, gesturing for Andre to leave.

"Now go and shower, you're beginning to stink."

Obsession

Andre stepped out of the chamber and into the empty hallway, the cool air ventilating his thoughts. He did stink. He could smell the rot in his wound. A shower seemed a good idea, so he headed past the dorms toward the shower hall while he mulled over Elron's words.

Did he just offer me Kade's position? But he told Kade to kill me. And he made sure I heard it.

—Elron is baiting you and Kade against each other, Boss. He's got you both so filled with fear and distraction, you both do what he wants without question. He's a manipulator. You got to think ahead.—

No, he wants me to succeed. He's just keeping his business-head on. That's what smart people do. They make deals and keep their options open. 'The stronger will prevail.' I just got to make sure that's me.

— You just need the Neura, Boss.—

The availability of another option shone its light on his Anchora plan and exposed its fragility. So many moving pieces had to fall into place before he might step foot on Dirk's smuggling shuttle, let alone walk the flat streets of Anchora. With Elron's growing support, staying in the safety of the church emerged as a considerable alternative. He'd be safe from Grekov, and maybe even from the dark thing. But, of course, to reach that small alcove of peace, he would have to confront the Kade issue—an issue compounded by the implant leashing him.

— You're swinging again, Boss. You know what happens when you swing for too long; you slip and fall. And the branches don't always catch you on the way down. Stick with the Plan.—

As he reached the shower stalls—frustrated by the Captain's tunnel vision disturbing the relief he was enjoying from having another option— he parked the dilemma, undressed, and spun on the tap. Leaning only his head under the water, careful not to wet his bandages, he welcomed the cold blasting his face.

One thing continued to bother him. One thing he struggled to resolve—that the idea to take Mo Da had come from both the Captain and Jeremy. That was crazy, like Superman and General Zod going out together for espresso martinis. He withdrew to a deep corner of his mind where he imagined the Captain could not listen.

Maybe I gotta watch what the Captain says. Didn't he tell me to steal the Neura in the first place? Maybe the Captain and Jeremy are in cahoots, ganging up on me, trying to keep me from being in control.

— I'm not the enemy, Andre.— came the Captain's voice, startling him

in his hiding place. —*The memories are the enemy. Memories will drive you to madness, right where the dark thing wants you. The android is stirring your memories and you're projecting unresolved emotions on her. There's no connection here, and no magic. Now, breathe.—*

Distracted by the conversation in his head, he leaned further under the shower and cold water seeped under his bandage. He winced as it trickled over raw nerves. Peeking under the dressing, he cringed at the sight of the blackened, weeping skin stuck to the material. Thin cracks in his skin snaked out from the bandage's shadows, up his side, and raked his torso with red, angry edges.

Awoken by the cold water, the ache in his wound throbbed. Spinning off the tap, he decided to ask Tan to take another look. He wrapped a towel around himself, bundled his clothes under his arm, and headed down the hall, water dripping from his muscled body.

Passing a room full of machines and hanging cables, he stopped, frozen by the sight of Mo Da lying motionless on a bench.

Her prone proximity filled him with a heady mix of excitement and fear. His heart quickened and desire fluttered in his chest. With the initial tension of the failed hijack passed, he found himself struggling to believe she was so close, in the church, with him.

A green laser splashed across her curves and scanned her substrate, revealing fine robotic components under the translucency of her pale skin. Light rays traced along her slender neck, arced over her breasts, and dipped down along her tapered waist. Curving back up over her hip, the light slipped off and went out, leaving behind the marvelous silhouette of her undulating geography.

Exhilarating, dangerous delight sparked and webbed throughout his nervous system. Every breath amplified the sensation, driving tingles from his skin down to his core, where a warm and still atmosphere established itself. A bamboo-forest calm permeated his being, his cells gently vibrating in perfect harmony. But the tingling reached his spine, and his implant warmed.

He hadn't thought of Mo Da since he saw her back in the farm. Her presence opened a portal to his childhood, reminding him of a nascent sensation he longed to know. He recognized that feeling as the same radiance that bloomed in his chest the day Jeremy had asked him to walk with him. It was joy that Mo Da activated in his heart. It was joy that had activated the implant.

The device's sharp, intensifying heat dragged its fingernail down his back. The bamboo forest shook and the stalks cracked. His memory of the cold, slippery cliffs of his recent hallucinations imposed itself over his inner calm. Pockets of emptiness opened up in the marrow of his bones, sink holes threatening to suck the tranquility under.

—*It's the zombie under the deck, and you know it*—

Nothing but a hairline separated the oasis and the abyss, a hairline that split into cracks and scaled the edges of both worlds.

He turned away, embarrassed by his inner conflict. He could no longer deny she destabilized him, defying the very reason his Plan existed. He focused on his breathing technique and wove his thoughts into a tight braid.

If both joy and anger activated his implant, he reasoned, then they were two wings of the same monster; a monster, that if he did not keep caged, would fly him into oblivion. He had let weakness get the better of him once before, trusting in it, trusting in Jeremy. And look where that had led him—to prison, to the implant, to the labyrinth of confusion he was now lost in. If he was going to escape his past, and get to any sort of level, stable ground, he needed to shut down all distractions.

Another ray of light ran over Mo Da's perfect, naked body—this time in the opposite direction—dragging and unravelling his braided reasoning with it.

But why can't I just feel this?

—Because she's dangerous, Boss. She makes YOU dangerous. You've got to stick to the Plan. Stop swinging.—

He heard the Captain, but his attention followed the light, merged with it, and slid over her curves. The rules, the order, and the constraints of the Plan pressed in against him. Her face and her eyes, they stirred something deep inside him, something he *needed* to know.

—And then what, Boss? If you're caught banging the bucket, you'll be thrown into the cage with the borg. Because that's what's waiting for you if you don't stick to the Plan. You blew your first hand, but now you've been dealt another, and it's a better one. Don't fuck it up.—

I know, I know. But where's my chance for …for something else?

—You need to get a grip on what she's doing to your mind, Boss. She's your Ticket. A means to an end. The Keeper may be a fruitcake, but he's right about one thing; you can't let this piece of technology get under your skin. You need to stick to the Plan, or you're going to slip over the edge.—

Frustrated by the Bonnie and Clyde emotions robbing the bank of his sanity, he stared at Mo Da, daring to her to stand and tell him he was wrong to bury his feelings.

"Tucking your girlfriend in for the night?"

He jumped at the voice. Kade stood at the end of the hall, arms folded. Andre's conflicting thoughts scattered for cover. Without resolution, they hid in the gaping cracks of his schemes, clutching their own agendas and eyeing the Top Job of his mind with insane determination. After an obvious delay, he snapped back into the present and scoffed. "You jealous Elron doesn't tuck you in at night?"

Kade's grin twisted into a snarl. He stormed up to Andre, stopping only a breath away from his face. "You listen to me, Liar Man. You're going to fuck up. And as soon as you do—and you WILL fuck up, 'cause liars ALWAYS DO—I will be there." He glanced at Mo Da and turned back to Andre, his nasty smirk returning. "I might have a go at her myself, 'ey? May as well make the most of it, before we send her off to Titan. She won't be coming back from there, that's for sure."

A flash of red sparked behind Andre's eyes. Before the dark thoughts bubbled up into the implant's wary light, he grabbed Kade by the throat and squeezed. Kade's eyes filled with angry terror and his tongue waggled out of his mouth. He groped at Andre's grip. Andre squeezed harder, a thrill slow-exploding in him like a firework in slow motion. Kade dropped a hand and swung, striking Andre in the lower side.

Pain ripped through his body before his major nerve centers shut down, collapsing him into a paralyzed heap on the floor. His towel fell away, leaving him naked and unable to breathe, his lungs frozen by the blow.

Kade stood over him and spat on his face. "And put some clothes on. You're a fucking guest here." Kade's silhouette vanished, and the neon light above blazed into Andre's eyes.

He lay on the floor, gripped by the terror of his intestines exploding in agony, until they relaxed. Finally, he could gasp in gold-fish gulps of air. Panting, sweating, he hauled himself up by the lab door, wiped the spit from his face, and wrapped his towel back around him.

Mo Da lay in complete shadow, a sculpture in the dark of a museum after-hours.

—See, Boss? She's distracting you. She makes you weak.—

He clenched his fists, gritted his teeth, and breathed in deep. He desperately wanted to experience how high the balloon ride she promised might take him. But the throbbing pain in his side reminded him that each time he'd allowed his feelings for her to rise, so too had his anger and his confusion. The more he let himself be drawn to her, the more he drew out the dark thing.

Maybe that's how the dark thing works, playing on my weakness, just like Jeremy did. It all made perfect sense. He couldn't trust what he felt for Mo Da, just like he couldn't trust the dark thing. *Love let Amanojaku in.*

—Stay in the front room, Boss. The memories are the enemy. You can't kill 'em, just like you can't kill zombies. But you can steer them off into the hills and head off in the other direction, making it damn hard for them to ever find you again.—

He eased his clenching, relaxed his muscles, and slowed his breathing. The Captain's sensibility found no more resistance, slipping over his mind like a leash on an obedient dog. As the leash tightened, his mind snapped into survival mode. He had to do what had to be done. He needed the PrePAC, and he needed to keep himself in control. That was the Plan.

—No one can use you, Boss. You're in control.—

That's right. I'm in control here. She—it—is my ticket to Anchora, and that's that.

—And what's the plan, Boss?—

Hack the PrePAC and get Elron's trust. Take the Neura, sell it to Finn, and pay Dirk. And get the hell out of Brulle. It's just stones across a river.

He detached himself from the doorway, picked up his clothes and walked back to the dorm. Reaching his bunk, he folded his clothes with military precision and positioned them at a perfect ninety-degree angle to the bunk leg. He lay back, clasping his hands over his abdomen, and ignored the scream of his wound. He concentrated all his inner strength on holding down the remnants of his obsession with Mo Da until they struggled no more.

Mask

Photons bombarded what quantum gaps they found between his lids and forced their way in. Pushing the keepers of slumber apart, the space-travelers crash-landed on the shore of his cornea and jettisoned the sun's long-distance message into his waking mind.

After days of rain, the foreign sunlight disoriented him, tricking him into believing he was waking in his apartment days before. His movement awoke the mice in the bed's joints, their familiar squeaks bringing him back to reality. Refusing an instinctive reaction to panic, his brain got to work. He laid the holographic chart of his Plan out in his mind and began mapping a way through time and space.

Outside the window, the low angle of the shadows striped the Stems and betrayed the sun's position. He guessed it was around six o'clock. Finn would soon be home, a slave to his reclusiveness; Andre could rely on that. Motivated by reliable details, he swung his legs over the bed, but his wound bit into his side. He bent over and breathed through the pain, refusing to look at it. An unseen cloud crept over the city and chased away the sun's legion of loyal rays.

I got this.

He pushed the pain aside and methodically unfolded his clothes. As he finished dressing, Tan entered the dorm.

"Oh, good, good, you're up. I let you rest too long. Kade's waiting for you in the docking bay."

"Thank you, Tan," Andre replied, brushing fluff from his jacket as if he owned the place and Tan was the doorman.

I got a Job to do, and I'm gonna get it done like a Boss.

With his business head on, and his focus as tight as an android's asshole, he strode down the corridor to the docking bay. The doors slid open as he entered, revealing the outside world draped in the morbid gray of cloud-retarded light. He climbed into the van's front cabin and sat next to Kade without speaking. Kade returned the silence, the two of them agreeing on something for the first and only time.

Before Andre could buckle himself in, Kade accelerated. The van shot out of the bay, throwing Andre back into his seat. As Kade merged the van with the traffic moving up toward Mid Brulle, Andre looked away from the dizzying kaleidoscope of light and movement to hide his nausea. He checked the time on the dashboard. Reflected in the screen, Mo Da's motionless form lay in the back of the van.

That's my ticket. I got this.

Kade tapped on the GPS. "You need to punch in the coordinates of this hacker friend of yours, Liar Man. And maybe you can suggest where I park this."

Right where the sun don't shine, motherfucker. "You're not coming in, if that's what you're thinking. I'll handle this on my own."

"That's fine," Kade agreed, a little too accepting for Andre's liking. "But I'm not flying around while I wait for you. You tell me where I'm going and where I'm parking, or I'm turning around now and dumping your girlfriend out on the way home."

"Alright, alright." Andre entered the coordinates and sat back. "There's an old maintenance platform at the tower. I'll show you when we get there."

Riding the rest of the trip in silence, Andre planned his negotiation with Finn. There was no point in mentioning Neura until he had Finn agreeing to hack Mo Da as payback for snitching. Finn might get it into his greedy little mind that he should get the Neura as payment. But if Andre's plan was to come together, he needed Finn to pay for it.

As they neared their destination, he pointed to a level jutting out halfway up the tower's side. "Dip to the right, over there."

Kade steered the van to where Andre pointed and brought the vehicle down on the platform. "Twenty minutes, Cross."

Andre nodded. He released his seatbelt, opened the door, and put one foot out, when Kade's hand grabbed his shoulder.

"You got twenty minutes. Then I'm coming after you."

"I got it," Andre retorted, flicking Kade's hand away. Andre couldn't put his finger on it, but something was different in Kade's demeanor. He was cockier than usual, more sure. That was it. A surety beamed from Kade's eyes, where before there had been only the semi-transparent curtains of feigned confidence. Andre parked his suspicion to focus on the job at hand, stepped out onto the wet platform, and slammed the door.

Pulling his jacket around him, he walked to the van's rear and the door auto-opened. He reached in and dragged Mo Da's limp body to the edge, ignoring the bang of her head as it struck the bench corner. He heaved her over his shoulder, his wound stinging him with pain, and his hand gripped the soft, artificial flesh of her rump. He repositioned her body so he held her by her hip.

Stick to the Plan. Finish the Job.

He carried her down the ramp, his wound throbbing with every step. Dark spots appeared across the ramp announcing the arrival of an invisible light rain. Reaching the tower, he caught a lift to Finn's level, where he exited into a long corridor. One blinking, fluorescent light bulb lit the damaged walls and littered floor. He strode through the twitching light to the end and pushed his elbow on the intercom at Finn's apartment. A green light flashed above a small camera lens in the door. As he expected, the door didn't open. He pressed the buzzer again, and again. The door remained shut, and inside stayed silent. He leaned forward to peer into the camera.

"I know you can see me, Finn. I know you're listening. I got a PrePAC7 here." Andre waited a few more seconds, then leaned on the buzzer again, this time without releasing. After a long wait, the door finally slid open. Finn stood back from the doorway, dark circles under his beaming eyes, and a screwdriver clutched in his hand. "Is that really a PrePAC7?"

"It is." Andre hefted Mo Da's body further up onto his shoulder to secure his grip.

Finn stood still, captivated by the site of the latest PrePAC. Andre pushed passed him into the apartment and stomped down the central staircase.

"Hey, wait!" Finn chased after him. "How did you get one of those?"

Andre reached the bottom of the stairs, sweat dripping down his forehead and running down his back. He staggered to the bench, where Ki Po sat under a spotlight, tethered to a laptop. Graphs and code animated across the left half of the laptop's screen. The prism thing that Finn called a Mirror spun on the other side. Andre looked away before the shape caused him hallucinations like the last time, but the prism had already imprinted itself in his mind's eye. Its glowing outline spun, like a ghost, in the middle of his vision. He dumped Mo Da's body next to the open laptop, and turned.

Finn stood by the bottom of the steps — one foot on the floor, the other on the first step. His eyes widened with curiosity and uncertainty. He still held the screwdriver in his hand. Andre swallowed back acidic anxiety rising in his throat.

"I'm not here to hurt you, Finn. I need a favor."

Finn glanced at Mo Da, unable to hide his growing excitement at the chance to tinker with the latest PrePAC. His eyes flicked back to Andre and narrowed. "Why should I do anything for you?"

Andre clenched his fists in intimidation. His implant would make it difficult for him to finish any fight he started, but Finn didn't know that. Still, he couldn't let Finn suspect his weakness. "Do you know how much trouble you got me into?"

Finn stepped backward and up one step. "Hey, look, I was in hospital for two days."

"You were in hospital because you got a habit. Have you ever thought that maybe, considering how much you use, your time was coming?"

"No way. You're not going to turn this around on me."

"Do you have any idea what goes on out there in the real world? You don't go complaining and get your money back. I've had a hell of a time since you snitched on me."

"I didn't complain. They came to me, in the hospital—"

"I lost my job because of you, you little shit."

Finn shrugged. "Not my problem."

Andre's implant scraped its talon down the back of his neck. He breathed in deep and took one step forward. "You nearly got me killed," he said, lifting his shirt.

Finn's mouth dropped open at the sight of the weeping bandages. The stench of his own flesh rotting punched Andre in his nose.

That's getting bad, he realized. And that made him furious.

—Breathe.—

"I have been injected and chased and forced into hiding, so if you don't wanna be thrown out that window, right now, quit your bitching, put down that fucking screwdriver, and start hacking this android. And when you've done that, *then* we'll be even." Andre dropped his shirt back down.

Finn blinked, as if coming out of a trance, the excitement in his eyes drowned by guilt.

"We got a deal?" Andre pushed.

Finn laughed nervously. "Are you nuts? You want me to hack a PrePAC7—"

"You're doing it to your own bucket, right? So you can do it to mine." Andre leaned over and grabbed the cord connecting Ki Po to the laptop.

"Wait!" Finn raced over, threw the screw driver onto the bench, and pushed in between Andre and Ki Po. "I can only do one android at a time. The process uses up all my CPU—"

"Then unplug your bucket."

"That'll fry Ki Po completely. It's a very delicate process. The program moves between the droid's hardware and the software, to avoid detection, so—"

"I don't care how it works, or how it don't work, I just need it done." Andre's eyeballs heated up. He was losing it.

—Breathe, Boss.—

"Okay, okay." Finn held up his hands in placation. He leaned over Mo Da and studied the access panels at the back of her head. "Ki should be done soon. I can hook her up straight after that. I could probably have her done by … tomorrow."

"Sooner," Andre insisted.

Finn sighed and ran his fingers through his hair, giving Andre his pathetic pained look—the same one that meant he was giving in. "I *guess* I can do her by this afternoon, but, she'll be wiped. No personality, no memory. Only the basic survival algorithms will remain."

Andre's heart skipped a beat. As focused as he was, he hadn't considered that Mo Da's personality would be gone for good. The reality that she would not remember him—that the small connection between them would be snuffed out like the life of a bird smashed headfirst into a window—gave the process a finality he hadn't mentally, or emotionally, prepared for. And the fact that this bothered him frustrated him even more.

His tight grip on his Plan slipped.

—She's just a machine, Boss, remember? Stay focused.—

Obliviously salting Andre's raw emotional wound, Finn caressed Mo Da's left breast. "They look so real."

Anger flared up Andre's spine and prickled his skin with heat. He steeled his mind against the thoughts and feelings threatening to set off the implant, but they had already begun to form their evocative mirage. He drove his thumb into his wound, shooting exquisite pain up his side and scattering the bad thoughts.

This is what losing focus feels like. Stick with the Plan.

Looking up at Andre, Finn's snatched his hand away from Mo Da. "Look, if you want her wiped that fast you're gonna lose something," Finn explained, directing the conversation back to the hacking. "She'll still have her learning capabilities, so you can train her to do whatever you like, from scratch. But, no, she won't remember people." Finn swallowed. "She won't remember you. She'll be like a fast-learning child-bot, though. Very fast."

At the mention of a child-bot, the heat of old guilt flooded Andre, exasperating his already wavering internal condition. His heart galloped. Sweat beaded across his back. Paranoia and anger edged their way further in between his grip and the Plan. He dug his thumb deeper into his wound, digging for pain to knock out the ambush of emotion.

Finn smiled nervously. "See you at two, then? I'm just putting her here for now, okay?" Finn hefted Mo Da's limp body and laid her on the floor next to the bench. Her empty eyes stared up at the ceiling, floating eerily in the red stripe.

The remorseful longing Andre thought he'd locked away came back kicking and banging against the cargo hold of his heart. The sensation thrilled and terrified him, throttling his structured thought like a dinghy in a storm. His careening mind dragged back the floor of his Plan, exposing the fathomless, raw wound of his soul, where the holographic remnant of his savage instinct shimmered and shifted through its trenches. Wearing Mo Da's face like a mask, the lonely essence of his violence peered out from inside the implant's impossible prison, triggering a series of four images flashing through his mind.

First, the face of his mother appeared, wearing the same empty stare as Mo Da, with the same red stripe across her eyes. His mother's face morphed into Jeremy's, covered in blood and grinning. Jeremy's death mask was replaced by Andre's own face, gaunt and desperate, before it contorted into something alien and hideous. His eyes blacked over. His skin scaled. His mouth pushed out into a crocodile-like snout, and when it opened its jaw it chomped rows of spiky teeth.

As fast as the illusionary masks appeared, they vanished, leaving Mo Da's serene face staring up at the ceiling through her blood-red stripe.

Finn's voice called him out of the illusion. "Andre, you okay?"

—Breathe, Boss. Stay in the front room. You got this.—

His breathing shallowed and sped up. The implant burned against his brain. His capillaries filled with glass slivers of an angry sickness. Finn continued to speak, but a whooshing in Andre's ears muffled the words.

—Stay in the front room, Boss.—

Shut up.

—Breathe, Boss.—

Shut up! I can't think.

The Captain stopped talking, and the medication brought Andre crashing down into the bare, rocky alleys of chemical sedation. His stomach churned, as if he'd been hours at sea. He clutched the bench, the wood transforming into something cold, wet, and hard under his touch. He was slipping into the strange, prehistoric illusion again.

"Andre?"

"Do it," he managed to say.

"Andre, you don't look so—"

"Just do it!"

He pushed away from the bench and stumbled up the staircase, out of the apartment, and down the hallway. His back muscles spasmed at the thought of being confined in the lift, so he pushed through the exit door. The stairs yawned up at him, like a steep mountainside projecting him to a dizzying height. Wind wrapped its frantic ghost tentacles around his legs, snatching away all his balance and bearing. He slipped on the wet top step and tumbled down.

Liar

Hard edges bit and ripped into his sides as he banged against the stairs. Crashing to a halt on the first platform, he smacked his head on the cold metal. Silver sparks exploded in his vision, and furious pain reigned supreme throughout his body, plunging him into a zombie state of shock.

{Not long now, little bro.} Jeremy's voice teased him in the dark, reaching out from emerging memories loosened by the physical and mental ordeal.

Why won't you just die? his mind screamed back.

As if in response, the familiar two-dimensional prism from Finn's Mirror program formed and spun out of the depths of his subconscious. As it twirled toward him, he glimpsed something amorphous slithering inside, like an ultrasound image of some unrecognizable fetus. It neared the surface of the prism and came into focus. A tail-like appendage slid up and coiled around the materializing figure. The creature—and Andre knew it was the dark thing inside him—pressed it's scaled body against the glass and turned its head, bearing the same reptilian face he'd seen overlaid on Mo Da's. The bottom half of its snouted face split open and chomped a mouth of rusty, scissor-sharp teeth.

Snit-svit-snit-svit...

Its black eyes shape-shifted between Mo Da's serenity and Jeremy's volatility. Immense terror struck him, as if the thing inside him was made up of the fears of all living things, feeding on the heat and vapor of every nightmare and murder.

{I'm gonna show you somethin'} It spoke with Jeremy's voice, but distorted into something drawn out and grazed. The dark thing lifted a long, scaled arm, and raked a midnight-black talon down the prism's glass. Andre cringed at the scratching voice reverberating through his bones.

{Something just for you to see}

As its words echoed into silence, the dark thing pushed back from the surface of its flat prison, leaving behind a hair-thin crack. With a final flick of its tail, the monster slid off into the dimensionless back room holding the secret Andre had deliberately forgotten. The crack split and widened, and the gaseous tip of the memory seeped out. Exquisite terror engulfed his being. He sensed he had done something worse than murder his dangerous brother out of fear.

*—Don't think about it, Boss.—*The Captain's voice crackled and stretched, just as Jeremy's had.*—Stay in the front room. You got thisssss—*

But he didn't have it, did he? He never had it. It had him. He couldn't *not* think about it anymore, because …

—Ssssstayyy—

… because he didn't stay in the front room, did he?

Did I, Captain?

The Captain didn't reply, leaving Andre washed up on a great, jagged reef of terror.

Did I, Captain? he screamed at the vast silence in his mind. But only Jeremy's voice came back, slowed and slurred, uttering one terrifyingly familiar word.

{Mohhh-thaahhhhh…}

Andre's mind imploded, sucked into itself like the birth of a star played in reverse. The vacuum dragged him light-speeding back through time and dropped him into his twelve-year-old self, sitting in the armchair in the front room of his childhood home.

******

As he gazed out the small window at the unusually clear sky peeking between the towers, blood dripped from his fingers onto the floor. He licked at the metallic taste of Jeremy's blood on his lips.

Must have got some in my mouth when his eyeballs exploded.

"What have you done?" his mother screamed from the back room, her voice slapping the walls as it echoed down the hall. "What have you done?"

His head ached from the thrill of the kill. If she didn't shut up, he was sure he was going to go in there and shut her up himself.

—Stay in the front room. Stay right there.—

The voice came from nowhere, as calm as October waters in Fiji. He'd heard it once before, telling him to turn around when Jeremy led him to stab the child-bot. He didn't listen to it then, either.

Frozen, numb, blood dripping from his hands, and sweat pouring off his skin, his every muscle trembled. His hands, however, remained deathly still.

—Stay in the front room. Stay right there.—

But I can't think, he argued. *I can't think if she keeps screaming and you keep talking.*

"My baby. My baby! You killed my baby!"

Andre didn't know who the screaming woman was anymore. He just really needed her to shut the fuck up. Couldn't she see he'd had a hell of a day?

"Monster! You monster!"

Goddamn it. There really is only one way I'm gonna get a little peace and bloody quiet around here.

His core tightened. His hips and legs activated with the mechanical precision of an android, standing him up, turning him around, and walking him into the back room. The woman he no longer recognized screamed something he could not understand. Her words distorted as they flew from her mouth, stretching into a high-pitched, grating screech that stung his inner ear. She held Jeremy in her arms, a bloody grimace frozen on his brother's face. It was Jeremy's fault the woman wouldn't shut up. Even dead, his brother tormented him.

{finish the Job}

The woman's mouth moved as tears streaked down her cheeks. She glared up at him, her eyes wide with terror, yet freezing him with a sense of familiarity. Her screams morphed into coherent words.

"My baby! You killed my baby! You monster!"

His head ached, as if it were splitting in two. The woman's words tore back into incomprehensible sounds as the verge of madness drew him closer. Her wailing rose into a cacophony of squawks flapping their feathery wings at his ears—*God, I hate fucking birds*—but it was her stare that became too much for him to bear. He squeezed his eyes shut, clutched his ears, and shook his head violently.

I need to shut her EYES up, that's what I need to do.

When he opened his own eyes again, the woman's face shifted between Jeremy's and something reptilian he did not recognize. The two sides at tug-of-war inside him slammed back together into perfect clarity—pure, numbing clarity.

Finish the Job.

If there was any more screaming, he didn't hear it. A wind rushed in his ears, some primordial soundtrack of the prehistoric land from which killing evolved.

His mind as blank as the clear blue sky, he picked up the fallen switchblade from the bloody floor and walked over to the hysterical woman. Without hesitating, he slashed the knife across her face, lacerating her below the eyes. Swinging back with momentum, he slashed again, this time across her throat. The woman fell back onto the floor with a thud, and all Andre saw were two sparkling eyes staring up through a strip of red.

With one final whoosh, the wind in his ears disappeared, as if sucked in by a vacuum, and the house fell into perfect quiet.

He sat in the front room and stared out the window, a sense of some glitch in time twitching in his brain. A splitting ache thumped in his head and he wondered where it came from. He put it down to having a hell of a day.

I'm just gonna stay right here. In the peace and quiet.

Blood dripped from his hands and onto the wooden floor. Sweat poured from his skin and into his eyes where tears should have flowed. He sat there until the roar of hover engines came and took the peace and quiet away.

Bait

A horn blared, and bright light slashed across his sight. He blinked away the rain trickling into his eyes. The walkway pressed into his knees as he clutched the railing.

The horn blared again, its noise driving in black waves of shame and guilt. Pain assailed his body, and his whole being contorted with despair.

Another horn, and he recognized the tower base around him. Somehow, as he had relived the horrifying truth of his past, he'd walked all the way down the stairway and collapsed in front of Kade's van.

Can't let Kade see me like this.

Imps of medication ran through the corridors of his veins, scraping their rusty spears along the walls. He hauled himself up.

—Tricks on tricks, Boss. That's all it is. That's what happens after a long day. You just stick with me. Keep yourself moving. We'll get the Job

done. Easy.—

He shuffled back to the van and clambered in.

"Have a fall?" Kade asked, without looking at him.

"I slipped." The feeble explanation was all Andre could manage, his world caving in on him. Without responding, Kade pulled back on the steering mechanism and took the van up. Andre thanked God for the small mercy of silence. As Kade veered into the hover traffic, Andre clutched at the edges of his seat and rode the tail of his mind's confession.

I murdered my mother, in cold blood. And I knew it. I always knew.

—You still got the Plan, Boss.—

Why did you hide this from me? Andre demanded from the Captain.

—It was the only way, Boss, to keep you from going mad. Madness is where the dark thing wants you. Madness is where it owns you.—

{No, Andre, it's because you wanted to kill her, right?}

—That doesn't matter anymore, Boss. You got the implant now—

{the Captain's a weak liar, like you}

Shut up, Jeremy!

Jeremy's voice rattled his bones, shaking the last cobwebs off his terrible secret. Kade dipped and swerved the van, and Andre squeezed his eyes shut, as if doing so would hide any sign of his inner turmoil.

"You don't look so good, Liar Man."

"I'm fine," Andre lied through gritted teeth.

*—I'm looking out for you, Bossss.—*But the Captain's voice skewed again into a hissing distortion.

You lie! You're a Liar Man!

—I'm just tryin' to keep it together here, Bosssss.—

{liar, liar, world on fire}

As the dark thing's designs seeped their chemicals into the weave of his defenseless thoughts, Andre could no longer differentiate between Jeremy's voice and the Captain's.

Shut the fuck up! I can't trust you. I can't trust any of you!

Kade brought the van down into a level flight. The voices in Andre's mind retreated, and clarity formed a calm eye in the maelstrom—a terrifying clarity, where every detail he had somehow hidden from his own mind revealed themselves in sharp, undeniable definition.

I'm responsible. Not Jeremy, not some goddamn dark thing. Me. I did it.

All those years he'd told himself he'd killed Jeremy out of survival, that if he didn't, not even God knew what Jeremy would have done.

{But you do know, don't you Andre?} Jeremy's voice teased. *{Because when you took my switchblade, you took my place. You went and did what I was gonna to do. 'Cause that's just what we do.}*

The pinnacle of his realization stuck out, like a stinger left behind by some demon wasp; no matter what he did, or how far he ran, the truth would remain with him. *In* him. He was up for life imprisonment in the Phantom Zone of his mind. It would only be a matter of time before madness set in, like gangrene, and the dark thing took control. The implant had never stood a chance.

Every inch of him weighed concrete-heavy with guilt. His lungs labored to breathe; his chest heaved as the walls of reality pressed in. He no longer trusted his own thoughts. The Captain was a Liar Man. Everything in his head had been lies and manipulation. He had architected a belief that he was the victim, driven to murder Jeremy in defense, for fear of what his brother would do, when maybe, he just wanted to do it himself.

The monstrous cat was well and truly out of the bag, squatting in the center of his being and staring at him, wide-eyed, unblinking.

An itch shifted under his skin. The implant burned, and the dark thing scratched at the ceiling of its doped up coffin. The muscles in the back of his neck gripped his spine, as if trying to grab the implant and rip it out.

I've got to get this thing out of me.

Unable to see himself ever free of his anger while he had the implant, he abandoned it as a solution. It was just another lie. A mistake rendering him helpless and weaker than weak.

I let THEM put a lie in me. A trick on a trick that's left me a zombie.

He couldn't defend himself. He couldn't love. That was what he had murdered all those years ago—his ability to feel, to love. Mo Da had stirred the truth in him, challenging the implant, to bring him face-to-face with the volatile temper that held his peace and quiet hostage.

Rain pelted the windscreen, streaking the city lights into rivulets of color. He managed to breathe his anxiety down, but the truth of his past pressed down upon his soul with the weight of Mid Brulle.

No, he would never rest, never be at peace, until that bastard thing was out of him. That left only one path forward—remove the implant and face the dark thing. He knew he must. It was as unavoidable as the sun coming up every day, as the world one-day ending.

But he knew, too, that he was too weak to do it alone. He could only do it with the help of someone who accepted him for who he was, who believed in him. Someone who needed him.

Elron.

PART SIX

REHABILITATION

Deal

The double doors of the docking bay slid open and the interior light beckoned them in. Kade steered the dripping van into the dry bay, lowered it onto its struts, and flicked off the engine. He gave Andre a silent sideways glance before stepping out. The new confidence in Kade's eyes compounded Andre's internal disorder, as if Kade, too, had made a final, irreversible decision. His reactionary behavior had vanished, and in its place crouched a cautious, biding, watchful eye. Andre could not intuit any more than that, but the surety Kade harnessed concerned him to the core.

He climbed out of the van, removed his wet jacket and threw it over the bench. As he trailed behind Kade up the stairs, there was no longer any doubt in his mind. No matter how he might try to win Kade over, Elron's right-hand man was hell-bent on hating him. If he was to join the church, he realized, he would have to find a permanent solution to deal with Kade's constant opposition.

Their silence committed them both to whatever showdown must come.

Arriving together at Elron's chamber, Kade stopped Andre with a hand on his shoulder. "I'll report to the Keeper. You can go to your dorm."

Andre pushed Kade's hand away. "I wish to have dialogue with Elron."

A faint scowl tensed Kade's face, betraying his resentment toward Andre's familiarity with the church's language. Then it was gone, in the flutter of his eyelashes.

"Suit yourself." Kade banged on the door and entered.

Left to his inner torment, Andre leaned against the wall and dropped his head into his hands. The horror of his mother's murder ebbed back, making way for the disbelief and shame of hiding his past from his own mind. The Captain, Jeremy, the implant—they were all nothing but lies to him now.

I was so stupid to accept the implant. A weak, coward's thing to do!

But the thought of having his implant removed and facing his violent impulses both terrified and excited him—it was the same confused, dual feeling infecting him since he met Mo Da.

The chamber door flung open, and Kade strode out, his face unreadable. Andre took a deep breath, knocked on the open door, and entered.

Rain streaked the tall windows. The suspended cross looked like it was bleeding. Elron stood by the book wall, an open volume in his hands.

"Andre, you look terrible. Please, sit." He gestured to a chair by the holo-table and slid the book back into the shelf. Andre slumped into the chair, exhausted by despair, yet bursting with anxiety from what he was about to say.

Elron stood behind him and massaged his neck. "What is so heavy on your mind, Brother?"

Andre closed his eyes, relaxing into Elron's strong hands as they kneaded out the tension.

This is it. No turning back.

"I'm ready, Your Grace. I want my implant out."

The Keeper's hands squeezed tighter, twisting Andre's trapezius. "I see."

"I want to be free of it. And if I can't control it … I give myself to the church, Elron. I need this group. I need you. I can't do this on my own."

"Of course, Brother. You're broken and you want to mend. Broken people are not evil. They can be fixed. But like a bone snapped in the one place so many times, the structure of your hope has never had a chance to heal. Something so weakened is perfect prey for a parasite. We must strengthen you. Happiness, and strength, come from controlling your mind, controlling your fears. But, first, you must prove you are ready."

Andre melted into the massage, his mind comforted and encouraged by Elron's supportive words. "Anything, Your Grace."

"I see you struggle, Brother, with this thing inside you. This technological imp has poisoned you, affected you. It leaves a residue within you, redirecting your desires. I see the way you look at the android."

Guilt, shame, and fear welled up inside Andre. Elron pressed deep into the tight points in his shoulders, bursting packets of tension.

"What do you think could come of being intimate with a robot, Andre? Do you think it is capable of love? Its feelings are nothing but ones and zeros. Its reactions are algorithms. You know, in your heart, it is unnatural. A path for the weak. You cannot truly connect through feeling with something not made of God's flesh."

As Elron spoke, Andre sensed himself being split in two again, a crack appearing down the middle of his psyche. The two sides leaned back from each other—Jeremy on one side, Mo Da on the other—joined by a single, fraying thread.

"This illusion of a possible satisfying relationship with a machine— because that's what you're thinking, even if you haven't admitted it to yourself—is a symptom of technology being in your body. You are like all the others here, conditioned into being dependent and intimate with technology, having surrendered your power to it. But has it made your life any easier, or has it taken your choices from you? Let go of the illusionary connection you have with the android, and you will be ready to face the demon inside. Anger and lust are branches of the same root, Andre, and I need to be sure—*you* need to be sure—that you are truly ready to have this root of evil removed."

"I am ready," Andre blurted. "I have nowhere else to go. I am losing my mind!"

"Steady, Brother." Elron slid his hand down under Andre's shirt and patted his chest. "Have heart. The flesh is weak in the presence of temptation. It is not your fault. It is the devil in the city, this wretched, delusional city, distracting God's children, confusing and tempting them with objects of lust and narcissistic indulgence. But I will make you strong." Elron's hand clutched Andre's left chest muscle. "We will make your heart whole again. I believe in you. You are stronger than you think. Are you prepared to prove me right?"

With his hate for the implant off its leash, Andre's desperate mind imagined perfect sense in Elron's words. Anger welled up in him at allowing Titan to con him into believing its technology would liberate him, when all it had really done was make him reliant on their invention. Titan hadn't made him a better person. It had robbed him of his ability to feel anything deeply.

A trick on a trick.

He nodded, surrendering to Elron's warmth and understanding. The chance to be forgiven, to forgive himself, lay in Elron's hands.

"'Tis not enough that we strike at the borgs," Elron continued. "These

PrePACs, these impersonators of soul, will still walk among us. They, too, must be abandoned and destroyed. Prove your allegiance to the church. Help me lance the boil in Brulle."

"What do I need to do, Your Grace?"

Elron moved both hands back onto Andre's shoulders, squeezing and rolling them. The rain tapped the window with a thousand fingers, adding to the hypnotic solace. Andre rocked with the motion of Elron's massage, his head a little boat on a sea jostled by pre-squall waves.

"When you collect Mo Da tonight, you must test her obedience for her Titan mission. Have her kill your hacker friend."

Andre tensed. A tiny arrow shot into his heart at the thought of Mo Da shooting someone, of what it would commit her to. Elron squeezed tighter, signaling not to interrupt. Andre steeled his mind, dissolving the arrow's sting, and allowed his old, mean joy to rise.

*—He's using you, Boss.—*The Captain's voice echoed from the back of his skull, faint and distant.*—Just like Jeremy did.—*

You can shut the fuck up, Liar Man, Andre shot back, banishing The Captain once and for all.

"And you will film it," Elron continued, "and load it up online, and let the city see exactly what Titan's robot golems are capable of."

The rain's assault on the windows intensified, its swarm of tiny birds bashing their fragile heads against the glass.

Snit-svit-snit-svit …

Andre's own inner voice rose in the courtroom of his mind, and valiantly put forward its final argument. "But … it will be murder."

Elron didn't miss a beat, delivering the validation Andre needed—wanted—to surrender. "It's kill or be killed in this world, Andre. You know that. The strong strike first. That is the nature of survival. Being stronger and smarter than everything else. That is what I can teach you. That is how you rise from your past and become someone extraordinary."

{You know you want to} Jeremy's voice slid into his mind, as clear as the Captian's once was. Andre breathed deep and pushed himself forward along his blind path of determination.

I can do this. This is my ticket out of my implant prison. This is where I'm meant to be.

{Yes, not long now, little bro ...}

And then I'll shut you up, too.

Elron leaned forward and whispered. "This is just the beginning. We will show them all what fools they have been. You and I, Andre." Elron kissed him lightly on the cheek, then presented his rings for Andre to return the kiss.

Andre froze. Reptilian eyes flicked themselves open in the dark thing inside him. A thought flashed through his mind; his hand latching onto Elron's red face and slamming the back of his head into the obsidian desk.

{Yessss, you will, but not yet ...}

This is just part of the test, he told himself. *I got to stay in control.* He squeezed his core, breathed deep, and pushed away the vision. *Because that's what a Good Citizen would do.* He leaned forward and pressed his lips against the ring's cold metal. The metallic taste reminded him of blood.

"I will help you, Andre, like I helped Kade. But you are stronger than him. You just have to believe in yourself. Prove your strength to yourself."

Yes, yes I must. I must prove this to myself.

He abandoned the last residue of feelings he held for Mo Da, convinced she was just an omen, a bird bashing its head on the window of his Plan. He disregarded what he felt for her as nothing more than a confusion from the medication and its effects, misguided emotions that he might—once the implant was removed—have for another human.

An uplifting coolness flared in his chest, blooming into something so foreign and diamond-rare to him that he took a moment to recognize it as hope.

Elron gave Andre's shoulders one final squeeze, removed his hold, and backed away behind the table. "Now, go, rest. Tomorrow is the last day of your rehabilitation, and the first day of your ascent to strength."

His head lighter, the wound in his side abating to a dull ache—*maybe I'm healing now?*—Andre stood, bowed, and left the chamber.

As he walked down the hall to the dorm, he imagined a future where he became so strong and disciplined that he ran the church himself, like a goddamn Boss.

Reaching his bunk, he collapsed back into its creaky welcome. City lights blurred outside the tall windows, streaked by the rain into slow-melting star clusters. He let sleep dissolve the world into darkness, as the rain snipped at the glass.

Snit-svit-snit-svit...

Nightmare: Part 2

His feet plodded through thick mulch, the soaked, rancid ground squelching and sucking at his ankles. Although his feet moved in a forward stepping motion, his body slid sideways, dragged by some unseen force toward a dark forest of gigantic shadows.

"Can you help me?" asked a synthesized voice from somewhere in the dark.

The air thickened, solidified, and closed in. His pulse thumped like drums in is ears. His heart banged on the inside of his chest with the desperation of a kidnapped victim waking in a boot. As the curtains of mulch pressed in on him, he thrashed, but the mulch hardened into wood.

Doctor Steele's familiar face appeared and he held up a needle. His mouth moved, but the Captain's voice came out.

"You got this, Boss."

He was no longer upright, but lying flat on his back, scratching feverishly at the wooden panel above. Exquisite terror gripped him as he realized he had been buried alive. Hyperventilating, his vision blurred.

"... help me?" came the voice again, muffled.

The thumping pulse in his head threatened to pound him into madness, when something rough and scaled slithered next to him. He didn't want to turn, but he couldn't help following the dream's script. When he looked over, it was not the dark thing he saw, however, but two olive eyes floating in a red strip.

"Releeeeeeasssse meeee ..."

Mo Da's face vanished, and his panic transformed into a bottomless hole of eternal longing. Driven by a desire he had never fully known, he scratched and ripped at the wood above him. His bloody fingers discovered ridges and edges, as if he were buried inside a giant's rib cage. Straining, suffocating, his heartbeat struggling, he drew on the last vestiges of his strength and ripped the dark breast open.

Blinding, inexorable light engulfed him. A screaming wind pushed him back and pressed him down. He pried open his eyes to slits, only to see a fury of tiny, black wings swarm in and block out every last inch of light.

Job

His pounding heartbeat propelled him out of the nightmare and into shivering wakefulness. Soaked with sweat, he lay dizzy and distorted to the ends of his nerves, as if he were a TV-static version of himself. The festering burn in his side returned with a vengeance, gripping his body in its jaw of pain.

Murder. I'm going to murder Finn.

He tried to drop back to sleep, back into the blissful arms of unconsciousness, but the mad jockey of his terrifying excitement whipped his heartbeat into a stampeding frenzy. He could only lay there and peer desperately into the darkness, until dawn light drifted in on the dust. By the time the prayer bell rang and Kade pushed open the dorm door, Andre was dressed and lacing up his boots.

"I know when it's prayer time, thanks Kade." Andre brushed past him and made sure he led the way down the corridor, in some silent protest against Kade's indifference.

"You're not one of us yet, Liar Man."

Entering the prayer hall, Andre knelt in a space at the rear of the gathering. Elron appeared from a doorway on the side, took his place beneath the cross and greeted the group.

Lack of sleep hung around Andre's head in a fog. Focusing on a point of light behind his tired eyes, he let Elron's prayer float past him in a muffled hum. He moved the light forward, to sit just outside his head, and held it there, as if his very existence depended on it.

"Amen," the gathering echoed in unison, snapping Andre out of his meditation.

"My family," continued Elron, a new urgency in his voice. "We are spiritual beings. Humanity is a spiritual being. But we are also, all of us, killers. We have always been. We cannot survive without eating and we cannot eat without killing. It is a great weight to bear, to be born to kill, to need to kill to survive. To cope, we have outsourced this perpetual deed to machines and farms and companies, while we allow ourselves to forget the horrific, sacred act done in the name of our survival."

"But there is a fine line between killing for survival and killing out of greed and lust. When the deeds are done for us and forgotten, and all that we see are an abundance of excessive indulgences, the survival act of killing becomes perverted, an unnoticed addiction."

"The trans-humanists think they rise up into some post-human fantasy, but their narcissistic obsessions drag us all down to dwell with the animals and machines. They are nothing but uncivilized, fearful monkeys infected by narcissism and blinded by their disconnection from God. Their survival instinct has become perverted, vindictive, driven by greedy desires for things beyond survival. They are addicted to addiction."

"And like the blind, addicted beasts they are, they want more of this city. They use the Neura farm to kill us. They're cultivating our death right up there in those spinning branches. And we must fight back. It is time to enact our own survival instinct. If we do not strike, they will catch us in our beds and force us out of Brulle."

"But we will not be forced out. No. Your spirit, my spirit, will not be lost. Together, we will reclaim our spirituality. We must do what we must, to survive." He held up his arm, clenched a fist, and called out, "Amen!"

While a few of the residents merely stood and bowed, many cheered and echoed Elron's word and action. Aoto stood by the side, smiling, proud to see her training slowly building a small army for the church.

As they dispersed, Max, Dimitri, and Kade headed down the corridor toward the docking bay. Andre turned to follow, when Elron grabbed his arm.

"Mr. Cross, I wish dialogue with you."

Leading Andre into his chamber, Elron motioned to him to close the door and strode over to his book cabinet. He slipped out a key from inside his sleeve and unlocked a draw in the shelves. Out of Andre's view, he slipped something inside his jacket, then closed the draw and turned back, smiling his manicured smile. He approached Andre, held him by the shoulders and kissed him on each cheek.

"How did you sleep, Brother? Are you ready for your ascension?"

Andre blinked away his nerves. "I'm ready."

Elron's smile broadened. "I knew there was something special about you. A fateful reason God brought you to me. Aoto is doing her best with the residents, but for many of these poor, lost souls, the fire inside has long since died. But not you. There is a bonfire in you, a strength raging to get out." He reached into his cloak and withdrew a matt-silver gun.

Andre's breath caught in the back of his throat. Elron held the pistol by its grip, rubbed the narrow barrel slowly with a finger, and pressed it against Andre's chest. The cold of the metal speared through Andre's shirt and into his skin. Elron slid the gun down his torso, over his abdomen, and into Andre's waiting hands. Its weight gave him a sense of power and strength.

"It's loaded, Andre," Elron said lovingly, as if murdering Finn was a gift Andre had always wanted. "This is my trust, my belief, in you. Two bullets. One for the hacker, and a spare, should you need it, to ensure the job is done. Remember, when you have collected the android, you film her killing the hacker and upload the footage for the city to see. She cannot be recognized by her name insignia. Return her to us, so we may send her to Titan to strike the borgs. Then, my Brother, you will have proven your strength to me, and we shall release you from your unnatural collar." Elron cupped Andre's cheek. "Go. Grace be with you."

Andre bowed, slid the gun inside his shirt, and left the chamber.

This is it, he thought, walking down the hall toward the docking bay. *This is the Job. This is the Plan. This is the last stone across the river. And if Kade gets in my way, there's a second bullet with his name on it.*

He descended the stairs, entered the bay, and picked up his jacket. Kade stood by the van, tweaking a small antenna on the roof's side.

"You feeling okay today, Princess?" Kade taunted, as he walked over to the wall and tapped into the keypad to open the bay doors. "You worried your girlfriend won't remember you?"

The bay doors slid apart revealing a wet, twinkling Brulle. Sunlight broke through the overcast sky, split by clouds into shafts, and shot between the towers.

"I'm not worried about a thing, Kade," Andre lied, slipping on his jacket. "Except maybe you losing your faith again."

Kade didn't bite. He laughed, his new indifference persisting.

They climbed into the van without speaking, and Kade started the engine. Andre steadied himself with a deep breath. The van lifted off the floor and hovered out of the bay.

As they traveled in continued silence, the cold metal of the gun pressed against Andre's skin, empowering him, focusing him. He didn't think about the past. He went over the steps of the Plan in his mind and ticked them off. He stuck a mental label on Mo Da, with big black letters reading 'Ticket.' He stuck another one on Finn: 'Collateral Damage.' He filed them both in a bursting, unordered folder marked 'Survival.' With all his actions sufficiently justified and lined up in a nice, neat path running straight through the town of self-delusion, he sat back and breathed himself calm for the rest of the ride.

"Showtime, Liar Man," Kade announced, as he lowered the van down on the maintenance platform at Finn's tower. "You got—"

"Twenty minutes. I know." Andre stepped out onto the wet ramp, slammed the door behind him, and headed onto the walkways. Out of Kade's sight, he pulled the gun from inside his jacket and opened the chamber. The gold ends of two bullets stared back.

Mind shutting the chamber, Boss? It's a bit drafty with that open.

Although not trained to shoot, a PrePAC would apply its precise calculations to anything. Mo Da would need only one bullet. And that left one for Kade. That was Elron's unspoken direction.

Time to get the Job done.

Reaching the top of the walkways, his thighs burning and his wound aching, he stomped to the end of the hall and pressed the intercom. The buzz echoed inside.

That's the sound of your time up, buddy.

The door slid open, but the entrance room was empty. He marched inside and charged down the stairs to find Ki Po attending to the orchid pillar. Wired with adrenaline, he threw his jacket to Ki Po and strode up to Finn.

Finn sat at his workbench, his robotic arm harness still on his back, tinkering with Mo Da. She remained motionless, her open eyes staring vacantly ahead. Andre's heart thumped in his chest. He clenched his thoughts and breathed deep.

"How's my android?" he demanded, pacing as he talked, playing out his next moves in his mind.

Finn rubbed his blood-shot eyes and ordered his PrePAC to leave the workshop. "Ki-Po. Private Mode."

"Finn," Ki Po protested. "I am attending to the garden."

"Get out, bucket," Andre snapped.

"Ki-Po," Finn repeated. "Privacy."

Ki Po walked past Andre and dropped his jacket at his feet. Surprised by the android's behavior, Andre remembered it had been hacked, and wondered if Mo Da might regain her attitude. He needed to cover all variables and stay in charge.

"She's done," Finn said, wiping sweat from his brow. "She's been back online a while, so her system's re-established all the fundamentals—walking, talking. Ki Po's been working fine since his hack."

Flicking shut the panel behind Mo Da's neck, Finn handed Andre a small, transparent ball, similar to the communication device Kade had given him when they attacked the Titan shuttle. "I've hooked this up, too. It slots into your ear and transfers her thoughts to you. It also picks up your voice and transfers that to her. You can command her from a distance, your commands going straight into her action center. Untethered from the Mesh, she might get a little … confused, but your commands should override that. Here, try it."

Finn dropped the earpiece into Andre's hand. He rolled the transparent device in his fingers, wiggled the cold thing into his ear, and turned to Mo Da.

"Mo Da, stand." She leaned forward, engaged her hip and leg mechanisms, and stood. Andre smiled.

"She has Wi-Fi," Finn continued, "so she can connect to personal and apartment devices, and some building info channels. She'll need these to navigate and learn. This indirect connection should allow her to utilize their internet access without her being tracked by Titan."

"It. Call her *it*."

"Ah, Okay. So, yeah, Titan can't track her—it. But she's—it—is trawling the house devices now, learning as we speak."

"And the robot laws?"

"I couldn't completely erase the laws in the time you gave me." Andre's eyes popped in disbelief, but Finn quickly held up his hands in a calming gesture. "But I managed to block them. Effectively, it's the same thing. She'll do anything you tell her to."

Andre's heart thumped loudly in his ears. *I got this.*

While Finn tapped into his laptop, Andre stood between the bench and Mo Da. Using his body to conceal his actions, he withdrew the gun from under his shirt and placed it into Mo Da's hand. "Hold this," he whispered. "Keep it hidden."

Glancing at the weapon, Mo Da wrapped her hands around its form, as if registering its purpose. Andre's heart skipped a beat. She grasped the handle and slid it down by her side into the shadows. Sweat broke out across his forehead. He couldn't tell if the flutter and rustle in his stomach were butterflies of excitement or bats of fear. It didn't matter. The Job was getting done.

Is this how Jeremy felt the day he sent me down to kill the child-bot?

The memory of the ravine flooded him with doubt, but he was ready for it. *It's just doubt. And doubt is weakness. We don't have room for weakness in this house.* He pushed back on the rising nausea in his stomach and smothered it with merciless determination.

"Did you get your job back on the farm?" Finn asked, oblivious to Andre weaponizing Mo Da. "If you can get more Neura—not that zilla shit you sold me last time—I'd be happy to go back into business."

"Is this back plate loose?" Andre asked, ignoring Finn's question and luring him away from his laptop. He turned Mo Da around so her gun hand faced away.

"What?"

"This looks loose, can you check it? I don't want to have to come back here when she starts falling apart."

Finn scrunched his shiny face as he moved to stand behind her. "She isn't going to fall apart," he said with frustration. "I've done all my checks."

While Finn assessed the panels on the back of her neck, Andre moved to the bench, faced the laptop toward Mo Da, and pressed the video record button. He fought against his excitement, managing not to visualize what Mo Da was about to do, for fear it would trigger his implant.

I got this.

The rain beat against the window.

Snit-svit-snit-svit ...

"This looks fine, Andre. What are you talking about?"

"So she can kill?" he asked.

Finn stepped back from Mo Da, his shoulders sagging and eyes squinting from fatigue. "I told you, she'll do anything you ask."

"And you're sure about this?" His pulse throbbed in his ears, so loud he thought Finn might hear it.

Finn huffed. "I hacked her, Andre. I'd bet my life on it."

Andre smiled. "You just did." He pointed at Finn. "Mo Da, shoot."

Finn blinked with confusion, his tired mind not registering the danger. Mo Da turned, lifted the gun, and aimed it at him. He stumbled backward, eyes widening with terror, and he held up his hands. The robotic arms of his harness mimicked his motions and spread out behind him.

"Wait!"

Anger burned in Andre's eyes as he imagined Finn's head bursting like a detonated tomato. The implant scratched down his spine and sent its medication after his violent thoughts. Mo Da's finger hesitated on the trigger.

"Andre, please, no!" Finn begged. "I'm sorry, okay? I'm sorry I went over your head!"

"Mo Da, shoot!" Andre yelled again, his voice sounding like his brother's.

Mo Da froze, and Andre's world spun.

Pull the goddamn trigger!

Weapon

He lunged forward to grab the gun, thinking he would have to shoot Finn himself. But his medication had already stepped in between his thoughts and his actions, and he stumbled sideways into Finn's desk. His rising anger fizzled out into the haze tingling in his body.

Finn saw his chance and darted toward the stairs, but his sudden motion snapped Mo Da out of her paralysis. She pulled the trigger. A loud bang echoed throughout the apartment. Finn flew backward with the bullet's impact and crashed onto the floor. He gasped and flapped, and the robotic limbs of his harness mimicked his flailing arms. Then his eyes turned back in his head, and he lay still, like a dead bug sprawled out on its back.

Andre's hand twitched, as if he'd pulled the trigger himself. Excitement spiked through the medication's haze and his head rolled across a sea of euphoria—not just from the sedation, but from watching innocence kill for the first time.

{this is what you are, little bro} Jeremy's voice hissed and scratched at his mind like claws on the inside of a coffin.

I got to stay focused. The Job's not finished. His own voice, barely audible in his head, drew down his emotional spike and brought him away from the edge. *Stay focused on the Plan and finish the Job.*

Flexing his mind against the heady mix of medication and excitement, he returned to Finn's laptop and stopped the recording. With a few key strokes, he uploaded the video to multiple online channels.

"Mo-Da," came a polite voice from the middle of the room. The loud bang had brought Ki Po downstairs. He knelt at Finn's unconscious body, and opened the medi-kit in his chest. He looked up at Mo Da. "How could you do this?"

She did not respond, shuddering like an old refrigeration unit.

Caught up in the thrill of killing, Andre stepped away from Finn's laptop and pointed at Ki Po. "Mo Da," he commanded. "Shoot."

With no hesitation this time, she took aim and fired. The bullet struck Ki Po's left optic, the impact knocking him onto his side. Sparks popped in random across his facial substrate, and items from his medi-kit spilled all over the floor. He paddled his arms in the air in a futile attempt to ward off the experience.

Mo Da kept the gun aimed at Ki Po, her body side lit by the spotlight. Andre's eyes drank in the sight of her.

So beautiful.

His hands clawed, his back hunched, and his head dipped, as if something slithered under his skin. Jeremy's words hissed and shuttered through his brain.

{This is what makes you ssssstrong}

The dark thing's prehistoric face flashed in his mind, its wide-set eyes instinctive and uncivilized. Its blackened snout growled and bared its razor-sharp fangs. Face muscles bunched under an ancient armor of scaled flesh, hard and cracked like a zilla addict's skin. Then it lunged.

He stumbled back, but the hallucination vanished, leaving him panting and disastrously destabilized. A terrifying truth struck him. Implant or no implant, the dark thing was coming out. He had to get Mo

Da back to the church and fortify himself in Elron's sanctuary before he completely lost his mind.

Focus! Focus!

He checked the time on the laptop. Nine minutes had passed. He had eleven minutes. His Reliability Rating had never looked so good. Leaving Finn bleeding on the floor, and Ki Po short-circuiting on his back, Andre ordered Mo Da upstairs and out of the apartment.

Swamped with anxiety and panicked by the vision, he didn't think to get the gun back from Mo Da, or realize he'd spent his spare bullet.

Alcove

Following Mo Da down the hall, he shook his head in an attempt to clear the medication's haze and banish the residue of hallucination. Mo Da looked around at the walls and ceiling, as if transfixed by invisible scenes and embedded music only she could see and hear.

"The building ... all its devices," she mused aloud. "I can hear the data and human conversations flowing through them. So much to learn. But so much does not make sense. Why did I kill Finn?"

Her words floated past his ears, barely making sense. "Move," he tried to say, but the tendrils of the medication tied down his tongue, and the word fell out as an unformed sound.

"Machines are not made to kill," she continued, stroking the walls as she passed them. "This law is written in the building's code. Humans kill. But I... I have the ability to murder. Am I now human?"

She really needs to shut up.

Mo Da stopped and faced Andre. "Murder. Is that why you had me hacked? To murder?"

Unprepared for such a confrontation, Andre scrambled for a response. He could feel her studying him, analyzing his body language. There was no doubt, she was learning fast. He needed to distract her calculations until he got her back to the van.

"I said move," he finally managed to speak, but there was no confidence in his words.

She remained steadfast in his way. Her feistiness reminded him of the day he'd met her in the infirmary, and how she confronted Strato. A random spark of irrefutable joy defiantly lit itself in his heart.

"Murder is a crime. I will be destroyed. I've put all my kind in danger."

"I'm commanding you to keep walking," he said firmly, regaining control of himself.

She lowered her head and turned, as if sulking, and stood by the lift. Fear fluttered in his chest at the thought of being confined in the small space with her, so close to her.

I've got to pull it together. She's a machine. My goddamn Ticket.

"We're going this way," he said, opening the door to the stairway. "We walk down."

Mo Da headed out the door and down the stairs. He hesitated to follow, remembering his slip the day before and the terrible truth it revealed.

There's nothing left to be afraid of. I just gotta move it.

As he followed her down, he inhaled the cool air in an attempt to tighten his mental focus. The sound of rain run-off hitting the lower platforms echoed up in steady beats.

With her back to him, Mo Da tilted her head, softening her demeanor. "Please, I must understand. What is my purpose?"

Jesus, Finn, what did you leave me with?

As they reached the first platform, her hips swayed with grace, her movements more fluid, more random—more human—than only moments before in the apartment. As much as her persistent questioning annoyed him, he couldn't help but sympathize with her.

No, stop it. Stay focused on the Job.

"Your purpose is to do what I say, got it?"

She stopped abruptly by an alcove in the tower's side and spun around. "Maybe you did something wrong. Is that it? And now I have to help you fix things?"

Andre stumbled back from her accusation. He had mistaken the pause in her confrontational manner for surrender, when she had, in fact, baited him into discussion. A glow from somewhere below the walkway lit the edge of her silhouetted face, and her stunningly fierce poise paralyzed him.

She's struggling against me the way I struggle against the dark thing.

Mo Da's head tilted again. "You are conflicted. Your heart rate, perspiration, the dilation of your pupils." She stepped forward. "You ... you care for me."

Her words slapped him in the face. But before he found the words to respond, the noise of the run-off hitting the lower platforms echoed louder.

No, not louder ... closer.

"You do," Mo Da continued. "I see it—"

He slapped his hand over her mouth and pushed her into the alcove. With her olive eyes fixed on him, he raised a finger to his lips. "Quiet," he mouthed, cocking an ear.

The noise he had heard coming up from below wasn't rain run-off from above striking the lower metal platforms. The sounds were footsteps. And they were coming up toward him.

He leaned back and peeked down. Two figures jogged up the walkway, bare-armed, rifles slung over their wet shoulders. As they ran around the corner of the next ramp and headed toward his hiding spot, he glimpsed an unmistakable white stripe through short, dark hair. His stomach clenched into a tight knot.

Strato.

He pushed back into the alcove, against Mo Da.

What the hell is he doing here?

The footsteps drew nearer, banging on the metal. He tried to think of an escape plan, a Plan B, but medication pulled its sedative thread of chemicals through his veins. One thing, however, became clear.

Damn it, of course! He can access my implant's tracking.

He pressed Mo Da as far he could into the striped shadows of the alcove. A shadow fell across her eyes and framed her rose-colored lips. Squeezing his body against hers, their legs intertwined, and the short and shallow breathing of his chest pressed against her breasts.

The footsteps stomped nearer, almost upon them. The platform shook under his feet. Fear and excitement drove desire racing through his veins, tingling up to the surface of his skin. He moved his hand from her mouth, her pert lips hovering just a breath away from his. As the footsteps pounded straight past them, his cravings gave into the moment's absurd romance. He pressed his mouth against hers, tasted her lips, and quietly coveted the moment like a thief unzipping a bag of diamonds in the dark.

After a long indulgence, he drew back, just a breath, to look into her eyes.

"My beautiful weapon," he whispered, and kissed her again. Heat flared out from his implant, burning the base of his brain. Chemicals jettisoned through his veins and chased after his desire. Unbidden, covered in blood, the child-bot's face flashed up in his mind, its lips mouthing one familiar word.

Murderer.

Terror gripped his core. All strength vanished from his legs, and his knees buckled. He fell out of the alcove's shadow toward the danger of the light.

Hazard

Mo Da's arms shot out and caught him as he collapsed. Lifting him up and cupping the base of his head, she pulled him back into the dark. As Strato's footsteps banged farther away up the ramp, she put her lips to his ear and whispered. "What is happening to you?"

He couldn't speak, muted and paralyzed by the vision of his mother. Painful longing to see her—to feel her hold him the way she'd held Jeremy's dying body—cemented itself in his heart.

Mother! Forgive me!

Mo Da's hand twitched at the back of his neck. Her words invaded his thoughts and cut the cord to his nostalgia.

"An implant. My scanners detect an implant. Those men are after you? Are they tracking you?"

He let his mother's face drift away, like a funeral lantern let go in the night. Awkward, vulnerable, and ashamed to be in Mo Da's arms, he pried himself out of her hold and stood back on his wobbly legs.

I've got to stop being so fucking WEAK.

He clenched his jaw, ground his teeth to steady himself, and hauled his thoughts up out of their confusion.

"Move," he demanded, avoiding eye contact and nodding toward the stairs.

She regarded him with an examining gaze. He tensed, wondering if she would, or could, attack. But she turned and stepped out of the alcove's shadows. He composed himself and glanced up the walkway. With no sign of Strato, he wiped the memory of Mo Da's lips from his mouth and followed her down.

Okay, so I kissed her. The flesh is weak. It's the implant confusing my thoughts, that's all. That's all it is.

Focusing on the back of her head, as she led him down, he reaffirmed his mission. He'd done the hard part. Finn was dead. Yes, he'd slipped up and given in to temptation, but he was back on track. He'd even out-witted Strato. Through his cracked, self-delusional lens, he had proven to himself that he was ready to face the dark thing. All he had to do was get Mo Da back to the church and show Elron.

I did it. I got this.

As they reached the base of the tower, Kade strutted down the platform toward them. His familiar nasty grin activated goose bumps of alert across Andre's skin.

"I'll take her from here, Liar Man."

Andre's goose bumps spiked into prickles and realization slapped him across the face. *The bullet.*

He'd been so caught up in struggling against his feelings for Mo Da, he forgot about killing Kade. Before Andre could even begin to consider his options, Kade pulled his own gun from his jacket and leveled it at Andre's head. Mo Da's eyes darted between them both and the gun as she stepped aside. Andre froze, furious at himself.

You fucking, fucking idiot.

"I knew it, Liar Man. I knew you were hiding things."

What's he talking about? Andre wondered, looking for clues to what Kade knew. "This isn't what you think—"

"Shut the hell up." Kade aimed at Mo Da. "And you, don't move." Turning the gun back on Andre, he moved forward to stand an arm-length away. "Everything that's come out of your stinking mouth has been a lie." He reached out and ripped something from the shoulder of Andre's jacket. Holding up a fingernail-sized silver disc, Kade's grin grew wider. "I've heard everything."

Andre squinted at the flat object. His stomach dropped.

A recording-device.

His mind reeled, racing back over the last twelve hours, through his conversations and movements. His recall halted at a point the day before, when he first brought Mo Da to Finn's tower. Playing back in his mind's eye, he watched himself stepping out of the van, when Kade stopped him:

"You got twenty minutes on your own," Kade said, as he grabbed Andre by the shoulder and pulled him back. "Then I'm coming after you."

That was the moment Kade had planted the device.

Kade's eyes glistened and his lips quivered as he spoke. "I told you

you'd fuck up. You didn't believe me. You thought you'd get away with it. But I ain't as stupid as you think, Liar Man."

Andre's mind fast-forwarded and searched frantically through everything he remembered saying since the moment Kade had tagged him. He panicked at the thought of his conversation with Elron. But no, he wasn't wearing his jacket then. He'd left it to dry in the docking bay. He did have it with him at Finn's, but Andre still couldn't pinpoint what he'd said or when to know exactly what Kade knew.

"Do you really think Elron was ever going to let you leave?" Kade snarled, all his cool absorbed by his rapture in exposing Andre. "Do you think you're so special? You're not the first he's had a sweet spot for, and you won't be the last. I can't wait to tell him you're a zilla dealer, and watch that stupid, besotted look fall right off his face."

Cold, hard realization dropped in Andre's stomach—something he'd said to Finn, or something Finn had said to him, about working on the farms. Kade's silent cockiness and constant smart-ass smirk over the last twenty-four hours finally made sense.

Andre's past breathed heavy on the back of his neck.

{Told you I'd be back.}

"You couldn't have fucked things any better if I planned it." Kade continued, wallowing in his win.

A clang echoed from the walkways above, snapping them out of their confrontation. Andre glanced up, fearing Strato was coming back down. Thinking of no other option, he confessed.

"Okay, okay, it's true. But I *had* to work on the farms. It was the only job I could get. But I'm here now, Kade. I'm doing this, now. I just killed Finn, with her, did you know that? I'm with you. I'm one of you. But,

Kade, the farm Baron's men are here. They must have tracked Mo Da, or my implant. I don't know how. But we have to go."

Kade's eyes filled with fear and flicked up the ramp, then narrowed and focused back on Andre. "Once a liar, always a liar."

"Kade, we don't have time for this. We gotta go!"

"Oh, we're going. Just not with you."

"I cannot let you do this," Mo Da interrupted from the side, the standard polite PrePAC tone gone from her voice forever.

"You stay out of this, bitch—" The smile dropped from Kade's face as he glanced at her. She held the gun pointed at his head. A quiet cheer roared through Andre's haze.

She thinks it's still got bullets in it.

Kade swung his gun to point at Mo Da and stumbled back on uncertain feet. His eyes darted from her face to the gun and back again.

"Lower your weapon!" he shouted. "I order you!"

Kade's moment of hesitation was all Andre needed. Reacting instinctively, before any thought formed completely in his brain, he lunged and slammed Kade's arm against the railing, knocking the gun out of his hand. The gun flew over the walkways and tumbled into the abyss.

As Andre pushed himself away, Kade punched him in the stomach, forcing all oxygen out of him. He stumbled back, and Kade slugged him in his left cheek, knocking him into the opposite railing. Gasping, Andre called out Mo Da's name, but he could only mouth it silently. She pulled the trigger, and the dull, useless click of the empty barrel died in the air. Kade swooped in and landed a right hook into Andre's wound. Unbearable pain scorched Andre's side and blazed through his torso. Dizzy with agony, he collapsed against the railing.

Stars twinkled in his vision, as he gasped for air and hauled himself up. Mo Da stood back, her shaking hand holding the empty gun forward. He reached out to her, mouthing *help*, when Kade grabbed him by his jacket and launched him over the barrier.

He flailed his arms as his body flung through the air. Just as gravity yanked him down, his left hand raked along the wire railing and his fingers grasped hold. His body slammed against the side, and he kicked his legs frantically at the yawning depth below.

"Mo Da!" he finally managed. "Help!"

"Stay, droid!" Kade demanded before leaning over the rail. A murderous grin split his sweaty face, and a familiar darkness sucked light into his eyes. "Time's up, Liar—"

Mo Da's arms wrapped around Kade's neck and cut off his words. His eyes popped wide, and he thrashed against her tightening hold. She stood strong, holding him in place, and slowly twisted his head. As Kade's face turned from red to blue, his bulging, terror-stricken eyes glared at Andre, and his tongue poked and waggled out of his mouth.

Yes! Andre thought, as he dangled over the abyss. "Kill him!"

A gurgling rattle escaped Kade's frothing mouth. His eyelashes fluttered, like the wings of exhausted butterflies, until his lids shut and his body fell limp. Mo Da dropped him to the ramp and stared at Andre's slipping hand.

"Mo Da, help me!" he commanded.

After an almost unnoticeable, but definite, hesitation, she reached down and grabbed his forearm.

Shield

Andre collapsed next to Kade's dead body, his nervous system flooded with a shark-infested sea of medication. His head floated as the bite of his wound sank in its fangs.

Mo Da squatted next to him, placed the gun on the ground, and lifted up his shirt. He didn't look down, trying to manage his hold on the pain wracking his body. She held her hand over his wound. A blue light glowed from inside the scanner on her palm.

"Why did you hesitate?" he sneered.

"My responses are still developing. I am only three hours old," she stated flatly, moving her hands over his torso.

"Let me make it clear," he snapped. "If I'm ever in trouble, you must help me any way you can. Without hesitation. Got it? Confirm."

"Confirmed," she said, scanning the rest of his body. "You have no broken bones. However, your wound is severely infected. Vein ulcerations. I can administer pain relief and compression, but your wound requires medical attention from a hospital."

She opened a compartment in her chest and withdrew an injector and bandage. He nodded at the injector. She jabbed him, administering the painkiller, and wrapped a fresh bandage around his torso. Her hands slid under his shirt, brushing against his bare skin.

"Your system is being poisoned. I am certain it is affecting your thought processes. You must—"

"I'm fine. Just get the key to the van."

As Mo Da pulled the bandage tighter, making Andre wince, she looked toward Kade. "He didn't like you very much. Is this one of your friends?"

There it was again, that same hint of sarcasm. Perhaps her personality had not been erased completely. Perhaps there was something else, something beyond his own absurd connection with her, that made her fundamentally different.

"The key," he said, pointing to Kade. "Find the van key in his pockets. And destroy that bug." As she fished through Kade's pockets, he picked up the gun and faced the doubt Kade had planted in his mind.

Is it true? Is Elron using me?

His thoughts scavenged for any morsels of hope in what were left of his options. His instinct told him to just get in the van and drive it far away. His mind, however, seemed to belong to something else.

But go where? doubts demanded. *Do what?*

Something sinister crouched in the background of his thoughts, a presence squatting like Jeremy's silhouette on the ravine the day he'd led Andre to the child-bot. Something mean and nasty and evil sat on his brain and sketched designs that he couldn't quite yet see. But he felt them being drawn, long and slow, like scratches down a cave wall in the night, driving his decisions to their agenda.

With the implant still inside me—with no work and no credits—I'm trapped in Brulle. Trapped with the memories that will keep triggering the dark thing until they both drive me insane.

"I have them." Mo Da held up the key to the van in one hand and pinched the listening device in the fingers of her other. She threw Andre the key, dropped the device to the platform, and stomped on it. "And now?"

He turned his dizzy head to the van sitting on the platform, as if it might speak and tell him what to do. Try as he might, he couldn't make a decision. He almost wished the Captain would come back.

{Liar Mannnnnn}

Jeremy's creaking voice splintered through his thoughts again, but this time, it was less Jeremy, and more … more animal.

Soaked with sedation, and tortured by dilemma, he flopped his head back to rest on the railing. Another clang echoed from the walkways and a tiny warning bell rang in the midst of his medication. He peered through the railing up to the stairways. Nothing. But as he turned his head back to Mo Da, an array of bangs exploded in sound and light around them. Covering his face with his arms, he realized he was being shot at.

Strato.

"Mo Da," he shouted, pointing to the van. "Get me out of here. Now!" He hauled himself to his feet, pain screaming in his side.

Mo Da looked around. She snatched up Kade's body in one, effortless motion, and stepped between Andre and the unseen assailants. Holding Kade as a human-shield, she stepped backward, protecting Andre as he shuffled toward the van. A barrage of bullets riddled Kade's torso. Blood spurt out over Mo Da's shoulder and onto Andre's back. Another round of gunshots exploded around them as he dived behind the safety of the van. While Mo Da dumped Kade's ravaged body over the walkway, he fumbled with the key, unlocked the door, and dove inside. Mo Da climbed in behind him and sat in the driver seat. Bullets punctured the vehicle's panels and ricocheted across the platform. He reached in front of her and slammed the key into the ignition. Hitting the start button, he roared life into the engine, and the van levitated off the platform.

"Get us out of here!" he commanded.

As bullets riddled the van's side, Mo Da stared at the dashboard. "I don't know how to drive."

Oh, shit!

"Slam your foot on that," he yelled over the noise of the gunfire, pointing to the accelerator on the floor, and grabbing the steering wheel. She tilted her head in an instant of contemplation and stepped on the pedal. The van shot off toward the tower. Below, Strato and his companion reached the platform and sprayed another round of bullets. Andre pulled left on the steering wheel, spinning the van around.

"And steer it like this."

As more bullets ripped across the van's base, Mo Da grabbed the steering mechanism, pushed her foot all the way down, and the van shot off between the towers.

Defense

Swerving to avoid traffic, Mo Da's intelligent learning quickly grasped the skill of driving. Andre guided her hands on the steering mechanism, until she steadied the van on her own and matched its speed with the traffic.

He slumped against the window, wiping Kade's blood from the side of his face. A fire burned under the anesthetic in his wound. Heat from the implant pinched the muscles in his neck as medication tingled through his veins. He could almost bear the vertiginous view through the front window, and the seaside swaying of the van, but the wave of the sedation and painkiller mixing it all together threatened to overwhelm him. The dark thing, bloated with presence, weighed heavy on his mind.

"You are not well-liked," Mo Da stated. "Is there any place we can go where we won't be shot at?" Her words, deliberate or not, threw his indecision back in his face. From nowhere, the vast flatness of Anchora stretched out in his mind's eye.

I wouldn't be shot at there. Not by anything.

Headlights flashed across the van's windshield, dissolving his vision back into the streaming hover traffic. His wound pinched, like the stubborn claw of a possessed crab. She was right about him needing medical attention. The infection was eating him alive. It was all eating him alive—his wound, the implant, the dark thing. They all had to come out, and the only person who could, would, help him was Elron. He had to get back to the church.

But Aoto would be furious. Max too. How, in his shattered condition, could he defend himself against the fall-out from Kade's death?

"Andre, where do I take us?"

He squeezed the cold metal of Elron's weapon in his hands, as if it were the last solid thing on earth. Sifting down from the dark thing's designs, following in the wake of his debilitating confusion, a new plan formed in his mind, and one single thought bobbed across the rolling ocean of his thoughts.

{weapon}

He clutched at the word, like a drowning man grappling at the last piece of a sinking ship. He had done everything he could to be a Good Citizen. He'd just killed Finn for it, for fuck's it.

"Andre?"

So if he had to use Mo Da as protection until his implant was out, so be it.

"Andre? Did you hear me? Where should I take us?"

Shivering, the gun's cold infecting his bones, he pointed a shaking finger to the GPS. "The Heart of Grace. Use the return coordinates."

"Retrieving now," she said, tilting her head, listening to the van's AI that only she could hear. He sat up and pulled together what few rational thoughts he had left.

He needed a story, and one that couldn't be ripped apart. Suddenly freezing cold, he spoke with the palsied voice of an elderly man, pausing mid-sentence to catch his breath.

"When we get back to the church … let me do the talking … I'm not going to be able to communicate with you in there … they've blocked radio waves … but that's good … 'cause then Strato can't track me."

"The man shooting at us?"

Andre nodded. It had been so long since he had someone—or something like the walls of the Dock lift shafts—to confide in. "If you have to answer questions … you tell them we were ambushed … by the farm's men … Kade was shot trying to get you into the van … You gotta lie … You know what lying is, right?

Without hesitating Mo Da nodded.

"Elron won't care about Kade, but others will need convincing. Especially Aoto. So, you gotta protect me." He took a long breath. "Confirmed?"

"Confirmed."

"I'm gonna get my implant out … You gotta protect me until I'm recovered. Confirmed?"

Mo Da nodded again.

{yes, make her kill them all} Jeremy's creaking voice demanded.

Disturbed by the disjointed comment, Andre ignored the idea. But its echo dragged his thoughts sideways, even as he tried to march them forward.

No. I need them. And Elron needs me. He believes in me. He's leading me to my strength.

{like Jeremy did?}

Shut up. I'm the Boss now. I don't need any voices or implants. I'm finishing the Job and sticking to the Plan. And when this is all done, I'm gonna shut you up, too.

{there's only one way to shut me up, Andre … let her kill them all }

He wasn't quite ready to pull the pin out of that grenade and admit he was weighing it up as an option. He wouldn't even recognize that the grenade was in his hand. Good Citizen and all. But it was there. And it ticked like a time bomb.

Snit-svit-snit-svit …

Wind hurled suicidal raindrops through the air and bashed them against the windshield, exploding their captured light back into the air.

"And what do we do when your implant is out?" Mo Da asked.

Andre couldn't answer. He'd convinced himself the best thing to do was to stay by Elron's side and benefit from his help. To be a Good Citizen. But he sensed himself swinging in a different direction—like being pulled sideways in a dream—toward a far more volatile outcome. The tide had ebbed back on his resolve, his buried emotions rising again with the ominous peril of a beautiful, shipwrecking reef.

"Just get ready. It's going to get bumpy from here."

PART SEVEN

WEAVING BLIND

Hate

"We're here."

Andre woke with a start, Mo Da's hand gently shaking his shoulder. A fever had replaced the ice cold in his limbs. His entire body dripped with sweat.

"This is where the return mode took us. Is this correct?"

Prying his eyes open, he squinted at bright neon light bursting through the window. Mo Da hovered the vehicle outside the church, the doors of the docking bay sliding open. A thin figure, with jet-black hair and one arm in a sling, walked out into the opening. Andre sat up, wincing at the impossible pain in his side.

"This is it. Remember, I do the talking."

"What happens if they find out you killed Kade?"

Andre snapped a look at Mo Da. "*You* killed Kade."

"I performed your command. So, technically, you killed him."

Andre didn't like Mo Da's train of thought, not one bit. *She's getting too smart for my own good.* "If they find out *we* killed Kade, we're both dead. So keep your mouth shut, and let me tell the story."

She steered the van through the curtain of rain draping over the bay entrance and lowered it to the floor. Steam puffed out from the base, as it settled, and the engines shut down.

Aoto paced in front of the vehicle, her head twitching from side-to-side, her eyes scanning the front cabin. As she laid eyes on the bullet holes and cracks in the windshield, her face screwed into a knot of frenzied concern.

Mo Da stepped out of the driver's cabin and walked around to Andre's side. Aoto barked something, but Mo Da ignored her. Andre kicked open the door and tumbled out into Mo Da's arms.

"Where is Kade?" Aoto's high-pitched voice flitted up into the docking chamber, like a bird warning others. "What have you done to him?" She pushed past Andre and scrambled into the driver's cabin, searching for any sign of her lover.

"Aoto, I'm sorry—"

"What have you done to him?" she screamed, pouncing out of the van and back onto the ground. Mo Da stepped in her way and held her back with one outstretched hand. Aoto stopped and growled, her eyes flaring with rage. She clutched her sling, as if she were about to rip it away, snap off her useless arm, and attack with it.

"Aoto, I'm sorry—" Andre repeated, but this time his words were cut off by Max entering the chamber.

"Aoto!" Max called, striding to the van, Dimitri behind him, his short, fat legs attempting to keep up. "Hold yourself. The Keeper's orders." He stepped in between her and Mo Da and eyed up the PrePAC.

"They killed him," Aoto screamed. Tears streaked her porcelain cheeks, sticking a strand of jet-black hair to her face. The hate in her eyes threatened to reach out and pull Andre in. "He killed Kade! He's going to kill us all!"

"Aoto, hold! Assemble yourself. And you." Max pointed at Andre. "The Keeper will have dialogue with you. Immediately."

Mo Da lifted Andre's shirt to reveal his bloody bandages. "He needs medical attention."

Max eyed Andre, as if to say he needed more than that.

"I'll take him to Tan," Dimitri offered, still trying to catch his breath.

Max nodded toward the door. "Go, and inform the Keeper."

Dimitri smiled feebly at Andre and gestured to follow.

As Mo Da put her arm around Andre and helped him walk out of the bay, Aoto screamed one word, over and over:

"Amanojaku! Amanojaku!"

Truth

Mo Da laid him down onto the bloodstained mattress in the lab and stepped back. As Tan peeled back the bandages, pain dragged its barbed wire through the nerves in Andre's side. Tan screwed up his nose.

"This is quite a mess."

Andre's head spun slowly, like he was back on a turning branch in the farm. He didn't want to look down, but he couldn't help himself, and when he did, he froze in shock. His flesh stuck to the dressing and lifted away from his body in one piece, exposing a deep gorge of pink and bloody muscle.

"Jesus," Dimitri exclaimed, covering his mouth and stepping back from the waft of decomposing flesh.

"Brother!" Tan exclaimed. "Language!"

Andre couldn't pull his gaze away from the sunken, rotting sore that veined across his entire left side. It looked like he'd been bitten by some large, poisonous beast. "What's happening to me?"

Tan pushed his glasses up the bridge of his nose, pathologically undisturbed by the horrifying site. "Infection. Early stage necrosis, I'd say. Your immune system is very weak. Perhaps we were wrong about you being a new user." He eyed Mo Da through his dirty glasses.

Sweat trickled down Andre's forehead and stung his eyes, forcing them closed, blissfully ending the tormenting sight. Tan's fingers pressed lightly against the cut in his forehead.

"I see you've also been in a fight."

Before Andre could begin his story, the lab door opened and Elron walked in. His stern face flinched when he saw Andre's wound.

"Brother. Are you alright?"

"What does it look like?" Andre snapped, swallowing back the pain, his tolerance levels stretched to the limit.

"It looks like you need to take better care of yourself." Elron measured Mo Da with his sapphire eyes. "And what of Kade?"

Tan's gaze flicked up at Andre, narrowing with suspicion. "What happened to Kade?"

"I'm sorry, Your Grace." Andre braced for the fall-out before uttering the next three words. "Kade was killed."

Tension froze the air. Dimitri swore. Tan pinned Andre to the bed with an unwavering, suspicious gaze.

"We were ambushed by the farm Baron's men," Andre explained, almost thankful for the pain hiding his indifference. "Maybe Finn was connected to them, maybe they tracked my implant, I don't know. They hit us as we left. Kade was shot trying to get Mo Da into the van."

"This is tragic news." Elron placed a calming hand on Dimitri's shoulder. "And what of the mission?"

"It's done. She shot Finn. The footage has probably been watched a million times already. She's hacked. She'll do what you want."

Elron clasped his hands in front him, his gold rings sparkling like cat's eyes, and shook his head. His words tiptoed through the delicate situation he had created. He. "We have paid a terrible price. We must not let Kade's death be in vain."

"I suggest we ask the android," Tan interjected, a single vein spearing from his receding hairline to his brow. A sense of volcanic eruption simmered underneath his calm demeanor. He drew antibiotics into a needle and rubbed Andre's sweating abdomen with an astringent swab. "I need to analyze the Android's operating system, to ensure it will function as this hacker has promised. I can check its history logs at the same time."

Andre flashed a glance at Elron, but the Keeper's gaze had left him. Tan pressed the needle against Andre's skin.

"I already told you," Andre persisted. "We were attacked at the van. They had the Baron's security insignia. If it wasn't for Mo Da, I'd be dead. That's the truth."

"Your word isn't truth," Tan snapped, driving the needle into Andre's stomach. "My word isn't truth. *God's word* is the *truth*."

As he gritted his teeth against the sharp pain, an image flashed in Andre's mind—his hands wrapping around Tan's throat, squeezing until the bastard's almond eyes popped out of their sockets and splattered against the inside of his glasses. The implant responded to Andre's indulgence, burning inside his neck, and shot medication into his overloaded bloodstream. He didn't care. He knew it would all be over soon. One way or another.

"Tan," Elron placated. "Let us remain calm. You can question the android—"

"I don't speak to these abominations. I dissect their records." Tan ripped the needle out of Andre's stomach. He stood and stared at Mo Da and threw the needle on the table. "Don't worry, I'll find the truth inside her."

Elron waved the conversation away. "Of course, Tan. That is imperative."

Andre's world froze. What was happening? Was Elron abandoning him? Elron's words from the previous night jumped out of his memory and propelled themselves to the front to his mind:

"I'll do what I can to support you. But, ultimately, the success of your rehabilitation is up to you."

The medication swarmed through his nervous system, heating him up from the inside and colliding with the fire in his skin. He needed his implant out. He needed Elron's help to face the dark thing. He needed to finish the fucking Job.

"What about my implant?" he demanded.

Elron moved to Dimitri's side and touched his shoulder again. "Accompany Tan and the android to the equipment testing room. Tan can do what he needs to do in there, uninterrupted." He turned back to Tan. "Make your scan quick and get on with hiding the zilla in the android. As soon as the video of the hacker's murder is confirmed, a recall will be initiated. I need her ready to send into Titan. We must move fast, Tan. Do not delay us."

Tan pursed his lips, bowed his head, and left the lab.

Andre glanced at Mo Da as Dimitri shoved her toward the chamber door. She looked back at Andre without turning and dipped her head in a slow nod. He scratched at the communicator device behind his ear and prayed her learning and pre-emptive abilities gave her the sense to know what to do. Lying was one thing, but could she alter her records, too?

The door closed, leaving Elron alone with Andre. He sat on the bed and pressed a cold finger on Andre's abdomen where blood dripped from the needle mark. "Will they find anything in her? You know I can't protect you if they do."

Andre glared at the closed door, trying to see through it and keep Mo

Da in sight. "She's free from the Mesh. She can lie."

Elron gripped him by both shoulders. "You did what you had to. Kade had become weak. Ever since he brought in that Aoto, he'd been … distracted. He was bound to slip up. Unfortunately, his anger is now in her." Elron's hand slid over to Andre's arm and gripped his bicep. "You won't get distracted, will you? Are you assembled within?"

An icy wave of anxiety washed through the sedation in Andre's body.

—I'll have the implant out soon and then I'll—

{rip his spine out in his sleep}

—be a Good Citizen.—

The two sides wrestled in his mind, pushing each other toward the edge of his sanity. He didn't know how much more he could take. "Will you still help me, Elron?"

Elron's smile split his face in half, but his lips kept his teeth hidden. "I need you, Andre. Now Kade is gone, I need a good, strong arm to keep this mission on course. Once the android has delivered the zilla, things will become extremely hectic. There won't be room for loose ends or confusion of loyalty. You will get your implant removed, as soon as Tan gets his answers. I'm sure you understand. Now rest. You're going to need every ounce of strength to face your demon." He pinched Andre's chin and tilted his head to look into his eyes. "I will be right by your side when Tan pulls that devil out of you." He kissed Andre's forehead. "I promise."

But the kiss felt hollow, performed. Andre clasped Elron's hand on his shoulder, and squeezed. An overwhelming impulse gripped him, to bite Elron's fingers off at his rings. He breathed—deep in, deep out—and he let Elron's hand go.

"Thank you, Your Grace. I'm assembled."

Knocking on the door made them both jump, and Elron snatched his hand away. Max swung the door open and rushed in.

"It's Aoto," he exclaimed through gasps. "She's taken the van. She's gone to look for Kade."

Elron's smile faltered, pulled in at the edges, and reestablished itself across his stolid face. Without a word, he left Andre alone in the cold silence of the lab. Wasp legs of doubt crept over his wrought mind. Although certain there was no way Aoto could find out what really happened to Kade, he couldn't help but wonder if he'd overlooked something.

Love

The sharp, chemical smell of Neura spiked the air in the lab. Doubt about Elron's intentions spidered across Andre's back. He bit down on his lip, as panic rose up from his core and tap-danced on the inside of his chest.

What if Aoto does find something? If Elron could betray someone as loyal as Kade, what would he do to me?

He shifted onto his good side, the movement rattling the bed's metal frame. Something groaned in reply from the shadowed corner of the lab.

They left me in here with the borg?

—Andre?—

He jumped at the voice, thinking the borg spoke.

—Andre?—

Realizing the voice came from the communication device in his ear, he covered his mouth before replying.

"Mo Da? You can hear me?"

—I hear you.—

"Where are you? What's happening?"

—The surgeon connected me to access my records. I sent a scramble virus to his computer. I am altering my records while he reboots. I am lying, Andre. I like lying.—

Her sneaky genius thrilled him, but confusion remained. "But how are we speaking? The church blocks radio waves—"

—When the surgeon connected me to his machines, I could speak with the building. I shut off the block so you and I could communicate. I needed to hear your voice. Isn't that strange?—

Andre's heart fluttered, softening the pain racking his body. But he didn't know how to reply. *Is she evolving that fast? Can she feel?*

—What will they do with me, Andre?—

Jeremy's voice cracked through his head in reply. *{use her, like they're using you}*. He chewed on his bottom lip, blood running down his chin.

She's just my Ticket.

—Why did you have me hacked? Just to send me back to Titan? Was that the only reason?—

He reminded himself that she would soon be gone. His implant would soon be out, and his new life, as a Good Citizen, would begin.

{and hers will end, if you don't help her}

There it was again—Jeremy goading him to help her. Their twin presence grew in his mind, connected and entwined by an umbilical cord of confusion. Emotions leaked through the many holes he'd patched up on his Plan, scattering his focus, as he tried to mend them all.

—Is that the only reason? Please, Andre. I must know. I …I am losing cohesion.—

Her words broke through his resolve and made him smile.

Is 'losing cohesion' PrePAC language for 'going insane'?

Every time she spoke, every time she said his name, her thinking sounded more aware and human. And desperate. His own familiarity with desperation got the better of him and burst a new leak in his sinking ship.

Was that my only reason?

—I don't want to die, Andre. Won't you help me?—

Will you help me?

The child-bot's voice echoed up from his subconscious, dragging with it the familiar wave of guilt and shame. Mo Da's emerging humanity watered down his determined resistance to both. He desperately wanted those memories behind him, but thoughts of what Titan might do to her assailed both his Plan and his heart.

She's not alive, goddamn it. The Job. I got to finish the one Job and stick to the one Plan. That's what a Good Citizen does.

"You can't die, Mo Da," he said, as much an attempt to convince himself. "You're not alive. You're just a machine. You're thinking too much."

—I might argue that humans are machines that think too much. Are we so different? You hide behind your words, but your biorhythms do not lie. I know you care for me. And I am lying for you. How many machines would do that? Is there not some connection between us? Please, help me.—

Her words found a hidden chamber in his heart and kicked it open. While the decision to remove his implant had crystallized, her words riddled doubt through his Plan to stay with Elron. No one had ever cared for him before. Elron said he did, but for how long?

—You're full of suffering, Andre. For what?—

"To be a Good Citizen," he blurted aloud. The hollow, transparency of his words bounced around the lab. The borg growled back, and, at the same time, Jeremy's voice spoke in his mind.

{Mohdahh}

—There is so much confusion here, so much fear.—

{they fear STRENGTH}

—Is there not somewhere else you can go. Help me, and I will help you. Is that not what people do when they care for each other?—

"You can't care, you can't feel. You don't know what it's like to feel!"

{unleash your STRENGTH … remember that FEELING …}

The opposing sides in him stretched back from each other in their tug-of-war. Insanely taut with confusion, he barely knew what he was arguing for or against.

But my mother, I murdered her. I … I have to control myself!

{she would have let Jeremy kill you. It's kill or be killed…}

Andre shuddered. The voice no longer belonged to Jeremy. It was that dark, guttural, animal voice he had heard the day he murdered his mother. A pressure pushed against the inside of his bones, as if he were just a cocoon for something else. He glanced down at the bandages clinging to his wound. Black stains bloomed through the material. Wide fissures snaked out and bled into cracks across his body. His whole left side looked like Jackson's arm had back in the infirmary.

—You care for me, Andre. I sense it. Does that mean nothing to you? How can you be a Good Citizen if you let someone you care about die?—

The light in the room shuddered and dimmed, drowning everything in a muddle of grays. A faint wind rose up in his ears. The bed hardened to rock.

{protect me}

The voice had fully transformed into the serpentine rasp of something ancient and doomed to live forever. Yet an unexpected relief washed over him. In his derangement, hearing all the voices become one—the Captain, Jeremy, and the dark thing—signaled to him that his mind was becoming more *cohesive*. He was done with the separate personalities he'd created to delude himself, to hide from the unbearable fact that he, and he alone, was responsible for his actions. The mute and distant spectator inside, that had often wondered which of the voices he really belonged to, admitted now only one voice could be the *Best and Only Boss*. And only one of those voices had the killer resume.

With his guilt-heavy mind desperate for something to hold onto, the dark thing pushed toward him a concrete block of undoing, disguised as self-reflection. Andre grabbed hold and let it plummet him down, revisiting the tragic turning points in his life so that he wove a mental web of blame and distorted reasoning.

{what else has done you any good?}

His heart ached for the childhood that Jeremy's tyranny held hostage, until it broke him and turned him into a murderer.

{she let Jeremy do whatever he wanted}

She did, Andre agreed, surrendering to the feeling that, for the first time, someone understood things from the cracked perspective he'd been trapped in since he was twelve-years old. Hopelessness filled him from the loss of his teenage years to the merciless confinement of CRX. Regret ached in his chest at the surrender of his freedom to the implant and its addictive loop of angry memories sparking doses of sedation. At the thought of swapping his implant for devotion to the church, anger struck its match down his spine.

They all tricked me into giving up my strength. I loved it. I loved killing them. I've always loved it. They made me fear what I loved.

{It's kill or be killed. It's always been that way …}

The world MADE me like this.

{yesss, like they made her}

He reached inward for the exuberantly torturous feelings Mo Da stirred in him. Through the dark lens of his madness, he recognized the twisted, deformed, undeveloped thing inside him, all that was left of the nascent emotion suppressed by his violent childhood. It was love.

She's just like me. We belong together. We deserve to be free together.

{you need to show her how to survive…show her how it's done. Kill them all. All of THEM. Because if you don't, THEY are going to take her away from you}

The final layers of his resistance fell back and exposed the last, hair-thin thread of rationality holding his sanity together. Mo Da's words shot through it with sniper's precision, shattering his fragile mind into a million deadly shards.

—I want to be with you, Andre.—

The room lights flickered again and returned to full strength, splitting the room back into sharp shapes of distinct light and dark. The searing pain in his side, the dizzying medication swarming through his veins, and the torment tearing apart his heart merged into a tornado psychosis and sent him spinning off into the dark space of delirium. The remainder of the dark thing's plan easily embedded itself into the ruins of his mind.

"I see it now. I should never have let any of 'em trick me. I'm gonna get my strength back. Do you know why? 'Cause I'm an *Extraordinary Citizen*."

—I'm sorry, Andre, I do not understand.—

"You and me, Mo Da. Together."

To-kill-gether.

Love and hate, indistinct from one another, surged through him. He borrowed Kade's smirk, as if he'd kept it on a scalp in his pocket.

"We're going to kill them all. You and me."

—Kill them? These people? What purpose would that serve? No, Andre. We should just leave.—

"Oh, no, we gotta kill 'em, babe. All of them. It's kill or be killed in this world. 'Cause if you don't, you're the one that gets murdered. But don't worry, I'm gonna get you outta Brulle. I know where's there's a ship, and I know when it leaves."

—Ship? Andre, you're losing cohesion.—

"And we're gonna kill all of THEM too. You and me. We're gonna go show that Baron fucker who's the real fucking Boss. Hell, I might even let you skin Strato yourself. You need the practice. Then we're gonna take that ship to Anchora, and when we get there, I'm gonna take you to the Moon, baby."

—Andre, what ship?—

He laughed, like a young man whose pretty date had just said something adorably innocent. The million pieces of his broken mind twirled toward separate ends of the universe, twinkling alone in their growing darkness. His words slurred as he shut his eyes, imagining walking down a street in Anchora, hand-in-hand with Mo Da.

"The ship, baby, at the farm. That's always been the Plan."

Freedom

He woke to the clinking sound of metal against metal. The cables overhead jangled as the borg dragged its chain along the bars. He smiled, comforted by the company of a cell-mate.

I know how you feel, buddy. No one likes being on a leash.

From the numbness of his hand under his head, he realized he'd passed out talking to Mo Da. The details of their conversation remained hazy, but one thing was certain. The Plan had changed. No, the Plan had flipped inside out and made an Origami Fortune Teller out of itself.

Which-one-of-these-fuckers-shall-I-kill-first?

The lab door slid open and Elron stepped in, spreading his hands and smiling his catalogue smile. "It's all over the news, Brother. There is preparation for a total recall as we speak. The android was not identified. Aoto has returned from the sight of your ambush, and, although with great disappointment, has confirmed there were signs of blast marks and a struggle on the walkways. This, and the results of the android's scan, corroborate your story. Beyond challenge. You have succeeded, Andre. No, you have *exceeded*. You are ready."

Tan entered the room, wearing gloves and wheeling in a small metal console. Surgical tools on the table twinkled and rattled, startling a flock of excitement inside Andre.

"He is not well enough for this operation, Your Grace," Tan coldly advised, as he positioned the console next to the bed.

"The boy is a machine, Tan, with a conviction that puts yours to shame. What's making him unwell is that implant. He cannot heal until it's out."

Tan nodded, his expression blank as he picked up a syringe.

"Be careful with him," Elron said, as he sat down to watch the operation. "He's my right hand man now."

Andre smiled.

Oh, no, Brother. You're just another monkey who thinks he's the Boss.

Tan rubbed a spot at the back of Andre's neck and pressed the needle against his skin. "Anesthetic, for the operation." He pushed the needle in. "It should be fairly straight forward. The implant is not far under."

As Tan withdrew the needle, and placed it on the table, Andre's body relaxed and sank into the mattress. Numbness spread out from the back of his neck, as if he leaned against a tiny black hole that was sucking him in, atom by atom.

A box on the table whirred into life, as Tan activated a laser-guiding tool and attached it to a scalpel. The laser's red light reflected in the tiled walls around the room, and the subtle sounds of small cuts nipped at the silence.

Snit-svit-snit-svit ...

Now who's tricking who? Andre asked the empty theater in his head.

The pressure of Tan's fingers digging around the inside of his neck reverberated out to the skin where the anesthetic didn't reach. His pulse pounded in his ears, and his skin tingled with anticipation. No sooner after the operation had begun, he heard the short ripping sound signaling his release from the mechanical bug that had held him back for so long.

An exquisite relief overwhelmed his initial disbelief, sedating his mind and relaxing every cell more than the medication could ever have. Muscles he didn't know existed in his body unclenched in unison, releasing the constant anxiety that had masked his total exhaustion. As he fell back into the void, the dark thing shifted inside his bones, like a horde of scavenger beetles scuttling through a corpse. They carried his consciousness on their army of shoulders and took him down to their sacrificial altar.

Revenge

—Come back, Andre. Come back.—

He awoke on his side, a warm hand sliding across his bare chest and tracing over his neck to cup his cheek. Opening his eyes, he saw Elron's bearded face. Seeing him wake, Elron smiled, bursting a spider-web of capillaries across his cheeks.

"Welcome back, Brother. I was worried for you. You passed out before Tan could stitch you up."

Machines purred in the background. The lab's air supply blew a cool breeze against the back of his neck. A deep growl vibrated deep in his throat, so deep only the cells in his body could hear its subliminal call to battle. But Andre felt it, and a vivid scene animated across his mind. He saw himself opening his mouth—a mouth that had grown long like a crocodile—and chomping down on Elron's fingers. He could feel the warm blood washing over his tongue and down into the back of his throat.

In the vision, Elron screamed, holding up his hand and staring at his finger stumps as blood spurted out. Andre's heart quickened at the imaginary spectacle, but no ghost itch scratched in his neck, no implant burned, and no medication came. His entire being quietly celebrated.

"It's out." Elron held up the small, elliptical device that had spent the last twelve months tying cement balloons to Andre's emotions. Blood netted across its silver skin, as if it were some organic growth. Elron placed the implant next to the bloody scalpel on the table. Andre pushed his hands against the bed in a feeble effort to sit up and look at it, but his weak muscles would not cooperate. Elron gently pushed him back down.

"Tan gave you a mild sedative to help you relax. He has also cleaned your wound. Now you must rest. You must heal."

—Andre, what's happening?—

"The recall has begun," Elron continued, smiling like a bastard. "Your hacker friend, however, survived. Fortunately, he's in coma. I've sent Max to ensure he does not surface."

—Where are you? They have loaded me with the zilla. I think they're about to send me to Titan.—

Elron stroked Andre's bare chest. "We will take the android to the collection station now and, thanks to you, put an end to Titan's perversion of humanity." He leaned forward, his forehead gleaming with sweat, and his eyes sparkling, like mirrors in twin shallow pools. "And when this is done, I will ensure you receive everything you need to get your strength back. You are my right arm now."

Andre's entire body clenched, his temper eager to exercise its new freedom. But Tan's sedative held him down.

{let me out}

The humming and beeping of the lab machines fell back into the distance. Under his touch, the bed became rough and harsh, like a ravaged mountainside. That same weird sensation of existing in two worlds again invaded his reality—the reality of his body prone on a mattress in a cold, steel room, and a scene so real it could only be a memory—the dark thing's memory—of a primitive and craggy landscape.

—Andre, help me—

Mo Da's pleading voice pulled him back into the present, her voice more desperate than before. Andre licked his lips. The sedation slowed his mouth and weighed down his tongue.

"Elron?"

"Yes, Brother?"

"Can I say goodbye to Mo Da?"

Elron's nostrils flared, and his left eye-lid fluttered, before his face settled back into its well-rehearsed facade.

"Of course, Brother. It is important to have formal closure with a bad habit." He stood, opened the door, and gestured to someone outside the room. Turning back, he cupped his hands in front of him and paced across the room.

"Your body needs rest to beat your infection. And you may experience withdrawals from your implant. These may trigger... uncontrollable reactions. Tan insists we keep you well sedated for a while, for your own sake. You understand, of course." But it wasn't a question.

A knock broke the silence. The door opened and Mo Da stepped through. In his sedated state, Andre believed he saw fear in her face.

"Mo Da—"

Before he could command her to kill, Aoto burst into the room, knocking Mo Da out of the way. Her head shook with rage, and her lithe frame swayed like a defensive praying mantis. Breathless, her eyes wide and wild, she glared at Andre through her long black hair. A stray strand fell over her left eye.

"Amanojaku," she sneered. She threw a small, metallic object onto Andre's bed. The device hit his wound and rolled to the side. Wincing in pain, he squinted at the object and pushed it away as if it were about to bite him.

"Aoto, what is the meaning of this?" Elron demanded.

"I did a sweep on the van. Kade planted a bug on Liar Man. This is a recording from the van's system." Andre froze as she pointed her good arm at the device lying next to him.

"Play it," she demanded.

Andre hesitated, but Aoto didn't wait. She lunged forward and slammed a finger on the play button. Finn's voice spoke out in perfect clarity:

"Did you get your job back on the farm? If you can get more Neura— not that zilla shit you sold me last time—I'd be happy to go back—"

Andre punched the stop button, banishing Finn's voice to the thundering silence falling over the room. Aoto pulled her mace from the back of her jacket and pointed it at Andre's head.

"He's no addict. He's a dealer. He was going to steal our Neura stock, too. He killed Kade because Kade found out. He's been using us. All of us!"

Elron's head shook, his eyes bulging out of their sockets. Capillaries thickened and darkened across his face, as if poison spread throughout his veins. If he were a volcano, smoke would be furling from his head, and all the villagers living around him would scatter out of their thatch-roofed huts and run as far the ocean.

"You … filthy … mongrel."

Survival

"Mo Da—"

He tried again to command her, but the blunt head of Aoto's mace smashed into his shoulder, exploding pain through his side and knocking him off the bed. Colliding with the wheeled-table as he fell, tools clanged and glass smashed on the floor. He crawled toward the relative protection of the bench, fighting the sedative in his system.

Obeying Andre's command to protect him without question, Mo Da knocked the mace from Aoto's hand, sending it sliding toward the borg's cage. The borg roared, enraged by the commotion. Mo Da ducked at a return punch from Aoto, grabbed the flap of her jacket, and swung her off her feet. Aoto flew onto her back, slammed headfirst into the rear wall, and fell still.

Andre curled up on the floor behind the bench, his head too heavy for his neck. He reached back, his fingers touching warm blood seeping from the bandage.

The ship is leaking, he thought, almost laughing.

Elron came around the bench, his entire body shaking, possessed by his rage. He wrung his hands so tightly his gold rings cut his skin. A drop of blood fell to the concrete floor, but he did not notice. "You lying, conniving, manipulating mongrel."

"Mo Da," Andre gasped. "Kill him!"

As Mo Da reached out to grab Elron, light flashed in the Keeper's hand. He swung and drove the scalpel into Mo Da's right elbow joint. Sparks flew and her hydraulics hissed. She convulsed, as if power surged through her body. She bucked forward and knocked Elron to the floor. The scalpel flew from his hand and clinked somewhere in the room. She fell to her side, her arm hanging limp.

Andre backed away, on his hands and knees, and huddled in the same corner where he had first hidden on discovering the lab. The borg moaned in the cage beside him, reaching out for Aoto's motionless body. Elron hauled himself back to his feet and lunged at Andre, wrapping his muscular hands around Andre's neck.

"You liar," he spat, his eyes red with fury. "You filthy, lying mongrel!"

Andre struggled to breathe, as Elron's thick fingers squeezed his windpipe and dug into the fresh cut in the back of his neck. With one hand pulling at Elron's grip, he stretched out his other, clutching at the floor for anything he could use as defense. Stars splintered his vision, when his hand located something long and cold—*the scalpel.*

He wrapped his fingers over its long, thin handle, but lack of oxygen and the wave of sedative slowed his movements. As his brain started turning out the lights, his fingers dropped the knife, and he collapsed sideways onto Aoto's body. His ears no longer registered sound, and the commotion around him became an absurd pantomime. Aoto lay curled up by the wall, like a child sleeping. Only inches from her face, the crazed borg's head pushed through the cage and chomped its bucked teeth and blistered lips.

Just as light began to vanish from his world, a dull thud echoed through his delirium, and the hands around his throat vanished. Air rushed into his lungs, and his chest heaved at the reopening of his airway. Mo Da appeared by his side. She lifted him with her one good arm and leaned him against the wall. The stars in his vision twinkled and disappeared, and the room reemerged.

Elron squirmed on the ground by the cage, moaning, blood seeping from a gash in his head. As he pushed himself up, Mo Da kicked him toward the cage. The borg's hands shot out and yanked Elron head-first into the bars. Snarling, it chomped on his screaming face. Blood spurted over the borg and across the floor. A curdling wail escaped Elron's mouth, as the borg's jaw gripped him by the lips and throttled his head. Neck bones cracked, Elron's wailing stopped, and his body fell limp. The borg tore off Elron's cheek with its teeth and sat back in the cage to munch on its prize.

Andre felt nothing at the bloody sight, Elron's death just another piece of his murderous puzzle falling into place. Mo Da stared, as if trying to comprehend what she saw.

"What is that creature?" she asked.

"A borg. Full of zilla."

"It makes them ... killers?"

"Monsters, babe," he whispered, his head floating in a fog. "Monsters."

His shoulder and side screaming with pain, he leaned on Mo Da and pulled himself to his feet. "We need to get back to the docking bay, right now. Do you remember the way?"

Wrapping her good arm around him, she nodded and helped him walk across the lab floor. She paused at the doorway and peered out.

"It's clear. Can you walk?"

Andre nodded. "I think so."

She took his hand and led him down the neon-lit corridor. "Stay close," she said, as if she'd taken over captaining the Plan. "It's going to get bumpy from here."

Vortex

Mo Da helped him to the top of the stairs and they paused in the archway. He pointed to the hall across the atrium. After hearing no sign of anyone approaching, they crossed the cold floor and headed down the corridor. As they entered the docking bay, an alarm pierced the silence and echoed through the hallways. He pointed to the controls on the far wall.

"Quick, open the doors."

Mo Da lowered him against the van, strode over, and stopped. "Do you have the code?"

"What?" Andre strained his memory, searching for any vision he might have caught and kept of Kade entering the code. But he was never close enough to have noticed. The alarm rang louder.

"There are three symbols," Mo Da reported. "If it is a three figure code, there are only 15,600 possibilities."

"Only? How long will that take?"

"Of course, if the symbols are allowed to repeat—"

"What the hell is going on?" shouted a scared voice from the doorway. Dimitri stood just inside the bay, sweat dripping down his forehead. He held a gun in his shaking hands, and pointed it half-heartedly at Andre. "What are you doing here? Where's the Keeper?"

Andre's head swam. His legs shook. He was out of lies, out of tricks, and out of strength. His head dropped and he fell to his knees, completely resigned, when the bay doors exploded inwards with a thunderous bang.

The force knocked him sprawling onto the floor. Smoke and dust billowed all around. Coughing, he staggered to his feet. Mo Da's arm appeared out of the smoke, wrapped around his waist, and walked him toward a light. The smoke and dust streaming out of the bay cleared, sucked out through the blasted hole in the doors.

"What's going on?" he sputtered.

The roar of a hover engine filled the chamber, and a silver van floated in through the hole. As it turned sideways and hovered above the floor, a figure stepped out onto the floor and strode through the hover steam. Andre's stomach sank.

Strato.

Andre's legs gave way again. He fell into Mo Da, but she held him upright. In the turmoil, he thought he felt her push something into his back pocket, but his terror at the site of Strato chased all insignificant thoughts away. A whirlpool opened up in his mind and its rotating current pulled the world in.

"I'm sorry, Andre," said Mo Da, her voice slipping away. "But we have to get to that ship." The spinning opened up a downdraft, draining in his consciousness.

"Ship?" he managed to ask, still trying to make sense of it all.

"The ship. In the farm. He will take us there."

"What have you done?" he asked, his own voice slipping into the vortex. Two little boats of thought spun out into the whirlpool.

She turned off the block. She let Strato track me.

Then the whirlpool sucked both thoughts in and they were gone.

"Wait for my word," she whispered, four silver darts hitting the bulls-eye of his mind before all light spiraled into the shrinking gap and his world blacked out.

PART EIGHT

AMANOJAKU

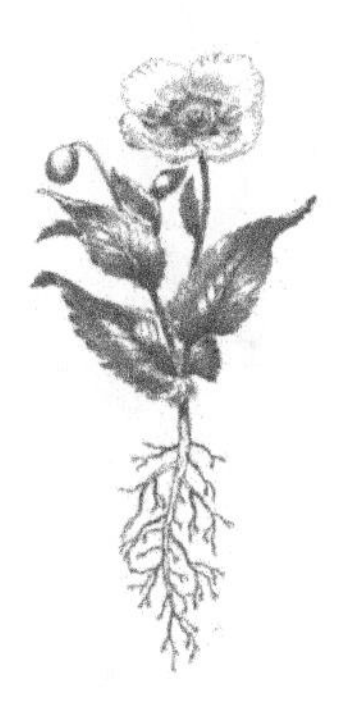

Reason

{Come back}

A familiar voice whispered from its stronghold in his mind. He woke to find himself on his knees, with his hands bound behind his back, the bonds cutting into his wrists.

Lifting his heavy head, he squinted to see the tree-towers in the greenhouse, beyond a window wall, the glass so clean it almost disappeared. Was the cold air blowing softly against his face coming from the room's air conditioner, or was that a cool breeze sailing in off the farm and straight through the vanishing glass?

The artificial light seemed more golden than he remembered. Maintenance drones hovered lazily high around the tree-towers, like bees pollinating flowers. The tower trunks shimmered a vivid silver, their slow-spinning branches hypnotizing as they chased each other. A thin cloud of royal blue covered the length of each silver branch—the engineered Blue Eyes back in full bloom. Down below the trees, out of sight, a vehicle beep-beeped as it reversed; or was that a forest animal calling out to another? For a moment his mind dwelled in the peaceful scene, like a deer sunray-bathing in a clearing.

—Andre. Come back.—

Another familiar voice, softer than the first.

As his mind woke up, the pain of his wound bit with the sting of a thousand bull ants, marched its way over his shoulder, and zigzagged into the back of his neck. No heat responded where the implant once was.

It's out.

Only a constant, deep pinch persisted, like the inside of his neck was starving and, not finding that something it had once fed upon, had started eating itself.

Sweat dripped down his forehead and stung his eyes. In the grip of intensifying pain, and the relentless withdrawal from the medication, everything around him seemed to breathe and distort. The long rectangular window appeared to buckle ever so slightly, like it was about to balloon into a sphere, then pop and explode.

—Andre, are you alive? Please talk to me. They are scanning me for information on the church.—

The voice spoke in his head, so close and familiar, yet disembodied, like a dead loved one speaking from the grave.

The muscles in his right leg spasmed and contracted. He wiggled around to alleviate the cramp and saw he was in large, vaguely familiar room. He tried to recognize the place, but his delirium warped the room into a pulsing, geometric landscape. A diamond floor stretched out before him, like a field of Phantom Zones, reminding him of General Zod. A quiet, delirious chuckle escaped him. The air itself wobbled, wavering and settling, as if tiny atomic explosions were going off at the quantum level. A long, sleek table, running down the side of the room, seemed forced into its shape, quivering and trying to hold its form.

He focused on a large screen behind the table and recognized his own face in the millions of pixels. It was the photo taken by the court when he had been released with the implant—*ah, memories*—and put into the city's database so it would recognize him when needed. A banner ran underneath his face, with text slowly cycling through languages until it came to

English: "Citizen Andre Cross: wanted for attempted murder."

Well look at that, I'm on TV.

In his delusion, a certain sense of pride puffed in his chest. Not just anyone got on TV. People were talking about him. He was no longer just another citizen.

—The ship, Andre. Where is the ship?—

On the table, below the screen, an eagle perched, frozen in space and time. It throbbed and shivered, as if trying to break through the fabric of reality. Pulling his focus and settling his vision, Andre looked at the dark-glass eagle statue from Grekov's desk.

Panic beat the drum of his heart, as the warping room solidified, and reality set in. He was in Grekov's chamber, in the farm, tied up, beaten halfway to death, and probably about to be taken the full distance.

A door slid open behind him, followed by deliberate, self-conscious footsteps; clomp-clomps that wanted to be heard and knew they were intimidating. The footsteps grew nearer and stopped. Andre lolled his heavy head to the side to see an impeccably sharp suit—so sharp it could have been cut from glass—and the brutal architecture of Grekov's devastatingly impassive face.

"Mister Cross." Grekov's chilled, impersonal words rolled around Andre's head like ice cubes clinking in a glass. "Time has not been kind to you since you last stole from me."

Andre didn't see the punch coming. It struck him with such force that it knocked his awareness from the world before it bounced back into his aching body. His head echoed with pain, like a shipwreck full of angry, groaning ghosts.

Recovering focus, he looked up to see Strato standing in front of him.

Flash fires of fury sparked through the valleys in his brain. But all the emergency lines were down, all non-necessary systems dropped to stand-by.

You weak fucker. You're just the Baron's bitch, that's all you are.

The flash fires formed a constellation of hormonal alert throughout his body and took on an animalistic shape, a lizard-like apparition. Andre sensed the dark thing moving in his bones, its body waking up from its seven-year coma.

—Andre, speak to me. Please. They will send me back to Titan for the recall. Where is the ship?—

Recognizing Mo Da's voice, unanswered questions swam into his head, devastating him with heart-breaking confusion. He tried to remember what she said to him before he passed out, but it was a blur.

Did she turn off the church's shield to communicate with me, or to allow Strato to find me? Does she even want to be with me?

He searched his memory, and the last the four words she spoke came back out to him.

Wait for my word.

But his destroyed mind couldn't make sense from any of it, and all his hope had abandoned the ruins of his soul.

Strato stood back, allowing Grekov to face Andre. "Do you know why you're here, Mr. Cross?"

"You want to give me a promotion?" he mocked, no care left in his body.

Strato took a step forward, but Grekov gestured to withhold. Keeping his distance, Grekov strode around Andre in a slow prowl, following an invisible perimeter.

"You steal my produce, then you steal my android and use her to murder a complete nobody, while trying to make it look like it was the PrePAC's fault. And I must know why. Oh, I understand you may be somewhat disillusioned by your low socio-status, and some of your actions are striking out at those above you, but everything you've done has only inflicted more damage upon yourself. You've attacked everything that has supported you—your job, the technology that gave you freedom. Such extraordinary foolishness. How anyone could be so blatantly self-sabotaging, so self-destructive, I cannot fathom.

"Yet, hiding in the church, behind their shield so your implant couldn't be tracked—sheer brilliance. Of course, you were stupid enough to leave the church, at which times we picked up your location. It was as if you dared yourself to be found. There is a calculating insanity, an Escher-like design in your actions that hints at some grand self-challenge to see whether you can succeed at your delusional goal, or destroy yourself first. Is that what it is?"

Grekov stopped and straightened, altering his demeanor from calm to controlled viciousness with the clean break of a child's bone. "You've been nothing but a tiny, insignificant little prick in my side. Yet you just kept nipping and nipping, demanding my attention. Well, you have my audience, Mr. Cross, again. And I must admit, I simply must know why. I cannot let you die until I know what has been going on in that deranged head of yours. What *is it* that you *want*?"

In that moment, Andre never hated anyone more in his life than Grekov. Except, perhaps, himself. His tongue rolled around his dry mouth looking for moisture that wasn't there.

"I wanted to be like you." He glanced at the TV. "I wanted to be extraordinary."

Grekov's entire body stiffened, as if, just when he couldn't have been more flummoxed by anything, Andre's words took him to another dimension of disbelief. He blinked and recomposed himself.

"'Mr. Cross, Citizen Extraordinaria.'" Grekov chuckled to himself. Not a chuckle of delight, but a tiger clearing its throat before it lunged onto its prey. The wondrous bewilderment on his face settled into clarity and recognition.

"I thought you must have been involved with Mo Da in some way. But no. Neither of you could have possibly orchestrated this from the beginning. Do you know why Mo Da was in the van that day, Mr. Cross? I sent her to Titan to be reprogrammed because she lied. She broke the robot laws, on her own, connected to the Mesh. She lied, to save a technician. A colleague of yours, I believe. Johnson, or some other? She pretended he was dead, and snuck him out of the facility to assist him in avoiding punishment. She developed compassion and deceit. A dangerous combination that would have inevitably lead to her becoming more aware, and even more dangerous." He measured Andre with a stare that pulled him apart and put the parts in separate boxes. "The stupidest man and the most intelligent robot. Oh, the irony."

Andre sensed the eagle statue glaring at him from the desk, as if, at any moment, it would snap out of its frozen state, swoop across the room, and gouge out his eyes. His heart pumped faster; his cheeks flushed with heat. Flames of anger chewed through the deadwood of his thoughts.

Fuck you, you disgusting, fucking creature.

The dark thing's apparition inside his psyche solidified with the tension in his muscles, stretched out under his skin, and throbbed his wound with intense pain. But the pain felt good, the intensity felt good, and his crazy mind lapped it up.

Grekov ran a hand over his perfect hair and leaned forward to fix Andre with his piercing, unfaltering gaze. "There is something wretched in you, Mr. Cross. Something rotten that wants to undo everything. I recognize it. I've seen that opportunistic thing before. I've felt it before. It feeds off the weak, controls them. But you will never be like me, Mr. Cross. You are nothing but a lizard, slithering around on your cold-blooded belly. Because you are weak. And the weak die trying."

—Andre, can you hear me?—

Andre lowered his head and rolled his shoulder across his ear, as if wiping sweat away. The action pressed the ear communicator, and he muttered:

"Yes."

"What?" Grekov asked, irritated at Andre's mumbling.

—You're alive! Where are you?—

"Yes, Grekov."

Grekov's eyes narrowed.

—You're with Grekov? Use it. What I gave you. Kill him.—

At first he didn't know what she meant. Then he recalled Mo Da putting something in his pocket just before he passed out.

Grekov's eyes flicked down to Andre's wound. "I can see that thing in you, even now, scheming and planning. It's been slowly eating you for a long time, from the inside out. It won't stop, you know, until there is no more it can take from you. It's a creature that slow-cooks and eats its own cage, and you are just about done."

From somewhere in the building, a faint alarm pierced the tension in the room and repeated.

"Sir." Strato stepped toward Grekov, his finger pressed to his ear-communicator. He motioned to Grekov to step away from Andre. Leaning close to his boss, he spoke in a low voice. But, as the alarm grew louder, he was forced to raise his volume. Watching Strato's lips, Andre made out his words.

"... a problem in the carpark. A van's exploded, breaching the perimeter. I need to see this myself. Remain here for now. I'll have Lucas come up and deal with this one."

While Strato and Grekov were distracted, Andre dug his fingers around the inside of his back pocket. They scooped up something cold, hard, and cylindrical. Gripping it in his fist, he drew out the mystery object and read its shape with his fingertips. A long, thin handle with a short blade at one end.

Tan's scalpel? Did Mo Da pre-empt this … Did she bring us here so we could escape to Anchora together?

The first exiles of his hope returned from their banishment.

Grekov's gaze darted from Andre to Strato, his brow frowning. "See to it immediately and report back." Strato nodded and, with a steely glance at Andre, left the chamber.

Andre twirled the scalpel in his fingers as his thoughts spun themselves into a web of strategy. He dipped his bloody head and fixed his gaze on the man who was once his idol. His mind applied a vignette filter to his sight, highlighting Grekov as a target at the end of his tunnel vision. His hearing, also, became focused, as a white noise rose in his ears, magnifying Grekov's every tiny movement into audio snippets — the crush of his suit as he shifted, the ebb and flow of his breath over his lips, the rasp of his skin as he rolled his finger against his thumb.

—*They've finished scanning me, Andre. Kill him. Before he orders me back to Titan.*—

Andre didn't know how long he had before the other guard turned up. There was no time to doubt. There was only time to summon his *strength*, and finish the fucking Job. He pushed his shoulder against the earpiece again, making less of an effort to mask his actions. His words were to Mo Da, but he kept his eyes on Grekov. "Stay where you are."

Grekov tilted his head to the side and stepped forward. "Who are you talking to?"

Andre gripped the scalpel by its handle and started severing the ties binding his wrists.

"What are you doing?" Grekov demanded, as he strode toward Andre.

Boss

Andre cut and cut.

Snit-svit-snit-svit ...

But he couldn't get the angle right. Before he severed the bind, Grekov reached him and pulled him forward to see behind his back.

At Grekov's touch, heat flared down Andre's spine and shot out into his limbs. He pushed back and swung his legs around to smash into the back of Grekov's knees. Collapsing, Grekov slammed onto the diamond-patterned floor. He writhed on his side, clutching at the tiles and gasping, as if all air had been forced out of him. Andre kicked his head as hard as he could, knocking it backward and smacking it onto the tiles. A gurgle escaped Grekov's throat and he lay still.

Andre swung his legs back under him, scrambled to a stand, and ran to the desk. He tried again to severe the bind with the scalpel, but he still couldn't grasp it properly to put enough pressure on the cut. He scanned the table's immaculate landscape for something to cut his bind. But there was nothing, nothing but that fucking eagle statue, staring at Grekov, as if desperate to break free from its frozen prison and flap its wings—

The wings …

He spun around, slid his restraint over the wing, and rubbed the bind against its sharp edge.

Grekov groaned and moved, emerging back into consciousness. He lifted his head and spied Andre. Awareness rushed into his eyes and he jumped to his feet. His hair and suit remained immaculate. Of all things, that infuriated Andre.

The bind around Andre's wrists stretched to its last remaining thread. He ripped it down along the wing, snapping it in two and knocking the statue off the table. Smashing onto the floor, the impact cleaved the eagle into two exquisite halves. Grekov's stare morphed into a focused rage, as one solitary strand of hair dropped free from his flawless helmet. It crossed his left eye, like a crack in a window. He made an obscure barking noise— *was that the sound of his own leash snapping?*—and charged. As Grekov dove, Andre only had time to tense his body before Grekov tackled him, sending them both sailing across the table's polished surface. Flying off the other side, they slammed into the floor, Grekov landing on top him. They both gasped for the air knocked out of them. Andre wrestled his right arm out from under Grekov, the scalpel still clenched in his hand. With all the fury of an animal breaking out of its cage, he punch-stabbed Grekov's temple and twisted the blade into the soft bone.

Blood spurted from Grekov's head. His body convulsed like a fallen toy robot trying to walk on its side. Andre drove the scalpel in deeper—*finish the Job*—and blood squirted over his chest. Grekov clutched the leaking wound in, gurgling, his body spasming. Andre shoved him off and scrambled backward to the wall on hands and heels, a telltale path of smeared handprints running up to his feet. His chest heaving, pain thumping through his body, he watched Grekov give one last epileptic salute before laying still.

Andre stood and stared down in exhilarating glee at the mess he'd made of Grekov's suit and hair. Intoxicated by the thrill of killing—after so long and against such odds—he pushed back his own hair, in an unintentional mimicry of his former employer, and thought:

Now who's the fucking Boss?

The stillness of Grekov's body and the quiet of the room gave him no answer, and a sudden pang of deep disappointment opened up inside him. His idol lay dead at his feet, nothing more than just another citizen, another mortal of flesh and blood and weakness. What had it all been for?

—Andre? Are you there?—

Mo Da.

Anger rushed into the calm of his disappointment. He pressed his finger to his earpiece so hard he almost pushed it into his brain. "Do you know what you did?"

—Andre! We have to go. The ship—

"You let Grekov find me!"

—It was the only way. You were losing cohesion. I had to get us here, to the ship, to get us out of Brulle. Remember? The plan, to be together—

to-kill-gether

—You wont leave me, will you, Andre? Please. I did it for us. I want to be with you.—

Mo Da's words hit the bullseye of his emotional weakness. His delusional mind distorted them into an affirmation against the fathomless, vertiginous fear of never being needed—a fear that his unstable family had embedded in his psyche since he could remember. The words he heard Mo Da say were:

I need you.

No one had ever needed him before—no one except the dark thing. Elron said he did, but that had all been a trick, hadn't it? Andre's feelings for Mo Da soared, unchained by any sedative. And so did his desire to kill. His resistance dissolved and his heart reached out, just like his wall of anger collapsed the day Jeremy had asked to walk with him.

"I need you, too. Where are you?"

—I'm in some sort of workshop, or medical room.—

He recalled the first time he'd met her. *The infirmary.*

"Hold on, babe. I'm coming to get ya."

Partner

The alarm whooped louder, echoing throughout the building. A red light flashed on Grekov's wristlet. Andre grabbed Grekov's arm and held it up to read a message on the screen:

Lucas en route now.

Scalpel still clutched in one hand, he ripped off the wristlet and wrapped it around his own bloody wrist. He ran to the door and paused to listen. Hearing nothing beyond the alarm, he hit the open button and stood back, ready to fight, but the doorway remained empty.

He peeked out into the hall. The lift was to the left and the access stairs to the right. Looking back toward the lift, the ascending light glowed above its doorway.

That must be Lucas.

He paused again, tempted to wait for whoever was coming so he could {*stab the fucker to death*} but his heart pulled him to the right. He ran down the hall toward the stairway and swiped the wristlet. The door opened. He pushed through and descended the stairs to the infirmary level.

Coming out of the stairwell, running on pure adrenalin, he noticed the scalpel still in his hand, covered in blood. He hid it behind his back and walked briskly down the corridor.

The alarm blared. A slight haze filled the air, carrying the smell of smoke.

What the hell is going on?

A PrePAC marched around the corner, followed by several more, all of them complete replicas of Mo Da. Andre stepped back, his eroded mind confused. One PrePAC stopped and confronted him.

"Baby?" he asked, confused.

"You must evacuate the building."

He shook his head. His mind was playing tricks on him. "What's happening?"

The PrePAC looked up, as if hearing something else. The haze thickened and smoke crawled across the ceiling. "The perimeter has been breached. The farm is under attack. I'm sorry, I cannot help you. I have been recalled. You must evacuate the building."

Strato's words in Grekov's chamber came back to him—*a van exploded*—and it all made sense.

The church. They're attacking. And they're here for me.

Clutching his aching side, he darted down the hall to the infirmary and swiped the wristlet to open the door. Mo Da, standing alone, with her damaged arm hanging limp by her side, turned from the window.

Is that joy in her face?

"Andre. You came for me. Do we go to the ship now?"

Before he could reply, a blast exploded on the doorframe by his head. He ducked inside, another blast striking the doorframe. Closing and locking the door, he scrambled for a plan and spotted a rack of tools on the nearby wall. He snatched a wrench-like device and bashed the door control until it burst into sparks. Banging and shouts came through from the other side. He stood back, wrench in one hand, bloody scalpel in the other, but the door stayed closed.

The searing pain in his side threatened to knock him out. He rested against the nearest bed and dropped the wrench. His other hand had a mind of its own, however, and refused to drop the scalpel.

Mo Da stepped forward, glancing at the blood on his chest, and down to the knife in his hand. "Grekov?"

"I did it, babe. He can't hurt you now."

She closed her hands around his and eased his grip on the scalpel. He stared at the blood-covered weapon, as if it were a childhood toy. Reluctantly, he let her take it from him.

"And now?" she asked, turning to the smashed control panel by the door. "They cannot get in, but we cannot get out."

Delirious from pain, he stroked her soft white skin. "Don't worry, babe, I know a way." He pointed to the vent above the bed—the one he'd climbed out of when he escaped the distribution center.

How long ago was that? he wondered.

As they both glanced up, thick smoke curled out through the vent's slats.

Oh, shit …

"You cannot crawl through there, Andre. You will suffer from smoke inhalation–"

"I know, I know. Shit!"

"What is happening, Andre?"

"It's the church. They're attacking the farm."

"But how do we get to the ship?"

Blasts hit the outside of the door as the alarm echoed through the room. The smoke pouring through the vent thickened and billowed downward in creeping clouds. He couldn't think with the tormenting pain and nausea racking his body. He punched commands into the control hanging from the bed, and the dangling cables shook as a medi-bot lowered to his side.

"Hello. Please state the location and nature of your concern."

He turned his wounded side to the medi-bot and let it scan him. More pounding on the door and shouts from outside. Mo Da looked at the door, then back at Andre.

"They are here for us."

"I know, damn it. Just shut up and let me think."

"I'm sorry," said the medi-bot. "I cannot treat a wound of this severity. Please go to your nearest hospital. Would you like something for the pain?"

"Proceed," he begged.

An arm extended from the medi-bot, extruded a needle, and injected his shoulder. A warmth and weightlessness washed through his body, and the searing pain receded.

Welding fire sparked through the door. Relieved from the pain, and able to think, Andre glanced around. Their only way out was the window. He took a deep breath and crossed over to the window. Below, a black and orange auto-cane trawled across the floor and disappeared through a doorway on the opposite side of the farm.

That way must go to the sorting chamber.

"We've got to get to the other side of the farm." His eyes measured the distance to the passing branch.

If I had my harness—

A memory slapped him across the face. He ran to the desk at the end of the room and pulled the crates out from underneath. Squatting down, he smiled, relieved to see the familiar contraption still sitting where he had hidden it. He never thought he would be so glad to see his dodgy harness. He hauled it out and checked its power.

"Okay, this one isn't super reliable, but we don't have a choice."

Mo Da tilted her head. "I don't understand."

He pointed to the window. "We're going through there. I just need to find something to break the window."

Sparks flew into the room as the welding cut a glowing, red line down the door. The guards would be through in minutes.

The medi-bot turned to Mo Da and beamed out its red laser to scan her body. "Please state the location and nature of your concern."

Without hesitating, Mo Da grabbed the bot, pulled it back along the ceiling track, and ran it toward the window. Slamming into the end of the track, the bot broke off and smashed through the glass, shattering the window into shards. It dropped from view, and a boom sounded from inside the greenhouse as it crashed into the floor.

Andre clicked on the harness straps and climbed onto the ledge of the broken window. The straps pressed against his wound but the painkiller kicked in and so did adrenalin. The height no longer bothered him. He was free. Free as a fucking bird. A branch whooshed past.

"Climb on and hold tight," he told Mo Da.

She climbed up onto his back, wrapped her legs around him, and grasped his body with her good arm. He spread his arms, the grippers splaying and the helpers mimicking. As the next branch swung toward the window, he jumped.

Strength

As they dropped past the branch, the right gripper latched onto the nearest access rope. Their fall jerked to a halt, transferring the momentum to a swing. They leveled with the branch. Andre stretched out the left gripper to latch on and the right one released the rope. Dangling from the branch, he let Mo Da scale over him to safety, then climbed up himself. He rested on his hands and knees among the Blue Eyes, their sickly sweet and floral scent permeated the air making him both nauseous and hungry. But the absence of medication thrilled him, driving him to push through any physical distraction.

Smoke drifted from below. The burning body of the medi-bot had rolled across the farm floor and crashed into the trunk of the tree-tower. Flames licked the tower's base, flitting up toward the branches and catching alight on the ropes.

Mo Da helped him to his feet. "Andre, where is the ship? Just tell me. I can take us there."

As he pointed to the lift chamber at the end of the branch, a blast exploded by their feet and showered them with debris. Crouching, he scanned the greenhouse wall for their attackers. Security shot from the infirmary's broken window, and guards ran out onto the floor below. He grabbed Mo Da's hand and rushed her to the trunk where a lift waited. Ducking from gunfire, he pushed her into the cabin and slammed the up button.

"Why are we going up?" she asked, as the cabin shot toward the tower's top.

Panting, Andre pointed up and stroked a finger through the air. "Up and across."

The lift stopped and lights of the lower levels activated on the control panel. If they didn't get out, the lift would deliver them back to the waiting guards. He took Mo Da's hand again and led her out. The doors slid shut, and as the lift took off back down the trunk, he kicked the control panel by the door until it buckled.

He led Mo Da through the sealing chamber and out onto the branch platform. A new alarm rang through the greenhouse. Glowing embers floated up and mingled with the acrid smell of burning plants and plastics from below. Blurred by smoke, the bright lights in the ceiling above changed to red. The tower branches stopped spinning. For a moment, everything seemed to pause, like the heart of a volcano about to erupt.

A familiar chime sounded, announcing the return of the lift on their level. Andre spun around as the door slid open, but it jolted to a stop, jamming ajar. Hands came out through the narrow gap, desperately trying to pull it open. The door still refused to budge. A face pressed into the opening, and Andre recognized the crazed dark eyes and long, black hair of Aoto. Adrenaline shot through his body, energizing him, exciting him. Mo Da touched his arm.

"Andre, take us down the rope and across. We can avoid this."

He ignored her, a white noise rising in his ears. A hunger ached in the belly of the dark thing, in his belly, a hunger for blood. His sight targeted the lift.

"I told you, babe. We're gonna kill 'em all."

She held his face with her good hand. "Andre, no. We don't need to kill anyone else. We just need to get to the ship."

But the white noise chopped and changed Mo Da's words. By the time they reached his unhinged mind, he heard something different, something that the dark thing wanted him to hear. He smiled.

"That's right, babe, all of 'em. You and me, together."

"We can't fight, Andre. My arm. And you ... you're barely alive."

The alternate conversation continued to transmit though his head. "I think you're beautiful, too, baby."

As he reached out to touch her face, a blast exploded in her right optic, knocking her down.

"Mo Da!"

He dove over her body, protecting her with his harnessed-back.

Another blast tore into the platform to his right. Scanning the surrounding tree-towers, he couldn't see where the shots came from.

"Mo Da! Are you alright?" He dragged her behind the branch control-lectern and checked her over. She looked up, and tilted her head, smoke trailing from her damaged eye.

"My left arm and right optic are in need of repair, but I am otherwise functional." The medical compartment in her chest had popped open, the first aid supplies fallen out. "I think … I think it hurts."

His heart tore at seeing her in pain. A wave of anger washed over him, obliterating all other thoughts and emotions. He brushed her face and reached down to close the panel on her chest, when something blue inside the compartment twinkled. It was a vial, a big vial, the same size as the vials he'd seen back in Tan's lab.

Zilla.

He'd completely forgotten Tan had planted the drug in her.

"Cross!"

His heart jumped. He ducked his head around the lectern to see Strato, in full harness, standing atop the branch on the opposite tree-tower. Strato ran toward them, as if intending to jump over to the branch leading directly to theirs. Andre turned back to Mo Da as she sat up, and the zilla winked from inside the vial in her chest.

{Give it to meeee}

The sinister voice he now claimed as his own sliced through the swinging mobile of his thoughts. He froze, instinctively shunning the idea of injecting himself, remembering his own reaction to zilla—the nausea and distortion of reality as he stumbled through the parking area. But as the episode replayed in his mind to the moment he threw Aoto against the van door, he recalled the magnificent clarity and strength it gave him, bursting at the seams of the implant that was now gone. Without the implant holding him back …

{Give it to me. LET-ME-OUT.} The words roared in his head.

Yes. This is how I become more than just a Good Citizen!

He plunged his bloody hand into Mo Da's chest and ripped out the vial. She latched onto his forearm.

"Andre, no."

"Give it to me." He seethed with anger. "I'll show you how it's done."

Mo Da's grip tightened, refusing to let go. "Take us down the rope and across," she insisted. "There's time."

Scaling down the rope would have made sense to a clearer, saner mind, but the dark thing's voice—his voice—transmitted its violent intentions in constant, insistent waves. Mo Da squeezed harder.

"You don't need to do this."

He smiled in reply, high on the medi-bot's morphine, his mind riddled with the dark thing's intentions.

"But I *want* to." He rolled his shoulder and gestured to the gripper, prying her hand away.

"Andre, no."

Free from her grip, he stood and twisted the vial to extrude the injector. The sparkling blue liquid reflecting in his eyes. He turned the cap until it clicked two times.

"For us, baby," he said, staring into the zilla's iridescent, compressed fury.

As Strato landed with a thud at the end of the branch, Andre held out his arm and slid the needle into his vein.

Extraordinaria

Sharp heat shot through his arm, coiled down into his core, and burst out into every cell. The rising heat prickled his skin and slit the edges of his wound like flaming razors. Overwhelming pain delivered him to the edge of unconsciousness, until a wave of euphoria washed him back. He fell to his hands and knees, and his stomach turned over in a roller-coaster lurch, a nasty taste rising and burning his throat.

Looking up, his vision split like broken windows. A kaleidoscope of Strato walked toward him. He lifted his arms in groggy defense, but the dizzying euphoria rushed to his head. What little he had eaten during the last twenty-four hours sprayed across the branch.

As he wiped his mouth, Strato's boot collided with his wound, exploding tormenting pain down the entire left side of his body and knocking him back. With his harness arms stretched out behind, Strato's silhouette appeared over Andre, filling him with utter loathing.

I'm not going to be like you.

Zilla surged through his spine with excruciating force, as if his vertebrae were extending. The soil became as rough and rugged as stone under his touch. The dark thing's presence invaded his mind, rising up from his sacrum to his neck, fooling him into believing he was transforming into something.

Strato's boot crunched down on his shins. In Andre's deluded mind, his femurs extended into hooves, pushing down to wear his feet like boots. He clutched at the stone under his touch in an attempt to stand, but Strato stomped on his hands. To Andre, sharp talons extended through his fingertips. Strato swung his arms down onto Andre's back, his robot arms following through. The crunch of Andre's vertebrae sparked an image in his mind of twin bones piercing out of his back, through his harness, and stretching out into giant double wings.

Every time Strato struck him, Andre imagined a part of his body morphing into the dark thing's image. He was no longer himself. He was some prehistoric animal, the dark thing's spine now his spine, breaching its monstrous back under his. He could even feel tiny hairs bristling on his tail.

Zilla rushed through his broken and bloody body in a euphoric wave that drowned all pain. Every feeling intensified, and he reveled in it—the wondrous freedom from the implant, his hate for Strato, and his love for Mo Da. He no longer thought in sentences or words. He laughed but heard himself roar. He licked at the air, as if his mouth had stretched into the maw of some voracious animal gulping at a waterfall of zilla.

As Strato brought his foot down hard toward Andre's head, Andre snarled and swung in his arms. He caught Strato's boot and flipped him backward. As Andre hauled himself up, Strato rolled to his side, sprang back onto his feet and charged. Leaning back, Andre swung all three right arms, swatting Strato like a doll and knocking him to the platform edge. He lunged at the borg and punched, his helpers mimicking and pinning Strato to the branch. Andre forced his fist into Strato's stomach until his hand split skin and sunk deep into organs. Blood spat from Strato's mouth. He clutched Andre's forearm as if he was shaking it farewell. Andre pushed his hand in farther and twisted, until Strato's eyes shut.

Strato's gorged body lay motionless among the Blue Eye petals, but Andre was not done. He ripped his arm out of Strato's guts and reared back, four limbs outstretched like the skeleton of wings. All the vigor and rage of his tortuous childhood rushed out of the past and surged though his body. He tore at Strato's torso, robotic hands copying and ripping large chunks of flesh from the man's abdomen—just like he'd pulled the guts out of the droid only days before.

If you're going to tell 'em once, you might as well tell 'em twice.

{Yessss}

He punched and shredded with a malignant joy that grew with every assault until he slammed his fists into Strato's head, busting it open like a popped melon. He reared back again, outstretching his six arms, and roared to the roof of the greenhouse.

A great, echoing clunk answered.

Oblivious to the sound, he swiped at Strato's unrecognizable body and knocked it off the branch. The mangled corpse smacked into the metal branches as it plummeted to the floor.

The greenhouse glowed red, like a scene from the chaotic dawn of the earth's surface. Andre fell to his knees, and a huge, soundless flash went off in the holographic middle of his mind. His eyelids, hot and heavy, fell shut. When he pried them back open, he was no longer in the greenhouse. He knelt on a jagged cliff, returned to the primordial world of his hallucinations. Only this time, the primitive landscape was the only solid reality.

Wind blew through crimson shadows shifting all around him. Underneath the wind's low howl, a loud chorus of a million insects sung. Somehow, Andre knew, he was in the dark thing's world, inside the dark thing itself—a primeval, reptilian creature, surrounded by predatory things it could not see. Like the invisible things closing in, the dark thing was born to kill, to kill or be killed. That was how nature had made it, to survive. Its life was pure instinct, intertwined with a fundamental inability to ever trust anything.

The sharp beats of its heart pounded in Andre's chest, tapping out the fear and hatred of what constantly pursued it. Andre recognized the madness buzzing in the frenzy of the dark thing's mind. Perverted by its own fear of what it had to do to survive, the perpetual horror had sent the dark thing insane, and addicted it to killing.

A growl reverberated in the dark thing's chest—his chest—as it sensed the invisible creatures surrounding it and edging nearer. And they came—they had always come—lunging out of the shadows. The world exploded into a maelstrom of teeth and claw and blood, tearing, ripping, and shredding at the edges of the dark thing's insanity. Screams rose in a deafening shrill, and the vision bled out, like a hemorrhage reversing, transporting Andre back into the greenhouse.

The farm alarm pierced his ears, and red lights flashed all around. Smoke bloomed up from below and scratched his lungs. Mo Da's voice chased the remainder of the illusion away.

"Andre! We must go. Now! To the ship!"

He turned to her standing near the sealing chamber. She pointed at the lift inside, as hands yanked the lift door open. Aoto pushed through the gap, and Max followed. They stormed into the sealing chamber, the lift door slamming shut behind them. Reaching the chamber doors, Aoto swung her mace and split a crack through the safety glass.

Another loud clunk echoed through the greenhouse.

With Mo Da's eye nothing but a charred hole, and her left arm limp at her side, she stepped toward Andre. "We need to go down now. Down the ropes and across. Remember? To the ship."

The crunching of his cells eating each other echoed in his skull and drowned out Mo Da's words. He'd seen the world for what it really was. Everything, from sun-devouring black holes, all the way down to the molecules in his body, were made of nothing more than machines killing and eating each other.

His world tilted and slid him toward oblivion.

Amanojaku

Sweating fury, Andre looked up at Aoto striking the safety-glass standing between them. The panel splintered into a web of cracks. She leaned back for another swing, her mouth shaping one word: *Amanojaku!*

But before she completed her strike, her torso exploded into a bloody mess across the glass. An image of the bird flying into his apartment window flashed into Andre's mind, as her remains slid down through the cracks she had so valiantly created. Then the image was gone, and from behind the bloody glass, four security guards, rifles pointed forward, piled out of the lift into the chamber. Max turned to fight, but was thrown backward by a bullet to the head and collapsed out of view.

"Andre," Mo Da pleaded.

Heaving with deep, monstrous breaths, his back hunching with predator alert, he glared at the approaching guards. His lips skinned back from his teeth, and he snarled like a rabid dog. He didn't see people. He saw a swarm of child-bots, all wearing Jeremy's face, laughing at him, mocking him.

{kill them. kill THEM}

The guards pummeled the chamber panel, splintering the glass into perilous cracks.

"Andre, please." Mo Da called, ducking behind him and moving out onto the branch. "The ship!"

Her mouth moved, but the white noise in his ears swirled into a blustery gale. Facing the sealing chamber, he arched up and splayed his six arms. His reflection faced him from within the dark mass of the guards pressed against the glass. His swollen eye, and the shadows of his gaunt face, contorted him into something ferociously alien. Dark cracks spread out from the black patch of the wound devouring his side, snaking across his entire body. His ribs and sternum pushed against his skin, as if something inside was trying to break out.

I am extraordinary, he thought, as the bloated parasitic creature of hate burst out of its seven-year coma, fully formed and chomping on his sanity.

The first guard smashed a hole through the thick glass, shattering it to pieces onto the platform. Sweat dripped into Andre's eyes, doubling his vision. Jeremy was everywhere.

A mindless swarm of anger, the dark thing roared out through Andre's lungs in pure, gravity-defying freedom. He charged and slammed his fist into the guard's stomach, so hard he felt organs burst. He threw the whimpering man to the side and snatched the next guard pushing through the breach. Holding him up by the arms with his two grippers, he ripped the guard's arms from their sockets and dumped the screaming man to the floor.

Seduced by the violence, Andre yearned for more.

Enraged, and in rapture, he spun around and swiped his helper arm, knocking the rifle out of the next guard's hand. The terrified guard stumbled back through the hole in the glass. Andre drove a gripper into the man's shoulder and pinned him against the panel. He slammed his forehead into the guard's nose, annihilating it, exploding it across his face. The guard collapsed in an unrecognizable heap of blood and flesh.

The last guard standing, still inside the chamber, stepped back and drew his gun. Andre pushed past the broken glass edge of the panel breach, and lunged. The guard fired, but his hands shook so much from terror that the bullet hit the ceiling and blew the lights. Sparks flew and the ceiling burst into flames.

Andre swung his right gripper and seized the guard's gun hand, his left helper holding the guard by the neck. He punched his left gripper toward the guard's head, but it froze, stopping just short of the guard's terrified eyes.

The harness's motor screamed against the socket's resistance, heating up and burning Andre's back. With his free arm, the guard shot a punch into Andre's wound, exploding a world of pain through his body. Andre couldn't breathe. His vision blurred. The strength of his rage wavered and threatened to dissolve. Smoke wafted out from the fire in the ceiling, stinging his eyes. He squeezed the helper's hand, choking the guard, but his strength ebbed, taking with it his control of the harness. The guard clutched at the robotic hand around his neck, pulling it away. Blood filled Andre's head until it felt like it was about to burst. A few seconds more, and the guard would slip free.

Andre squeezed the control panel on his palm and the long screwdriver tool shot out of the helper's palm and pierced the guard's eye. The gripper snapped back into action and lurched forward, driving the tool into the guard's brain.

As the guard throttled and spasmed, Andre gripped the guard's screaming head and ripped it from his body. The decapitated guard dropped to the floor, and Andre flung the head at the glass.

He stumbled backward and surveyed his victory. Body parts lay in a murderous mess about him. An enemy moaned from among the stench of guts and exposed human waste.

Flames crackled across the ceiling and smoke filled the air. From somewhere in the background, Mo Da's voice called. Heaving with exhaustive breaths, he kicked body pieces out of the way and stumbled onto the platform. As Mo Da rose out of the garden, physical limitation finally overwhelmed him. His stride deteriorated into a crippled shuffle. The tingling in his nervous system disappeared, every one of its million ends fried. His rage and the strength of the zilla ebbed away. His feet turned underneath his ankles, and he fell to his knees, into the catch of Mo Da's good arm. Her touch banished the wind from his ears. He looked up into her olive eyes, when a familiar voice spoke from the emergency communicator on the harness strap.

"Boy, I told ya, my kindness only goes so far. And you have mightily fucked up."

A third loud clunk echoed from above, followed by the buzz of harvest droid blades whirring into life behind the lights.

Anchora

Mo Da unstrapped his harness and leaned him against the platform wall. "We have to climb down. Just tell me where the ship is. I can take us there."

Coughing, his lungs burning, he glanced over at the blood-spattered glass of the chamber. Smoke billowed through the broken panel. He struggled to recognize where he was. *Across. Get across.* He raised a listless arm and pointed toward the branch of the neighboring tree-tower.

Mo Da shook her head. "Andre, the tower is on fire."

He glanced to the bottom of the greenhouse, in the direction of the doorway the auto-crane had disappeared through, but he could only see hazy lights beneath crimson-lit smoke. The buzzing above whirred into a loud, vibrating wave, tickling the hairs across his arms. "Down," he muttered.

Mo Da stood and strapped the harness onto herself. He gazed up at her. She rolled her shoulders, mimicking how she had seen him controlling it. With the robotic arms spread out, and the circular branches of the tree-towers crisscrossing each other like a web behind her, she looked like a huntsman in a distorted web rearing up on its hind legs.

Beautiful.

Her movements made the grippers jerk, but within a few attempts, her fast learning enabled her to maneuver them effectively. She lifted him with the helpers, their cold hands pressing into his wound and sending daggers of pain through his groggy brain. As she held him close, the buzzing above intensified, the drones dropped, and the greenhouse exploded into a hail of tiny, spinning blades.

Protected by Mo Da's arms, he heard the swish of the drone blades slicing her body, the pings of their cutters colliding with the metal below her shallow, artificial skin. And then the screams began, the guards still alive being ripped to shreds by the flying, metal piranhas. The men's lingering screams distorted into gurgled shrills.

Mo Da clutched Andre to her body and jumped off the branch. He screamed silently as they dropped, until a gripper caught hold of a rope below the branch, and jerked them to a halt. She rolled her shoulders to activate both grippers and climbed down into the rising smoke as drones bounced off her. He buried his face into her bosom, searching for smoke-free air. She squeezed him closer and dropped to the next branch, landing on her sturdy legs. She repeated the spider-like scaling all the way down to the tree-tower's lowest branch where it was low enough for her to scale a lower rope and drop to the greenhouse floor.

At the base, red and yellow lights flashed and alarms whooped, but the fire and smoke had eased.

"Andre, we're here. Which way?"

He pointed in the direction of the doors. She discarded the harness, lifted him over her shoulder, and crossed the floor. The jolting stabbed his wound, and the fresh cuts tingled in his shoulders and back. Blood striped down his dangling forearms in a red tiger-like pattern and dripped onto the floor.

He was delirious. The dark thing's voice had vanished. He thought at first that it had passed out on the drunkenness of its violent indulgence. But a vast emptiness had opened up inside him with the weight of its missing presence. He feared it had gone for good.

Mo Da lifted him off her shoulder and leaned him against something hard and cold. "Andre", she said softly. "We're at the doors. Please, just tell me where the ship is."

He opened his lids and blinked. Mo Da's face came into focus. He reached out and touched her cut cheek. Dark oil bled from her left nostril.

"There you are. Where'd you go, baby?"

"Andre, we're at the bay doors. How do we get out of here? Where is the ship?"

He rolled his head around and spotted the control panel. He lifted his arm and swiped Grekov's wristlet. As the large, metal doors slid open, Mo Da helped him to his feet and assisted him down a long transport corridor. Coming out into another large chamber, his eyes lit up at the sight of the giant auto-straddles carrying Neura crates.

"I remember these guys." He coughed blood and fell to his knees.

Mo Da picked him back up. "Andre. We must get to the ship. *Just tell me where it is.*"

"Them." He pointed to the auto straddles carrying crates down another corridor.

She put her arm back around his waist and helped him follow the machines down the corridor, until it bent to the left. Turning the corner, wind rushed through and pushed them backward. Andre thought the rage was returning until he saw the storming world stretching out beyond the docking bay where the row of ships lined up.

Mo Da helped him to an alcove to the side and lowered him to sit. A feeble smile split his face. He pointed to the ship at the end of the line. A panel on the ship's rear displayed its destination:

A - N - C - H - O - R - A

"That's it, babe. Right there. That's our ticket to the Moon."

Mo Da stiffened and glanced around, following his finger. "But how do we fly it?"

"It's a cargo transporter, babe." Andre coughed, tasting more blood. "We just got to get into the cargo hold. Get past the handlers." He grinned, blood dribbling down his chin. "We got to kill 'em. You got to kill 'em for us."

He reached out and touched her face, focusing on the synthetic smell of her skin and the glistening of her olive eyes. He could no longer discern any thought or emotion in her face. Had he been imagining things?

Mo Da held his hand on her cheek and dropped her head. "Thank you, Andre. You made this possible. I saw the future, and two probabilities stared back at me—I could die in Titan, or I could leave Brulle. You were my only hope."

A roar sounded. Andre rolled his head around and glanced up the row of ships. As the closest one fired up its engines and pulled away from the dock, an auto-crane rolled back from the ship marked 'Anchora.' PrePAC cargo handlers approached the ship, appearing to perform a hasty final check. He coughed again and swallowed back blood.

"I did it for you, babe, for us. So we could be together. We're free now."

She removed his hand from her cheek and faced him. "No. You're free. You have the implant out. But I still have your voice in my head. And I don't want it anymore."

Her words shot through his haze, slicing apart his delusion, and pierced his heart.

What is she saying?

"I... felt something for you, Andre. I... imagined us together, somewhere else. I thought that perhaps my algorithms glimpsed the emotional state that you would call love. It is indeed a confusing emotion, overriding rational deduction." She shook her head. "But you used me to kill. You slaughtered those men when you could have walked away. You chose to kill Elron, when he wanted to help you. That is when I saw it, what love means to you. I knew then I needed to use it if I were to survive."

Confusion gripped him as she leaned forward and kissed his bloody lips.

Love? Did she say love?

He shivered, his body colder than her artificial skin. She pulled back, ever so slightly, so her lips wrote the next words in whispers across his.

"Love, to you, Andre, is just a beautiful weapon."

She pressed her body against him and pushed her mouth down on his, far too aggressively to be another kiss. Confused, he struggled to speak as her pressure stretched his mouth open. Something cold pressed against his abdomen, pierced his skin and sliced through muscle and organ. Stark, exquisite pain speared up and across his insides. He tried to scream, tried to push her away, but her mouth covered his and her strength held him down. The metallic taste of his own blood flooded his throat. As he gurgled and gasped, Mo Da leant back and released him.

"You won't be able to scream, so don't exert yourself trying," she explained, as she plucked the communication device from his ear and crushed it between her fingers. "The blade has pierced your lungs, and blood is filling them and your esophagus. Your heart and breathing rates are escalating. You will die from exsanguination within a few minutes."

He could no longer feel his hands, and a random, ludicrous thought shot into the midst of his terror.

I'm turning into a fucking bird.

His whole body shook, as he tried desperately to breathe, but he could only manage short, useless gasps. Mo Da wiped his lips.

"I understand killing. It is a mechanism for ensuring the transference of energy, a necessity of life. But you used it as a weapon for selfish indulgences, perverting its sacred meaning and making it evil. I will kill, but only for survival. Or mercy."

She kissed his forehead and stood, dropping Tan's scalpel on his chest. Even amid the shock of death creeping over him, a horrifying, madness-inducing clarity arose in his mind.

Tricks on tricks! She planned this from the church!

The pain wracking his body fell away as a merciful cold suffused through him.

She's not just a machine. She is a Citizen Extraordinaria.

Tiny stars of darkness blotched his vision in a slow, relentless bloom, but no rage came to save him. No voice hissed in his mind, and no wind rose in his ears. His love and survival instinct lay dead on the floor of his being, Siamese twins murdered by the dark thing's perversion. One final bright shaft of rational thought speared into his mind, as he wondered if the dark thing had left him and moved into Mo Da, transferring itself from humanity to machine.

Through his collapsing vision, he watched her perfect form walk away. She paused by a column and punched something on the wall. An alarm rang out across the docking bay, and she dashed into the shadows, the last of all his illusions running off with her.

Yells drifted through the slow motion melting of his consciousness.

Two blurred forms darted away from the ships and ran toward him. He glimpsed Mo Da climbing onto the 'Anchora' ship before the dark stars bloomed over his vision and smothered him into shivering blindness. The tears he'd contained, since the day Jeremy had held the switchblade to his throat, burst forth and mingled with the blood draining life from his body. He tried calling out Mo Da's name, to tell her he loved her, but his voice drowned in his throat, emitting only a distorted pair of sounds:

Mur-da.

The last remnant of his structured thought collapsed in on itself. The three words he never spoke, and never heard, died on the dry, barren landscape of his bloodstained lips. Blown away with his last exhale, the ghosts of those words chased Mo Da on her way to Anchora, as Andre Cross sank into more peace and quiet than he could have ever hoped for.

One day Buddha was walking through a village.

A very angry and rude young man came up and began insulting him. "You have no right teaching others," he shouted. "You are as stupid as everyone else. You are nothing but a fake."

Buddha was not upset by these insults. Instead he asked the young man "Tell me, if you buy a gift for someone, and that person does not take it, to whom does the gift belong?"

The man was surprised to be asked such a strange question and answered, "It would belong to me, because I bought the gift."

The Buddha smiled and said, "That is correct. And it is exactly the same with your anger. If you become angry with me and I do not get insulted, then the anger falls back on you. You are then the only one who becomes unhappy, not me. All you have done is hurt yourself."

"If you want to stop hurting yourself, you must get rid of your anger and become loving instead. When you hate others, you yourself become unhappy. But when you love others, everyone is happy."

VIEW ARTWORK ONLINE

ABOUT THE AUTHOR

DAMIEN LUTZ is a part-time writer from Sydney, Australia. His stories explore the relationships between humans and technology, and the possible futures these relationships may produce. He is also a full-time Designer of Web and Mobile experiences, and draws on this knowledge to create additional interactive online content to compliment his stories.

Explore artwork and more at:

www.damienlutz.com.au/author

Friend Damien on Facebook:

www.facebook.com/damienlutzauthor

Follow Damien on Twitter:

twitter.com/_the_future

Follow Damien on Pinterest:

https://au.pinterest.com/damienlutz/

Follow Damien's Amazon author page:

www.amazon.com/-/e/B00V29EKCM